Born in Oamaru and educated at Otago and Toronto, Fiona Farrell has been writing since the 1980s. To date she has published two books of poetry, two collections of short stories and three novels. Her first novel, *The Skinny Louie Book*, won the New Zealand Book Award for Fiction in 1992. She has won many other awards, including the Bruce Mason Award for Playwrights and the Katherine Mansfield Fellowship in Menton. Her last novel, *The Hopeful Traveller*, was runner-up for the Deutz Medal for Fiction in the 2003 Montana New Zealand Book Awards.

book book

FIONA FARRELL

V
VINTAGE

 The assistance of Creative New Zealand
is gratefully acknowledged by the author.

ARTS COUNCIL OF NEW ZEALAND *TOI AOTEAROA*

National Library of New Zealand Cataloguing-in-Publication Data
Farrell, Fiona, 1947-
Book book / Fiona Farrell.
ISBN 1-86941-619-8
1. Books and reading—Fiction. I. Title.
NZ823.2—dc 22

A VINTAGE BOOK
published by
Random House New Zealand
18 Poland Road, Glenfield, Auckland, New Zealand
www.randomhouse.co.nz

First published 2004. Reprinted 2004, 2005, 2006

ISBN-13: 978 1 86941 619 5
ISBN-10: 1 86941 619 8

Text design: Elin Termannsen
Cover photo (chickens): Getty Images
Cover design: Katy Yiakmis
Pages 146–147 'Personality' lyrics and music by L. Price and H. Logan
© M. C. A. / Universal Music Publishing. Reprinted with permission.
International copyright secured.
Printed in Australia by Griffin Press

For Bob
UAL Flight 175
11 September 2001

One day a hen walks into a library. She goes up to the desk and says to the librarian, 'Book book! Book book!' So the librarian gives her a book. The hen tucks it under her wing and goes off out the door.

The next day she comes back. She goes up to the librarian and says, 'Book book! Book book!' So the librarian gets her another book and the hen tucks it under her wing and goes off out the door.

On the third day the hen comes back again. She goes to the desk, says, 'Book book! Book book!' and the librarian fetches her yet another book. But this time the librarian is really curious so she follows the hen up the road. The hen goes into a park. In the middle of the park there's a pond and by the pond there's a frog sitting on a whole heap of discarded books. The hen goes up to the frog and hands him the book. The frog looks at it briefly, then tosses it over his shoulder.

'Reddit,' he says. 'Reddit. Reddit.'

Children's joke

1.

Xenophon was distressed as well as the other Greeks, and unable to rest, but having at length got a little sleep, he had a dream in that, in the midst of a thunderstorm, a bolt seemed to him to fall upon his father's house, and the house in consequence became all in a blaze. Being greatly frightened, he immediately awoke and considered his dream as in one respect favourable (inasmuch as being in troubles and dangers, he seemed to behold a great light from Jupiter) but in another respect he was alarmed (because the dream appeared to him to be from Jupiter who was a king, and the fire to blaze all around him) lest he should be unable to escape from the king's territories, but should be hemmed in on all sides by inextricable difficulties.

What it betokens, however, to see such a dream, we may conjecture from the occurrences that happened after the dream. What immediately followed was this. As soon as he awoke, the thought that first occurred to him was, 'Why do I lie here? The night is passing away. With daylight it is probable that the enemy will come upon us; and if we once fall into the hands of the king, what is there to prevent us from being put to death with ignominy, after witnessing the most grievous sufferings among our comrades, and enduring every severity of torture ourselves? Yet not one of us is concerting measures or taking thought for our defence, but we lie here sleeping as if we are at liberty to enjoy repose.

From what city then do I expect a leader to undertake our defence? What age am I waiting for to come to myself? For one thing is sure: I shall never be older if I give myself up to the enemy today.'

After these reflections he arose, and called together the captains . . .

Xenophon's *Anabasis*

One restless Sunday, fog over the valley, she took down Xenophon. She was supposed to be working. She had the house to herself for the week. Rory was away tramping with some mates, the phone was off the hook, there were no visitors, no meetings, and a deadline pressing at the end of the month: episode five of *McGibbon*, a detective show in which the bodies washed ashore in a variety of picturesque locations around the Marlborough Sounds. Enough local colour to market the show at MIPTV, enough tension to keep the viewers slumped on the settee between ad breaks, enough blood and sex to satisfy the 35+ male who demographic studies showed controlled the remote in the majority of the households targeted by the major sponsor.

It paid well, of course. Much better than any of Kate's novels ever would. And thousands would watch this episode when it finally came to air. Its star was a popular man. He smiled from the covers of the magazines, arms about the blonde PA who had become his second wife, bravely detailing his struggle with dyslexia or his brush with skin cancer, or holding his third child in his arms and lauding the newly discovered joys of parenthood. This week's episode involved some particularly nasty disarticulation.

But this week, murder and the step-by-step identification of its perpetrator seemed silly stuff. Pallid and thin.

Kate could not settle.

She walked about the room, picking things up, putting them back, made a coffee, sat at her desk, shuffled some paper, stood idly by the bookcase, found Xenophon.

The Anabasis and Expedition of Cyrus, literally translated from the Greek of Xenophon by the Rev. J.S. Watson, M.A. M.R.S.L., published at Covent Garden in 1878.

The book stood on the second shelf, bound in grey cloth ornamented with a discreet curvilinear pattern. All her life it had been somewhere nearby. To begin with, it had occupied a shelf behind her father's chair, one of a company of texts in sober uniform: Xenophon, Catullus, Ovid, Livy, Herodotus, Horace, Strabo and Suetonius. She had noticed the title especially because of the X. The only other name she knew of that began with an X was Xavier, which appeared in one of the December boxes on the Columban calendar tacked to the wall above the dining table. She liked that X. She liked the sound of the name 'Xenophon', and his *Anabasis*, whatever that might be.

The other books in the grey series had disappeared, along with Josephus, Layard's *Early Adventures*, *At Home with the Patagonians*,

The Brendan Voyage, *Commandant of Auschwitz*, paperbound copies of *Johnny Enzed in the Middle East*, novels by Priestley, Wells, Orwell's *Road to Wigan Pier* and several slim red volumes from the Thinker's Library. Kate's sister Maura had the ten-volume history of Ireland and the leatherbound copy of Mungo Park's explorations in Africa. Kate had the regimental history of the 19th Battalion, *Buller's Birds* and a copy of Richard Baxter's sermons, a strangely puritan purchase for a determined Catholic like her father, but present on account of its beautiful binding and for the spidery inscription on the fly-leaf: *Hannah Wright, Her Booke*. But the bulk of the assortment of biographies, travel books, novels and histories that her father had retrieved from the dusty shelves of second-hand shops and auction rooms had dispersed, gone to other shelves or to the dump or the fire.

Some of these books had been ruined when the storm drain outside the front gate flooded in a thunderstorm back in 1960. The house was a cavernous villa set in a valley and its section was prone to flood in winter. Kate and her sister had looked forward to it. They took out the old tin baby bath, which could hold them both, and set off to paddle about above the lawn and the potato bed, fancying themselves explorers in a new world. When the water drained away it left a layer of mud that seemed to do wonders for the vegetation: never were the peonies so extravagantly crimson, the delphiniums so heavy with blue flower, the potatoes so prolific as after a flood. It was like Egypt, like the flooding of the Nile, a blessing in disguise.

That was until a new subdivision was built on the land at the end of the street above the cemetery. The first winter after the houses appeared, sprung like fungi overnight from rough paddocks fenced with African thorn, the drain became a geyser. Water the exact colour and texture of mustard surged against the wall her father had constructed painstakingly all one summer holiday. For weeks he had lifted the limestone blocks into place and set them there with a slurp of mortar like the icing on a cake. The flood surged at his handiwork, then pushed it flat before flowing over the flowerbeds into the house. Kate did not see it happen. She woke to a quiet lapping in the dark, and her mother standing in the doorway holding a torch and saying, 'Don't turn on the light, whatever you do!' An object floated between them and it took a moment for Kate, still confused with sleep, to identify it as her bedside table. The table bobbed on its side, knocking gently at the tallboy where all her jerseys lay ruined. And her shoes in the wardrobe.

And all the books on the bottom rows of all the bookshelves.

They swelled like strange seeds and burst, spitting pages, and had to be thrown out, along with metres of soggy broadloom. Some were dried by being spread on the rack over the coal range where they lay like birds cast ashore by an oilslick, and though they dried, they were never quite the same. The Patagonians swimming in the icy waters with their babies clasped to their shoulders sprouted a spotty mildew, and *Buller's Birds* smelled for ever after of damp and mould and the feeling of faces distorted in torchlight and nighties trailing in dark water.

Xenophon, however, survived. He had been safe on one of the upper shelves along with his grey brothers and when Kate's father died and her mother was released at last to move to a smaller place in Dunedin, only half an hour's drive from her sister Izzie's home at Millerhill, Xenophon for some reason made the cut. He was packed along with a random assortment of books into a box that had once held two dozen cans of Black Doris plums — the 500g size — and carted to Dunedin. There he occupied a kind of memorial row on a new bookshelf that was principally taken up by her old nursing texts and her family histories (maternal and paternal lines), four copies of *The Book of Mormon* (because she had felt sorry for the young men, so earnest in their white shirt-sleeves on her doorstep, so far from their own people), three Bibles, an assortment of Jehovah's Witness *Watchtower*s, Adventist publications and Presbyterian *Outlook*s.

Before her husband's death her books had had a shelf to themselves next to her bed, for easy reference as she readied herself for sleep. The *Watchtower*s and *Outlook*s had been stacked under a Windsor chair in the kitchen, tucked in the corner between the electric stove (which was practical) and the coal range (which was for comfort). With an old unmatched pair of her husband's socks pulled on over her stockings she had sat, feet in the open oven of the coal range, within reach of the stove top to keep an eye on silverbeet boiling to khaki rags and potatoes bubbling to mush. She could turn the clothes drying on the rack above the range or pop another shovelful of anthracite from the scuttle into the firebox. She could reach under her chair and bring forth something interesting to read, about the Last Days, or the miraculous visions of John Smith, or an account of missionary activity in India. She was never at a loss for entertainment.

Now, in her widowhood, their books were not divided: his books and her books co-existed in an easy solidarity they had not shared during her husband's lifetime. Xenophon suvived when Catullus and Ovid were sidelined to the bin or the second-hand stall. Maybe she, too, liked that initial X. When she died in her turn, curling to sleep alone in her bed, facing the wall, Xenophon stood by as the room grew still and cold in the middle of a Dunedin winter. Her little radio played on the bedside table, tuned to the National Programme, and her Bible was under her pillow with a bookmark embroidered with violets at a passage underlined and annotated in her unsteady hand: *My Daily Prayer. Praise him with the psaltery and harp! Praise him with the timbrel and dance!* The hymn of the ecstatic shepherd who danced before the ark. *Praise him with stringed instruments. Let everything that hath breath, praise the Lord!* Her cheek lay against song, the cancer run riot in the takeover bid, clusters taking possession of brain and liver and bowel, gaining a foothold in all the secret bloody crevices of her body. Xenophon stood on the bookshelf, small and grey in his square cloth coat.

And when that shelf was cleared and the books made another division, goats to the left, sheep to the right, he arrived in Kate's home on the Peninsula. She chose him from the pile on the green carpet in her mother's room.

'I'd like the Irish history,' said her sister.

'I'd like *Baxter's Sermons*,' said Kate. (She had always liked that book especially. She used to take it to school for her morning talk. 'Goodmorninggirls'nboys. My talk is about this book. It is old. It is an olden days book. It has olden days writing in the front . . .' And she used to show them the olden days writing: *Hannah Wright, Her Booke*. They couldn't spell properly in the olden days.)

She put *Baxter's Sermons* on her pile on the carpet.

They were being fair, sharing out the bits and pieces that had been their parents' as carefully as they had always shared: one lolly for you, one lolly for me; one sticker for you, one sticker for me.

'I'd like Mungo Park,' said Maura. She had always liked the engravings of strange beasts, the tiny black figures before the towering waterfall.

'I'd like Xenophon,' said Kate.

She put him and her share of the books that had belonged to her parents on her own bookshelf. Her mother's piano moved into the living room too, beneath the engraving of Edinburgh's Princes Street from Calton Hill, which had hung above the piano when Kate sat as a child in an icy front room stumbling through 'Für Elise' and 'The Robin's Return' on fingers like wooden pegs. Xenophon and his mates took their place among Kate's non-fiction with Elaine Morgan's *Descent of Women*, Norman Cohn's *Warrant for Genocide*, Arbeau's *Orchesography*, Charlotte Macdonald's *A Woman of Good Character*, Bill Bryson's *Notes from a Small Island* . . . Ranked above

Xenophon were the short stories, the poems and the longer fiction; below, were the dictionaries and the reference books.

On Kate's father's shelves, books had co-existed in a casual disorder, like the men in a wartime mess, scholars and scrubcutters elbow to elbow at the bar. On Kate's mother's shelves, books had been catalogued in terms of memory: this section belonged to her youth and her career at Oamaru Public Hospital, this to the time of her marriage, these were her daughters' books (the ones they had left behind), these belonged to her husband. Just as cupboards held cardboard cartons full of old toys, her nurse's cape and stethoscope, receipts dating back to the purchase of the villa in Oamaru in 1948, guarantees for appliances long discarded, and electrical leads, plugs, picture hooks, hanks of string, paper bags neatly folded, Christmas cards and knitting patterns — all the things someone, sometime might want again — so the bookshelves stood as evidence of a life. The books were part of the record.

Everything in her house had been labelled: *Kate's School Uniform. Maura's Pony Club Cup. Pat's Books.* Behind the engraving of Princes Street was a card sticky-taped to the frame: *This picture was brought to New Zealand by my great grandmother, Jane Grant, on the* Glentanner, *1856.* Under the silver sugar basin was another label: *This was part of a tea set belonging to my grandmother, Isabel Falconer, Kenmore, 1883.* When Kate had the piano tuned — its first tuning since the flood thirty years before — the tuner showed her the middle-C key. On the wooden side beneath the ivory her mother had written: *This piano belonged to Alice Falconer and to her daughter, Tollie Stuart.* Kate added her own name: *And her daughter, Kate Kennedy.* Her daughters were visiting, a Christmas pit-stop between apple-picking, the Annapurna circuit, driving a 1972 Toyota to the Gulf of Carpentaria, whatever.

'That's cool,' they said. They added their names: *And her daughters, Hannah Dobbs and Bridget Dobbs.* They made a tight little cluster of descent, there in the crack between the semitones.

Kate thought of them whenever she played the piano. It jangled with rust, lending the most pensive of Chopin nocturnes a jazzy honky-tonk, but she liked to play it, with the candles lit in the sconces dripping hot wax onto the ivories and the walnut burr pulling faces in the gleam of flame. The engraving of Princes Street, the sugar bowl, her old walkie-talkie doll with its sticky yellow nylon hair had all found their places in her house. Xenophon, however, remained untouched, preserving a kind of anonymity among the ranks of non-fiction and reference.

Then came that restless Sunday.

All week the papers had been full of war: the first strikes had featured on the front pages, detonating in spectacular balls of flame above the grey city. Kate recorded the BBC News overnight and played it each morning. The tally had begun: seventeen Iraqi soldiers surrendered to US Forces, one US marine killed in southern Iraq, eight British soldiers and four Americans dead in a helicopter crash . . . The television screen showed the same footage over and over: tanks charging across a featureless plain, pennants flying. 'We're in this now,' said the commander of the USS *Abraham Lincoln* battle group, in a voice like caterpillar treads grinding over stony ground, 'and we're going to win it *fast*.'

Kate had drunk her morning coffee watching the weird exhilaration of the tank charge, and the equally weird stillness of the waiting city. Families were waiting in those sleeping towers, children were climbing into their parents' beds at the thud of the first salvo in the mission to disarm Iraq and free its people. She felt a resurgence of that familiar hopeless fury she had felt at intervals throughout her life and remembered her father flinging a teacup at the television and Muldoon smirking and shattering all over the Feltex in a little storm of broken china and milky Amber Tips.

She had done her best. She had walked around the Square one

sunny afternoon in the usual column with the usual cardboard placards. *NO WAR. PEACE NOT WAR.*

What do we want? No war! When do we want it? Now!

She had tried to keep herself informed, reading the overseas edition of the *Guardian* every week and *The Press* every day. *The Press* had begun to run a special feature headlined War On Iraq, bracketed by photos of Bush on one side and Hussein on the other, as they did for other important events such as parliamentary elections or the Rugby World Cup. She had signed various email petitions and ruined a perfectly good dinner party arguing with someone who thought invasion 'justifiable'.

'It's justifiable,' he said, 'though not necessarily legal.' He had spent eight years working in Washington. He could recommend a book that would explain the background to the war — he could send her a copy in fact, if . . .

'What about DU?' said Kate. 'The babies born without heads? Three or four of them born every month and that's in just one Iraqi hospital! In Basra or Baghdad or . . . somewhere.' Fury made her inarticulate. 'Every month! What can possibly justify that?'

He was taking out a pen so that he could make due note of her address for postage.

'Well, that's regrettable, of course,' he said. 'No one can defend that.' Kate could feel her face going red. Beside her, Rory was scraping every vestige of lemon mousse from his plate. 'But even in peacetime, bad things happen,' said the man. His voice was deep and his speech was soothing. 'Babies are born deformed. It's natural.'

'Regrettable!' said Kate, and this time her voice was definitely too loud and somehow she had managed to knock over her wine glass as she put down her spoon. 'What a feeble, stupid, legalistic word to use! Sorry, Morag, sorry,' as Morag dabbed at the stain with a handiwipe.

'It'll be fine,' said Morag in her bright that's-enough-of-that voice. 'Now: more mousse, anyone?' Her party never quite recovered from the headless babies.

Kate had engaged in all the trivial rituals of dissent and of course it had done no good. Not a single life had been saved. Nothing she did or said would make any difference. She wandered about the house, restless with uselessness. Fog had rolled in out of a clear day, one of those inversion fogs that sometimes came down out of nowhere, blotting out the sea, the hillsides, the trees behind the house. She had gone for a walk on the beach to try to clear her head of the children in their parents' arms, the fireball breaking like the sun of freedom, the young men racing one another across the desert toward something or other. The fog had the effect of muffling sound. Just the crunch of her own feet on layers of broken shell, no future, no past, her footprints disappearing into nothing behind, nothing ahead but a small patch of sand. She came back to the house, stood in front of the bookcase seeking solace. She reached out her hand and found Xenophon.

The paper was crisp with age, like the dry skin of an old man. The pages strained at the binding strings and some sections had already come loose, but the text was complete within its tooled covers. She had no idea of its contents, other than some vague association with the Ten Thousand (Ten Thousand what?), and a picture dimly recalled from her *Arthur Mee's Children's Encyclopaedia* of a soldier, arm upraised, pointing to a gap in the horizon that was *The Sea! The Sea!* (Which sea? Why was the soldier so far from the sea?)

She turned the pages idly, the tanks still charging across the wide plain of the mind's eye, and read:

Cyrus now advanced through Arabia, having the Euphrates on his right, five days' march through the desert, a distance of thirty-five parasangs. In this region, the ground was entirely plain, level as the sea. It was covered with wormwood, and whatever other kinds of shrub or reed grew on it were all odoriferous as perfumes. But there were no trees. There were wild animals, however, of various kinds: the most numerous were wild asses; there were also many ostriches, as well as bustards and antelopes and these animals the horsemen of the army sometimes hunted. The wild asses, when anyone surprised them, would start forward a considerable distance and then stand still; (for they ran much more swiftly than the horse;) and again, when the horse approached, they did the same; and it was impossible to catch them, unless the horsemen, stationing themselves at intervals, kept up the pursuit with a succession of horses. The flesh of those that were taken resembled venison, but was more tender . . .

The Euphrates?

She looked up the atlas that she usually left on the kitchen table as she liked looking at maps while she was eating breakfast. Toast and blackcurrant jam and the Plateau of the Matto Grosso stretching between 10° and 20° south, webbed with the fine blue lines of rivers she had never seen: the Guapore, the Teles Pires. Or porridge and a boiled egg overlooking the Kunlun Mountains and the sepia expanse of the Turfan Depression. The Euphrates began as a web of faint blue lines in the yellow patches that were the uplands of Syria and Turkey, thickening as it gathered the tributary waters of lesser unnamed rivers nearer Baghdad. Rising in the higher country to the east was its twin, the Tigris. Between the rivers were Basra, Mosul, An Nasiriya, towns whose names she was beginning to pin to the mental map, as she had earlier learned the whereabouts of Saigon or Santiago or Kosovo. And there in the ornate letters that signified a Historically Significant Site was *BABYLON*, only a few kilometres south-west of the modern capital.

An army is marching over a vast plain. Xenophon has noticed the plants crushed beneath their feet or brushed aside in passing. He has recorded the wildlife and the sport of their hunting and the taste of asses' flesh when cooked.

The image rises from the foxed pages: a haunch of meat, roasted over a fire of scented wood, the spiral of smoke, the hiss of fat dripping into flames, the tearing of strong teeth at tender flesh.

But why was this army marching alongside the Euphrates? Kate flicked back to the beginning. The explanation was delivered with military economy:

Of Darius and Parysatis were born two sons, the elder Artaxerxes and the younger Cyrus. After Darius had fallen sick and suspected that the end of his life was approaching, he was desirous that both of his sons should attend him. The elder happened to be present; Cyrus he sent for from the province of which he had made him satrap. Cyrus accordingly went up, taking with him Tissaphernes as a friend. But when Darius was dead and Artaxerxes was placed upon the throne, Tissaphernes brought an accusation against Cyrus before his brother, saying that he was plotting against him. Artaxerxes was induced to give credit to it, and had Cyrus arrested, with the intention of putting him to death, but his mother, having begged for his life, sent him back to his province. When Cyrus was departed after being thus in danger and dismay, he began to consider by what means he might cease to be subject to his brother and make himself king if he could in his stead. Parysatis their mother was well disposed toward Cyrus as she loved him better than Artaxerxes who was on the throne . . .

It is the beginning of a fairy tale, the proper start to a story. Two brothers; a single throne; a mother who prefers one son. Their battle would be about not just power or wealth, but about some barely acknowledged antipathy: something that had its origins, perhaps, in some squabble by the king's door. Two kids fighting over a toy, one kid stronger than the other so the mother intervenes, says something along the lines of 'Cut it out, you two', and perhaps protects the younger, delivers a quick slap to the older. Or perhaps the older claimed the toy and so intimidated the younger that he has never forgiven him for that loss: of some little wheeled object, a terracotta figure of a charioteer, a soldier bearing a javelin, something coveted most desperately.

It's as good a reason for a war as any. Kate had always suspected that behind all the microphones and smart suits lay the child's fear of being too small, or of the dark — or, equally, the child's delight in making things go bang, or the thrill of ganging up and running amok, or the dark pleasure in tearing the wings off a dead bird or watching a kitten drown.

The little grey book listed the broken truces, the secret deals, the trade-offs, lies and promises by which a leader builds a willing invading force. Cyrus left his exact purpose vague. *To some he said he intended war on the Pisidians, to others, that he was going to war with Tissaphernes on behalf of the Miletan exiles.* Not once did he announce that his real intent was to break all the protocols of his time and cross the Euphrates, to commit treason and lay siege to his own brother, the Great King himself.

Kate curled on the sofa entranced. Beginning with the monocled Germans and those 'Gott in Himmel!' comics her cousin Bernard had read by the dozen when they were children, she had never been particularly interested in war stories. She had never finished *Catch 22*. For a few weeks when she was newly divorced and weak on discernment she had gone out with a man who liked arranging little plastic figures on large green-baize tables and re-staging the Somme Offensive. His idea of a good night in was fish and chips in front of black-and-white footage of Operation Barbarossa. The relationship had been doomed from the start. But Xenophon was different. He noticed the detail.

As he reports it, the mercenaries Cyrus recruited were not unduly bothered about their purpose. It was spring. They were soldiers. Like the GI on the front page of that week's *Guardian* with *KILL 'EM ALL* daubed on his helmet in cartoon letters oozing cartoon blood alongside a cartoon skull, their motives were simple:

fighting and booty. When their leader's motives did become clear, they were readily persuaded by some smart oratory to persist in treason, on the promise of steady pay and a bonus on victory. In the War On Iraq feature section, their descendants recline in a paddling pool on the deck of an aircraft carrier, tossing a beachball as they await instruction.

The Greeks marched and hunted. There were women with them, and children — not named, of course, but they appeared in asides when they had to be loaded with the baggage animals onto boats or when the column was forced through some defile. There were four hundred wagons carrying barley meal and wine, and an unknown number of merchants who conducted a mobile market, spreading their wares out for purchase at every halting place.

The plodding progress of the vast column, the dust, the campfire gossip . . .

Xenophon records the visit of Epyaxa the Cilician queen, who arrived in Cyrus's camp, hoping to divert the army or at least secure gentle treatment in exchange for a large sum of money. The troops, in consequence, writes Xenophon the mercenary, *received pay for four months*. Then he adds the tittle-tattle, *and it was reported that Cyrus had connexion with her*, before describing the review staged to impress — or intimidate — her and, in particular, the fine sight the Greeks made in their brazen helmets, scarlet tunics, greaves and polished shields. (*KILL 'EM ALL! KILL 'EM ALL!*) He records the way the Greeks staged a mock attack on their allies, the Persians, frightening both them and the queen herself, who ran in terror as did the merchants in the market who deserted their goods *while the Greeks marched up to the tents with laughter.*

The swagger of it! The confidence of the man who can make a show of terror with a real weapon in his hand! The bravado of the man in the immaculate uniform!

KILL 'EM ALL!

Kate is caught. All that week while *McGibbon* lies neglected on her desk, she reads. She reads while tanks race toward Baghdad and 1500 bombs fall there in a single day from British and American planes. While the city burns, Cyrus's army is marching south through Syria where the fat fish in the River Chalus are held sacred. They pass a riverside palace with a particularly large and beautiful garden where every kind of produce grows. They burn it, of course, and no doubt eat the sacred fish. They pass ruined cities where the statues of former potentates lie broken in the marketplace, crumbling to rubble. They march through country clearburned by the enemy to deprive them of sustenance. They arrive at last on the plain of Cunaxa, near the city of Babylon. Here, Cyrus, antici-pating resistance, draws them up at midnight in full battle array. The ground around their feet is marked with the print of many men and horses but of the High King's army itself there is no sign. The Greeks arm themselves and assemble as ordered, and Cyrus briefs them on what to expect.

'*The enemy's numbers are immense,*' he says, '*and they make their onset with a loud shout.*' But stand firm, he tells the men, and they will be duly rewarded with land and gold and governorship of regions in the postwar regime he plans. The army stand to that night, and all the next morning, but when the enemy does not materialise, they begin to advance, cautiously, keeping the river on their right across the trenches dug in the plain to link the Euphrates with the Tigris. Night comes, and day, and another day, and still they encounter no opposition. They begin to relax, to stroll toward Babylon *observing no order on their march and many of the soldiers' arms were carried on the wagons and beasts of burden.*

Bunker-busting bombs are falling in Baghdad. They will remove Saddam Hussein and his two sons as neatly as a pair of tweezers plucking out a thorn. These are clever bombs, smart bombs, not the stupid, thoughtless bombs of earlier wars. These bombs kill only wanted, ugly men. The news reports show a pile of smoking rubble where perhaps fourteen people have died; others have been wounded by shrapnel shredding the air 200 metres from the site. The postwar administration is poised to move in, according to *The Press*. The Office for Reconstruction and Humanitarian Assistance will install a civilian administration headed by retired General Jay Garner. Its first objectives will be to facilitate humanitarian aid and to set up dialogue with the newly liberated people of the country.

Xenophon walks toward Babylon. At about ten o'clock on the third morning, however, a man comes riding at the utmost speed with his horse in a sweat, calling out to all he meets, both in Persian and Greek, that the king is approaching with a vast army, prepared as for battle. The confusion is immediate but in short order the army scurries into formation: Clearchus takes the right wing next to the river, Menon and his company take the left, and the barbarians are drawn up with Cyrus at their centre in the midst of 600 cavalry, his head bare as is the Persian custom.

It was midday, *and the enemy was not yet in sight. But when it was afternoon, there appeared a dust, like a white cloud, and not long after, a sort of blackness, extending to a great distance over the plain. Presently, as they approached nearer, brazen armour began to flash, and the spears and ranks became visible. There was a body of cavalry in white armour on the left of the enemy's line (Tissaphernes was said to have the command of them). Close by, there were troops with wicker shields; and next to them, heavily armed soldiers with long wooden shields, reaching to their feet (they were said to be Egyptians); then other cavalry and bowmen. These all marched according to their nations, each nation separately in a solid oblong. In front of their line at considerable intervals from each other were stationed the chariots called scythed chariots: they had scythes projecting obliquely from the axletree and others under the driver's seat, pointing to the earth, for the purpose of cutting through whatever came in their way . . . and they approached not with a shout but with all possible silence and quietly with an even and slow step . . .*

The cloud, the silence, the clink of mail as the tide of men sweeps toward them . . .

Scythed chariot and smart bomb, British airman and Greek mercenary become confused in Kate's mind. The book lies ready on the kitchen table, wide open, awaiting the moments during the day when she can pick it up again. She reads the text, consulting the Rev. Watson's commentary: seventy-three painstaking pages based on an expedition of his own in 1840 *under the auspices of the Royal Geographical Society and the Society for Promoting Christian Knowledge, following the track of that gallant little corps*, and his Tabular View of the Marches and Stoppages. On 9 March, 419BC, 2422 years to the week before the Americans' opening salvo, Xenophon and his mates had enlisted at Sardis. (Kate looks that up in the atlas on the kitchen table. There it is, some hundreds of kilometres west of Ankara: *SARDIS*. The city of the Lydian king Croesus, built on the banks of the gold-bearing Patroclus, a city famed among the ancients for its splendour and opulence. By 1836, when the Rev. Watson made his visit, Sardis was a heap of ruins, its only sign of life a *few black Yuruk tents and a Greek miller who had taken advantage of the streams that flow past the acropolis to turn the wheel of his mill.*) On 22 July, Xenophon and the army had crossed the Euphrates. On 3 September he had stood watching the silent approach of the High King's army.

She reads in the morning as the bombs fall and the veiled women scream into her living room at seven o'clock with the BBC News. Phrases bat about the place newly hatched, becoming as familiar as the Warehouse jingle or the little song that sells Toyotas: 'weapons of mass destruction', 'shock and awe', 'Chemical Ali', 'the coalition forces'. She reads at night when the garden outside the window takes on the nun colours of indigo, black and iridescent white and moths beat at the windows, thinking they have found the moon. Bombs kill uncounted numbers of Iraqi soldiers, not by piercing or by fire but by sound: the sonic boom dissolves their internal organs before they can make a move. They die with a trickle of blood at nostril, mouth and anus.

Day after day Kate turns from the television and the newspaper to the narrative of a band of Greeks, whose leader brought them to exactly this place only to guarantee their defeat by his own weakness. At the crucial moment in the battle, Cyrus spotted his hated older brother, whereupon he *lost his self-command*. Shouting, *'I see the man!'* he acted on impulse, escaped the protection of his own bodyguard and rushed to strike his brother on the chest. A javelin caught him under the eye and he was killed outright. Artaxerxes had suffered only a flesh wound and retained sufficient composure to order that his younger brother's head and right hand be hacked off. His troops then turned on Cyrus's troops, who fled before them. The High King's army sacked their camp and took one of Cyrus's mistresses, *the Phocaean woman*. The other, *the Miletan woman*, escaped, naked, to the Greek lines, where alone on that vast battlefield she found safety.

The Greeks did not know Cyrus had been killed. The battle front was long and they fought on all day with discipline and furious intent, routing the forces immediately before them. When night fell they gathered, still ignorant of the failure of their general's cause. They were preoccupied with finding something to eat, as they had been taken by surprise earlier that day and had to fight before they had had their dinner. They slaughtered some of the baggage animals and cooked them on fires fuelled by arrows collected from the battlefield and *the wicker shields of the Persians and the wooden ones of the Egyptians and there were also many of the light shields and wagons emptied of their contents, and using all which materials, they appeased their hunger.*

A kitchen created from a battlefield. Kate exists now in two narratives. One is contemporary; the other is ancient. One is complete; the other is still evolving. She reads about the death of the Greek leaders, enticed to parlay with the victors and slaughtered as soon as they entered the enemy camp. In their shouts as they were dragged to summary execution she hears an echo of the voices she heard one afternoon on a radio documentary backgrounding the war: men who opposed Hussein shouting as they were dragged from a conference room to their deaths in some parking lot or service access. Remove the head and the body will flap about for a while before it lies down ready for plucking.

The Greeks were left leaderless, trapped in enemy territory hundreds of miles from home.

Then, Xenophon had his dream.

He woke in clammy terror from a dream of fire and lightning and said to himself, *'From what city do I expect a new leader to come to our aid? What age am I waiting for to come to myself?'*

The words snap as if they have been spring-loaded. They take hold.

What age am I waiting for to come to myself?

Kate has read all night to this part without noticing the arrival of dawn. Outside the sky is becoming milky. A bird has woken and is singing. Just a single repeated note, the one that presages rain. Kate hears it sing in counterpoint to a young man refusing to wait passively for the knife to strike. Instead Xenophon persuaded the Greeks to action by appealing to their good sense, to their power as citizens of a democratic state to engineer their own preservation.

'The enemy thought that on destroying our general we should perish from want of direction and order,' he told them. But restraint, that self control that Cyrus had so signally lacked and a sense of responsibility for the mutual good would see them safe. *As he was uttering these words, somebody sneezed and the soldiers hearing it*

with one impulse paid their adoration to the god.

Good sense, and a sneeze — an omen from Jupiter the Preserver, signalling that they were under his protection — became their salvation.

Kate is stiff, her feet are cold. She drags the duvet over herself on the sofa and switches on the TV. The Greeks could not return by the way they came. They had stripped that trail bare of all provision. Getting back is always the difficult part. How does a man whose helmet is decorated with KILL 'EM ALL return to parent-teacher meetings and local body elections? How does a nation recover civilisation and courtesy when it has charged over frail protocols and the delicate conventions of international agreement? The Greeks chose uncharted territory, across the Tigris and into the mountains of the Carduchi and the northern tribes. They tossed aside what was not necessary, to travel light. They burned their tents, turned their baggage animals to cavalry. They marched and skirmished, passing villages and ruined cities: one with shells in its tumbled walls, though they were many kilometres from the sea; and another legendary as the place ruined by Jupiter's thunderbolt, which dropped one afternoon from a clear sky and drove all its citizens mad.

Tomahawks and MOABs rain down on Baghdad. There is a long history here of attack from the sky, from indifferent gods within their machines.

The Greeks directed their march toward the mountains where the Carduchi gathered on the summits and rolled rocks down on the slender column. They crossed the Tigris, which had been a broad barrier near Babylon but which up here in the narrow ravines had shrunk to a torrent a man might leap in a single bound. They struggled through deep snow. When they lit their cooking fires the burning logs sank steadily toward the earth, so that by morning they found themselves at the bottom of deep pits. They suffered from bulimia — not the disease of supermodels but the disease of hypothermic men, which led them to reject food and to fall into a deep and fatal torpor. They encountered people who lived in this savage place in homes carved beneath the ground, snug with all their animals and feasting, their hair crowned with coronets of hay, while the Greeks suffered, as intruders always do, on the surface. They met tribespeople who fought, women as well as men, with a desperate ferocity. When the high redoubt was taken, the invaders found it empty, for the defenders had flung their children and themselves from its summit. They entered villages where the people lived on chestnuts and pickled dolphins. The sons of the villagers' great men were fair and fat *and not far from being equal in height and breadth, painted on their backs with various colours and tattooed all over their foreparts with flowers.* In one mountain village they ate honey that drugged them all so that the soldiers lay about as if dead or raged out of their senses. (The peculiarities of the honey arose, notes the Rev. Watson, from *the herbs to which the bees resorted: goats bane and a species of rhododendron.*) They passed through the Mossynoecian villages, which were perched on crags. Though it took many hours to walk between them, they could call to one another, *so mountainous and hollow is the country.*

And on a mountain-top called Theches, on 27 January 400BC, they caught sight of the sea. *When the men who were in front had mounted the height, and looked down, a great shout proceeded from them. And Xenophon and the rear guard, on hearing it, thought that some new enemies were assailing the front, for the people from that country that they had burnt were following them and the rearguard, by placing an ambuscade, had killed some and taken others prisoner and had captured about twenty shields made of raw ox-hides with the hair on. But as the noise still increased and as those who came up kept running at full speed to join those who were continually shouting, the cries becoming louder as the men became more numerous, it appeared to Xenophon that it must be something of very great moment. Mounting his horse therefore and taking with him the cavalry he hastened forward to give aid, when presently they heard the soldiers shouting, 'The sea! The sea!' and cheering one another. They then all began to run, the rearguard as well as the rest, and the baggage cattle and horses were put to their speed and when they had all arrived at the top, the men embraced one another and their generals and captains with tears in their eyes.*

The soldier's upraised hand is explained. That wedge of blue glimpsed between hills that can never be claimed as the territory of any one country. The possibility of freedom.

Kate reads about this man in a book she received from her father. He had been a soldier too, and he had known also about escape from encirclement.

He had enlisted in 1939 up on the East Coast, where he was working as a labourer. He had joined up as an ordinary infantryman, gone to Egypt, been wounded at Alamein, come home again to Oamaru. The evidence of his soldiering had lain all around them when Kate was growing up. His kitbag lay folded in a drawer in the tallboy in his bedroom, along with his dog tags and puttees. The brass plate from Egypt hung over the mantelpiece, the little box with the sphinx on the lid sat on the sideboard holding bills and receipts. A copy of Josephus, which he had been reading at the time he was wounded, and which still released when it was opened a fine trickle of desert sand, sat on the bookshelf. He drank at the 2nd NZEF clubrooms, avoided Anzac and all that ballyhoo, sang 'I've Got Sixpence' when they were driving in the car and 'Sari Marais' and 'She'll be Comin' Round the Mountain', which were soldiers' songs.

Happy is the day when a soldier gets his pay.

And we all come rolling home!

He told them nothing about the war, except for the story of the truck, which he told Kate because she had insisted. Each year she made an Anzac Day wreath for the school gate. It was always the same: rusty brown chrysanthemums laboriously stitched onto a cardboard cross. One year, during the week when the crosses and bunches of flowers hung withering on the gate, her class had to do a project on The War.

She sat at the table, carefully writing *THE WAR*. She had made each letter into a gun with a little puff of smoke coming out of the barrel. She was colouring the letters in with her Lakeland pencils and feeling the usual disappointment at the pale colour they made when they promised such brilliance lying in their box.

'Tell me a story about the war,' she said.

'You don't want to know about that,' said her father. But because she said she had to write something, it was a *project*, he relented.

'All right,' he said, and he told her about the time when the Germans were all around them and they had to run away, to break through. It was kind of like bullrush at school, when the kids in the middle had to break through the ring to get to safety, but with no chance of saying pax, of crossing your fingers and saying you didn't want to play any more.

'Were you scared?' said Kate.

'Bloody scared,' he said. 'Then some Maori fellas up the back started up a haka and everyone just took off, flat to the boards.'

The way he told it, it was a funny story, because as he was running along, a truck came up and he got a lift, bouncing along with a lot of other jokers in the back and there was petrol all over the floor.

'Why?' said Kate.

'Because the petrol tins were useless,' he said. The only decent ones were the German cans they found lying about sometimes, the ones they called jerrycans, which had been properly welded. But anyway, that night they were sitting up to their ankles in petrol because the cans were crook, and the whole shooting match could have gone up any minute because they were under fire, and this officer scrambled on board and do you know what he said?

'No,' said Kate.

He said, 'Mind if I smoke?' Which just went to show that officers were a pack of clowns. The other funny thing was that his mate Mulherron was sitting in the back of the truck with him and after it was all over Kate's father had said to him, 'What were all the Hail Marys in aid of?' Because Mulherron was a hard man, not the kind who would pray all that often, and he had been praying HailMaryfullagrace the whole way, and do you know, he had no idea he was doing it?

And Mulherron had said, 'What about you? With all that bloody singing?' Kate's father had been singing his head off.

'What were you singing?' said Kate.

'Ferdinand,' said her father. 'You know: the one about the bull?'

Kate knew it. A silly little song about a bull who sat among the flowers and didn't want to fight.

'What about that?' said Mulherron. 'I thought you were never going to stop.'

And the funny thing was, Kate's father had not known he was singing either.

My dad went in a truck, wrote Kate carefully, in her best printing. *He sang Ferdinand.*

It wasn't a very good story.

Years later Kate read another, slightly more heroic version in the regimental history.

The breakout at Minqar Qaim

27 June 1942

The moment when the New Zealand Division found itself encircled by Rommel's forces and in imminent danger of annihilation. To the north, south and east were the 21st and 15th Panzer divisions; to the west were the Italians, the XXth. For days tanks had been arriving in increasing numbers, their swastika flags barely discernible through the desert haze, and the New Zealanders were coming under greater pressure. The German commander, General Bismarck, contemplated a full attack on the evening of the 27th, but decided at the last minute to 'wait to destroy the enemy' (as he confidently put it) in the morning, when his troops would be rested and in possession of full supplies of fuel and ammunition.

Freyberg had been wounded, hit in the neck by flying shrapnel, and a message thought to have originated with General Gott, commander of the Eighth Army, suggested that he thought the New Zealanders had already 'fallen out of the bedstead' — code for defeat — and were no longer in existence as a fighting force. Their supply lines had been blocked; the artillery was down to thirty-five rounds per gun; contact between battalions had become difficult and in some cases had been lost altogether.

The division was presented with a simple choice: wait until morning and be annihilated, or blast their way through. They could cross known ground through a narrow quarter-mile-wide col between German encampments on Bir Abbu Batta and Mahatt Abu Matta, or detour further south, where there would be less resistance but the ground would be completely unknown and encountered for the first time in the dark.

The command decided to move directly through the col: a silent approach fought with bayonet, bullet and the newly issued Bakelite grenades, led by the 19th Battalion — Kate's father's battalion — with the 20th and 28th (the Maori Battalion) on either flank. They would punch a hole through the German lines, clear mines and prepare the way for the transport that was drawn up in tight night formation behind the field guns, Vickers guns mounted on trucks, and anti-tank batteries across the rear of the column. The brigade HQ occupied the centre and a field ambulance stood behind each battalion. Zero hour would be 12.30am so that the column of men and transport might stand some chance of being through the gap before the short midsummer night ended and daylight exposed them to enemy fire out in the open.

Once through the gap, the division would reassemble at an embussing point south of Bir Abbu Batta, from which, in tidy desert formation, they would head east to Deir el Hassa, ninety miles away on the route to Alamein.

It was a moonlit night. The 19th Battalion took their places, bayonets fixed, forming a tight rank of men about 200 yards deep along a 400-yard line, which the brigade intelligence officer had drawn with screened lights along the length of the forward defence positions. The 20th and 28th drew up also, though there were delays as parties of men returned from destroying abandoned German vehicles and investigating what had been left behind during the previous few days' fighting. By the time everyone was in place it was late: 1.45am. According to the official historian, men reported a strange absence of apprehension. Many dozed while they waited and one at least reported that at Minqar Qaim he felt, oddly, 'completely happy', and went into a deep sleep until woken at the moment of advance.

No audible command was given. The men simply began to advance: bayonets at the high port, Bren and Tommy guns at the ready. Kate read the official history hearing the muffled tread of hundreds of pairs of dusty desert boots, the rattle of stones underfoot as the slit trenches that had provided their skimpy shelter for the past few days slipped away to the rear. Two hundred yards, five hundred, a thousand.

And then there was a gunshot, a rattle of automatic fire, the pink and green flash of tracer bullets. The line hesitated but from the 28th Battalion there came the sound of a haka — none of the histories mention which — and as the voices rose in the darkness, men began to run, all of them, at machine guns hastily focused by Germans jolted from sleep and scrambling to occupy their trenches. The Germans milled about in the dark, barefoot and wearing pyjamas, according to the New Zealanders who survived the engagement: striped pyjamas. It struck them as odd — one of those peculiar, vivid details recalled from the general mayhem as they emerged from the darkness, yelling, bayonets driving into soft flesh, guns firing, grenades finding their startled, shattered targets. The New Zealanders met little resistance at Bir Abbu Batta, so overran it before turning south, where the German transport had been drawn up in a laager and men were fighting fiercely hand to hand around the burning trucks.

Rommel next morning would call it savagery. He complained that all the ethics of military engagement and the standards set by international law had been violated by the New Zealanders. German bodies were found with multiple bayonet wounds, but what choice did a soldier have in the dark and chaos, said the historian? How could anyone tell who was dead and who was merely lying doggo, awaiting the chance to rear up and strike from behind? It was in this battle that Upham flung grenades into a truck full of fleeing Germans, killing them all and earning his first Victoria Cross. The New Zealanders fought their way through, and from beyond the col, at the embussing point, they could hear the cries of the wounded. They sounded, a soldier said, like a great flock of sheep bleating in the desert.

Behind the infantry, the vehicles had accelerated: 900 trucks, nine abreast on an eighty-yard front led by Bren carriers and two-pounder anti-tank guns with troop carriers to the rear. Behind them were the field ambulances carrying more than 300 men seriously wounded from previous fighting. The plan was to drive through, maintaining a steady pace and in an orderly fashion under fire — but a truck is an easy target, a big lumbering thing met head on, and in the event, the column broke. Bolting, maddened, the transport thudded across rough ground, men flung this way and that as the drivers went with feet flat to the boards, concentrating simply on breaking through to the relative safety beyond the guns. Some swung around entirely and fled, driven not by orders and reason but by a primitive instinct for survival, like bullocks stampeded, and went some distance before they could be turned and driven east.

Come morning, units of the New Zealand Division were scattered all over the desert. Until midday commanders had no idea where their men were, or whether they had survived. At the assembly point at Deir el Harra they waited while trucks and men slowly came in from all points of the compass. It took two days before they were regrouped and able to commence the march to Alamein.

One hundred and sixty New Zealanders died in the stampede. Churchill described the action as heroic. *They have acquitted themselves in a manner equal to all their former records*, Hansard reported. (*Cheers*.)

The sun is over the hill now and the birds are singing in chorus, all claiming first dibs on the day. Kate is stiff from sitting so long and Xenophon's account has trailed away into a list of raids and counter-raids. The Greeks have reached Byzantium where, unbelievably, most of them, Xenophon included, have promptly re-enlisted in the service of a Thracian prince.

Two helicopters have crashed in mid-air, one journalist has been killed by a suicide bomb, another by friendly fire. Men have trailed through smoke, hands raised. Fire billows above Baghdad, a child in a frilly frock screams for the camera. A thousand cruise missiles, a hundred air-strike sorties, five captured soldiers, people killed as they pick over onions and peppers in a street market, blood trickling from dirty bandages, a cluster of photographers, proboscises erect on top of a truck, catching images.

Deep ravines separate Kate from Xenophon. Chasms filled with many years and many people and many voices, but perched at her vantage point on the living-room sofa she can hear him speaking as clearly as if he were in the next room. His voice accompanies the voices of the living, interrupting what they say, echoing it, making some elliptical comment, lending it a context. Xenophon says to Kate: some things remain constant. There is always the glorious embarkation in spring, the journey toward battle, the adventure and comradeship, and the curiosities of foreign lands and people. There is always the blood and slaughter and it comes always, it seems, as something of a surprise, something the soldier had not entirely anticipated. Then there is the despair of defeat, or the commencement of the skirmishing that is construed as victory, and then there is the long, long journey back to peace. Where, after an interval, the process starts all over again. Xenophon says all this, but he also says: some things change; they are odd, memorable on account of their idiosyncracy. Wild asses running, evading capture, so tender when cooked. Fat boys with their bodies painted with flowers. Citizens driven mad by Jupiter's thunderbolt.

Kate sits in a room, centuries distant, on an island Xenophon had never heard of, reading his thoughts expressed in a language he would not understand in a translation by a Victorian cleric of a faith yet to be born. A miraculous collusion of chance, ingenuity, invention and human empathy has made this possible. Cyrus's military expedition would be construed a failure. But Xenophon turned it into literature.

2.

'Doughnuts!' said Robert. 'For all of us!'

Robert and His New Friends by Nina Schneider

There was an instant. A specific point when the words appeared, as leaf and branch can shimmer and settle to the form of bird or deer. There was a moment when marks on a page, no more remarkable until then than a random scattering of twigs, separated from their white background and formed themselves into significant shapes.

'Doughnuts!' said Robert. 'For all of us!'

Kate recalls the astonishment of their emergence.

The book was called *Robert and His New Friends*. It was a Little Golden Book, one of the few books she owned. There were books everywhere in the house: on chair arms, on the kitchen table alongside the breadboard and the cake tins, by the bath, in piles on the pink Feltex beside each bed. But they were library books, borrowed each Friday night to be returned the following week, gritty with crumbs or cigarette ash after their brief sojourn at 55 Greta Street. Kate's father earned six pounds a week walking up and down the streets of Oamaru reading the meters for the Power Board. He liked the open air. There were photos of him when he was young, years and years before he met their mother and got married in his black suit, and in all the photos he stood in the open air: stripped to the waist and leaning on a shovel with a gang of men by a railway line somewhere in the North Island, nonchalant in togs and towel at a beach, in funny big shorts outside a dugout in the desert. He couldn't stick at an indoor job. He'd never be an office wallah. He preferred the freedom of the streets. Kate thought he was lucky. He knew all the back doors in Oamaru, who had dogs and who had cats, what lay behind each hedge and inside every gate. But the price for such knowledge and freedom was that there was never a lot of money. Books were for Christmas and birthdays.

Robert and His New Friends was a birthday book, like the pop-up *Cinderella* that could be tied with a blue satin ribbon to make a tiny circular stage. One scene was the kitchen in gloomy 3D where Cinderella swept and slaved, the next a pumpkin coach with tiny mice footmen in white pigtails and gold-buttoned jackets. Then the ball and the handsome prince. The owned books had a permanent place on the shelf next to Kate's bed, where their covers became worn from much handling and their margins were scribbled with awkward letters and the scrawls that were intended to be princesses or horses. The blue satin ribbon frayed and twisted. The white mice footmen bowed low at their cardboard waists.

'Doughnuts!' said Robert. 'For all of us!'

There was a picture accompanying the moment of revelation. The little boy was wearing a red jersey and long trousers and his father's fireman helmet. He had been running about exploring his new home. It was a place where different people lived behind each door, like the gollywogs, dolls and rocking horses hidden behind the flaps on the glittery Advent calendar each Christmas. It was an 'apartment'. It sounded so much more interesting than Kate's own unremarkable villa, where only four people lived: father, mother, sister, Kate and a succession of half-wild cats, inveigled into dossing down in the washhouse with surreptitious saucers of milk. On their street, each house was separated from its neighbour by groves of blackcurrant bushes, the dusty crimping of an olearia hedge or a stout wooden palisade.

Robert's mother was unpacking the furniture in the new 'apartment'. She rushed across the page with a hammer clenched between her teeth, too busy to be bothered, so Robert put on the helmet and set off to find someone to play with. He knocks at one door and behind it there is a doctor's surgery: the doctor wears a round mirror thing on his forehead and can fold his white handkerchief to make a rabbit — but he is much too old to be a friend. Robert knocks at another door and finds a baker and his plump wife who give him a whole bag of doughnuts. Behind other doors live an artist, an angry carpenter, a woman who plays the trumpet, an old lady who owns a talking parrot. Finally, right across the hall from his own apartment, he finds the Teacher Family: big boy wearing a tie, big girl with plaits like Kate's own — only they are called 'braids' — a little girl sucking her thumb, a black puppy, and a boy who is just right. He wears long trousers like Robert's and slip-on shoes: another oddity, for all the boys Kate knew wore grey shorts, woollen jerseys knitted by their mothers, and brown sandals.

'What's in the bag?' the children asked.

And Robert said, 'Doughnuts! For all of us!'

Kate had asked her mother about the doughnuts. 'What are they?' she said. They were clearly something desirable, the kind of thing that would earn one instant acceptance from strangers.

Her mother shoved aside a *Watchtower* with its promise of eternal salvation. 'I'll look them up,' she said. She opened the kitchen table drawer that held the recipe books, all swollen around bulging hoards of newsprint clipped from magazines and notes scribbled in haste: *Izzie's Steamed Pineapple Pudding*, *Halfway Bush Cake*, *Freda Pinder's Lemon Sponge*. Her mother was always careful with attribution. The bits of paper were dog-eared and splattered with the vestiges of cakes and stews consumed long since, and they were held in place by stout rubber bands, wound once, twice, around the straining covers. Her mother unwound a rubber band and the book flew open, disgorging memories of food onto starry Formica.

'Doughnuts . . .' she said. 'Hmmm . . .'

She found a recipe at last and Kate stood beside the table to watch as the doughnuts took shape. They began as a sticky substance like the flour-and-water paste she and her sister made to glue old Christmas cards into their scrapbooks. The dough attached itself in long tendrils to her mother's hands and transferred itself to her hair when she pushed her curls back behind her ears. The doughnuts were fried in batches in a couple of inches of fat scooped from the Dundee marmalade fat-jar under the sink. They bobbed about sizzling and when they had swollen and turned brown, her mother lifted them out with the big holey spoon and it was Kate's job to sprinkle them with sugar. Doughnuts were sweet, greasy balls tasting distinctly of roast mutton. They weren't half as nice as pikelets or scones but Kate ate one slowly, thoughtfully. At least she knew now what it was Robert carried in the brown paper bag.

'Do you want another?' said her mother. 'I can't say I'm that fussed about doughnuts.' She dumped them with the potato peelings and cabbage leaves in the hen bucket.

Doughnuts may have been disappointing as food, but they marked the line where the miracle happened.

Kate and her sister were snug in bed with their dad. It was a good Saturday. During the week their father got out of bed early, daubed his chin with soapy stuff that he scraped away in white furrows with a dangerous little razor, then he ate kidneys on toast for his breakfast, and set off to walk around Oamaru. On good Saturdays he stayed in bed and read. When Kate and her sister woke, they could take their books and climb in beside him and read too: Kate on one side, Maura on the other so they wouldn't squirm or fight.

The book is propped between them on the pink eiderdown over their father's knees. His cup of tea waits on the bedside table to be cool enough to drink, caramel brown in the big white cup with the spidery web of cracks in the china. Next to the cup is the ashtray with the carved tiki, which holds a packet of matches and some rollie papers. The tray is charred where Dad, reading, has not paid proper attention and has let the stubs burn down to the wood.

His pyjamas are soft and striped in blue and white. Between the jacket buttons the ginger hair on his chest is soft and curly and interestingly different to the hair on his head, which is thick and black and straight. Kate lies cuddled against his chest listening while her father reads to them. She can feel the tickle of ginger hair on her cheek and hear the words rumbling about like water in a deep cave beneath his skin. The eiderdown is pulled up around them all, and while he reads, she and her sister fiddle furtively with the ends of the feathers that poke through the fabric.

'Eiderdowns won't keep you warm if you take out all the feathers,' Mum tells them. 'Just leave them alone.'

But when you tug at the plastic tip, a whole feather slides out: sometimes black, sometimes white, sometimes striped, and that is why you must do it, even if you will all freeze eventually. For the surprise.

The feather curls itself around her finger, a brown breast feather from a duck like the ducks they go to feed in the Gardens, or from a hen like the hens in their house by the back fence. The eiderdown contains millions of surprises. The tips press through the paisley print like the shreds of metal that emerge from time to time through her father's skin. He got hit by shrapnel at Alamein and even now, years after the war and thousands of miles from Egypt, it materialises in the palm of his hand: a prickle to be tugged out with tweezers under a bright light. Kate and her sister lean close to watch as The War is drawn from beneath their father's skin.

The bed smells dreamily of pyjamas and detergent on crinkled cotton sheets and the warm dad-smells of tobacco and soap and sweat. Outside, through swags of net curtain, is the verandah with its handkerchief edging of white lace and the front garden: the pink pucker of sweetheart roses, a shiny broadleaf, twin rows of pansies lined up along the path to the gate. The garden ends at the wall her father built: the wall that marks the boundary between their place and the place of the people who walk to the Arun Street shops for a sliced Vienna and the Saturday paper, or who drive to the cemetery at the top of the hill to put bunches of daisies in jam jars on the graves where their mothers and fathers lie under grey concrete covers.

Across the street Mr Anderson is already out mowing the lawn: Kate can hear the steady whine up and down the driveway and the short choppy strokes around the plinth where the seal sits, bearing a silver ball on its upturned nose. Mrs Anderson is polishing the front windows. Next door, Mr Nelson is cleaning his car with the radio on and Ellen Nelson is practising her scales. Her voice tiptoes up until it can't go any further, then it turns and tiptoes down. In a while she will begin to sing *I came to the garden alone while the dew was still on the roses*. She sings the solos at the Salvation Army. Her brother

Claude plays the trombone. Mr Nelson has let his pigeons out and every few minutes they circle over the house as if they are all whirled about on a single thread. In a while they will settle with equal single-mindedness on Kate's father's vegetable garden, and if he hadn't strung black cotton booby-traps the length of the rows, they'd have all his peas.

Everyone else is up and about. It is a good Saturday, and in a while Kate's dad will join them doing the Saturday things: he'll rescue the peas, plant potatoes. He'll get on his bike, sling a sugar sack over the handlebars and, holding his rod like a lance, bike off to the wild beach beyond the cape with its seals and African thorn and tangled kelp. There he'll stand on the rocks, casting for cod and trevally. If it were winter, he would bike out in the afternoon to watch Athies thrashing the opposition at the showgrounds. Or he might take his daughters to the swings at Awamoa Park, while he joins the thin emigrant line of Dutchmen and Scotties in their scarves and caps, keeping the dim memory of soccer alive.

Kate's mother is up already. She has gone through to the kitchen and stoked up the range. She has made a pot of tea and put on the porridge, and while its grey blisters pop blub blub blub in the pot she sits by the range with the door open to warm her feet, and reads. Kate and Maura have climbed into the warm nest she has abandoned, for a story. Their father reads to them slowly, giving them plenty of time to look at the pictures. There is Robert and the doctor, Robert and the baker, Robert finding the happy children. Kate tugs a grey striped feather from the eiderdown, and suddenly the miracle happens. She can see not just the picture, but the line of words underneath.

'Doughnuts!' said Robert. 'For all of us!'

It is an ordinary miracle. It happens to millions every day. But it is not diminished by repetition. It is the moment when the navigator, after months at sea, looks out and sees the cloud on the horizon form

45

itself into a mountain top. The words emerge like a new land, like shy creatures from dense forest. The marks that began life thousands of years ago, scratched into the dust in some desert encampment or scraped into mudbrick in some small dusty town, assemble into meaning. 'D'. *Daleth*, a door. It opens onto the circle of 'O', the pictogram for eye; and 'U', the image of a hook. In 'G' there is the camel's hump; in 'H' the palisades of *heth*, an enclosure for sheep or floppy-eared goats. Then the serpentine squiggle of 'N', a snake; another hook; the crisscross of 'T' or *taw*, a sign; and, finally, the nibble of 'S', the symbol for *shin* or teeth. Letter by letter, they line up for decipherment, the entire sequence no longer intended to be read as a series of unrelated objects — door, eye, hook, hump, enclosure, snake, hook, sign, teeth — but transformed in some unrecorded, ancient moment of human genius to signify the object word's initial sound: DOUGHNUTS

And after the word, the exclamation point — '!' — to colour the word with ecstasy.

Doughnuts!

It is the voice of a child who finds friends after a long quest. The voice of the voyager come ashore. The high-pitched triumph of the hero who holds the shibboleth that will make him welcome among strangers. This exclamation point, too, has had its moment of invention. It is a word, though Kate and her sister and father snug in the bed at Greta Street no longer register it as such. *Io*, it says. Joy. The Latin word inserted into manuscripts by medieval monks and nuns, squeezed end on between lines of text when the transcriber's joy at what he or she was copying became transcendent and demanded expression. The copyist sits at her desk, the light of some forgotten afternoon spread like a white cloth from the window, the quiet scratch of pen on vellum, the snick of a knife sharpening a feather. *Io*, writes the nun at the moment of the angel's apparition to the Virgin kneeling in her study. *Io*, at the empty tomb. *Io* at the blinded saint tumbling to his knees on the road to Damascus. The capital I floats in the air like an angel with its hands clasped, above the circle of light that is the O, dwindling to a dot.

'Doughnuts!' said Robert. 'For all of us!'

The miracle takes place one Saturday morning at 55 Greta Street, Oamaru, Otago, South Island, New Zealand, the World, the Universe. Kate sees the words for the first time. She can walk along the line as easily as she walks along the wall her father has built around their garden, block by limestone block. That 'D' has opened and let her into the world of reading.

Kate is old now, and has read many books, but she remembers that first reading with peculiar clarity. Even at the time it seemed significant. A few years later when she was seven and could write properly, she underlined the sentence and printed neatly in the margin at its side: *This is the first sentence from a book that I could read*. It seemed a moment worthy of record.

3.

The first memory is of a book. It belongs to the time before Robert and the doughnuts. It belongs to the time before her sister was born, when Maura existed only as a round bulge beneath her mother's cotton frock.

In the memory, Kate's mother is sprawled on the sitting-room floor. Kate is being pulled uncomfortably against her shoulder. Above them sways Kate's father, with the sewing machine in his upraised hands.

Years later, Kate stood in an Italian church looking up at a painting of Moses holding aloft the tablets of the law, prepared to smash them in pieces in anger at the backsliding of the Israelites.

'The sewing machine!' she said to her friend Maddy.

'What?' said Maddy.

'The tablets,' said Kate. 'They remind me of a sewing machine.'

'If you say so, dear,' said Maddy. 'You'd better keep out of the sun.'

'It's a long story,' said Kate. 'Too hard to explain.'

Her father had stood over them holding not the commandments that would govern the children of Israel for all time, but a Singer Electric. The machine was new. It had replaced the treadle machine which, with its ornate wheel and foot-pedal, now stood in the hall-way supporting a small jungle of asparagus fern and Busy Lizzie. The electric machine was set up now when required on the dining table at which her mother sat, frowning with concentration as she pushed cotton or winceyette tikkatikkatikka beneath the busy needle. Her hands moved in a small circle of light.

The machine's name was written in gold on the front, as if each letter had burst from sheer importance into tendril and leaf. In the memory, however, the machine is not remarkable for its newness or elegance. It seems big and black and very heavy, swept up into the air in her father's unsteady hands. It could fall at any moment; it could be dropped or thrown; it could come crashing down on Kate or on her mother and her mother is frightened. She is shouting something, her mouth all pink and rubbery; her arm is hurting Kate, who can hardly breathe, trapped between her shoulder and the big round bulge that is the new baby. Kate struggles and squirms and keeps tight hold of her book.

The Little Red Hen.

Kate carried the book everywhere. There is a photo from this time of Kate and her cousin Bernard seated on Rajah the pony out at Weston. Bernard has a firm grip of Rajah's mane, but Kate is hanging on to *The Little Red Hen*. Inside the book the plump little hen is bustling about asking who will help her sow the corn and water it and grind it and bake it into bread.

'Not I!' say the pig, the cow, the cat and the horse.

So the little red hen does it all herself and when the bread emerges from the oven, brown and crusty, they all want to eat it. But the little red hen says no. She has made it, so she can eat it all, and she won't be being greedy or selfish.

The Little Red Hen is there in the first memory, where Kate's mother sprawls on the floor with her petticoat and the tops of her stockings showing and her mouth pink and frightened. Kate has arrived at her side, flung somehow or booted, and her mother has her in such a fierce protective grip that Kate can hardly breathe. She squirms, fighting against her mother's bulk. *The Little Red Hen* is clutched against her chest, spread wide, as if by holding it against her body she might absorb its contents through her skin. She lays her hand on such pictures, or her cheek. They enter her. Here on the sitting-room carpet is a loud place of noise and shouting and tears and confusion. The event has rolled in like a big wave at a bucket-and-spade beach. She is tumbled by the unexpected.

The world of the little red hen is different. In the book, the world remains constant. In its even golden light, the little hen is always cutting the corn and baking the bread. The pig is always in his trough, the horse always munches the same mouthful of hay. In this world, the little hen is busy. She is good. Her moral adversaries — lazy pig, indolent cow, vain cat — are predictably themselves. They always say the same thing. They always do the same things. And the little red hen always has her bread in the end. It is her reward for industry and perseverance. This sunny world is neither generous nor particularly forgiving, but it is a world where what happens seems fair and possessed of a certain simple justice.

Kate understood the rules that operated between the cardboard covers.

It was, moreover, a world that was just the right size. It could be held easily in two hands. It could be opened whenever Kate wanted to open it, wherever she might be. The book acted as a talisman, such as the time she was seated on Rajah and it was meant to be exciting, when her Auntie Mary cupped her hand over the Box Brownie and they had to smile, say 'Cheese'. But it was not exciting. It was, in fact, a terrifyingly long way to the ground and Rajah shifted from hoof to hoof, moving beneath them like a sofa that had suddenly acquired a mind of its own and an uncertain temper. This was the time to take firm hold of a book.

Kate's real father gave her elephant rides so she swayed safely above the crowd. He got down on all fours so that she could ride on his back up the hall to bed, growling past the dark cupboard, the pot-plant jungle. He foxtrotted her around the sitting room balanced on his feet. So who is this giant with eyes like a drained glass? Viewed from the sitting-room carpet, he seems to reach all the way to the upturned bowl that holds the light at the centre of the ceiling. He holds the sewing machine aloft. He could throw it; he could drop it on the head of her mother or herself. This is also the time to take fast hold of a book. It is spread flat across her breastbone, bearing the words of the charm that guarantees the triumph of order.

'The sky is falling! The sky is falling!' said Chicken-Licken. 'I must go and tell the king!'

The Tale of Chicken-Licken (trad.)

The transformation of man to giant happened month after month, year after year, without warning.

In the story, the two sisters are seated by the fire in their cosy cottage. Outside, snow has fallen and the trees are bowed low beneath its weight.

Knock knock knock.

The thud at the barrier between darkness and firelight, warmth and cold, safety and chaos, routine and interruption. Snow White, who is the older sister, with hair like spun gold, goes to open the door, while Rose Red, who is the younger sister, with dark bouncing curls, picks up the poker, just in case. A bear walks in, the way bears do, and lies down by their fire. The sisters are frightened, but he seems to mean no harm so they let him stay, and after many such nights, one sunny morning he stands before them, shorn of his heavy coat and transformed by their patient kindness into a handsome prince.

Kate and her sister are seated by the fire before bed. They are perched on either side of the fireplace on the little gold boxes that hold the kindling. Each box has a picture of a windmill on the front and a girl in golden clogs. Kate and Maura have had their baths. They have their nighties on under tartan dressing-gowns. Kate has on her slippers, which have red pompoms, and Maura has on hers, which are just the same except the pompoms are blue. This is the way sisters' clothes are meant to be: the same in general outline, with some subtle distinction. (Snow White's dress is yellow with flounces and bows and Rose Red's is identical, but it is pink.) Their mother is sitting in the kitchen reading the *Oamaru Mail* and listening to the radio.

'Life with Dexter'.

They could hear the perky tune and Dexter calling, *Hi, family, I'm home*! in the funny foreign voice used by the people in the stories on the radio. Dexter has returned from the office where he works for stuffy old Mr Wilmott and he's going to take Jessie and the kids to the pictures for a treat, which sounds ordinary enough, but you know, you just know, that it is all going to become a muddle because that is what life with Dexter is like. He fixes the leak under the sink, though Jessie says he shouldn't, and the whole house is flooded within an hour. He wants to buy Jessie a surprise birthday present and ends up demolishing the garage. Tonight they have arrived at the picture theatre and already he has dropped things and lost things and forgotten to turn the tail-lights off in the car and the picture theatre audience is telling the whole family to stop talking and SIT DOWN, while the studio audience is laughing and laughing, because that is what they like: Dexter making a mess of everything every week.

Hi, family, I'm home!

Kate and her sister have had their tea. The table is still spread under a fine white veil. Their father is late home.

'Off at that darn club,' their mother said.

She meant the 2nd NZEF down by Gillies Foundry, a dark, bare room filled with smoke and the laughter and loud talk of men. Next door, the furnaces of the foundry belched from the bottom of a bank covered in bony carcasses of rusted metal. The furnaces emitted an acrid smell that caught at the back of the throat. Men with sooty faces and white eyeballs worked the furnaces and the fires leapt in a wall of flame up each tall chimney. Kate thought that hell would probably be like that: a larger, smokier version of Gillies Foundry. The RSA was several blocks away, with its memorial rose garden and white limestone pergolas, but that was for woofters, men who had sat the war out in Cairo and marched down Thames Street clanking with medals every Anzac Day. Real old soldiers didn't march. They went around to their mates' places where home-brew bubbled out in the wash-house. They drank at the 2nd NZEF. That was where Kate and Maura's father went while they waited until their mother clicked her tongue and said, 'Well, it won't keep for ever. It'll spoil. You'd better sit up and have it.' And she dishes them out a chop each and a scoop of mashed potato and some peas and puts their father's plate in the oven under a pie-dish to keep warm. There is sago for after, which is Maura's favourite. She asks for seconds while Kate pushes the slimy, lumpy stuff around her plate.

'I hate sago,' she says. 'It's like sick.'

'Don't be picky,' say her mother. 'It's good for you. It's nourishing.' She is not really paying attention. Her mouth is set in a thin disapproving line. Kate knows not to ask for a jam piece instead tonight. While she is out in the kitchen, Kate gives all her own share to Maura and their mother doesn't even notice. They eat their tea, have their bath, sit by the fire until bedtime.

Now they have their books open on their knees. Kate is reading her school book: *The Tale of Chicken-Licken*. It is a proper story, unlike *Janet and John*, which is also a school book but has big round letters and no story whatsoever. Nothing happens. They just run. Or jump. Or look. *Look, John, look. See Janet run*. Kate hates *Janet and John*. *The Tale of Chicken Licken*, however, gets bigger and bigger, page by page, as the birds join the expedition. Then they meet Foxy Loxy and follow him into his cave and the door slams shut. It's an ending as perfect as the BANG! of a party balloon. There was no need to worry about what might happen afterwards, behind that closed door. They had gone and that was that. The closing of the door marks The End to a proper story.

Maura is too small yet to read school books. She is practising her writing anyway, over the pictures in the *Children's Bible*. The infant Samuel kneels in a palisade of uneven Ms and upside-down As.

There is a thud at the front door, the fumble of a key in the lock. Far away in Ashville, the radio policeman is asking Dexter what he's doing breaking into his own house and the audience is in stitches. Out in the hallway the song starts.

And who is the gi-ant with long curling hair . . . sings the stranger at the door, loudly and unhappily, as if Kate and her sister and their mother were the bloody brutal British themselves. The song has started and the unsteady tread as the man marches down on the redoubt that is the sitting room . . . *who-oo strides at the head of the band* . . .

Another thud as he lurches into the door that divides the

hallway in two. The top half of that door is coloured glass: look through one of its panels of red or green or yellow and the hall becomes another place. The details remain the same: the barometer by the front door turned permanently to Fair, the door to the front room slightly ajar, allowing just a glimpse of the piano supporting the vase of plastic gladioli, the door opposite opening onto the front bedroom with its dressing table holding brush, mirror and comb on special crocheted mats. Viewed through the glass their house becomes a country where pianos can be red and dressing tables green and where the light is always sunshine yellow, even at night.

This evening, though, it all goes to smash. Crash goes the red panel, bang goes the green and the yellow is cracked right through so that for ever after the view of the hallway lurches like a car bouncing over a railway line, across the zigzag at its centre.

Why 'tis Kelly, the bo-oy from Killarne! sings the man in the dark hall. The sitting-room door opens. He sways in the doorway, red-faced, shirt loose and eyes that empty brilliant blue. This is a night to remain quiet and still, to stay out of the way while Mum brings through the tea, the peas dried to pellets, the chop a withered crescent, the potatoes set under a stiff white crust.

'Wass this pap?' says the stranger, and he tosses the plate at the wall. It strikes just below the citation from the King, gratefully thanking Grandad Kennedy for Making the Supreme Sacrifice for King and Country in France in 1918. The plate cracks in a shrapnel of green peas.

On such nights, Kate and her sister shrink. They become very small — so small that no one can see them. They take their books and the lavatory torch from the shelf by the back door and go outside to their hut by the hen-house, where they hide until the house becomes quiet and the stranger is sleeping, like those giants who rage *Fee Fi Fo Fum*! in their big boots, then doze off suddenly while the hero escapes with the golden eggs.

55

The hut is constructed from appleboxes and sacks. It smells of hessian, coal-dust and sugar. From the hen-house comes the contented sound of hens settling to roost with their scaly pink feet clamped to a dry branch. They snuggle in a row, with Moses at one end ready to burst into hiphoorahs at the hint of a new day. In the hut there are paua shells for plates and the mattress that used to be Maura's when she was a baby and an old tartan picnic-rug. Kate and Maura curl under the rug and read by torchlight, the thin beam picking out Chicken-Licken and Goose-Loose running to tell the king that *the sky is falling, the sky is falling*! From the house there are thumps and slams and the sound of raised voices but Kate and Maura listen instead to the hens, who are having a much better conversation up there on their branch.

'All right?' they say to one another.

And 'Yup,' they say. 'Yup, yup, yup.'

'All right?' says Kate to Maura.

'Mm,' says Maura. She is sucking her thumb and winding a tendril of hair around one finger the way she does just before she goes to sleep. Her other hand is between her legs.

'Do you want to go wees?' says Kate, and Maura shakes her head and snuggles closer. She's fibbing. In a few seconds the damp patch spreads beneath them but it is warm under the picnic rug and their nighties are nearly dry by the time Mum comes to find them.

'Shh,' she says, bending down to look under the coal sack. 'He's asleep.'

She has her tired face on and she winces at the movement required to gather up Maura and the picnic rug. Kate walks behind, dopey with interrupted sleep, carrying the torch and *Chicken-Licken*. The garden is blue and white under the eye of the moon. The nectarine tree, the plum and the apple trees are covered in silver leaf. The flowers on the broad beans shine pure as a candle flame and their scent is sweet and heavy. Kate can feel the wet grass soak through her slippers. The house is dark, only the hall light on. The bear-stranger has turned into Dad again. He lies on the sofa under a blanket, still wearing all his clothes, even his shoes, which poke out the end. He is snoring. A deep inbreath that rattles in his nose, followed by a funny whistle on the outbreath. His mouth is wide open. Kate can feel a giggle bubble up but her mother shakes her head quickly so she swallows the giggle and it lodges in her throat in a sago lump. They tiptoe past. Kate knows enough about giants to understand that it is not a good idea to waken them.

Fee fi fo fum!

Their mother tucks them into bed and switches off the bedside light with its little row of elephants racing around the shade, tail to trunk, straight into the hole the bulb burned through the vellum one night when it was knocked over.

'Prayers,' she says and she kneels by the bed while Kate rattles through the God blesses and Gentle Jesus meek and mild, skipping as fast as she can over the part where you have to say, 'If I should die before I wake, take me to heaven for Jesus' sake.' The very thought of that! That death could come sneaking up on you, while you had your eyes shut, taking tiny chicken steps! It could reach out and tap you on the shoulder before you had a chance to say it wasn't fair, you were asleep. It could tap you and you would be IT.

Dead.

Kate usually tried to stay awake as long as she could so that death would not stand a chance. She lay in the dark each night wondering what it would feel like: what would happen first? Would she find herself gasping for air the way she had when she fell into the creek at the Botanic Gardens? She could remember gulping and struggling, then a curious drifting, looking up at the water golden brown above her head where bubbles rose and burst in little glittering clusters, and then the crash of her father's hand reaching through to grab her sunhat and drag her to the bank, where it was cold and shivery and alive. She lay on wet earth among squashed buttercups. She vomited creek water. Her throat hurt.

Would death be like that? Each night she lay listening to her breath going in and out. She listened to the ticktock of her heart. She forced her eyes to stay open, focused on the white plastic fluorescent angel that glowed in the dark above her bed. And suddenly it would be morning. Her father was whistling as he shaved in the bathroom, the radio was playing in the kitchen and she was alive! She had escaped Gentle Jesus yet again — and heaven, which truly did not seem especially interesting, even if you were given wings and could fly about. There was a picture in her mother's room of Jesus sitting in heaven with a crowd of blond children — all presumably dead, the unlucky ones who had not made it through the night, the ones who had presumably suffered to come unto him. Heaven looked remarkably like the Rhododendron Dell in the Botanic Gardens.

'Night night,' says Mum after prayers on the night when the bear-stranger lies asleep on the sofa. 'Roll over, face the wall and you'll have good dreams.'

Kate does as instructed. She sleeps turned to the right, while Maura sleeps on the opposite side of the room turned to the left. Kate lies listening to their mother moving quietly about the house, closing doors gently, switching off the hall light. There is the creaking of the board by the bathroom, then the click of the door to the spare room closing. Their mother has moved from the front bedroom. Their father has the double bed to himself while she sleeps on a foldout bed among the suitcases and unused rolls of lino and Maura's old cot. The foldout bed is metal and jingles as she climbs aboard. Kate listens to the muted music of springs and the quiet rustle of pages turning. Their mother is reading the Bible, as she does every night, consulting one of the little red booklets she gets from Church, which tells her what to read, and making notes of her own in a sixpenny notebook. Once, when she was reading, she saw

Jesus. He came and stood by her bed and put his hand on her head.

'What did he look like?' Kate asked, because she liked to know all the details. She liked precision. Though there could be little doubt when it came to Jesus: in the picture with the children he was tall and blond with a straggly beard and wavy, shoulder-length hair.

Her mother thought for a moment, frowning, though her eyes were still bright and excited on account of Jesus' unexpected visit. She was standing at the ironing board sweeping the iron back and forth over one of their father's shirts.

'I only saw his feet,' she said. 'I had my head down so I could only see him from the knees down. He had on some sort of white robe.'

'Was he wearing shoes?' asked Kate. Her mother said yes, a pair of sandals, and Kate imagined roman sandals, such as the boys wore to school, not plastic sandals like their own, which were blue with shiny buckles.

'Did he say anything?' said Maura.

'Yes,' said their mother. The iron was sending out little puffs of steam and the shirt was smooth in its wake. 'He said my name.'

'Mummy?' said Maura.

'No, silly,' said Kate. 'Her name's not Mummy.'

'He said Tollie,' said their mother. It was her pet name, her family name, given when her little brother was three and could not pronounce her real name, which was Dorothy. Jesus, too, knew her pet name. 'He laid his hand on my head and said, "Tollie".'

'What did it feel like?' said Kate.

Her mother hung the shirt over the narrow shoulders of a kitchen chair.

'It felt lovely,' she said. 'Like electricity. Like . . . umm . . . warmth all through.'

Then he had disappeared.

She sang as she was doing the ironing. *Love divine, all loves excelling* . . . She was happy all that day.

Jesus could come again, as he did that night. He could arrive unannounced in the spare room where their mother lies reading, and place his hand on her hair.

'Tollie,' he'd say, while their father sleeps undisturbed on the sofa. Kate might hear Jesus in conversation with her mother through the bedroom wall.

'NO!' says Maura quite distinctly from somewhere under her eiderdown. She often talks in her sleep, long conversations with rabbits and other interesting creatures.

Around the blind there is a rim of light from the street-lamp, dappled by the leaves of the ribbonwood outside their window. Kate can make out every detail of the room: the wardrobe and chest of drawers, both unremarkable by day but at night heavy and unpredictable as a pair of bullocks on their bandy wooden legs. Above her bed is the fluorescent angel and the picture of the little girl whose name is Pinkie, who is walking about in a storm in only a thin white dress and a ribboned bonnet. Over Maura's bed there is a row of Bambi stickers and a picture of the Virgin Mary with a blue veil and dark bruised eyes. ('Not enough iron,' her mother had said when Kate asked her why the Virgin Mary looked like that. She did not like the Virgin Mary much. The picture was there because Kate's father had insisted.)

In the air around the house is the sound of the sea. Not the safe sea where Kate and her sister go with buckets and spades, where it is called Friendly Bay and pats at their feet with waves like kittens' paws. It casts up seaweed necklaces and the occasional jellyfish, big lumps of blood-spotted flesh that they catch on their spades and leave in their tin buckets to see if they will melt in the summer sun.

The night-time sea does not come from Friendly Bay with its kiosk and merry-go-round but from the shore beyond the breakwater where the sea roars in, white-crested, and tears at the shingle bank, strong enough to fling whole trees ashore, stripped to bone, and hillocks of seaweed, rotten and stinking.

As they sit at Friendly Bay eating their eskimo pies and waiting to see what will happen to the jellyfish, they can hear this other sea growling beyond the breakwater, trying to find a way through to drag them away. That is the sea Kate hears at night, surging in and out, like breathing. At intervals the town clock plays its little tune, broken neatly in pieces for the quarter-hour, the half and the three-quarter, before gathering itself together for the hour. The grand and formal beats tread the night air, announcing that time is measured, orderly and solemn. The night of darkness and Gentle Jesus hovering overhead like a hawk above a road has been organised into manageable segments. Time is an orange, neatly peeled.

This Saturday will not be a good Saturday. For days now, the house will hold its breath. Her father will waken on the sofa and he might still be angry. He could be angry all week. He will come home day after day angry with the meals, the way their mother looks or the way she tidies the house. He will be angry with her for leaving the Church and not taking Kate and her sister to Mass as she had promised she would when they married at the Basilica. She has gone back on her word. She has broken her promise, she has gone back among those Presbyterian bastards, she will go to hell and she will take Kate and Maura with her; she is a lazy bitch, a filthy, deceitful, idle . . .

The words will swill about the room, sticking to the chairs and curtains, seeping out into the dark hallway and the cold bedrooms. Kate's mother will stand by the stove crying into the custard and everything she makes will taste bitter. If she fights back it will be sudden and defiant and Kate and her sister will keep their heads down and move fast. They walk along the edges of their parents' quarrels like cats in a strange yard. They do not argue because it seems as if all the space for arguing has been used up. They cut out paper dolls in their room, or stay out in their hut pouring tea from the green plastic teapot and saying, 'Would you like milk?' in pinched, polite, grown-up voices.

When their father comes home from work their mother will say, 'Go and keep him happy, girls, until I've dished up.' They will run to the door. They will hug his legs and say, 'Daddy! Daddy!' like the children in books. They will stand in front of his chair and Kate will sing him 'My Pigeon House I Open Wide', with all the actions, and Maura will dance. She does The Blue Dance, hopping about from one foot to the other and twirling, or The Pink Dance, which is exactly the same. She did this once when she was much younger, too small to know that dances are each supposed to be different, and their father had laughed. Now she does proper ballet with first, second and third position, but The Blue Dance can still be relied on to amuse him. And while they dance and sing, their mother will bang the pots out in the kitchen and sigh over gravy gone to lumps.

And slowly, day by day, the house will become light again, and one day their father will bring their mother home a gift. Some little thing he has bought at Bartram's Hardware. A china dancer in a stiff lacy skirt, a painting of a boy in a blue velvet suit in a golden frame. Their mother will receive her gift as if it does not matter. She will open the wrapping paper slowly. She will lift the beautiful thing out of its box and set it on the table beside the teapot.

'Very nice,' she'll say. She will furl the ribbon around her fingers and put it in the sideboard drawer, though Kate strokes the china lace and says, 'It's so pretty. Don't you think it's pretty?'

She wants her mother to say thank you, as you should when you are given a present. She wants her father to be pleased that he has chosen the right thing. There is something uneasy about this phase: not straightforward anger but a kind of queasy truce as unreal as the transformation that had preceded all this. Kate wants that over too. She wants everything to be ordinary — not too angry, not too sweet, but like the porridge in the story: just right. Just ordinary. She wants to go to bed at night with prayers with their mother, and then a story from their father. She wants him to say, 'Sleep well,' then turn as he goes out the door after switching out their light to make them fireflies in the dark. He lights a cigarette and spins it in swirls and great loops. He writes their names in the dark: KATE and MAURA, writing backwards on a single swooping thread of light before he closes the door just so, with the darkness exactly divided so that Kate can sleep in the dark and Maura can sleep in the glow from the hall. Kate wants everything to be ordinary, with a good week and the promise of a good Saturday to follow.

That is a few days off yet. Tonight, the storm still rumbles in the distance. Kate knows it will take time to clear, but in the meantime she knows that the sky cannot fall, though a silly bird might think so. You must not panic, nor imagine that things are worse than they are. You must be sensible, you must be resourceful. You must manage on your own and make your own bread.

Those were the lessons that were taught by hens.

4.

As the Little House settled down on her new foundations,
she smiled happily. Once again she could watch the sun
and moon and stars. Once again she could watch Spring
and Summer and Fall and Winter come and go.

The Little House by Virginia Lee Burton

Dad's book was propped against the teapot. Maura sat on his right with her book open against the sugar basin and Kate, crammed on his left between the sideboard and the dining table, had her book balanced against the cruet set. Her mother sat out in the kitchen with her books and pamphlets spread among the pots on the Formica table. From time to time she called, 'Want any more?' and if they answered yes, preoccupied, turning a page, there would be a rustling of paper before she appeared bearing a saucepan and the big spoon. The fire burned in the grate; the radio played

'Popular Parade': 'How Much is that Doggie in the Window?'
(*wuff wuff*)

They sat peaceably reading beneath the King's letter.

'Five pound,' their father had told them. 'That's what came with that letter. Five pound for a widow with six children.' And the canary chirrup of emphysema already in her lungs.

That was typical, their father said. The King was British and upper class: how could he possibly know what was decent under the circumstances? Grandma Kennedy had put the five pound toward a passage to New Zealand, where her children would have a better chance. Spent the remainder of her short life scrubbing the patterns off Protestant lino until her children were old enough to cope on their own. By then her lungs were awash. She had died when Kate's dad was fourteen, and once a month they went to put flowers in the jam jar on her grave: daffodils, marguerites, chrysanthemums, according to the season. Kate's father tidied the grave as if he were picking lint from a woollen skirt. Then he stood for a moment and his hand flickered across his shirt in the sign of the cross.

'So if the King was so stupid, why do we have his letter on the wall?' said Kate.

Her father turned a page. He looked up briefly.

'So we remember,' he said. He meant that they should remember their grandfather, whose picture lay in the applebox in the spare room. He was a stubby man in the uniform of the King's Own Scottish Borderers. He rested one hand on the shoulder of their grandmother, who was delicate and had cheeks of a hectic rose-pink. She sat on a velvet throne in a hothouse dripping with ferns. That was Kate's sole image of Dundee, Scotland, where her father and his brothers and sisters had been born. When he was eight they had sailed away down the Irish Sea. His mother had taken them all to the railing to show them the coast of Ireland.

'What was Ireland like?' Kate asked.

Her father licked a cigarette paper.

'Green,' he said.

Naturally. He spat a few shreds of tobacco and felt in his shirt pocket for his matches.

He had seen the shining line of the horizon where Kelly had marched with his long curling hair, and people thought it was sweet to die for the faith of their fathers — they didn't mind a bit — and a pale moon rose above an endless succession of crystal fountains in vale after green vale.

They were to remember Ireland and their grandfather as they sat to eat their saveloys and upside-down pineapple puddings; they were to remember the five pound posted to a poor grieving widow by a regent too rich, too upper class, too British to care.

Their grandparents' picture could with due justice and elegance have replaced the King's letter, but their mother did not like to have dead relatives hanging about the walls. Her own were lined up where they belonged, in black and white on the walls of the Pioneer Gallery in Dunedin: men and women who had sailed from Scotland and then, hands clenched in crocheted mittens, lips pursed over dubious teeth, appeared to be regretting the decision. Or they lived in the applebox too, with their boater hats or Oxford bags or bonneted babies. All properly labelled with names that became familiar with repetition. When Kate and Maura were sick or when it was too wet to play outside, they would get out the applebox and tip its contents onto the floor.

'Who's that?' they would ask, and their mother would lean down, take the photo in her hand and hold it to the light at the window.

'Ah,' she would say. 'That's my cousin, Gwen Scott, at Halfway Bush. All the Scotts were tall, well over six feet. She was a beautiful dancer but she found it hard to get partners on account of her height. Then she met Maurice and he was six foot six. He had to stoop to get through doors. He couldn't dance, but it was a perfect match . . .'

'And this?' they'd say, though they knew already.

'That's my Great Uncle William,' she said. He had been a gentleman. He had been possessed of such perfect manners that he had got on the boat to go to Sydney and been too refined to go to the toilet. 'They had to . . . you know . . .' Her voice lowered with the indelicacy of it all . . . 'Go . . . over the side of the boat.' But not Great Uncle William. He had held on all the way to Australia and expired on the quayside on arrival. Kate and her sister put Great Uncle William reverently back in the box — a high-browed man with full beard and crinkly hair like Kate's own: Falconer hair, red and crimped into lambswool — imagining his sad demise. The crowd standing by the boat, the man lying on the wharf, the pop as he exploded from all that pent-up pee.

They left the sad photo to last: the one of their mother's younger brother seated astride an Indian motorbike with the little dog on his lap. Their mother held this photo to the light and stroked the surface free of dust.

'That's Tom,' she said. 'That's Tom and . . .' She would stop there always and peer more closely. '. . . Tug . . . or maybe it's Skipper . . .' Her voice trailed away. 'Such a waste,' she said. Kate and Maura would wait for the story that always followed, about the boy who was so clever, who knew more than the teacher at school, who had pointed out mistakes in the sums on the blackboard, who could play the violin not as others played — with music to read on a spindly stand — but 'by ear', which was much better. He could go to the pictures and come home and play all the tunes 'by ear'. He had a beautiful German violin that had cost a fortune. Their grandmother had bought it for him with all her teaching money, all the shillings amassed on countless afternoons spent listening to the children of the district stumble up and down C major at the piano in the front room. Tom had taken it out of the wrapping — 'green felt wrapping' their mother always said, for she liked to get the details accurate — and he had played it for Grandma right there in the kitchen: difficult things: Handel and whatdoyoucallhim? Bach. Yes. Bach. With lots of double-stopping. He had played 'The Londonderry Air'.

Kate's mother always stops there. She is hearing the music in her head. She is seeing the young man playing difficult things under a drying rack hoisted up to the ceiling with its load of work shirts and socks. 'The Londonderry Air' still makes her cry when she hears it on the radio.

'Then what happened?' says Kate, for the story did not stop with the German violin.

Her mother sighs. Tom got Matric and went off to Dunedin to study to be a lawyer. He shared a room in Cumberland Street with another young law student, Henry Parata, from down Wyndham way.

'He was such a nice chap,' says Kate's mother.

There is a photo of Henry in the box too, standing beside Tom, one arm draped companionably across his shoulders in front of the clocktower on the banks of the Leith.

'Tom and he were such great chums.'

They played music together — Tom on violin, Henry on piano — four evenings a week and Sunday afternoons at the Savoy.

Their mother stops again. She turns the photo over to read the names written on the back. *Tom and Henry P. Dunedin 1928*. She is hearing Czardas, Raff's 'Cavatine', airs and tangos played from the carved Tudor corner of a carved Tudor room to tiered cakestands of butterfly cakes, to diners chatting over silver and starched linen.

'Parata and Stuart!' Henry had yelled in Tom's ear as they roared home late one night along Cumberland Street on the Indian. 'Barristers and Solicitors!'

'And then?' says Maura. Because now the sad part is coming.

Then Henry got ill. They thought it was just a chill. The room was cheap and damp. Henry began to cough. Tom, too, caught a fever.

'They'd overdone it, you see,' says their mother. 'They'd got run down with all the swotting and every night out working. They'd let their resistance get low and there was a lot of TB around in those days.'

Henry died within the year. Tom went to the sanatorium up at Waipiata and survived. Then one afternoon out at Millerhill when he was chopping kindling, his father had said something to him.

'What did he say?' Kate asks. But their mother will not tell them. Something about Henry, something that made Tom pick up the hatchet and threaten his father.

'He wasn't right, you see,' says their mother. 'He wasn't right in the head.'

The TB germs had swum up into his brain and destroyed that part that makes people love their fathers no matter what they do or say, and he was taken away to Cherry Farm, where the doctors took away that part of the brain that makes people take up the kindling hatchet and hate their fathers.

And now, 'What a waste,' their mother says, holding her brother between her hands so that the light will fall full upon him. 'What a terrible waste.'

She means the saggy brown cardigan. She means the woollen slippers. She means the shining dayroom, the white villa. She means Cherry Farm.

It is a name like a place in a book.

Cherry Farm.

It should have thatched cottages, trees in white blossom, a barnyard of fluffy chicks. It is instead a treeless settlement of white boxes that grew on the banks of the Waikouaiti River between one summer holiday and the next, as if overnight, the way white things seemed to, with their white frills and white poisonous gills. They passed Cherry Farm on their way to their grandma's house at Millerhill. They looked down as they crossed the bridge to see how the water beneath had turned rusty red.

'To think we used to swim here!' their mother always said. The mud stank. They held their noses until they had driven safely past. Sometimes, though, they could not pass because their uncle lived there and must be taken for a drive.

'Hello, Tollie,' he would say, shuffling across the lino in the shiny room where men rocked to and fro in vinyl chairs or made sudden loud cries and the room smelled of damp and cabbage and dreadful waste.

'Hello, Tom,' said their mother, and she put her arms around him. The man who rode the Indian bike at breakneck speed navigating all the twists and turns of the Kilmog, until the TB ambushed him and wriggled into his brain so that it rotted like a bruised apple. It went brown and soft, and he became mad.

Photos and their stories belonged in boxes hidden away in the spare room. There was too much story for each photo to bear everyday contemplation. When Kate and her sister and father sat at their tea beneath the King's letter and the Columban calendar, they remembered, but not too much. Not a single saint among the many listed on the calendar was related to them.

They read their books instead, piling meat and potato and peas onto their forks with absent-minded dexterity. 'Pass the butter,' was all the conversation required. Chewing steadily, they read their way through the books they brought home each week from the Library.

Once upon a time there was a little girl.
  She had a Father, and a Mother, and a Grandpa,

*and a Grandma, and an Uncle, and an Aunty; and they
all lived together in a nice white cottage with a thatched
roof.*

Milly-Molly-Mandy Stories by Joyce Lankester Brisley

On Friday nights — good Friday nights when their father was safely
himself — they walked into town. Their mother took the pushchair
for the return trip up the hill. It was steep and Maura's legs got tired.
Kate, too, sometimes hitched a ride, sitting with her feet dangling
over the front, with Maura's knees pressed against her spine and
bags of shopping wedged about them both — shoes in awkward
shoeboxes, plants in punnets for the garden, groceries from the big
shop that proved week after week that Mr Budd at their dairy
charged more than he should for the convenience, not to mention
being prone to slip mouldy fruit in with the good oranges and
keeping a blunt thumb on the scales when he was weighing out the
mild or tasty.

Even when they were too old to ride in the pushchair their
mother took it for the shopping while Kate and Maura walked hand
in hand with their father, taking exact turns corner to corner with
the Bad Hand and the Good Hand. The Good Hand had all its
fingers. The Bad Hand was twisted and lacked fingers because of
The War, and neither of them liked the feel of it, the thumb and
pointer finger like a hen's claw. All the way to town and all the way
back, dawdling up the hill in the dark, they maintained a strict
rotation, running behind their father's back to swap. Their shadows
broke from pools of light beneath each street-lamp, stretching and
mingling and washing back like sand caught on a receding wave.

The week after Kate recognised the doughnuts, her father had
taken her to the Library. The Library was a massive edifice, an
athenaeum, a temple, one of several on the main street with columns

at the front carved with leaves, as if the stone went up and up until it could bear to be simple stone no longer and must sprout. Around the back, where a few cars parked among puddles in a rough and ready fashion, the carving stopped and the temples dwindled to unadorned blocks and corrugated iron, just as houses had brass doorknobs and verandah lace pinned on their fronts, but were wash-houses and coal sheds behind. The doors to the Library were of glass and heavy polished timber and when they swung to it was with a flump flump, a sound like velvet. Inside, people spoke in hushed voices as if they were in church, and women stood at a high counter, doing something serious. There was the smell of paper and the rustle of pages turning over on a long table where people were reading newspapers. Kate kept tight hold of the Good Hand.

'Now,' said her father, 'you must always take two books from here . . .' and he showed her some shelves where all the books had white numbers on their spines and were real, '. . . and two from here.' Those books had no numbers and were not real. They were just stories.

Kate dutifully picked two books from each section and carried them home, holding them close to her chest the whole way. She read *The Little House* before bed. It was about a house that might not have been real, but that looked like her own home, with windows either side of a front door. It stood happily among the blossoming apple trees until the city marched over the hill and surrounded it with traffic and high buildings. The little house became sad and neglected until one day a truck came and it was carried once more to the country to stand on a hill among apple blossom.

The little house was an image of perfection: a place lived in over many years, a house with a story. And its trees with their pink and white blossom against the green of fresh leaf, the crimson fruit, the golden fall, the frosted branches of winter, were an ideal of beauty.

The second book was about a little girl who lived in a nice white cottage with a thatched roof. The little girl ran errands and picked blackberries. Her life was simple and orderly. There was a map at the front of the book. You could walk your fingers down the road to the school or the village shop. It showed where everything belonged.

The third book had no story but lots of pictures. There were children playing dozens of different games, a woman walking on flowery grass among dancers whose dresses were so thin you could see their bottoms through the material, a room with blue walls and yellow chairs . . . Kate examined each picture minutely, touching the children, the flowers, the yellow chair so that years later, when she came upon them unexpectedly in some museum or gallery, grown huge perhaps, occupying metres of red velvet wall-space or framed in gilt, she felt the same pleasure at finding them there among anonymous hordes of goddesses and courtesans and kings as she felt meeting a friend from Dunedin, by accident, in the middle of Piccadilly.

The fourth book was about animals. There was a sloth hanging upside down in a jungle tree. It moved so slowly that plants took root in its fur. There was a frog that carried its babies in its mouth and a giant anteater with a slender snout and a snake that could swallow whole cows; there was a photograph where you could see the shape of the cow in the distended tube of the snake's body, like a toy crammed into a a Christmas stocking. The sloth, the frog, the snake were real, but every bit as mysterious as a bear that turned into a prince.

Each Friday night now she went to the Library for two of what was real and two of what was not. Down Wharf Street, past the fire station, crunching across the white gravel of the Garden of Remembrance, over the railway line where sometimes they had to wait while the bells rang for the people who sailed above them in their lighted carriages through the early evening, going somewhere. Past the white bank temples and the Post Office with its frilly tower and machines that spat stamps — pttt — when you put in a penny. Past the war memorial where the soldiers stood before ranks of elm trees drawn up two by two, all the way along the main street to the second war memorial, where a big black lion kept order at his end. Past the auction rooms where the shutters were down but around the louvres seeped the damp scent of King Edwards, leeks and cabbages. Past the Power Board where their father worked, its windows glittery with new heaters and a skinny tasselled bevy of standard lamps. Across the road to the Library.

The flump flump of the double doors, the muffled voices.

Outside, the Friday-night cars cruise the length of the main street where young men try a thoughtful swish swish at the drum kits in Beggs Music Store and the man at the bookshop who has half an arm furls a *Weekly News,* a *Woman's Weekly* and a *Chatterbox* expertly into a tube, then holds it steady with the stump while whipping a rubberband around the lot with his other, whole hand. It is one of the physical wonders, like the woman at the bakery who has a lump in her neck that looks like something swallowed incompletely — a whole Sally Lunn perhaps, or an entire sponge roll, like the cow in the snake — but is actually there because she didn't eat her nice fish in white sauce when she was a little girl. In the shoe shop, people walk about, seeing if their toes reach the end. They peer through the machine at their bones wriggling in the dark like flatfish spotted on a shallow night-time estuary. Outside Woolworths the pipe band is drawn up in a circle, white duck feet flapping, cheeks puffed with the glorious caterwaul of 'Scotland the Brave' and 'Road to the Isles' and a block south outside McKenzie's the Salvation Army is drawn up in competition, having marched down from the citadel playing hymns no longer slow and Sunday serious but recast with a cocky military swagger into brassy 4/4 formation. The bodgies, leather-clad, straddle their motorbikes outside the Excella or gather with girls backcombed and beehived, around the jukebox. Starlings chatter at roost in the darkening trees and the people stroll up and down from the banks in the south to the northernmost point where the shops dwindle to bike repairs and a petrol station. *G'day, George. How's it going, Gwen? Hear you've been crook. Izzat right? Well, hooray, then. Tataa.* Or they retire to the front seats of grey Morris Oxfords and beige Vauxhalls and Ford trucks powdered with the white limestone dust of country roads to sit side by side, sucking peppermints as if they occupy the front row of the balcony and it is Saturday night and they are here to watch the show.

There is the rustling of pages from the newspaper table. The rubber stamp leaves blurred blue numbers on the endpaper. The people choose what is real and what is just a story. Then they carry these things home, free as mushrooms from an autumn hillside, free as blackberries among the broom and wild roses on the banks of a swirling milky river, free as Christmas plums on a wild tree.

5.

'My dear uncle! How can I thank you? This is your doing! Your care and nursing . . .'

'And God's sunshine and mountain air,' interrupted the grandfather, smiling.

Heidi by Johanna Spyri

There were nights when what was real and what was not real became more confused.

Kate wakes in an echoing cavern. The cupboard at the foot of the bed has trotted off on its bandy legs and lurks about miles away. Above the eiderdown floats Kate's mother's face. Her hand is reaching across an immense distance to rest on Kate's forehead, cool and heavy. It is all that holds Kate from drifting off over the room, a stone anchor.

On such nights Kate wakes to find her skin splattered in red spots, or dotted with tiny blisters that must on no account be scratched no matter how much they itch. Or she finds, not spots, but curious lumps on either side of her neck. Her body takes on a fascinating independence. Her tongue might become coated in creamy fur. Her voice might disappear or wheeze so that she sounds like the weather man on the radio: as if her voice has taken up habitation on a storm-tossed distant island. Her neck might refuse to turn. Her eyes might water, her ears ooze yellow stuff, she might heave and find her dinner chopped up in tiny pieces in a sour puddle in the red plastic bowl that is kept in the cupboard in the bathroom for just such an occasion.

Kate's mother believed in getting illness over and done with.

'Go and play with your sister,' she'd say, should Maura wake up first with the spots or swollen glands. 'Take her this blackcurrant drink.' That way, they would both be ill at once. They could lie in their beds on either side of their room, taking turns with the silver mirror to examine the strange state of their tongues or the net of fine red threads on their eyeballs. If their eyes hurt too much for mirrors, they lay with a couple of big black umbrellas over their heads and the blinds drawn to keep out the light.

Time behaved erratically. One minute it was dark, the next the bell was ringing and from the school playground over the back fence they could hear the children marching about, arms linked, chanting, 'Who will play ti-igg-y?'.

They didn't want to join in. They didn't want to run like mad, tigging and being tigged, or beckon *Puss puss puss* from the corner of the shelter shed, or jump over the rope, knees bent, *all in together girls*, to find the initials of the name of the boy they would marry . . .

They drifted instead on the current of being ill. The house became hushed, the fighting ceased, their father biked home at lunchtime bearing raspberry iceblocks and comics: Donald Duck and Daisy with her round yellow shoes, Scrooge diving into the green banknotes in his Money Room, Casper the Friendly Ghost, Tiger Tim and the Bruin Boys. Kate and Maura sucked their iceblocks: so sweet, so cool, icy water seeping over swollen tonsils and sore throat. The pictures in the comics were lolly-pink and lolly-yellow. The stories made as little sense as a dream: Donald goes off to sell fridges in a cold place called Alaska, accompanied by his three nephews who are called Huey, Dewey and Louie, which should rhyme but doesn't quite: not in Oamaru at any rate, where it's Hew-y, Dew-y and Loo-y. The ducks paddle in a canoe — even though they are ducks and should not really need a canoe at all — along a river and over a waterfall and meet some Eskimos in fur suits and then the story ends and Donald is back home painting the fence and it doesn't matter: there's another story as sweet and inconsequential beginning on the next page, and so on until the comic ends with the advertisement for the wonderful Sea Monkeys, who wear crowns and live in an underwater castle and could be Kate and Maura's, if only they were permitted to send away the money. The stories dissolve, leaving nothing behind, like raspberry ice.

When they were ill, their mother became brisk and certain. She retrieved some of the authority they sensed in the photos of her when she was a 'sister at Public' and wore a starched uniform and a veil of stiff white wings.

She had begun nursing when she was sixteen, after she failed Matric. Kate and Maura were not sure what Matric was but it sounded important: if she had passed Matric, she would have become a missionary in China. She would not have become their mother; she would have become someone else entirely. But on the morning of Matric she had walked down a hill in Dunedin and been dazzled by a roof. A new roof of shiny corrugated iron, glinting in the early-morning sun. It gave her a migraine so that she could not see the examination paper. The questions shimmered, then broke into triangular pieces, then disappeared entirely.

Kate knew this because she had asked what a migraine was like and her mother had drawn one on the back of an old envelope. She still had migraines when the wind blew from the alps in dry nor'west gusts.

She might stop abruptly in the middle of choosing Kate's new school sandals at the Farmers' Co-op.

'I'm afraid we shall have to leave these for another day,' she says to the assistant in the black dress. 'I'm terribly sorry.' She is fumbling for her bag and her gloves, pink with apology. The assistant is not of a mind to forgive. She puts the shoes back in their box, lips pursed around nuisance like a mouthful of pins, while Kate's mother lays her hand discreetly on Kate's shoulder and Kate guides her down the stairs, past the rosy pong of the cosmetics counter and out onto the street. Once home, her mother lies on the sofa with a wet facecloth over her eyes until the rain comes. Thunder mutters in the distant Kakanuis, the clouds swell in purple velvet, raindrops plop and burst on dusty earth, there's the sweet-sour smell of tarmac gone to rainbows under the deluge.

'Ah,' she'd say, sitting up, rubbing her eyes, seeing Kate again. Her face is fresh as a flower. 'That's better.'

On the day of Matric she had sat in the darkness of a migraine for two full hours amid the scratching of busy pens, waiting to fail.

'But there you are,' she said, screwing the picture of the migraine into a ball and tossing it into the fire in the coal range. 'It was all meant to be, in the end.' She meant that it had led her to nursing, which was her calling. There were jobs done for money, like selling shoes at the Farmers'. And there were callings. Callings were jobs that God considered important. When she had glanced at the roof and become blinded she was like Paul on the road to Damascus. He had been going to kill Christians, but God was rough and directed him instead to become a saint who wrote lots of letters. Their mother had been led by God to become a nurse up at Public.

The evidence of her calling lay all around them, like the evidence of their father's time as a soldier. In the photo box, women in uniforms and veils stood in the hospital gardens, or smiled for the camera from the windowsills of the isolation ward where they had been locked in for weeks, their meals left on trays on the verandah, during a polio outbreak. Their names were printed carefully on the reverse: *Watty, Sonny Rewi, Rita McIvor*.

Rita McIvor had caught polio in the isolation ward and died.

That was what you did when you had a calling. You fought infection like a soldier in his trench, prepared to sacrifice yourself for the good of others.

On the bottom shelf of the bookshelf were her nursing texts: weighty tomes with terrifying photographs of tonsils blackened with diphtheria and arms withered by polio. Kate and her sister crawled behind the chair and looked at the photographs with the same queasy fascination they felt when poking at a dead hedgehog in a gutter, its body white and seething with a sequined citizenry of maggots, or a sheep dead in a gully, legs splayed, lips drawn back on yellow teeth, her baby still curled in a bony ball in the leather pocket of her belly. They turned the pages in the nursing books until they could look no longer and had to run out into the back yard, away from the child with the harelip, the withered arm, the tonsils.

A cardboard box at the bottom of the wardrobe held the nurse's cape of heavy blue serge lined with scarlet, wrapped in white tissue, and her medals, and a stethoscope through which they listened to the astonishing bubblings and drumming and tidal surging that were going on all the time, out of sight, beneath their skins. They unwrapped the dresses she had worn to the hospital balls: one filmy green with velvet roses at the neck, the other black net with silver daisies embroidered on the skirt. They slipped them on over tartan skirts and jumpers, twirled in front of the wardrobe mirror. The skirts flew out in wide circles, releasing the faint scent of face powder and roses and Happy New Year. There were shoes, too: beautiful shoes in green suede with patent-leather tips, brown and white shoes elegantly tooled, black leather shoes with laces, which belonged to that distant era when their mother was up at Public and was photographed arm in arm with Rita McIvor, lipstick smiles and trim little suits and Robin Hood hats with feathers, walking down Thames Street. They all belonged to the golden time before she had met their father.

He came into the hospital to have the stumps that had been his fingers examined. Kate's mother had been in love with someone else. At least, Kate and Maura suspected that. There was a photo of a young man in air force uniform with sleek hair and a moustache in a frame of robins, jingle bells and skaters on a pond in a snowbound village. *Happy Christmas and a Prosperous New Year, Yours ever, Findlay* was scrawled on the reverse in vigorous, angular writing.

'Findlay Todd,' their mother said when they asked, concentrating on her knitting, twofoursixeight, the stitches sliding along the needle. 'Nice chap. Twelvefourteensixteeneighteen . . .'

That was generally all. But bit by bit, by repeated interrogation, they had managed to piece together a biography. Findlay had lived across the valley at Millerhill, one of a numerous family to whom their mother was distantly connected — cousin married to second cousin or some such. They knew he had gone to school with their mother, sharing the buggy that her older sister Annie had driven up the road every morning, collecting all the children on the way. They knew that the buggy was drawn by a horse called Billy. They knew that Findlay had later played in a dance band with their mother and her brother Tom before his brain rotted and he came to the sunroom at Cherry Farm. They knew Findlay had played the drums while their mother played piano and Tom played the violin. They knew the band was called the Debonnaires. They knew the music they had played, for their mother played it still on the piano in the front room: 'Mexicali Rose', 'Side by Side', 'Bye Bye Blackbird', the tune picked out by the right hand while the left marked a steady, heavy beat. They knew this was called 'vamping'. They looked at the photo of the airman with his sleek hair and dashing moustache and around him there was the echo of 'Mexicali Rose', shining shoes, and vamping.

'What happened to Findlay?' they said.

'Shot down,' said their mother. 'Battle of Britain. Twentytwo-twentyfourtwentysix . . . darn . . .' She peered at the knitting pattern. There was a man carrying golf clubs on the front. He did not look in the least bit like their father. He had a moustache.

There would be no more. Kate and Maura laid the photo back in the box as if they were placing a dead bird ready for burial in the garden. And around the young man with his sleek hair and dashing moustache there hung the echo of a plane plunging from a grey sky, the shriek of skaters scattering in a hail of burning metal.

So when Pat Kennedy arrived at Oamaru Public with his wounded hand, months after Alamein, he met a woman who was neither engaged nor promised. She bent her head with its starched wings over the dressing, probing at the wound. He fell in love, Kate supposed. They married within six months, he in a black suit and round metal-rim spectacles, she in white georgette and orange blossom. A service in the Basilica, for their mother had converted. She had 'gone over', as if faiths were rival towns on either bank of a torrent of disbelief. She had taken instruction in the Faith of her husband's Fathers. Their wedding was no broom-cupboard affair devoid of music or due ritual at some side altar but the full ceremony. Her own father, Kate's grandfather — elder of Millerhill Presbyterian Church, descendant of Wee Frees to whom even Christmas smacked of Popery — refused to attend. Tollie walked down the aisle on the arm of her cousin Crawford, who drove a Morgan, sold insurance and was not bothered about religion.

'So long as you're happy, Tollie,' he had said. 'That's what matters.'

Grandad Stuart refused to have any further communication with her. He sent no telegram or gift and when Kate's mother and father called in for a visit on their honeymoon he left the room without a word, whistled to the dogs — *Here Bess! Here Tip!* — and went off up the hill to check on the lambs. He stayed away until late afternoon and did not return until after they had been driven over to Millerhill station to catch the five o'clock back to Oamaru.

He died a month later. Slipped on hill pasture, broke a leg and lay for three hours in heavy rain. He died with a shattered femur but his religious certainties intact.

Maybe Presbyterian elders could lay curses. For the wedding marked the end of the golden time. When Kate's mother talked about her life it snapped at the crack that was her wedding. Before that was the time up at Public when she was a nurse with a calling and a wardrobe full of smart shoes and elegant suits. Then there was the time when she had dwindled to housewife and mother with no uniform, no money and a wardrobe full of cotton-print frocks from Millers. From time to time, when the bills in the Egyptian box became pressing or the leak in the hall became insistent, she would suggest that she return to work.

'What for?' said her husband, paying no attention to the drip drip drip into the bucket in the hall, as loud as a rallying drum.

'I could help out,' she said.

Pat flapped the evening paper that he called the two-minute silence from the news to the racing page.

'I earn enough,' he said.

If she pressed, said she had training, it was all going to waste, he added the clincher.

'You've got a job: you've got children. You've got a house to look after.'

And within a minute he had added that a bloody poor show she made of it too, and why couldn't she smarten herself up, get the place looking decent? The two-minute silence flapped like the wings of a bird beating at a closed window.

Kate and Maura kept their heads down then, the guilty ones whose births had put the final bracket around the golden time.

But when they were ill she became superb. For however long it took for the spots to clear or the mumps to dwindle, the house ran like Ward Three up at Public. She took their temperatures, sliding the cool bulb of a thermometer tasting of metal and cleanliness beneath their tongues. She stood by as the silver thread rose, with two fingers lightly on their wrists and one eye on her watch, counting the beat of their hearts. She made them orange drinks from real oranges squeezed and heated with a spoonful of honey, then poured into one of Maura's old baby bottles, so they could lie under the blankets sucking blissfully on the worn rubber teat. Or blackcurrant drinks to be drunk hot from a rabbit mug with a teaspoon. When they were too wobbly to stand, they had proper bed-baths, sponged expertly on one side, then turned for the other. Afterwards they were brought clean nighties warmed on the shelf over the range and ironed so that no creases would press on feverish flesh. From time to time she mounted an all-out offensive on the germs that flew in invisible hordes above their heads. She walked about Kate and Maura's bedroom waving a coal shovel full of burning embers from the range onto which she had sprinkled dried lavender, leaving in her wake a drifting cloud of good health. Or she fetched a basin full of hot water and Friars Balsam and they would sit up in bed under the steamy towel tent, breathing in the scented steam. The germs did not stand a chance.

The fight against them was a constant campaign.

'We've got to build up your resistance,' she told Kate and Maura as she held out their togs for them to step into at the beach. Swimming in the ocean at Friendly Bay built up their resistance, as did playing outside every day, even when it was raining, and sleeping every night with the window open. Cod-liver oil capsules in their brown plastic skins aided in the fight, and malt extract in spoonfuls from the sticky tin every morning after a good cooked breakfast. Woollen singlets worn next to the skin helped, and sensible bodices with rubbery buttons to keep their kidneys warm. Things that lowered resistance were many and varied: sitting on cold concrete was one, or staying up too late or sleeping in stuffy rooms or eating bought apples with sprayed skins or playing with the Creeches.

The Creeches lived up the road. Their father was a fisherman who could conduct an entire conversation without removing his cigarette. It appeared to have been glued to his lower lip, where it smouldered to a waggle of ash. His brother, the Creeches' Uncle Reg, had a glass eye that he popped out for general entertainment and put in backwards. Their mum, Faye, sat on the back step painting her toenails and saying listlessly from time to time, 'Now cut it out, you kids, or you'll get a hiding when your dad gets home.' There was a stick in the bathroom, a mean length of bamboo that Kenny Creech said with a kind of nonchalant pride was used in the execution of these hidings.

It had little apparent deterrent effect. The Creeches ran riot. They were not, in Kate's mother's opinion, 'corker kiddies', but rascals and hoodlums who pinched sixpences and shillings from their mum's purse and made a run for the dairy, where Mr Budd sold them gobstoppers, smokers and pineapple chunks. They hurtled on homemade sleds named Flying Fanny and Beetlebomb down the rough ground behind the cemetery, heedless of hidden rocks and tumbling among the buttercups that grew in profusion around the drainage ditch at the bottom. They rolled cigarettes of dock leaves and birch bark and smoked them in the huts all the kids in the street built in the cemetery: not the new cemetery, which was an orderly subdivision of concrete tabs listing name and date, but the old cemetery, where cooch and hawthorn tangled over carved stone, fuzzy with the creeping frogs' hands of lichen. Beneath the lichen were whole poems written in silver letters, and accounts of shipwrecks and great floods that had taken people unawares as they lay sleeping, for they knew not the hour nor the day when the Lord came. There were little iron fences around each grave, and gates wedged open on rusted hinges. Their surfaces heaved and cracked. The kids peered through the cracks looking for coffins, the glint of a silver handle, a bony face peering back.

It was Kenny Creech who showed Kate how to get the pennies out of the Barnardos box. The box stood on the bench, a little red canvas affair in which they were supposed to put pennies to help feed the poor orphans in England. Two had their photographs on the front: Terence and Evelyn from Camberwell. Terence was a ferrety boy with wire-rimmed glasses and protruding teeth, and Evelyn wore a grubby pixie hat and strange woollen stockings crumpled from sheer despair about her skinny ankles. They stood hand in hand in the sad grey yard of England. The stockings disgusted Kate. They made her ruthless. She slid the knife into the slot as Kenny instructed. Terence buckled and the pennies fell onto the bench. Kenny made a rapid tally.

'Have we got enough?' said Kate. They were whispering, furtive.

'Yep,' said Kenny. 'Heaps.' He popped back two brass buttons dating from when Maura had been too small to know the difference between real money and pretend, and a couple of halfpennies so the box would still rattle. He led the way grandly to the shops.

They curled beneath dry grass and crimson hawthorn and sweetpeas the colour of smokers. Grass arched, heavy with seed, over their heads. A gravestone with a peeling poem stood warm at their backs and an angel flew above, arms raised in blessing. They lay sucking the fruits of crime — aniseed balls and jaffas and chocolate buttons — among glass domes of china flowers like the bony ghosts of lilies, roses and carnations.

And a few days later came the penance: worms or headlice or impetigo or ringworm. Their mother dabbed gentian violet onto the rings where the hair had fallen out and said, 'Tsk. Why can't you play with nice children like Virginia Craddock?' Virginia lived in a double-storey house with a proper banister for sliding on, the way they did in books. Virginia and her eight brothers and sisters lined up on either side of the tea table, not speaking unless to ask 'May I have the butter please?' while Mr Craddock, who was a lawyer, conducted one of his little quizzes: Who is the little old lady of Threadneedle Street? What is the capital of France? 3 times 6 is . . .? Their side of the table against the opposite side.

Kate's mother measured a dose of bitter worm medicine into a teaspoon. 'You are to stay away from those Creeches. Do you hear me?'

The Creeches were a bad influence and they had germs.

Kate's mother was ever vigilant. At the hint of a sore tummy, Eno's Fruit Salts to be drunk while it still fizzed in the glass; at the first sneeze, a gargle of hot water and salt. Kate stood in the bathroom singing, through the gargle, about the doggie in the window — as the germs died in their millions.

In situations of greater seriousness their mother called in God. She laid her hand on the part affected and prayed for healing. Sometimes there was a sensation beneath her palm, which Kate supposed was the Holy Spirit attending to their mumps or measles. The power of the Holy Spirit felt fizzy, like fruit salts.

Not everything could be cured. Some germs reigned supreme, with polio at the top of the list, and that ultimate horror, the iron lung. You mustn't swim in public pools during a polio epidemic, or you might end up in an iron lung. You mustn't go to the pictures or anywhere where there were crowds of people. If you did, you might end up in an iron lung, like the girl in the *Woman's Weekly* who lay in a massive metal can. Only her head was visible. She lay smiling, like Snow White in her glass coffin, waiting patiently for the Prince's kiss. Kate had experimented with an iron lung. She had tried it out by sliding into a roll of linoleum stored in the spare bedroom. She wriggled in until only her head was exposed. Her arms were pressed against her sides, her legs were trapped. She couldn't breathe. Sudden terror made her scream for rescue.

'What on earth did you think you were doing?' said her mother, tugging her out by the shoulders.

'Nothing,' said Kate. 'Nothing!' And she stretched her free arms. She skipped up the hall on her free legs. She breathed her own free breath.

. . . the once rosy face so changed and vacant, the once busy hands so weak and wasted, the once smiling lips quite dumb and the once pretty well-kept hair scattered rough and tangled on the pillow. All day she lay so, only rousing now and then to mutter 'Water!' with lips so parched they could hardly shape the word . . .

Little Women by Louisa May Alcott

Kate and her sister avoided polio but one morning Kate woke with the curious sensation of having swollen overnight to an enormous size. Her arms were too heavy to lift.

'I don't feel well,' she said to her mother. The words scratched.

'You'd better stay home,' said her mother. Kate crawled down into the warm burrow of blankets and slept. The next morning Maura, too, was sick. They lay in their beds watching the patterns on the wallpaper dissolve into faces with bulbous eyes or pointed chins. They did not want orange drinks. They did not want Donald Duck. They could scarcely be bothered to look in the silver mirror, and when they did, their tongues had become pink and swollen like strawberries and their chests were covered in a rash of minute pimples so densely packed they appeared to be one continuous flush. Their mother called the doctor.

Scarlet fever.

Their skin peeled away like the dry outer skin of an onion. They vomited and sweated and bled from the nose until the doctor had to come to stop it or they would have shrunk to nothing, to empty skins like balloons popped at the end of a party. They dreamed one long confusing dream, and then one morning they woke.

Sunlight dappled the wall above Kate's bed and a bird was singing in the ribbonwood outside the window. A rippling song, up and down and up and down. Kate stretched her toes. She stretched her fingers. She felt light and cool. The blood whirred in her ears as it was supposed to; her heart was beating a steady dubdub.

The scarlet fever had gone off somewhere else. They had been released into that glorious state known as convalescence. They had to stay in bed for a few weeks on account of their hearts. They made little caves in the bedclothes and arranged the dolls' house furniture inside as if the dolls had run away from their ordinary lives, arms bent stiffly in a permanent 'Oh my goodness!' gesture in the dolls' house with its painted shutters that couldn't really shut. The dolls camped among the bedclothes and had adventures out on the eiderdown mountains. Kate and Maura had ice cream for lunch and mashed potatoes for breakfast, and one day grapes, which were special fruit for people who had been sick — fruit that would make people well. The grapes popped, cool and sweet, in the mouth like the toffee shocks in the Faraway Tree.

They took exact turns looking at the Viewmaster. It was like a pair of black binoculars through which they could look at 3D images of Snow White, Tropical Fish and the Wedding of Princess Grace in Monaco. Princess Grace had been just an ordinary person but she was very beautiful, so naturally she married a prince. Prince Rainier was short and fat but at the wedding he was wearing proper prince's clothes with gold frilly bits on the shoulders. The last image on the reel was of fireworks, marking the Explosion of Joy over the Principality. Kate and Maura clicked happily from luminous angelfish to Snow White in the glass lung to the Explosion of Joy. They painted in their magic books with plain water, which turned a magically mucky pink or green on the page, they dressed their paper dolls in all their outfits, bonnets, baskets and crinolines until the white paper tabs fell off and the dresses had to be licked on instead.

One afternoon Kate noticed a blister on the wallpaper next her bed. It was just a bubble on the trellis of blue roses, like a scab or a mosquito bite with a crusty top, so she scratched at it. Underneath there was a tiny patch of crimson with two white dots. Kate tore a little more and the dots formed a fleur-de-lis. Maura looked over from her bed where she was cutting out old Christmas cards and gluing them into her scrapbook.

'You'll get in trouble,' she said.

'No I won't,' said Kate. There were three fleurs-de-lis in a line going up the wall. Kate tore at a rough edge and under the crimson was a patch of green, a sad green like boiled broccoli with a phlegmy yellow stripe. She tore at that and it came away in a clean strip. There was a face beneath: a lady's face, on newspaper black and white. She was pretty, with dark cow eyes and curly hair on which perched, when Kate had torn a little further, a perky feathery hat. She tore more. Her dress had a tight jacket and she carried an umbrella. Her skirt trailed on the ground and she wore tiny pointed black boots.

Maura glued in a kitten in a red stocking.

'Now you'll *really* get in trouble,' she said.

There were words under the lady's pointed boots, smudged and torn. 'A charmblankensembleblankblankter, that . . .' The words vanished at the edge. Kate tore a little more. The words formed a line, a block of print.

'You're wrecking the wallpaper,' said Maura. She sprinkled some glitter on the kitten.

A slender gloved hand extended from one edge of the hole. An arm, another lady, a gentleman in a top hat, a fluffy dog, more words, a whole column of print . . .

'What are you two up to?' said their father.

He stood in the doorway, hands behind his back so they would have to choose: Mickey Mouse or Donald Duck. Kate sat up. The hole, which only a second ago had seemed so entrancing, a gap through to the black-and-white world filled with words and pictures that lay beneath the one in which they lived, was now nothing more than a ugly patch in the nice blue roses that decorated their bedroom.

'Kate's made a mess,' said Maura.

'I didn't mean to,' said Kate. She could feel tears clotting at her throat. But Dad said, Mahleesh, he'd paint over it when they were better. He gave her a hug, and he told her, because she asked, what 'ensemble' meant.

Over the walls and earth and trees, the fair green veil of tender little leaves had crept . . . and the sun fell warm upon his face like a hand with a lovely touch . . . a pink glow of colour had crept all over him — ivory face and neck and hands and all.

'I shall get well! I shall get well!' he cried out. 'Mary! Dickon! I shall get well! And I shall live for ever and ever and ever!'

The Secret Garden by Frances Hodgson Burnett

Not long after, they were allowed up. Their father carried them, one at a time, out into the garden where it was spring all of a sudden. The last time they had looked it had been dead winter. The sun licked with its warm tongue at their new skins. The air smelled of daffodils and mown grass and wet earth. He carried each of them around the garden, stopping for them to sniff, to see the honey bees writhing in the pink lolly blossom of the flowering currant by the dunny, to touch the little green leaves that were just beginning again on the apple trees, furled and fuzzy in their brown winter ensembles. Kate and Maura's legs were wobbly still, their legs not sure about walking any more. They held on to the bed while their mother helped them get dressed properly, in their jerseys and tartan kilts with birds' feet holding the front closed instead of ordinary buttons. Their clothes scratched a little on their new skins and their shoes and socks felt tight.

'Your feet have grown,' said their mother. She pressed for their toes. 'You're going to need new shoes.'

The house, too, had changed. The front bedroom was no longer pink but white. It smelled of new paint and wallpaper paste. It was trellised in shiny silver leaves and the double bed was stripped of its mattress. They tried an experimental hop and then they were bouncing and Mum and Dad were standing in the doorway not telling them to cut it out or they'd wreck the springs, but laughing, and sunlight was brilliant through the curtainless window and they jumped in the sunlight until their legs were tired. Then they went through to the sitting room, where the table was a birthday: cheerios in split pink skins, meringues oozing cream, animal biscuits and a little cake each with candles. They had been sick right through both their birthdays and they had not even noticed, though normally they kept close count, marking the quarter, the half and the three-quarters, like the clock on the Post Office, until the moment when they sat in a paper crown and blew out the candles on another year.

There was a present each: a *Tiger Tim Annual* for Kate and a *Chatterbox Annual* for Maura. The Bruin Boys and Twizzle the Little Elephant and children who slid, chuckling merrily, down wonderful slides that wound round and round, unlike the plain straight slides at the playground in the Botanic Gardens. In the annuals, children swung on little boats operated by pulling on tasselled ropes, unlike the plain wooden benches at Awamoa Park. In the annuals, the Bruin Boys went to the seaside where the waves were flat and children ate ices and rode donkeys in straw hats with holes cut for the ears. The seaside was a grand version of Friendly Bay, that cubby-hole on a savage coast where beaches were more normally home to penguins with startled yellow eyebrows nesting under the barbs of African thorn; and the sea surged at the base of cliffs made up of bubbles of lava, red and black; and there were no kiosks but shattered shell and whole trees stripped to bone and (once) the massive bulk of a whale, its tail flapping uselessly, its small eye weeping because it was lost and alone, out of its proper place in the ocean. The seaside was straw-hat safe. The waves at the seaside twinkled, whereas the waves at the beach could suddenly make a grab, tangling their white fingers around your ankles, pulling you out to be lost among forests of kelp.

In the annuals, the Bruin Boys went to the countryside. The countryside was different to the country. In the country, uncles did the shearing with 'Blueberry Hill' on the radio, doubled over sheep whose legs were spread in surprise as their coats fell away. The country was uncles wearing old jerseys and woollen beanies on bald heads like the cosies on boiled eggs. In the country, boys went shooting at night for rabbits and dumped them on the back step with a bloody wound in one shoulder for dog tucker. In the country, the children were given a length of fencing wire onto which some inner tube had been threaded and set alight. They ran about, yelling, setting fire to the gorse bushes. Each bush, with its luminous golden flowers smelling of toasted coconut, exploded into flame as they thrust the wire at its golden heart, until the whole hillside was burning and they stood back, thrilled at the billowing wall of smoke, as the fire prepared the earth for the tender grass that would grow to feed next season's lambs.

In the countryside, no one burnt gorse. The trees were called woods and copses, and beneath their shade, rabbits played. Lambs were tended by Farmer George: lambs as unsullied as if they had been washed in Persil. The lambs Kate and Maura knew were stained yellow and wandered about trailing the bloody thread that had attached them to the big red jelly sacks that littered the wet springtime paddocks, food for gulls. The orphan lambs in the countryside were gathered up in the arms of Farmer George. In the country they were bundled three or four at a time in a sugarsack to be carried back to the house, where they lived in cardboard cartons on the back porch. They drank milk from old lemonade bottles, sucking furiously with waggly tails and weeing. When they were strong enough to clickety click about on little black high heels they were moved to the orchard, where they lived among the daffodils until they could eat grass and manage by themselves. Meanwhile, up on the hillside, their mothers' bodies swelled and rotted and were picked clean by gulls and hawks until they were nothing but bone: the exquisite linkage of backbone, the arching curve of the ribcage, the skull with its jawbone for playing dentists, the knucklebones for playing Scatter Ones, Big Jingles and Clicks. In the countryside, the sheep led neater lives, with their long black stockings pulled up to the fleece like schoolgirls in uniform. The children in the annuals were unlikely to fossick for knucklebones in their bare carcasses.

Kate and Maura ate their cheerios and meringues; they took their pencils and joined the dots to make a picture of a shrimp net; they traced the maze to Farmer George's barn. They entered the world of the countryside and the seaside, which was as unreal, as pink and sweet, as the dreams of fever.

They went out of Moonface's little round room and climbed up the topmost branch into a cloud.

The Faraway Tree by Enid Blyton

Sickness was a world that existed beneath the wallpaper of everyday. It was a dream place, a disturbing place, yet ultimately peaceful, where it was possible to think, to idle, to be.

Years later Kate read about Einstein and how, when he was five years old and sick in bed, his father had given him a pocket compass. The child lay in bed intrigued by the action of the needle. *That the needle behaved in such a determined way did not at all fit into the kind of occurrences that would find a place in the unconscious world of concepts . . . it made a deep and lasting impression on me . . . something deeply hidden had to be behind things.* She read about Matisse, who spent a year recuperating as a young man from complications caused by appendicitis. Until then, he had been set on a career in law. In bed, in convalescence, he discovered art. There was a later photograph of him sitting up in bed, in Nice. There were the plump pillows, the clutter of books on a sickbed table, a checked rug spread over the knees. In his hands he held a long stick and he was drawing, as everyone who has ever spent time in bed is tempted to do, on the wall.

Kate did not become an artist while she lay sick in bed, spotty and snuffling. Nor did she commence a process that would lead eventually to the most profound speculations concerning the functioning of the universe.

But she can understand why other greater people did.

6.

Millerhill church stood at the top of the hill, like the church in a storybook. It had white painted walls and a steeple raised like a little finger for the attention of the deity. It stood in a ring of macrocarpa and pasture grass kept down by a few of Ross McDonald's Romneys, which grazed safely throughout the week, depositing black beads of shit that had to be sidestepped, come Sunday, by best shoes.

The interior of the church was a nutshell of polished totara. Bare wooden pews lined up either side of a strip of blue carpet. There was a communion table spread with a white cloth at the front, between a little eggcup of a pulpit on one side and a carved wooden eagle on the other. The eagle bore the heavy weight of The Word, wings spread. It hovered above the sunburnt farmers, their hatted wives and scrubbed children like the hawks that hung on the empty air above the hill outside, waiting for a rabbit to make a careless move. The window glass was white as milk frozen in the can on a winter morning, and permitted no distracting glimpse of the sky. The minister, who had arrived a few minutes before in shirt sleeves, emerged from the door to the Sunday school room in black robe and white tabs as Kate's Auntie Annie wheezed out some triumphal chords at the harmonium: Diapason, Celeste, Forte Coupler at maximum extension. Auntie Annie had also done the flowers: vast confections of lilies and gladioli gathered from her own garden and around the district on Saturday afternoons.

'Help yourself,' the other women said, waving vaguely at the agapanthus and red-hot pokers that popped up around their houses. 'Take as much as you like. Take some plum blossom. Those plums are useless for bottling.'

Auntie Annie picked armloads and carried them in her Morris Minor to the church, where she snipped and wired according to the season: white and yellow for spring, red for Christmas, orange and purple for autumn, and dry flower-heads and whatever she could scrounge for winter. The results were as good as anything you'd see in a book — better than Constance Spry. The flowers were brocade and satin, they were embroidery and tapestry and incense and choir, in the bare little church.

'Psalm Twenty-three,' announced the minister. 'The Lord's my shepherd, I'll not want. Psalm Twenty-three.' The congregation straggled to its feet. Auntie Annie sang too, her red velvet hat bobbing away as she pedalled frantically, thighs pressed hard against the swell, opening and closing, diminuendo and crescendo. *My head he doth with oil anoint*, sang Auntie Annie, supplying the soprano descant. She did not need to read the words any more than did the farmers and their wives and children. They knew them all, from

'Lead Kindly Light', 'By Cool Shiloam's Shady Rill', 'Oh God Our Help' and 'Onward Christian Soldiers' right through to the triple Amen that closed every service. The hymn books were for prompting only. A lifetime of hymns, four a morning, every Sunday.

Outside the church the dead gathered on a sunny north-facing slope, some sporting fresh flowers, some with plastic roses, which were easier in terms of upkeep, but bore just a hint of convenience and filial neglect. The dead were assembled in family clusters, husband and wife side by side, a blank left on the stone for their children; cousins and neighbours kept up the elbow-on-the-gate propinquity they had shared in life. Magpies squabbled in the macrocarpa. The McDonalds' Romneys bleated to one another over dry paddocks. Cars like coloured beads slipped along the silver thread of the road on the flat below the hill. The Horse Range receded into a blue haze.

And the waters prevailed exceedingly upon the earth; and all the high hills, that were under the whole heaven, were covered.

Genesis 7:19

Kate sat in church looking at the bullethole. The minister was reading the lesson from the Old Testament. He looked like a turkey rooster: bald and pink with his white wattles. Kate sat with Maura among the cousins, grandmother, aunts and uncles. Behind them sat the patients.

The patients were driven to church at Millerhill from Cherry Farm. They occupied a double row at the back of the church: two rows of men in ill-fitting cardigans and trousers that seemed to have been worn previously by someone else entirely; men with blubbery lips who dribbled; men who twitched strangely; men who answered 'Yes!' when the minister asked a question no one was supposed to answer. 'Jesus said, "Come unto me all ye who are heavy laden." Are you heavy laden?' The minister surveyed the congregation and 'Yes!' said Charlie with deep emphasis from behind Kate. Charlie smelled of Cherry Farm: of cabbage and floor polish and pee and clothes kept too long in a locked cupboard.

Charlie was odd, but the man across the aisle was worse. Viewed side on, he was tall and slender, with floppy brown hair and a beautiful face. He wore a tweed jacket like Kate's uncles, and a scarf tossed about his neck, and clean trousers with a crease down each leg. And in the middle of his forehead there was a hole. It was the size of a shilling piece and half an inch deep, as if someone had pressed a finger into the flesh and left their mark, like the hole in a doughnut.

The other patients had names like Charlie or Arthur, but the man with the hole on his forehead was The Professor.

'He was such a brainy man,' Kate's mother said. 'A professor at the university. But he cracked up, like Tom.' His brain, as frail, as pure as a porcelain cup, had become too full of facts from all that swotting and when it got too full, it cracked. The Professor had tried to shoot himself when he cracked up. The bullet had entered his forehead, rattled around the white bowl of the skull and re-emerged, leaving him alive. He sat silent at the back of Millerhill church.

Kate's mother nudged her. 'Don't stare,' she said. But who could help staring? He held his hymn book in slender fingers. Beside him the other patients sang lustily, not caring if they were out of tune or saying the right words. The Professor retained a distant dignity, looking more like a real prince than Prince Rainier of Monaco who, despite the gold epaulettes, bore an unmistakable resemblance to Mr Budd at the dairy, like someone who could strip off his uniform, pop on a grocer's apron and say, 'That'll be two and threepence, love.' The Professor stood at the back of Millerhill church like the prince in Cinderella: so noble, so tragic, so brainy.

Her mother nudged her again. Kate tried to concentrate. She looked at her Bible, reading odd bits and examining the blurred pictures of Canaanite temples at Megiddo and olive trees by the Sea of Galilee. Immediately in front of her sat her cousin Graham. His neck was pink where his hair had been clipped the night before with the silver clippers. Auntie Izzie had done all five of the boys, lining them up for a trim like sheep on a stand. The light through the milky windows shone clear through Graham's ears. 'Red sails in the sunset,' Kate would have said, if this were not church and whispering were not forbidden. They shone on either side of his skull like iridescent insect wings. She would have liked to touch them. She liked ears: dogs' ears that folded back when a dog ran; cows' ears round and ruffled in contrasting fur, brown and white or black and brown; the ears of ponies. She liked looking ahead at the world bracketed between the ears of a pony. She liked the way ears did the talking for an animal deprived of speech, flicking back and forth in surprise or alarm or anger or simple curiosity. She liked her cousin's ears glowing in church, and the two bumps at the nape of his neck when he bent his head to watch as Bruce beside him surreptitiously allowed one of his ferrets to crawl up the sleeve of his church shirt. She could see the bulge of its slinky body wriggling across the shoulders. Its pink nose whiffled at her from Bruce's collar. Its pink eyes regarded her coolly, then it dived back into the tunnel of grey serge. Bruce loved his ferrets, not seeming to mind that they stank and nipped. He gave them names: Pinky and Whitey and Fang. He poured them from hand to hand as if they were water.

At last the minister said the prayer to bless the children and they could leave the adults to drink the miniature glasses of blackcurrant cordial and eat the squares of sliced white bread Auntie Annie had arranged on the communion table on a pink china plate.

The children clattered out with Alison McDonald, who was sixteen and in love with Kate's oldest cousin, Pete. Graham said he'd seen them pashing in Pete's car up behind the planny on McDonald's Road. 'The windows were all steamed up,' he said, 'and when I looked in, Pete told me to bugger off.' They were unsure what was most shocking: the pashing, the steam or the swearword.

Alison led the way to the Sunday School room. They had to be quiet, as every word could be heard through the varnished wall. She pulled out the felt board with its little figures of men who wore tea-towels on their heads and Mary in her veil and a selection of animals, and, very quietly, she told them one of the stories. Moses dropped by his mother into a river in a basket, Joseph put into a hole by his brothers, Noah building his ark.

She lined up a pair of sheep and a pair of felt giraffes. 'So Noah found two of each animal,' she said, 'and put them into the ark.' A giraffe's neck flopped from the board.

'What about the other animals?' said Kate. It was something that had bothered her ever since she had seen the illustration in the *Children's Bible* where the waters were rising around a flock of sheep, peacefully grazing unawares.

'Which animals?' said Alison, re-attaching the giraffe's neck.

'The ones that didn't fit in the ark,' said Kate.

Alison looked in the box for the dove.

'He could only take two,' she said. 'Two of everything. That's what God said to him.'

'So did all the other animals drown?' said Kate's girl cousin, Rosemary.

'And the other people?' said Bruce. The ferrets were asleep in the pockets of his jacket. 'Did they drown?'

'They'd been wicked,' said Alison. 'That's why God sent the flood.'

'Could they swim?' said one of the Crawford twins. They had no names. They were The Twinnies, duplicated like Freddie and Flossie in that fascinating Bobbsey fashion. They wore identical pink skirts and fluffy angora cardigans and would have been impossible to tell apart, except that one twinnie wore her pink hair-ribbon on the left and the other wore it on the right.

'I can swim,' said the left-ribbon twinnie. 'I can do a starfish.' And she spread her arms to demonstrate.

'But where did they swim to?' said Kate. 'Because there wasn't any land, was there?'

'No,' said Alison. 'The water covered the whole earth. That's what the Bible says. But Noah and his family were safe in the ark.'

The lucky little felt family stood on the deck of the ark with its jaunty red-and-yellow trim and its livestock: two cows, two pigs, two lions and two giraffes, one of which seemed to have lost its stickability.

'So they couldn't swim to the edge?' said the starfish twinnie.

'No,' said Bruce. 'They all drowned. Aargghh!' And he clasped his throat and gagged and fell on the floor thrashing. The starfish twinnie's brow crumpled in concern.

'Did all the ponies drown?' said Maura.

'All of them, except the ones Noah saved. Don't be silly, Bruce. Get up off the floor.'

'Crocodiles wouldn't drown,' said Gus Todd. 'There'd be two of everything except crocodiles. There'd be heaps of crocodiles in the water.'

'Only two,' said Alison. 'Two crocodiles.'

'Did all the children drown?' said the starfish twinnie. 'The ones that couldn't swim?'

'Yes,' said Bruce. 'God killed them all. That's what she said.'

'And the kittens?' said the other twinnie. 'I'd have held on to my kitten.'

She knew about drowned kittens. They all did: that squirming sack dunked in the creek when the numbers in the milking shed threatened to become too many. They knew that handful of wet fur, the pink tips of noses and eyes tight shut and barely born. They had watched them slip out of the mother cat's bottom and seen them suck, the mother cat's paws making bread dough in the straw and purring as if it were the most wonderful cosy thing in the world to lie in a warm nest with kittens in a row, suckling. They knew to keep such things secret if the kittens were to avoid the sack, the dark pool under the willows, the eels unreeling from beneath the bank with their rows of needle teeth. They all knew about drowning.

'There was a kitten on the ark,' said Alison. 'Two kittens. There were two of every kind of animal and for forty days and nights they floated on the flood.'

'What did they eat?' said Gus.

'They had food on the ark. God told them to take lots of food.' The giraffe had fallen off again so she gave up and put it back in the box.

'Like hay and that?' said Rosemary. 'You'd need a lot of hay for that many animals.'

'Yes,' said Alison. 'Hay. And oats.'

'And meat for the lions,' said Graham.

'Yes,' said Alison. 'And on the fortieth day, what do you think Noah did?'

'They could have fished for meat, I suppose,' said Gus. 'There'd be heaps of bodies in the water. They could have put a line over the side and hooked a horse or a zebra and fed that to the lions.'

The starfish twinnie was crying quietly by the felt board. Tears oozed down her cheeks and soaked into the fluff of her Sunday angora cardigan. Alison held up a black bird.

'That's a starling,' said Gus. 'I shoot starlings.'

'It's not a starling,' said Alison, pressing it into place alongside a puff of white cloud above the ark. 'It's a raven. Noah sent out a raven to see if there was any dry land.'

'Is a raven bigger than a starling?' said Gus.

'I think so,' said Alison. I've never seen one.'

'Starlings are hard to hit,' said Gus.

'What kind of gun have you got?' said Bruce, climbing back onto his chair and looking interested.

'It brought back nothing,' said Alison. Her big squiffy eyes were looking faintly desperate. ('Astygmatism,' Kate's mother said of Alison. 'All the McDonalds have problems with their eyes. Cousins married first cousins.')

'Slug gun,' said Gus. 'Point seven seven.'

'Was everything still under the water?' said Graham.

'Yes,' said Alison.

'Even the mountains?' said Maura.

'Everything,' said Alison. 'That's what the Bible says. The whole world was flooded.'

She held the dove in her hand but both the twinnies were crying, their faces puckered, their noses running, their identical pink mouths open like the mouths of birdlings in a nest.

'Shh,' said Alison. 'It was all right because: see? Here's the dove. That showed it was all right. It's bringing back the olive branch. Don't cry.'

The sobbing was gathering strength, a duet perfectly pitched.

'The ki— ki— kittens!' hiccupped the twinnie with the hair ribbon tied on the left. The twinnie with the ribbon tied on the right simply opened her mouth wider and howled.

The hymn next door had trailed off into the long drawn-out bleat of the Aaaamennnn.

'There!' said Alison quickly. 'And that's God's promise that it will never happen again!' And she stuck the rainbow to the board.

'Now, let's go and play Stiff Candle,' she said. 'Shh, twinnies. Shh . . .'

She did not want anyone to hear the twinnies crying. Most particularly Pete, who had told her last week that he wanted heaps of kids, a whole football team. One of the reasons she had agreed to take the Sunday School was the opportunity it gave her to leave the church, children gathered about her, demonstrating her maternal side.

And [the prophet Elisha] went up from thence unto Bethel: and as he was going up by the way, there came forth little children out of the city, and mocked him, and said unto him, Go up, thou bald head; go up, thou bald head.

And he turned back, and looked on them and cursed them in the name of the Lord.

And there came forth two she bears out of the wood, and tare forty and two children of them.

And he went from thence to Mount Carmel . . .

II Kings 2:23–25

The children, released, run into the sunshine while the adults turn to the consumption of the holy Ribena and the sanctified sliced white. They run and squeal along the concrete edges of the graves, ducking behind the trees around the dunny raising clouds of flies. They run and yell, 'Over here! Over here! Tag me!' Their legs are quick and can leap high, they can dodge and feint, because they are not, after all, drowned or paddling for dear life, bedraggled and mewing on the flood. If you want to escape, all you have to do is cross your fingers and yell pax! Then nothing and nobody can get you.

In the back room, Kate is left alone. The children's squeals have receded and there is a pious murmur from the church next door. The Sunday School room is small, with a fireplace set diagonally into one corner. The fireplace is never used and the grate is splattered with floury droppings from the starlings that nest every year in the chimney. There are some hooks by the door where the minister has hung his coat, and a table by the window with the Sunday School box and its felt inhabitants. The room smells of dust and old wood and musty birds' feathers. Against one wall is a cupboard. The upper shelves hold Auntie Annie's jealously guarded collection of jars and vases and florists' wire. On the lower shelves are the books.

They are piled anyhow, abandoned and unread. They are different from the books at the Library in Oamaru, with their shiny plastic covers to keep them clean. They are books from the olden days: books with covers embossed with garlands of flowers. When Kate's mother was a little girl the church had functioned also as the district's lending library. Now a big Bedford bus lumbers down from Christchurch every four months and comes to roost in the middle of the school basketball court. People come and choose books from the shelves inside: travel to distant places, biographies of famous people, love stories, and some economic history for old Stevie McGregor, who lives alone up on Millerhill Hill, votes communist and bikes every Friday night into Waikouaiti for his groceries. He never bothers with a bike light but everyone knows to keep an eye out for him, materialising like a startled night bird in the headlights around some corner on the road.

The books in the cupboard behind the church have been forgotten. No one reads them. No one takes them home. They have fallen out of fashion and lie in the cupboard, solid and solemn, with thick creamy paper, slightly toasted at the edges. There are real books and storybooks. The real books are sad: one is about Little

Pearl, the China missionary's daughter, who was very good but got sick and died and everyone from the chief missionary to the Chinese cook cried. Or the two Margarets who had been killed in Scotland for going to church. They had been tied to sticks and slowly slowly the tide had risen until one drowned while the other Margaret sang hymns to cheer her up. Then the water covered her too and she died. The real stories do not have pictures. The storybooks are more cheerful, with pictures of little boys in caps and boots and little girls in bonnets and pinafores. Their print is big and round and at the top of each page there is a subtitle in thick black letters that tells you what the story on that page is going to be about:

We must find them!

Murray finds a chum!

All a Mistake!

All the pictures have titles too:

Till dawn, the heroic girl fought her awful battle.

Marcia lay stunned, motionless, insensible.

These are the books belonging to Millerhill. Each place has its own books. Whenever they visited their great aunts in Dunedin they were given a copy of *Coles Funny Picture Book* to read while the adults sat in chintz chairs in the living room and drank tea. Kate and Maura looked at pictures of the Smacking Machine, which had a wheel with many rods attached. The bad boy stood with his bottom to it, his mouth stretched in an agonised grimace, while the teacher in his long black robe laughed and turned the wheel. They turned the page and examined the picture of the Boy Who Smoked, who was dark and sunken, and the Boy Who Did Not Smoke, who was smiling and sturdy.

'Why is it funny?' they asked their mother. And she said it was a book from the olden days and they thought different things were funny then. The books at Millerhill were also from that foreign place called the olden days, where a little boy called Murray sacrificed his dearest possession, a stuffed toy he called his "ickle 'amb' in the collection plate at church and the mischievous little Irish girl, Pixie, finally received the school prize for Kindliness and Consideration because she had been 'content to suffer for the sake of others'.

Kate knows about this place because each Sunday during the holidays when she went to Sunday School with her cousins she removes one of the books. She chooses the one with the prettiest cover, wraps it in her cardigan and hides it under the waterstand while she runs to join the others.

'Tag me! Tag me!' she calls as the harmonium wheezes the three part Amen and the men emerge from the church to talk lambing and rugby and how many inches of rain they've had that month, until the minister comes up for his bit of a chat. He's a brainy chap, a real Rhodes Scholar, but he does his best with the lambing and the rainfall, while the ladies circulate with tea trays laden with cups and some nice Albert Squares. They're all going home to roast and three veg, the leg left in the oven on low, the brussels sprouts all peeled with a cross cut in the stem. The patients stand to one side and the ladies say, 'Go on, Charlie, help yourself.' And Charlie takes four Albert Squares and puts two under his hat for later.

Kate is standing by the water tank in the shadows behind the church, tagged and turned to wax. The tank is rusted and sad. It oozes water in a long brown runnel down one iron leg as if it is old and has peed itself. Behind the tank, the boards of the church are coated in green lichen and there is the smell of damp and sticky snail trails.

'Over here!' shouts Kate, for her arms are tired with being held stiff. 'Over here!' The other children squeal and scatter like chooks in front of Graham, who is It for now. She considers ignoring the rules and running to join the flock, but it is not permitted. She must stand turned to wax, thinking about drowning, thinking about the people in the train who fell into the river, the year when the Queen came and the town was filled with boxes full of flowers with perfect names — gladioli, carnations, gypsophila — and she had a gold medal to pin to her jersey. That was when the river poured into the train and all the Christmas presents were torn from the racks and all the people drowned so that carnations, gladioli, gypsophila became the flowers for dead people. Kate stands looking down into the valley as water pours from the heavens and water pours in from the sea. A towering wall of water like the Tidal Wave or Tsunami on the Weetbix card. Graham had sent away for the book and glued in all the cards in the Great Disaster series. The *Titanic* going down, dwarfed by the iceberg. The buildings toppling in San Francisco, the volcano tossing flame and burning rock into the air above a tiny white city. Worst of all was the tsunami, one of Nature's Most Fearsome Spectacles! The wall of water stood over a sandy beach where tiny palm trees bent before the force of its coming and people the size of ants ran hopelessly from its fall.

She sees the McDonalds' Romneys tossed into the water, tiny hooves flailing, the gum trees on the flat torn from the roots, the houses in their rings of macrocarpa torn from their foundations, the barns and paddocks, school and dairy factory drowned and broken, and above them floats the little boat with its smug red and yellow trim and its privileged cargo. The water fills the valley until the hills are covered, the water is rising around her ankles, around her knees and up to her stomach, she can't breathe, she can't . . .

'Go! Go!' says Rosemary, hitting her hand. 'Go!' And she is freed at last to dash away from the water tank, the drowned valley, around to the sunny side.

Pixie O'Shaugnessy was at once the joy and terror of the school. It had been a quiet, well-conducted seminary before

her time, or it seemed so at least, looking back after the
arrival of the wild Irish tornado, before whose pranks the
mild mischief of the Englishers was as water unto wine.

Pixie O'Shaugnessy by Mrs George De Horne Vaizey

When Kate and Maura stayed with their other cousin, Bernard, out at Weston, they also went to church, but then it was to the Basilica. It was grand and snowy white and the priest wore robes of green and purple and the women of the congregation had black lace scarves that lent them an exotic, gypsy air. The floor was of white stone and hard on the knees when they knelt, and they had to kneel properly, on both knees, or Auntie Mary poked them in the back. Around the walls hung little theatres where Christ fell repeatedly, and there were whips and anguish and trickles of blood. At Christmas, in the Nativity at the back of the church, a life-size Mary and Joseph knelt before the baby Jesus in his white robe, lifting his arms to be picked up from a manger filled with real straw.

At Bernard's house they played science games because Bernard liked science. They gathered moths in old preserving jars and poured mixtures from his chemistry set onto them to see what happened. They made explosions with baking soda and red food dye to blow the corks from bottles. Bernard collected stuff and made model aeroplanes out of balsa wood and delicious glue. A Fokker Eindekker hung in one corner of his room, and on the shelf beneath lay his principal treasure: a real dinosaur tooth his father, Kate's Uncle Frank, had found in a lump of limestone at Weston Quarry. Bernard thought it might have come from an ichthyosaur or maybe a plesiosaur. He had printed the names on a bit of paper under the tooth. Bernard's books stood beside the tooth: *Rupert Bear*, who was a strange white bear in checked trousers, and *Now We Are Six*, with the pictures of the little boy who looked like a girl, and Cuthbert

Caterpillar setting off for the Pink Tea at the Queen Bee's castle. Gentle things alongside that huge incisor with its savage cutting edge from the mouth of some creature that had once swum, predatory, above where they sat now in a companionable row on Bernard's chenille quilt, reading 'I am Sir Brian ker-splash!'

Everywhere around them had once been under the ocean. The garden, the road, the hills, the distant mountains. The limestone from which Kate's father had made their garden wall was made up of billions of tiny shells. There were places on the hills around the town where the shells were still visibly shells, exactly like the cockles and pipis at Friendly Bay, only conveniently crushed by millennia to exactly the size for feeding chooks. They collected bucketfuls to make the hens' eggs nice and strong so they did not smash in the nest. The hens ate their grit not knowing that they were eating dinosaur bones, or that their hen runs had once been under the sea. Everything about them had risen dripping from an ancient dinosaur ocean.

This was a different kind of fact to the fact of Noah. Noah was true, but the giant tooth on Bernard's bookshelf was true too.

When Agnes was thirteen a rich man asked her to marry him. Agnes said 'NO!' It would be wrong for her to marry anyone, because she had promised her love to Jesus. The man was so angry he had Agnes killed. She was a martyr — that means she died for Jesus.

Dear Saint Agnes, help me to suffer rather than do anything bad.

A First Book of Saints by Father Gales

111

At Bernard's they also encountered saints. Auntie Mary read them a story about a saint every night before they went to sleep. There was St Teresa, who was too little to do big things for God but who made her bed and shelled peas with great love instead. There was little St Agnes who said 'NO!' when a rich man asked to marry her, though she was only thirteen. St Francis, St Margaret Mary, St Patrick and St Benedict had all loved God and become saints, which meant that even after they were dead they had a job to do, looking after things. There was a saint who helped Auntie Mary find her car keys. God was naturally too busy to be bothered about such trivialities, but saints were available upon request.

You had to be very good to be a saint, and you had to be Catholic. Presbyterians could not be saints, even if they had been tied to sticks and drowned singing hymns. At Bernard's they said their prayers, leaving off the end of the Lord's Prayer, because Catholics stopped short at the request to be delivered from evil, without adding 'for thine is the kingdom' and the compliments Presbyterians clearly thought necessary to ensure divine favour. When they had said their Catholic prayers their aunt turned out the light, closed the door and went out to play cribbage in the kitchen with Uncle Frank and Kate and Maura's father. From the bedroom they could hear the chink of glasses and the sound of adult talk, 2 for his heels, 15 for 2, 15 for 4, and a pair for 6, the pegs advancing hole by hole up and down the board.

Bernard stood, arms spread, on top of the wardrobe. 'Banzai!' he whispered, so as not to disturb the adults, and he leapt down onto the bed. It bounced hugely and grandly and tossed its pillows onto the floor. Maura followed, nightie billowing around skinny legs. Kate awaited her turn, balanced on the tallboy. On the wall hung the picture of Jesus in his crown of thorns. Blood trickled down his forehead and his eyes were twin bruises, clenched tightly against the pain. But if you looked at him for longer than a second, the eyes opened. They stared back at you. Kate scrambled up onto the wardrobe, keeping her face studiously averted. They had three jumps each, then tucked themselves in, Maura on one side, Kate on the other, and they tickled Bernard, who lay in the middle. Bernard had a penis that stood up when tickled, small and pink as a birthday candle. He possessed the enchanting ability to pee precisely on huhu beetles or slaters. Kate and Maura had tried to emulate him, standing legs astride to direct the flow away from socks and shoes, but somehow they never managed it with quite Bernard's casual flair. They tickled and giggled and then curled to sleep, while Jesus opened and closed his eyes at the foot of their bed.

7.

First a hidden door; and then a secret room that had been closed for seventy years, and now an imprisoned maiden in a golden frame. Clarinda, 1869. What more could you ask on a wet Sunday?

The Four-Storey Mistake by Elizabeth Enright

There were two houses at Millerhill. One held Auntie Annie, Uncle George, Bruce, Rosemary and Grandma. The other contained Auntie Izzie, Uncle Ted and eight cousins, ranging from Pete, who was almost grown up and had his own bedroom outside in a caravan with iron wheels and its own little wood stove, to Diane, the baby.

Uncle George and Auntie Annie milked cows, which queued in an orderly fashion in the yards to be ushered, udders swaying grandly, into the byre, where the radio played and George and Annie sang.

They sang 'Some Enchanted Evening' as they slapped the cups on swollen teats. And 'Oh What a Beautiful Morning'. And 'Old Man River'.

Around the byre sat a ring of half-wild cats, waiting for the moment when George would direct a teat in their direction. The cats bred indiscriminately, ginger and striped, fluffy and short-hair. They hunted rabbits and kept the mice at bay, and twice a day they sat like a small skinny choir with their pink mouths gaping, waiting for their reward.

'Open wide!' said Uncle George, and doused them with milk.

Auntie Annie sang all the time. She sang as the cows came and went and she sang as she walked on swollen ankles across the yard to the house, where she sang as she popped on some sausages for breakfast, and an egg or two to keep their strength up, and a few slices of fried bread. When she was a little girl, Kate's mother said, Annie had stolen a whole pound of butter from the churn and run away up the hill and eaten it all.

'No one told on her,' their mother said. 'She was the oldest. We were all a bit scared of her.'

Kate and Maura did not like staying with Auntie Annie much, even though Uncle George played jokes and slid his teeth out at the dinner table.

'Oh, George!' said Auntie Annie, laughing until her eyes watered. 'Don't be silly.' He waggled his lips so his cheeks shook. His whole face seemed to have collapsed in on itself. His skin was as limp as a popped balloon.

I'm Popeye the sailor man, he sang. *I'm Popeye the sailor man!*

Then he said, 'Tataa for nownow!' and went out and jumped on Star, the little grey mare, by leapfrogging over her tail. He whistled the dogs, set Star to a steady canter and stood up on her haunches. 'Yee har!' he called as he galloped off over the flat.

'He should have been in a circus,' Kate's mother said. 'He's no farmer and that's a fact. But then he's a Roper from Waitati.'

Bruce had his ferrets and Rosemary had a Manx cat. She had made it herself. She had caught one of the wild cats, the whitest, fluffiest one, held it down on the woodblock and docked its tail with the kindling hatchet. The kitten left a long graze on her arm, but was tamed eventually and came when Rosemary called it ('Fluffy! Fluffy!'), twitching its little stub.

Grandma lived with Auntie Annie. She was thin and gentle, with grey hair pulled into a bun. When she got up in the morning she dressed slowly and tied on a clean pinafore.

'Can I help?' she said, standing in her slippers in the kitchen that had been hers before her husband died and Annie and George took over the farm. ('And it's gone back ever since,' said Kate's mother. 'Fences broken, ditches left to block and flood. It was never like that in my father's day, I can tell you.')

Auntie Annie swept some onions into a frying pan.

'No,' she said. 'You just put your feet up and take it easy, Mum.'

Grandma sat in her pinafore and slippers by the window and looked out at the garden where the roses she had planted arched in red and gold over the horopito hedge and a grey warbler rippled among overgrown dahlias. Sometimes she shelled the peas. Sometimes she just sat.

In the afternoons she went through to the living room and played the pianola. Uncle George and Auntie Annie had bought a pianola with dozens of paper rolls, which turned and produced miraculous music as unseen hands pressed the keys on the keyboard.

Uncle George pedalled away happily, singing that seven lonely days amounted to one very lonely week.

The pianola was large and occupied an entire wall, so Grandma had given her piano to Kate's mother, so that Kate and Maura could have lessons. Grandma sat to play at the pianola instead, bending carefully to switch off the automatic player and pushing the player pedals back into the body of the machine. She stretched her fingers over the keys and very quietly, so as not to disturb anyone (for George and Annie had a lie-down every afternoon after lunch without fail), she picked out as much as she could remember of some dreamy nocturne, a minuet, a song without words.

Kate and Maura preferred to stay with the other cousins on their mother's side, sleeping top and tail in the double bed with the girls. The boy cousins slept in a row of beds in the sunroom like the seven dwarves in their cottage. The house was noisy with guitars and loud singing in Elvis voices. At night Auntie Izzie sat on the floor in front of the fire while Uncle Ted brushed her hair. She had long hair. When she was a girl it had reached to her knees. ('Sapped her strength,' Kate's mother said. 'All her strength went into her hair.') Her hair no longer reached her knees but it was long enough. It spread over Uncle Ted's lap, crackling and springing away from the brush. Her face was uplifted, her eyes closed.

'Oooh, that's lovely,' she said. 'Lovely.'

If she had been a cat she would have kneaded the hearth rug. Kate had seen Uncle Ted shearing, shoving a ewe between his thighs, holding it firmly while the blade swept over belly and back, then dispatching the sheep, which looked surprised and naked, through the flap to the yard. He worked hard and fast. But when he sat brushing Auntie Izzie's hair he was so gentle. He brushed with concentration, careful not to tug. The hair fizzed with static electricity. Kate watched them side on, feeling embarrassed at witnessing such pleasure, such gentle rapture. This, she decided, must be true love.

At Millerhill, Kate and Maura and the cousins played with the past, squabbling over whose turn it was to straddle the broad leather seat of the Indian motorbike out in the barn and head down that invisible straight. Brrrmmm, they said. Brrrmmmm. They made their huts in tumbledown houses that had been abandoned long since as smallholdings coalesced into bigger and bigger farms. Doors opened stiffly on rotten floors covered in straw and wallpaper gnawed through to the boards by rats. Around the rotting walls old plum trees burst into blossom each spring and the pathways to out-buildings long gone emerged again, marked out by daffodils with frilled golden heads bearing the sweet scent of spring and rain and damp earth. On wet days, the cousins played endless games of Monopoly or looked at the *National Geographic*s that were stored in a box under the windowseat.

— *Each move has meaning as a be-jewelled member of the Asante court performs a ceremonial dance.*

— *Inside their 'chum', a tent skilfully constructed at every camping place from larchpoles and reindeer skins, a Nenet mother and her son drink spoonfuls of reindeer blood.*

— *A woman of the Divali tribe veils her face, believing that the camera's lens will steal her soul.*

How could people walk about in those big fur trousers? How could they drink blood? How could people walk about with droopy breasts and bare bottoms? The children turned the pages, giggling, astonished and appalled at the world that lay beyond the hills of Millerhill. When they had seen enough, Graham took out the shock box from the windowseat and made them stand in a circle, holding hands.

'Now,' he said, spinning the handle, 'shut your eyes and no one is allowed to let go.' They stood and from hand to hand a shivery trill passed. It fizzed right through them, head to toe and down the arms. It was like the buzzer hitting a nerve at the murder house. It was like biting a chocolate still coated with silver paper. It was like touching the evil white bristles of ongaonga. If you let go, the shock stopped all at once in the person before you, whose hand you held, and they died. Just like that. All the electricity filled them up, as water builds behind rocks damming a creek. Then they fell to the floor, twitched a bit, and died. The cousins stood staunch in a circle, hanging on tight while Graham spun the handle faster and faster and the shock zipped between them and no one was a cowardy custard; no one let go.

'That's enough,' said Graham finally, and they were able to open their eyes. And there is the circle of cousins, brave and resolute, and they are all alive. There is the cat batting at flies on the windowsill, and the canary is singing out in its cage on the porch. They tumble together onto the sofa, wriggling and scrapping from sheer relief. Then Rosemary gets out the Monopoly board and they argue for the rest of the afternoon over piles of money, Park Lane and The Angel, Islington. They buy up hotels and railways. They demand extortionate rents. And as they trade and sell, their hands tingle still, remembering their earlier brush with death.

High up on the hill they called the Saddle Back, behind the ranch and the country road, the boy sat on his horse, facing east, his eyes dazzled by the rising sun.

My Friend Flicka by Mary O'Hara

Kate and Maura and the cousins sit, two to a pony, down by the creek. Thick cloud has gathered overhead, there is a roll of thunder then a flash of lightning coming to earth somewhere beyond the McDonalds' plantation. They slide from the ponies' backs and shelter beneath Star's belly as the rain comes down, hammering dusty summer earth, releasing the smell of dry grass. Hailstones skitter and shred the leaves of the willows. Beneath Star's big round belly the children crouch. Star can be trusted. She stands unmoving, head facing the storm. Kate looks up at the swirl of hair on her belly, swept this way and that as if it has been curled specially. The nipples are swollen already for the foal Star is carrying. Kate reaches up and squeezes tentatively and creamy milk oozes onto her hand. She tastes it, thick and sweet, Highlander Condensed straight from the can.

'Yuck!' says Rosemary. But Kate says it is nice, truly. She licks her fingers, thinking that this is how it would feel to be a foal, born in a field, standing under your mother's soft belly.

'Give us a go then,' says Rosemary.

They sit under the pony, taking turns to squeeze the little pink teats while Star stands patiently and the storm drums its way across the paddock and off up the hill toward the Kilmog. The grass when it has passed lies flat, and there is the scent of bluegums in the air. A bird begins to sing in the willow trees by the creek, a bellbird repeating its little tune over and over. Ping ping ping pingety ping.

Star stamps her hind foot.

'All right,' she says. 'That's enough.'

So the children crawl out from her protection, damp and safe and a little cramped from kneeling so long on wet grass, as if they were indeed foals new born, trying out their legs for the very first time.

8.

'I've been watching you carefully, and it looks so easy and so interesting, and I should like to be able to tell my friends that once I had driven a motor-car!'

> *The Wind in the Willows* by Kenneth Grahame

When Kate was seven she came home from school one afternoon to find Mrs Nelson seated at the dining table with their mother. Kate and Maura stood trailing their schoolbags uncertainly in the doorway. Mrs Nelson had never to their knowledge set foot in their house before. The closest they came to contact with the Nelsons was when their pigeons landed, nodding and dipping, among the peas and had to be dispatched with a lump of coal, a clod, whatever came to hand. Or when Kate or Maura had to retrieve a ball strayed over the fence. They entered the Nelsons' garden with awe: standard roses lined up along the Nelsons' drive, like dancers en pointe in a froth of gypsophila. The lawns were green rugs bordered with pansies, and around the back the Nelsons' vegetables grew lush and orderly. And undisturbed. The Nelsons' pigeons knew better than to fossick in perfection. Every morning Mrs Nelson stood on a special concrete step behind the washing line by the fence, cup of tea in hand, and called, 'Ooo-hooo!' to Mrs Evans, who was a widow and lived on the other side. Mrs Evans emerged from her kitchen with her cup of tea and stood on a step on her side of the fence and they chatted amicably for fifteen minutes while the sheets bellied white on the line behind them. Mrs Nelson never called 'Ooo-hooo!' to Kate's mother, who couldn't be bothered wasting time gossiping anyway: she had her cup of tea by the range, with her book.

Mrs Nelson turned and frowned at them.

'Shh,' she said, though they hadn't made any noise. 'Your grandmother's dying and your mother's upset.' She had brought over a chocolate cake with coconut sprinkles to mark the seriousness of the occasion.

Their mother went down to Millerhill that night on the bus. A week later she returned. She had nursed Grandma and when she died she had laid her out. After all, she was a nurse and trained to do such things.

In death, Grandma had shed her years and become young once more. Her skin had become smooth and white and all her freckles had reappeared, a brown sugar sprinkling over the nose, just like Kate's. And while Kate's mother was laying her out, Grandma had said, 'Don't cry, Tollie,' though she was already half an hour dead. She had sighed, her roses knocking at the window, and said, 'Don't cry, Tollie.'

Their mother inherited a share of the farm when Grandma died. She sold her share to her sisters and with the money, she bought a car.

Their father had already bought a car: an Austin Standard with blue tartan seat-covers and two little black indicators that popped from its sides at intersections like stunted fingers. It was painted red. Red was not a colour that could be lost in a crowd. The reason he had insisted upon a car of that colour was that he had gone to a test match in Dunedin with his mate Trethewey, who drove a grey Morris Minor. When they emerged from Carisbrook, the Springboks down 10-6, the crowd ecstatic, vengeance for 1949 in the air, it had taken them four hours to find Trethewey's car in a sea of grey cars.

'Red,' he said. 'That's the only colour for a car, I reckon. You can't lose a red car.' The Standard was red as a cherry, red as a phone box. He drove them in it that first weekend to view the Parade of Homes. Their mother sat in the front and Kate and Maura sat in the back, careful not to knock the upholstery with their shoes. They joined the procession of cars slowly inching along a cul de sac that had only a year before been a rubbish dump. Where seagulls had previously squabbled among scraps and heaps of garden clippings, there now stood a double row of houses with picture windows and white sheers and front doors with deer etched on frosted glass. Kate's family would never own such a house themselves. They would live all their lives with damp rot and a sunless kitchen and a row of buckets the length of the hall runner whenever the rain came from the south. They would never be able to move to tapestry brick and picture windows, but at the Parade of Homes they could dream. They could imagine life in a kitchenette with a breakfast bar and a roof tiled in permanent materials, impervious to storm and tempest.

Their father drove with a fine careless air, one arm crooked in the open window, the good hand turning the wheel this way and that as they drove the length of the street, then back to examine the houses on the other side, and their mother said, 'Ooh, I like that one, don't you, Pat? Look at that one with the boomerang design. Now, I'd say that one would get all the sun.'

Then they drove to a milk bar out on the Main North Road, a new milk bar called the Carolina, with a black silhouette of a lady in a crinoline on the front wall, and they got ice creams: double dips bigger by far than the ice creams from Mr Budd's dairy. The Carolina added peanuts at no extra charge and a serviette around the cone to catch the drips.

They sat in the Standard eating their ice creams while their father drove them down the main street and around the corner to park overlooking Friendly Bay. And though it was cold they were warm inside the car, not huddled on the beach like the people who did not have cars. They ate their ice creams then drove home singing 'I've Got Sixpence' all the way through to the part where the soldier had spent everything he had and had Sweet Fanny Adams for his wife, poor wife.

In the Standard they could go on holiday. Their mother stayed up all night baking biscuits and fruit loaves and bacon-and-egg pies for the journey, then Kate and her sister sat wedged in the back, crammed among bedding and suitcases and cake tins and cartons as the Standard chugged up the Waitaki Valley to the Power Board's crib at Hakataramea. The river churned somewhere off to their right behind bands of swaying willows dipping their long hair in the water. On their left stood limestone outcrops marked with strange creatures sketched by people who had walked this way hundreds of years before Kate's father drove by in the little red Standard. The family peered through the wire that kept the dream figures on their curve of limestone.

'Taniwha,' said Kate's father. 'Or maybe a giant eagle.'

And somewhere above their heads there was the rush of great wings as the bird fell from the eye of the sun, and somewhere at their bare necks was the brush of talons big enough to grip moa or child, to carry them to a high bluff to be torn into morsels for the gaping beaks of its fluffy nestlings.

They ran back to the car and off went the Standard, bumping across the black bridge at Kurow and zigzagging through the gap into the valley where heat created mirages of water on the road ahead and the air smelled of sheep and dry grass and a million briar roses, pink as burnt skin, pink as summer.

The car Kate's mother's bought was a 1948 Morris. She arrived home with it one night without warning. She simply pulled in behind the Standard in a car as round and brown as the little red hen's newly baked loaf. The car was registered and insured. She had taken lessons and had her licence.

'It's my money,' she said.

The next afternoon, Kate and Maura came home from school to find a note on the dining-room table.

Gone to pick apricots, said the note in their mother's quick, jagged hand. *Back around 7. Tea in oven*.

There was a mutton casserole and some potatoes all peeled and soaking in salt water on the hob. The table was spread beneath a filmy throw.

Their father was furious. 'What does she mean, running off like this?' he said, mashing potato as if it would bruise. 'Leaving you children on your own?' At seven she returned. They heard the quick tread of her footsteps in the hall. The door opened. In her arms she held a wooden fruit box.

'There's two more in the car,' she said.

'What the hell are you playing at?' said their father, and he would have hit her but she was serene, untouchable, her arms carrying apricots.

'They're half the price of the fruit at the auction rooms,' she said. 'I've got enough for bottling and for jam.'

Next afternoon the kitchen was sweet with the scent of stewed fruit. Rows of jars filled with fruit arranged like petals in syrup stood cooling on the bench, and on one shelf stood twenty jars of apricot jam, their father's favourite. He could hardly object. He had been outflanked by apricots.

The following week she ventured further afield, up Central for raspberries. And after that she picked strawberries at Geraldine, nectarines near Kurow. The cupboards were crammed with jams and pickles and chutneys and preserves. On her way to pick and gather, she took to dropping in on relatives she had not seen in years: elderly aunts and distant cousins. She began to collect dates: a wedding here, a birth date there, and note them down. She began to bring back family along with the fruit. Peaches in their velvet skins, the brown saucers of mushrooms plucked from some roadside paddock, blackberries oozing inky juice through the cardboard box she had used as an impromptu container. And dates and anecdotes: the great-great uncle, Drysdale Stuart, who lost all his money and went to Canada where he made a fortune in timber. The second cousin who had married a man who had another wife across the mountains in Westport.

'He drove the coach,' she said, 'and she had no idea until the day of his funeral that there was this other woman and four kiddies over on the Coast.'

She cleared a space on the kitchen table among the jars for a Remington portable from Harris's second-hand shop and a shoebox full of cards and photographs. She was going to write it all down (omitting, of course, Drysdale's bankruptcy and the second cousin's perfidious husband. Some things were best forgotten.). She was going to preserve her family.

In time she took to staying away longer. Sometimes she visited her sisters in Millerhill. Sometimes she needed to gather information from relatives in Gore or Wanaka. Sometimes she simply left, driving off along Highway One, unpicking the white line between herself and home like a row of stitches. She took a thermos and a sleeping bag so she could pull over wherever she pleased and sleep curled up on the back seat beside a river or among the tossing heads of tussock in the Danseys. She returned home, calm and happy.

'Cope all right?' she said to Kate as she lifted a tray of Black Doris plums from the back seat of the Morris.

'Sort of,' said Kate.

'Of course you did,' said her mother. She patted her hand. 'Our family always cope.'

> *'Those men last night did bring very bad news, and Father will be away for some time. I am very worried about it, and I want you all to help me, and not to make things harder for me.'*
>
> *'As if we would!' said Roberta, holding Mother's hand against her face.*
>
> *The Railway Children* by E. Nesbit

Kate's mother and Izzie talked at the kitchen bench as they stood buttering bread and cutting cold mutton for the shearers' lunches, and talked as they knelt in the garden dragging out armfuls of chickweed and couch. They spoke quietly, laughing in a secret giggly fashion that stopped the minute one of the children approached.

'What do you want?' she said as Kate stood on one leg, then the other, shy of this stranger who materialised in her mother's place whenever they came here to Millerhill. Their mother seemed younger here, once more the youngest sister. She became Tollie, the one who left home to go nursing, the adventurous one who married out of the district, the bold one who told jokes and spoke her mind. There was a streak of earth over her forehead and her hair had come loose under an unfamiliar sunhat with daisies on the brim.

'I can't find the others,' said Kate.

Auntie Izzie and her mother looked about absently, as if it did not matter at all where the other cousins might be.

'We were playing sardines,' said Kate, 'but no one found me, and now they've all gone.'

She had been so clever finding the cupboard in the laundry, tucked in behind all the boots and outdoor coats. She had heard the footsteps on the lino from her safe nest behind a raincoat where a mason wasp was busy whipping up a tube in a long fold of japara. Its tiny drill squealed beside her head as it smoothed the clay ready for the store of preserved flies for its babies to eat when they hatched. It was warm in the cupboard. It smelt of all the people who had ever worn these clothes, a thick odour of belonging. She felt contained by it. Maybe she dozed a little. It's hard to sleep four to a bed; there is always a stray foot nuzzling at your neck. When she woke in the cupboard nest, the house was silent. She climbed out on stiff legs to find only the house cat curled on rug by the range, and out in the garden, her mother and aunt in their sunhats, kneeling among the weeds.

Her mother tugged at a dandelion.

'Have you tried the caravan?' she said.

'Yes,' said Kate.

'The barn?' ventured Auntie Izzie.

'I've looked there too,' said Kate.

'They'll be around somewhere,' said her mother. It was a dismissal. Kate turned to go and as she did she heard her mother say, 'So what did Ted say when . . . you know . . .' They were talking Grown-up, the code of glances and silences that was not to be understood by children. As Kate trailed off across the yard, her aunt's soft conspiratorial giggle emerged like the scent of daphne or winter sweet from the overgrown flowerbed.

Her mother was determined to go to the opening of the Millerhill Hall. All winter the farmers had been pouring concrete and hammering away on a patch of ground opposite the church and the school. Their wives brought them scones for smoko. They paused briefly to sit on saw benches and piles of timber, teasing one another the way men did, poised for the joke that would put them ahead, like puppies play-fighting for the grip on the neck. By spring, just before lambing, the hall was ready.

'Are you coming down for the opening, Pat?' Kate's mother said. Pat shook his head.

'Not likely,' he said.

'I want to go,' she said.

'Suit yourself,' he said. He turned a page.

Auntie Annie was in charge of the catering. The phone rang incessantly, long short long. Pause. Long short long.

'So can you manage some sausage rolls?' said Auntie Annie, and it was not a real question despite the rising inflection. 'Four dozen? . . . Grand . . . Toodle-oo.' She ticked sausage rolls on the list pinned to the wall.

Kate and Maura sat with the other cousins on the morning of the opening, folding crêpe-paper streamers at the kitchen table: red

129

over green, yellow over pink, until their fingers were brightly stained. They were dressed in their best clothes mid-afternoon and then hung about, rustling with sticking-out petticoats and white socks while the adults rushed about taking forever.

'There,' said Auntie Izzie at last, twisting in a pair of crystal earrings. 'Let's have a look at us all.' She lined them up and surveyed them with satisfaction. 'My,' she said, 'aren't we flash?' And they were. Uncle Ted had on his Sunday suit, and his hair — which was thinning on top — was smoothed in individual strands across his skull as if it had been neatly darned. There was a rustling in the doorway behind them.

'Wheet-whewww!' whistled Uncle Ted and they all turned to look. Kate's mother stood there, wearing a dress Kate had never seen before. It was toffee brown, but when she moved it changed colour. It had rainbows concealed in it, like the rainbows on a road after rain. Her waist was tightly cinched and the skirt swirled out. There were amber crystals at her neck and matching earrings and her hands were concealed beneath long white gloves.

'Oh, you beautiful doll!' sang Uncle Ted and he tried to dance her off around the kitchen, though she resisted, said, 'Don't be daft, Ted!' but not meaning it, for her eyes were shining and her red lips were smiling. Auntie Izzie gave her a hug. 'You're a cracker,' she said. And then, if everyone was ready, 'Into the car, kiddies!'

Crammed into the back of the Vauxhall, Kate's mother gave Kate's hand a squeeze.

'All right?' she said, and Kate could only nod. Her mouth was stuffed full of excitement and strangeness.

At the hall cars were drawn up in the dark but light poured forth from the new door and all along the walls were the streamers they had made that morning and bunches of balloons, like Christmas. The band — the Rhythm Boys from Palmerston, drums accordion and two guitars — were standing on the little stage in glittery jackets and someone was sprinkling powder on the floor and behind the kitchen slide were dozens of sausage rolls and devils on horseback and sandwiches, plain and club. There were no drinks except orange cordial but out the back in the carpark the car boots were up and men were standing about in the dark having a few beers. Uncle George made a speech, then the Rhythm Boys did a drum roll and Mr Brown the school teacher, who was MC for the evening in a proper black suit and bow tie, grabbed the microphone, which whistled and clicked, and said, 'Ladies and gentlemen, take your partners, please!'

Kate had kept close to her mother during the speech and the jokes about Bert Crawford who had left a couple of bags of cement out in the rain and if anyone wanted weights for the tractor, well, he knew where to find some! Laughter had hung about like a bright cloud above the forest of white furry stoles and evening bags and pressed trousers, but suddenly her mother was moving away to join the ring of women forming in the middle of the slippery floor. A circle of men surrounded them and the Rhythm Boys were setting off, tee dum tee dum, and everyone was moving. The men took the women in their arms, two steps to the right, two to the left, then the women spun under the men's arms and they all knew how to do it. Her mother knew how to do it. She was laughing up at a man as she passed from him to the next man. And when it was over she walked over to their side of the hall with a man who looked a bit like Mr McGregor but all polished and smiling and not like the dour man who kicked his dogs and swore at them, his anger bouncing from the hillsides and amplified the length of the valley. He was saying thank you to their mother and almost bowing and as soon as he had turned away the MC was announcing a Gypsy Tap and another man had come up.

'Tollie Stuart, isn't it?' he said.

And Kate's mother was smiling.

'Alex! I didn't expect to see you here!' And off they went. Heel toe and step step step.

'Come on!' said Rosemary, grabbing both Kate's hands. 'Come and dance!' She hopped and Kate had no option but to hop too, and Maura joined in, and before the Gypsy Tap was over all the children had joined hands and were hopping about and skidding over on the polished floor in their best clothes and no one was saying they shouldn't.

The dancing in the middle became more crowded and as the men drifted in and out from the carpark, the laughter grew. Kate's mother danced, light on her feet, her back straight, her arm at just the perfect angle, then Mr McGregor took her into a snappy foxtrot and everyone stood back and watched as they swooped into all the corners, and turned and executed deft little twinkling steps from one side of the hall to the other. The brown taffeta dress swirled about her slim legs and caught all the colours and they were the best dancers by far. When they'd finished everyone clapped. Then Graham got down some of the balloons and the children danced balloon dances, and when the balloons popped it didn't matter because there were so many more, pink and yellow clusters of them, ripe for plucking.

Then Auntie Annie slammed up the kitchen slide and they ate sausage rolls and sponge cake and devils on horseback all on the same plate until they could eat no more and the dancing began again. Kate was sleepy now so she went into the cloakroom and slept on a pile of coats, and when she woke it was morning and she was back in bed at Auntie Izzie's.

There was the sound of quiet talk in the kitchen next door, so she slid out without disturbing the others and found Izzie and her mother in their dressing gowns sitting either side of the fireplace having a cup of tea.

'So how did you like your first dance, Kate?' said Auntie Izzie.

"Sall right,' said Kate, but she knew as she said it, snuggled against her mother's warm side, that it was not enough. Her mother was herself again this morning, hair tangled, no make-up, but now Kate could see the dancer in her. She could hear the quick light step as she rushed back from the shop, late with the tea. She could see the straight back and the elegant lift of the head. She knew the dancer was there.

9.

Mary sorrowfully left the gay court of France and came back to troubled times in her own kingdom. She was one of the most beautiful women of her time. She married her cousin Darnley, and their little son became James the Sixth of Scotland.

Arthur Mee's Children's Encyclopaedia

Two fact, two fiction. To begin with, the distinction between fact and fantasy was immaterial. The sloth slung from his branch sprouting his own personal jungle was as real as the little house in its orchard of apple blossom, and as unlikely. In play, reality ran together with fantasy like currents in a single river in which Kate swam without a sensation of having crossed any boundary.

She lies under the house, which has become a rabbit's burrow. And she is the resident rabbit, with furry paws and long, long ears.

But she is also Kate, hidden down here where the earth is grey and possesses that smell distinctive of all secret places: the scent that wells up from the drain outside the front gate or from closed cupboards or from the tiny private crevices of the body, the smell of tummy-button fluff, ear wax and the flaky skin between the toes. Above her head she can hear the beat of shoes: her mother's staccato tap across the kitchen lino, Maura's skip hop run down the hall, her father's heavier tread toward the front door. There is treasure here in the dark: bottles with marbles in their necks, a rusted dog chain, and above all, the secret pleasure of listening to others undetected. Her long ears waggle. Her pink nose twitches. She is rabbit and child.

As Kate grew, the gap widened.

There was a fact.

There was what was imagined.

Some things belonged on one side, catalogued with numbers on their spines. Some belonged on the other side, in a more random arrangement. Kate knew now that when she knelt over the wood-block with her tender neck exposed to the axe her friend Marilyn Rasmussen held in her hands, that Marilyn was just pretending to be Elizabeth and she, Kate, was just pretending to be Mary Queen of Scots. So her mother did not have to scream, finding them there when she came out to chop some kindling. She screamed; she grabbed the axe as if it were real, as if Marilyn really would have chopped off Kate's head. They knew about Mary Queen of Scots from the *Children's Encyclopaedia*, ten red cloth volumes Kate had received for Christmas, which were largely dedicated to what was real: *The Interesting World of the Protozoa, The Land of Egypt and its Long Long History*. From the encyclopaedia they had learned that Mary was beautiful and Elizabeth wasn't, but Marilyn would not have cut off Kate's head. They were *pretending*. Kate felt embarrassed at her mother's panic. (Though it had to be admitted that Marilyn had not wanted to be Elizabeth, any more than she wanted to be the mean teacher when Kate was the naughty schoolgirl, or the servant when Kate was Cleopatra and lay on a curtained mattress in the playhouse reading while Marilyn swept the floor. So it was just conceivable that Marilyn could have brought down the axe and that Kate's mother could have found her daughter lolloping woozily and headless toward the hydrangeas.)

Reality possessed a special terror. Storybooks tried to terrify with one-eyed giants and witches. Cinderella's sisters cut off heel and toe to fit the shoe, the Happy Prince tried to make the little swallow fly south for the winter. But none of these horrors could equal the terror of fact. No one-eyed giant could equal the Professor at Millerhill church with the hole in his forehead. No witchy wood could equal the train in the year when all the shops in town suddenly sprouted boxes on their fronts filled with carnations, gladioli and gypsophila because the Queen was coming and everything had to be perfect.

Except that the train fell into the river.

There were photos of it in the *Weekly News*: an ordinary train like the ones she saw passing over Thames Street carrying their passengers in illuminated carriages to some unimaginable other place. A flooded river. The lights extinguished, the water rushing through broken windows, the people drowned, the Christmas presents torn from the racks.

And no ogre could compete with the boy Kate read about on a scrap of paper torn from the two-minute silence, the boy from New Plymouth who had filled a bath with petrol, then climbed in and set fire to himself. His story was contained on a six-inch by six-inch square of newsprint from the little wooden box by the lavatory. Kate had been sitting on the warm wooden ring reading the stories first: a ripped-up picture of the Blossom Festival Queen, a scrap of an advertisement for cigarettes. *Albanys! Hillary's Choice for the Everest Exped* . . . The story of the bath was complete. Kate held the scrap of paper and saw the bath, an ordinary bath such as anyone might fill with warm water, where you might soak or make soapy gloves from the foam. She thought of this bath filled with flame. She imagined the boy lying in the flames, burning. She screwed the story up, dropped it into the bowl and flushed it away. It swirled and disappeared beyond the S-bend but when she shut her eyes for nights after there was the fire and the boy in New Plymouth crying and an ordinary bath transformed in an instant of unimaginable despair to a flaming pyre.

Now and again an arquebus popped and flashed, and a bullet sang.

'Got him!' said Angela in a tone of deep satisfaction.

Alan looked around at her. She was laboriously winding back her crossbow for a second shot.

The Hills of Varna by Geoffrey Trease

She chose a middle path: not the fantasy of giants and dragons that growled and raged only for effect, while the outcome of the tale remained inevitable. (The hero would overcome the giant, the princess would live happily ever after, the pretty poor girl would win the prince.) Nor the factual world of the newspaper, which between advertisements and the Blossom Festival could spring such horrors. She chose, as her two fiction, books in which realistic-looking children spent summers exploring or winning prizes at gymkhanas or thwarting smugglers. She read about children who attended boarding schools with dorms and tuckboxes and children not very much older than herself who escaped from German soldiers or marched north to fight the Picts, or girls who dressed as boys and roamed about rescuing valuable manuscripts from perilous places.

She chose a world that was utterly unlike her own, but which acquired its own coherence and reality.

She began to live in two separate places. It required a special kind of thinking, like the thinking required to make the two candles in *Coles Funny Picture Book* transform into a witch's face.

She rides her pony — a pony called Nugget borrowed from the herd at Miss McQuaid's Riding School — along the gravel road that leads to the beach. The road cuts, white, clean, across the fertile black soil of the market gardens with their rows of cabbages and lettuces. The rows break around outcrops of limestone that burst from the soil in curious formations. In one part of her mind the landscape is just that: the Chinese market gardens, hillocks of vegetable crates around bare houses dedicated to toil, cabbages, lettuces. But in the other part of her mind, the part that has been colonised by books, the limestone outcrops are villages and castles, the kinds of places where knights might joust or precious manuscripts might be concealed. Nugget tosses his shaggy head at a plastic bag tangled in overgrown mallow. He can smell the sea already in the wild gallop along the beach, leaping driftwood, the sea grabbing for his hooves. And he too will pretend. He will pretend the sea is alive, though he sees it every Saturday. He pretends that it is something to be treated with the deepest suspicion, snorting and pawing. He snatches at the bit and dances a little with excitement as the students of Miss McQuaid's Riding School trot, posting properly as they have been taught, past the Hills of Varna.

George was surprised. Why did a spook-train run about with boxes in it? She shone her torch on to one — and then quickly switched it out!

*She had heard a noise in the tunnel. She crouched down
in the truck, put her hand on Timmy's collar, and listened.*

Five Go Off to Camp by Enid Blyton

Kate and Maura rode their ponies and their bikes around Oamaru, desperate for adventure. They formed clubs with friends dedicated to this purpose.

The Adventure Club met on Saturday mornings at the top of Tamar Street, where the road climbed toward the cape with its cap of pines, crewcut and sinister. From up here, the town was a toytown of little streets arranged in neat squares over the coastal plain and the terrace that had once formed the cliff face to a primitive sea. There was the post office with its frilly tower, there were the railway yards and the clang and bang of mechanical coupling and shunting. A sign at the centre of the Lookout carpark directed visitors away from here to London, Antarctica, Sydney. The sign was a little woozy and in a puddle at its cracked concrete base floated one of those rubber tubes Wayne Norris at school called a frenchie. He had flicked one they found in the gutter one afternoon on their way back from softball at Awamoa Park, so that it had landed flat on Caro Williams's foot.

'Yuck!' she had said, and kicked it off. They had all squealed and scattered then, not certain what it was exactly but knowing that they did not under any circumstances want to feel the frenchie's clammy touch.

Kate poked at the frenchie with a stick. It floated like a pale jellyfish in a puddle of petroleum rainbows. There was a puffing and a wheezing behind her and there at last was Marilyn, eyes popping with the effort of biking all the way up Tamar Street, just to see if she could. Marilyn, Kate, Maura and Virginia Craddock. The Adventure Club was assembled. They concealed their bikes behind a gorse hedge and entered the pines.

The trees sighed overhead, making that strange sad sound pines made that was the next thing to silence. The trees were planted in rows like some army that had taken the high ground and stood to, alert and watchful. Beneath them lay a thick bed of rusty brown pine needles that deadened the sound of the Adventure Club's feet as they scrambled through over dead branches. There was no birdsong. They were entering the place where the funny men lurked. The funny men haunted such dark corners: the overgrown edges of parks, streets after dark, empty houses. They drove silent, sinister cars and offered children lollies to climb in beside them. They had no faces. They were shadows beneath the brim of a hat. They cruised the edges of the little town like the grey sharks who lurked beyond the safe waters of Friendly Bay, creatures of some nameless, unexplained menace.

'But what do they *do?*' Kate had asked her mother, and her mother said they interfered with little girls and sometimes, though less often, with little boys. Kate did not have to enquire further. 'Interfered with' was some awful rude thing like having holes in your pants. The words bore a sticky, queasy quality, like 'brassiere' or 'number twos'.

The Adventure Club entered the realm of the funny men carefully, mindful of every snapping twig, every shadow. Given a choice, Kate would not have chosen this as the morning's adventure, but they took turns in strict rotation to choose, and today was Virginia's turn. She wanted to find the volcano.

Each Saturday the Adventure Club did something that frightened them. They climbed the rocks at Bushy Beach, right to the top where the rock turned to slippery rubble and they had to hang on to treacherous iceplant and roots and not on any account look down to where the surf surged below. They climbed the slate quarry too, where the rock shattered into perfect rectangles and slid away to smash with a musical ding on the debris behind the little square blocks that were the quarry offices. They walked along the sea-wall, daring the sea to rise up, as it so easily could, and sweep them over into the forests of kelp. They explored the wild reaches beyond the Botanic Gardens where the little kids slid down the high slide, thinking themselves daring for doing so. The Adventure Club disdained such childish bravado, pushing its way through to the shrubs that grew longer and more dishevelled the further they were from the grand trees that stood about the lawns sporting their silver medals: *Sequoia gigantea*, *Fagus sylvatica*, *Quercus robur*. The Adventure Club sought the source of a creek that might easily have been filled with blood-sucking fish amid jungles of suckering elm and feathery groves of fennel.

Today they were looking for the volcano.

A branch had left a long scratch down Kate's leg and another was caught in her plait, dragging out hanks of hair. 'Are you sure it's this way?' she said to Virginia. Virginia crawled under a fallen trunk. Her shorts were irritating: yellow check, with little folded cuffs.

'Yes,' she said. 'It'll be right at the top.'

She knew all about volcanoes. She had done a project, painstakingly constructing a papier-mâché cone with crinkly red cellophane at the top and a torch in the middle to make the fire. It had taken pride of place on the Display Table, next to the frog tank and the pa with its palisade of burnt matches. She knew where the vent must be — somewhere beneath these pines — from which the lava had flowed to form the bubbly rocks at Bushy Beach. She marched ahead down a long dark aisle of pines, seeking it there, braving the funny men.

'There!' she said. 'That's it!'

The Adventure Club surveyed the vent. It was a hollow in the earth ringed by boulders. There was no sign of fire or molten rock, simply a soft dimpling covered in thick moss. Virginia jumped down to stand at its centre and Marilyn joined her. Kate held back, nervous that their combined weight might be sufficient to plunge them all into the molten centre that surged beneath their feet, maybe only a torch length away.

Now that they were there, they were uncertain what to do next. Their adventures usually ended like that. In books there would have been a rumbling beneath their feet, or failing that, they might have found a trapdoor barely concealed by the moss, or they would have come upon a gypsy encampment among the trees, where swarthy individuals made devious plans they could have overheard. Reality was such a disappointment. The Adventure Club stood around the volcano and the pines sighed overhead, and now the sigh was not of sadness but of the most profound boredom.

Then, somewhere to their right, they hear the cracking of a twig. There is some movement over there, where the trees are thickest. There is a sensation that creeps the length of the spine that someone, behind them, is watching them, someone is approaching on stealthy feet, there is that cold draught at the nape of the neck that could be the breathing of a funny man — he has tracked them through the trees, he is coming closer, he is prepared to interfere with them, all of them, he is reaching out and suddenly Kate finds herself running, and Marilyn too, and Maura and Virginia. They are all crashing back through the trees, dodging the gnarled hands that reach out to grab and trip and the trees are lined up on all sides like a crowd so that right and left look exactly the same.

'Over here!' Over here!' yells Virginia. And they can see where she is pointing, and there is light there, a flickering of emptiness beyond the ranks of terrible pines with their scars oozing resin and their dead arms and suddenly they are through, they are out in the open. And there is the Lookout, pointing the way to the whole world. And there is the town doing all the usual Saturday things. Going to

142

the dump. Playing tennis. Clipping hedges. The Adventure Club stand gulping in sunlight and safety. Their breathing slows. Their hearts steady. They find their bikes where they left them behind the gorse and they ride off down Tamar Street to the dump, where they spend the rest of this free and beautiful morning hunting among squabbling seagulls for old telephones to be pulled to bits to find the bell, discarded account books with useable pages, some bedsprings that might be tied to the feet for an experiment in jumping over the fence into the Nelsons' garden. They ride home laden with booty and giddy with triumph. They are reckless and brave. They have found the volcano and they have escaped the funny men.

'We must leave Warsaw for good and go and find Father,' she said.

'Find Mother too?'

'Yes, Mother too. We must go to Switzerland.'

'Where's that?'

'Millions of miles away,' said Jan. 'And you'll have to walk, without shoes.'

The Silver Sword by Ian Serraillier

It was Kate who decided to get out of the car. They were driving home from Weston: just Kate and Maura and their father. Their mother did not visit Weston any more than their father visited Millerhill. Weston was His Family. Millerhill was Her Family. The afternoon had been muggy and endless. Kate and Maura had argued with Bernard over Ludo while the grown-ups played cards and laughed a lot as it was New Year's and everyone had to stay up until midnight to see the Old Year out. At last their father lurched toward the car.

'Nigh',' he called to Auntie Mary and Uncle Frank. 'HabbyNewYear!'

Kate and Maura sat in the back seat and the Standard moved unsteadily off down the hill and out onto the main road. Revving mightily, it ground toward town, swooping from verge to verge, a groggy boat on a dark stream. A short distance down the road, it slowed. Their father was going to visit Walker, his old mate from the battalion.

'Juss'a minute,' he said. 'Won' be long.'

The door to Walker's little crib opened and closed.

He'd be gone for ages. They could have waited inside but they did not like Walker. He had bleary eyes and his crib stank of mutton fat and tobacco and the shaggy sheepdog that lounged about the place gnawing at its bottom with fierce enthusiasm.

They waited outside. The car grew cold. When they had driven out that afternoon it had been sunny, a brilliant blue day, but the wind had risen, driving the wisps of cloud over the moon. From inside the crib came the shout of laughter, the clink of glasses.

Kate opened the car door.

'Come on,' she said.

'Where?' said Maura. 'I'm not going in there. I don't like it in there.'

'Home,' said Kate. 'We'll walk.'

'But it's miles,' said Maura.

'It's not that far,' said Kate. 'And there's a moon. You can sit there or you can come with me.'

Maura sat there, so Kate set off. Before she had gone twenty yards, there was the sound of the car door closing softly and the tap of summer sandals on the tarmac.

'Wait for me,' called Maura.

They walked together in the moonlight along the road home.

The way ahead was lit fitfully in luminous indigo and white. There were hawthorn hedges on either side and onion flower in brilliant white flower in the deep ditches that edged the road. There was little traffic but when they heard a car coming they bobbed down in the ditch, which was dry and lined with crackling leaf. The headlights swept overhead.

After a while they heard a car approaching slowly, revving in second gear. They hid and saw the Standard pass, their father's face peering intently ahead in the reflected glow from the lights. They watched him pass in one direction, and about a quarter of an hour later they saw him return, driving back towards Weston.

'Do you think we should wave?' said Maura. 'Won't he worry?'

'No,' said Kate. 'We're walking the whole way.'

They were caught, however, half an hour later, trapped in the headlight beam of Uncle Frank's Vauxhall as they were crossing bare ground around the sale yards on the edge of town.

'What the hell do you think you're playing at?' he said, dragging them from behind the saleyard fence with a grip so fierce it left blue bruises on their arms. He flung them into the back seat.

Kate said nothing. A dumb resistance had swept over her. Maura was crying but Kate said nothing to either Uncle Frank, or, when they got back to Weston, to Auntie Mary. She watched their mouths opening and closing with a curious detachment, and the way their skin had gone a peculiar purple and the way their eyes blazed with a pale blue fury. Her father, too, was silent. He stood a little to one side while his sister and her husband asked Kate why? Why had she done such a thing? Why had she put her little sister in such danger? Anything could have happened to them. They could have been picked up by anyone. Didn't she think of her father? Didn't she realise he would be worried sick? She deserved a good clip around the ear.

Kate said nothing. She looked at her father and he was looking straight back at her. Eye to eye. It was strange. She had expected anger, but he wasn't angry. He was dead white.

He was frightened.

They climbed once more into the Standard and he drove them home, still drunk, but more careful now, judging the corners with silent attention. When they got home he went to bed. He said nothing to their mother, and nor did Kate.

The moonlight edged the blind, the wind blew in the ribbon-wood outside the window. Kate lay awake in the early hours of this new year, feeling a muddle of sensations. One part was akin to that feeling when she stood at the top of the cliff at Bushy Beach after scrambling up. It was that feeling that made her want to spread her arms wide — the feeling that she could, if she wanted, fly. It was the simple feeling of triumph George must have felt when she outwitted the smugglers.

But mingled with that was a new sensation she could not quite identify. It was pity, perhaps. For the man in the car.

10.

For a moment Anne hesitated. She had an odd, newly awakened consciousness under all her outraged dignity that the half-shy, half-eager expression in Gilbert's hazel eyes was something that was very good to see. Her heart gave a quick queer little beat . . .

Anne of Green Gables by L. M. Montgomery

Kate lay on the sofa in the front room with the door closed, hoping no one would find her, eating salted peanuts and reading about love. Through the wall, Maura was playing her record on the radiogram in the sitting room.

Oh-oh-over and over, sang Lloyd, *I'll be a fool for you!* for the twentieth time that morning. She had spent all her birthday money on a single disk.

Over and over, what more can I do?

It made a change from the records the radiogram normally played. Light classics of a pensive disposition. 'Pavane for a Dead Infanta', 'To a Wild Rose', 'The Swan'. Or Mary O'Hara and her harp and the song where the spinning wheel slowed to a stop.

Cos you've got PERSONALITY!

Lloyd belonged to America and movies and love on a beach, ponytails and gingham bikinis, convertibles with chrome trim and boys with straight teeth. Saturday night love. Love encountered from the stalls of the Majestic, with hundreds of others all sighing or laughing or surreptitiously sniffing at the same time. Love encountered in the main feature after the Queen on her horse and the cartoons and interval, when Kenny Creech's older sister Jugs, her hair backcombed under her little white cap, stood like a filmstar, alone in the spotlight in front of the audience, to sell chocolate dips from the Nibble Nook tray.

STYLE and PERSONALITY!

There were so many kinds of love. Kate studied them all with acute attentiveness, mostly alone in the front room with the door closed. This love had nothing do with the booklet that had arrived mysteriously in the drawer among her handkerchiefs and clean pants. The booklet was an earnest pallid blue. It was called *You and Your Body*. It contained disgusting pictures of tubes and sacs that were the Female Reproductive System, cut clean through the middle and viewed side on. On the opposite page, a parallel diagram with a small hose attached was the Male Reproductive System. The diagrams had the same queasy reality as the pictures of diphtheria and measles in Kate's mother's nursing books. The words, too, were repellent.

Penis.

Penetration.

Vagina.

Intercourse.

Kate read a couple of pages quickly, then thrust the booklet back deep beneath her underclothes and ran outside where the sun was shining as usual and the air smelled of mown grass. She went to talk to the hens. Usually she found them calming, with their amiable chat of this and that. But this afternoon she could not help noticing how Moses strutted in his golden wig and how the hens bobbed down the moment he approached, tail feathers flared in submission, and how he nipped them on the neck, leaving speckles of blood on their feathers, and how they did not seem to mind afterwards but simply returned to their dust baths, scooping particles of earth beneath their wings, eyes glazed with ecstasy. Today she hated Moses, and she hated the hens. She hated their silly scrawny pink necks and their stupid forgetfulness.

The little blue book sat unread in her drawer like a trap spring-loaded, like something that could take fast hold of her fingers whether she liked it or not. She did not want any of it. Not Penis. Or Penetration. Or Vagina. Or Intercourse. She did not want the thimble swellings beneath her shirt, nor the pin-prickles of hair at armpit and groin. She wanted nothing to do with the entire business.

'Did you find something in your drawer?' said her mother a day or so later.

'Yes,' she said, furious with embarrassment. How could her mother have put such a thing among her most personal clothes? Her pants and socks and handkerchiefs would for ever after retain a whiff of Penis, Penetration, Intercourse.

'Good,' said her mother, and went back to her typing. The kitchen table was littered with file cards crammed with birth, coupling and death. She never asked about *You and Your Body* again and a few days later it had disappeared.

So when the blood came, a curious cramping as Kate was playing French cricket at Millerhill one summer morning, it was a surprise.

Auntie Izzie was sitting with her feet up listening to 'Dr Paul'.

'What's the matter?' she said when she saw Kate's tearful face.

'I'm bleeding,' said Kate.

Auntie Izzie put down her cup and reached out to give her a hug.

'So, you've got your granny,' she said, as if it were something to be pleased about, and she fetched Kate a kind of towel nappy, which was fixed in place with safety pins and an elastic belt. Outside the window the other kids were running about squealing and Rosemary was batting, knocking the ball for six right down the drive.

'Now,' said Auntie Izzie, 'let's have a cup of tea, just you and me.'

And she made Kate a proper grown-up cup with one sugar and a couple of malt biscuits to dunk and they sat at the kitchen bench on high stools, Kate on the thick bulk of her pad, her auntie beside her, listening to the episode where Dr Paul has to tell Eileen her cancer is terminal. Out in the sun Rosemary was saying she wasn't out; she wasn't; Graham had hit her above the knee and it wasn't fair. Viewed from the kitchen bench it seemed a very childish dispute.

Her body was intent on developing. Another word she hated. 'Developing'.

'Now that you're developing,' her mother said, regarding the swellings beneath the school shirt, 'you'd better wear a bra.' She took her to the Farmers', where a woman in a black dress fitted her with a lacy bra that scratched and felt tight as if she had been firmly bandaged to prevent breakages. Kate looked at herself side on in the wardrobe mirror. The bra was visible as twin hillocks beneath the fabric of her shirt. An overshoulderboulderholder. That was what Kenny Creech had called bras when his older sister had to wear one.

'Jugs has got an overshoulderboulderholder,' he said, lighting up a cigarette he had pinched from his mother's bag, and he had laughed so much that he choked at the absurdity of it.

Now Kate had to wear one too. Her body seemed intent on following its own set of instructions, whether she wanted it to or not. Once she had wanted to grow up, carefully marking the inches on the kitchen door jamb with dates and initials. Now she wanted to stop. She sprouted and swelled like a seed in spring, and with as little control and as little knowledge.

She was perplexed by sex. She was curious about love.

As they reached the end of the terrace and paused to look at the view before them, she said softly, 'Gerald, it is almost too beautiful. And to think that our lives are to be spent here, together! It seems too much. I do not know how to believe it all!'

He looked down at her with a tender smile and silenced her with a kiss . . .

Gladys or Gwyneth by E. Everet-Green

There was the kind of love encountered in the books from Millerhill: old-fashioned love, where the stories ended with the declaration, the tremulous acceptance with eyes where smiles and tears mingled like an April sky, and finally, the kiss. The heroines usually achieved love by being beautiful, or orphaned or good. Like Elsie Dinsmore, who was all three, and who arrived in the southern mansion of her relations where her life was made miserable by her pretty, spoilt cousins. Twelve solid volumes later her story ended when, as Grandmother Elsie, she settled to the peaceful enjoyment of the substantial profits of a life of gentleness and forbearance.

There was Anne, who was more likely than Elsie, being quick-tempered and capable of breaking a slate over a boy's head. The boy fell in love with her anyway. Gilbert, the most handsome and desirable boy in the class, did not choose Diana who was sweeter, or Ruby Gillis who was prettier, but Anne who was clever. Just as Laurie loved Jo best. Who would swap Laurie's vow of undying friendship for the dull formal proposal of Mr Brooks to dull, unimaginative Meg? Kate tipped the last of the salted peanuts into her hand and licked the salt from her fingers. Anne and Jo were a vindication for all competitive, plain girls everywhere.

'It never can be the same again. I've lost my dearest friend,' sighed Jo.

'You've got me, anyhow. I'm not good for much, I know: but I'll stand by you, Jo, all the days of my life; upon my word I will!' And Laurie meant what he said.

Little Women by Louisa May Alcott

Then there was the love encountered in her mother's magazines, in which careless heroines dropped their handbags or tripped over kerb edges and lost their door keys and were rescued, week after week, by insufferably arrogant men whom they later came to love.

And there was the love encountered in the book Maddie Greenleaf brought to school.

She had found it in a rubbish bin as she was helping tidy the front double at Bella Vista. Maddie's mother was alone, tragically widowed when Maddie's father rode his motorbike into a train at a railway crossing somewhere in the North Island. Maddie had only been a month old when her mother fled to Oamaru to escape the painful memories and opened a B&B ('Sea Views from Every Room') on Wansbeck Street. The book had shiny paper covers declaring *Explosive Best Seller*! and in its pages dwelt teenagers who drove in their own cars to a lake where they swam naked and got pregnant and talked about lovers and virgins and orifices.

'Orifices?'

'Openings.'

'Like what?'

Norman half turned onto his side and ran the top of his little finger around the opening in Allison's ear . . .

Maddie formed a club, the Peyton Place Club, expressly for the purpose of reading about them. Each lunchtime in the first term of their second year at Junior High the members of the club assembled on the benches behind the school toilets where Maddie read to them aloud.

His fingers found the tie of her halter and in less than half a minute the garment lay on the sand next to the blanket. Betty's back arched against his arm as she thrust her breasts up to him.

She read well, with lots of expression.

'Please,' murmured Rodney against her skin. 'Please. Please . . .'

Between sessions, club members referred to the book only as 'PP'.

'What did you think of PP/61?' Maddie said to Kate as they waited for Miss Ronald to tap her long red nail on the window from which she addressed them lined up in their houses — Weka, Tui, Huia and Kiwi — like a small grey army in the small grey yard. And Kate knew that Maddie was referring to the page where the evil, drunken Lucas drags the shirt from the back of his stepdaughter, the beautiful, doomed Selena. *You're getting to be quite a gal, honey*, he says, as she backs away beneath the bare room's one unshaded electric lightbulb, her bare breasts exposed to his lascivious gaze. Then Selena's scream rips the stillness with a sound like tearing fabric . . .

'It's fab,' said Kate, and all the club members nodded agreement. Yes. Scary, but definitely fab. Above them Miss Ronald's irritable Monday morning face appeared at the window, lips red as if she had spent the entire weekend sipping blood. Tap tap tap went the nail.

'What's PP?' said Marilyn Rasmussen. She and Kate had not argued exactly, but Marilyn was deputy captain of Weka House. She had got off her bike in town and told Kate to put on her gloves. It was a hot afternoon, a nor'wester blowing grit in their faces all the way along Thames Street: serge uniform, black stockings, hat and gloves damp with sweat at the end of the day. Kate had waited until the corner past the Post Office, then peeled off her gloves. She was just wondering if she could roll down her stockings too, when Marilyn turned the corner, pedalling seriously with her hat jammed down firmly against the wind and her little silver badge winking in the sunlight.

'But I don't want to wear my gloves,' said Kate. 'It's too hot.'

'I know,' said Marilyn. She was in Sea Scouts. She liked the sailor hat and the whistle. 'We're all hot.' She smiled a smile that was full of comradely understanding, but with just the faintest hint of authority. 'But those are the rules.' Kate had dragged her gloves back over sticky fingers and decided that she would never again be friends with Marilyn. The days of her Mary Queen of Scots to Marilyn's Elizabeth were over, the long afternoons seated on the bed at Marilyn's house swapping her *Girls' Crystal*s for Marilyn's *School Friend*s. They had reached The End.

So when Marilyn asked her, 'What's PP?' she had to say, 'Oh, nothing. Just something Maddie and us are talking about.' Because the club had been sworn to secrecy, and not telling was also a rule.

The PP Club leaned back in the sunlight, stockings rolled to their ankles, lunches abandoned half eaten on the wooden bench.

You are truly beautiful, says Maddie, in a deep and thrilling manly tone as Brad strokes Allison's virginal body. *You have the long aristocratic legs and the exquisite breasts of a statue.*

Kate surveyed her own legs, white and sprinkled with freckles. Legs that might be called 'sturdy' and would never, in a million years, qualify as 'aristocratic'. Caro Williams was sitting next to her. Caro's legs were slender and brown without effort because Caro's grandmother was Italian. She had been an Italian opera singer and Caro's grandfather had met her during the First World War and it was terribly romantic because he was wounded and she had bound up his wounds with her petticoats. Kate longed for an Italian grandmother, opera singer or not: anything would have been better than the Irish-Scottish blend that had cursed her with ginger hair and pasty skin.

'Your grandmother used to take such care of her skin,' her mother had said. 'She rubbed olive oil into it every night for suppleness, and lemon juice to bleach the freckles.'

Kate had tried for solutions, in a lotion guaranteed to confer an instant glowing tan, and in a foil box she constructed to a design in the *Woman's Weekly*. It was supposed to direct the sun's rays at just those parts of the body most in need of tanning. The foil box left her scorched and peeling even on the insides of her thighs, which had never been burnt before, while the lotion made her nauseous and turned her the colour of a carrot. It did no good to be told for the hundredth time about Grandma and her beautiful skin.

'I don't care about Grandma!' she said. 'I want a tan!'

Brown skin, lustrous dark wavy hair, straight teeth without that annoying little gap at the front, and green, or maybe grey, eyes. And today, listening to Caro, she added aristocratic legs to the list.

Dr Barry rose to his feet and stood looking down at her red curls tumbled on the pillow, at her startled brown eyes. 'Do you know,' he said, 'that you're a very lovely person?'

For a moment, Sue could find no words. Then she said simply:

'Thank you.'

Sue Barton — *Student Nurse* by Helen Dore Boylston

Kate wanted long legs, but not too long. Caro's legs were actually a problem when it came to Winks. They played Winks a lot the year Kate turned thirteen — at Bible Class socials in draughty halls

155

where Girl Guide promises to do one's best for God and the Queen still adhered to varnished wood. The girls stood in a circle and the boys stood behind them. It was like musical chairs, but instead of an absent chair there was an extra boy. He had to wink to get a girl. The girl he winked at had to run immediately and stand in front of him before the boy behind her could put his hands on her shoulders and prevent her.

Caro was tall. When she stood in front of boys they had to reach up to her shoulders. They did not want to wink at her.

Suddenly such things mattered. At primary school, if you so much as sat on a seat recently vacated by a boy you said, 'Ugh, yuck! Boy germs!' Now, boys you had only a couple of years before ignored, or ambushed from the hut in the ribbonwood with a rain of clods, boys whose hands you had to be forced to hold for folk dancing, boys with whom you played only when no one else was around to see you both happily building dams across the gutter to flood the road, boys who were otherwise absolutely and irre-deemably boring — being content to spend hours practising bowling overarm — these boys began to be interesting. One year there was Winks; the next there was dancing class.

Kate sat with the other girls in her school uniform in the Eveline Scout Hall while Roderick and Lois of the Elite Dance Academy gave a quick demonstration of the waltz. As danced by Roderick and Lois, it was an ornamental routine of swoops and flourishes, each of them leaning away from the other, faces averted as if they were breathing pure onion. They held each other's hands with a fastidious distaste. After one rotation Roderick ran lightly to the record player and switched it off.

'There,' he said. He had a delicate voice, as light and flyaway as the orchids he wired and posed in the window of Forget-me-not Florists. 'Easy, isn't it?' He paused for a second as if expecting applause. The girls looked down at their black brogues, the boys stood in a huddle by the door with grass stains on their knees above their socks. 'So, gentlemen,' said Roderick, 'take your partners, please, and let's begin!' No one moved. The gentlemen hugged the doorway, clearly wishing they could burst as a herd straight through the vestibule into the open air. But something prevented escape. They stood immobile instead, while the girls waited on the benches beneath taggles of crêpe-paper chains left over from Christmas.

Roderick gave an exaggerated sigh.

'We haven't got all day,' he said. 'If you won't do it for yourselves, I suppose you must want me to do it for you.' He scanned the huddle. 'You,' he said, and he drew forth Kenny Creech. Kenny had grown short and skinny, a perfect model for *Cole's Funny Picture Book*'s dire warnings on the risks attendant on smoking. His hair stood upright in a greasy cowlick.

'And . . .'

Roderick's eye travelled dispassionately along the line of girls as if he were deciding between Weetbix and Cornflakes at Four Square.

'. . . you.'

Caro got slowly to her feet. When Roderick brought Kenny to stand beside her, the cowlick reached just above her breasts and just below Caro's scarlet face.

'Now, take your partners, please,' said Roderick. The gentlemen had got the hint.

Wayne Norris walked coolly over to Angela Avery. Her hair was backcombed and a kiss curl was firmly glued to each cheek. She was Gidget-cute, demure as a little china shepherdess, though she was reputed to have gone All The Way already with a fifth-form boy, a boarder, one exeat weekend at the golf links. Caro said you could tell for sure by the way Angela walked. After they had gone All The Way, girls walked differently. Caro and Kate had watched Angela closely for signs of ambulatory change but it was hard to tell.

Certainly, Angela's neck bore a telltale rash of lovebites, and she had taken to wearing her Weka House sash slung low at the hips and pinning the brim of her school hat to the hatband in a kind of Robin Hood peak, both signals of deep and deliberate rebellion. At the end of the first term, the fifth-form boarder was expelled and rumour had it that it was for having frenchies in his locker, not to mention a small home-brewery in the dormitory attic. Caro said that proved it, and that Angela would definitely end up Getting Into Trouble.

'MayIhavethepleasureofthisdance?' said Wayne to Angela, as instructed by Roderick. He made it sound like an insult. Angela shrugged as if it were immaterial to her whether he had the pleasure or not, but said, 'Yes, thank you,' which was the correct reply. Slowly the other boys followed Wayne's ground-breaking lead across the white lines marked out for badminton on the hall floor. Kate sat on the bench in an agony of dread. What if nobody chose her? A boy was approaching but at the last second veered left and took Heather McFadden instead. The girl on Kate's other side was taken too, by a heavy-set boy chewing gum who, instead of asking for the pleasure simply raised his eyebrows. She stood with alacrity anyway, and Kate was left on her own at one end of the bench and Marilyn Rasmussen at the other.

'Everybody organised?' said Roderick. 'No? . . . Over here!' he called, pointing to Kate and Marilyn. 'There's a couple left over here!' A gangly boy lurched toward Kate, tripping over his feet and scarlet with embarrassment and flowering acne.

'At last!' said Roderick. 'Now, let's dance!' The gangly boy took Kate's hand in a stick grip. Her eyes were on a level with the adam's apple on his thin neck. He gazed over her head, making no attempt to talk, as they circled onetwothree onetwothree around the hall. She was glad of the silence, as it required all her concentration not to back into other people. 'Sorry,' he said, when he stood on her feet. 'Sorry,' she said, when she trod on his. His jersey smelled of sweat and he had ink stains on his knuckles. When Roderick and Lois interrupted to demonstrate a particularly telling point, Kate and the boy stood awkwardly, unsure whether to drop hands instantly or remain in clammy engagement. They tried both before the music finally reached an end and they were free to walk, arm in arm as instructed, back to the wooden bench where the tall boy said, 'Yeah, well, thanks.' For the first time their eyes met and he gave a quick smile. Quite a nice smile, really. And Kate said thanks too, and he was free to retreat, sliding the final ten feet on the slippery floor across the badminton lines to the security of the huddle by the doorway.

Kate saw him by the bike stand outside after the class had ended. 'See ya!' he said, then he pedalled off, dragging his bike up to rear onto its back wheel — Hi Ho, Silver! — as he turned the corner and headed out into the badlands of Thames Street, ridin' out of her life for ever.

Grant smiled.

'I fell in love with you that morning you came thundering down the paddock toward me on Russetty, bare-back, bare-legged, remember? We talked about the larks singing in Maoriland. I fell in love with you against my will. Oh, what a fool I was!'

The Lark in the Meadow by Essie Summers

Kate biked home each afternoon with Heather McFadden, who was her best friend now, though Heather was doing Commercial and Kate Professional, so they did not share classes. It didn't matter. They had fallen into a habit of stopping off at the Rendezvous on the way and spending their lunch money instead on cappuccinos and toasted corn rolls. To begin with, they had gone to the Excella Milk Bar and drunk lemonade spiders, but the Rendezvous was more sophisticated. It had a wheezing Gaggia machine and a model of the Eiffel Tower by the cash register. The ceiling was painted black with a web of white string tacked across it. Each table had a red gingham tablecloth and an empty Mateus Rosé bottle in the middle covered in stalactites of candlewax. They sat eating their corn rolls and picking the wax from the bottle and talking about school and boys.

Heather was in love with a boy who travelled on the Hampden bus. They biked into town each afternoon, dawdling until the bus passed, crammed with grey serge and farting clouds of diesel. Kate had to look up to see if the boy was there and if he was looking at them.

'Is he?' said Heather, concentrating on an interesting dog that was running along the street opposite.

'No . . .' said Kate, trying to look up and not wobble into the rear of a parked car. 'No . . . Yes!'

'Is he looking at me?' said Heather.

The boy was seated in the back seat: fair hair, square jaw. He had turned and was staring at them over one shoulder. The bus was slowing for the corner by the war memorial outside the Farmers'.

'Yes,' said Kate. 'He is. You should wave at him.'

'I can't!' said Heather.

Their bikes narrowly avoided collision. The bus was accelerating. It was turning the corner.

'Quick!' said Kate. 'He's still looking.'

Heather glanced up. The boy winked. He quite definitely gave that little duck of the head that said 'Hi!' as clearly as if he had yelled it through the bleary glass of the rear window.

They discussed that wink at length at the Rendezvous, as they discussed all such momentous issues: what had happened to that girl in the fifth form who had suddenly had to go up north, why

Marilyn Rasmussen was so awful, what to wear to the Bible Class social on Friday night, how old Jack Palance, who starred weekly in *The Greatest Show on Earth* on the McFaddens' new television, might really be. A hail of little wax spheres formed between them on the gingham.

Kate discussed Malcolm Trotter with Heather. He had walked home with her after the rehearsal for the Bible Class concert. He was one of the boys who marched onto the stage with handkerchiefs sewn to their caps as members of the French Foreign Legion, singing, *In some Abyssinian French Dominion . . . I'll be full of grit, you won't see my heels for the dust*!

Kate was in the following item, as a flower-seller in Covent Garden. Malcolm was a year older than her but short and plump, and he took her hand with a certain casual expertise as they walked up Wansbeck Street after rehearsal in the spring twilight. She had never held a stranger's hand before. It felt hot and she wondered if she could detach to wipe her hand on her skirt or if that would seem critical. She decided against detachment. The street-lights cast dappled shadow through the branches of cherry plums in fresh leaf. Malcolm was telling her about the Maloch U2 he was building with his uncle, who was a panelbeater, to some plans they had had sent out from England. They were building it up from the chassis they'd got from a wrecker's — Ford parts because they were the best: a 109 motor, which was pretty good though a 115E would have been better; and some wheels that needed heaps of work — they had had to split 'em on the lathe, whip the centres out, bang in a fillet, that kind of thing.

'Oh,' said Kate, since there was a pause and some kind of comment seemed to be called for. 'That'll look nice.'

'It's got nothing to do with looks,' said Malcolm with just a hint of impatience. 'It's stability. You gotta aim for the maximum amount of rubber on the road.'

They turned the corner into Greta Street as Malcolm described his last race, a hill climb out at Herbert where he'd got second FTD, even though he'd overcooked one of the corners and taken out a couple of fenceposts, and how his ideal would be a Lotus Super 7, and then he'd work his way up to a C type and then maybe head overseas, work at Brabhams, or one of the other big factories, take in the Isle of Man, Monte Carlo . . .

His voice in the darkness had taken on a dreamy tone. They had arrived at her gate.

'Well,' he said, and he turned to her, clutched her to his nylon parka and kissed her. Her first kiss. It landed on her lips as if skidding into a tight corner, almost by accident, narrowly missing the tip of her nose. His lips were like puckered silk. Up close he smelled faintly of engine oil. He had to stretch slightly to reach her mouth and she was glad her Sunday shoes were almost flat with tiny Louis heels. She bent her knees slightly to accommodate the kiss. It lasted less than a second.

'See you round, doll,' said Malcolm, and he was gone.

She went inside.

'Have a nice time?' said her mother, looking up from her Bible study on the sofa.

'Yes,' said Kate. A petroleum whiff lingered on her top lip.

Next rehearsal, the dress, she tried to meet his eye, but he was preoccupied, marching about with the others flourishing his hand-kerchief kepi. She didn't really care. He was too short, too fat. He wasn't Gilbert Blythe, or Brad, the one everyone else wanted. Just to be sure, she mentioned him to Heather one afternoon at the Rendezvous. Nothing too revealing: just, what did Heather think of him?

'Malcolm Trotter?' said Heather, biting into her corn roll. 'He's a drip.'

It was confirmed. If Heather would not want Malcolm Trotter, Kate did not want him either.

11.

---

*Miss Matty made a strong effort to conceal her feelings —
a concealment she practised even with me, for she has never
alluded to Mr Holbrook again, although the book he gave
her lies with her Bible on the little table by her bedside. She
did not think I heard her when she asked the little milliner
of Cranford to make her caps something like the
Honourable Mrs Jamieson's, or that I noticed the reply —
'But she wears widows' caps, ma'am?'*

*'Oh! I only meant something in that style; not widows',
of course, but rather like Mrs Jamieson's.'*

Cranford by Mrs Gaskell

At school they were reading *Cranford*. It offered little advice when
it came to Malcolm Trotter and the waltz at the Eveline Scout Hall.
Cranford was finicky and difficult, like other female things: like

flaky pastry, French seams and blanket stitch. A group of old ladies of fifty-two and more, living lives of elegant economy, fierce passions gloved in lace mittens, in an English village a hundred years ago. Who could possibly want to read about *that*? But *Cranford* had to be read, however puzzling, because it belonged to a new breed of book: the set text.

Arabella entered the room to find both its occupants laughing, and thus had the felicity of seeing Mr Beaumaris at his best. That she herself was looking remarkably pretty, with her dusky curls and charming complexion admirably set off by a high-crowned bonnet, with curled ostrich feather tips, and crimson ribbons tied into a bow under one ear, never entered her head.

Arabella by Georgette Heyer

Books now came in two categories: there were the books Kate chose as she had always chosen. Fact and fiction, selected on a Friday night or picked up from some bookshelf or second-hand table. She had crossed the lobby from the children's side of the Library to the adult section, where she chose heroes sporting Stanhope crops, coats of olive green superfine and gleaming hessian top boots, and heroines blessed with a rose-petal complexion and an independent streak. She liked their clothes and their houses and the cotillions and the London Season and the hefty dinners with boiled duck and 'serpents of mutton' and Rhenish creams, without having the faintest idea what those might be. She chose mysteries with a dash of sex, reading and re-reading the bits where the heroine sat with the 'dry roughness' of the hero's tweed coat around her naked body as they hurtled in a borrowed fishing boat over the Mediterranean in pursuit of villains.

She chose books set in country houses in Cornwall, whose customs she could name with more confidence than the customs of the world that lay immediately beyond the confines of 55 Greta Street, Oamaru. She knew that clothes were laid out on beds by discreet servants and that dinner was at eight and that one wrote letters on heavy cream notepaper to one's acquaintances. She knew about meres and moors, shooting parties and dinners at the club, holiday villas on Greek islands, cleaning ladies with names like Mrs Tinker who dropped their aiches and Oxford dons who drank single malts.

She chose books where bodies were discovered in shrubberies or conservatories, and their deaths mattered as little as the deaths of Chicken-Licken and Hen-Len. The story was simply a puzzle for solving, and the victims usually deserved death anyway, for being generally unpleasant.

She chose big books by big brooding men whose photos appeared on the covers, pipes clenched between their big teeth. She liked size in an author: authors whose books occupied at least a foot and a half of shelf space, authors whose books had lengthy lists of 'Other Titles' by the frontispiece. She liked working her way through whole sets. She liked books about major topics, like international security or nuclear radiation. When Moira waved goodbye to Dwight Towers as he sailed off to certain death in his submarine, leaving her alone to swallow the suicide pills with a brandy chaser, Kate was impressed. She closed *On the Beach* with the satisfaction of having read about something very important: the creeping nuclear death of the entire world. Of course it could not have a happy ending.

She chose heroes who were manly and who survived against terrible odds: she chose Bruce Wetheral venturing out at great personal risk to warn men who had only a few hours before been his enemies that the dam was about to collapse and drown them all. She chose Richard Hannay, the master of disguise, evading his pursuers by the simple genius of slipping on a roadworker's cap, a man uniquely capable of detecting the essential German-ness that lurked beneath the apparent Englishness of the men dwelling in the villa on the cliffs. The vicious members of the Black Stone could ape English manners all they liked but Hannay had twigged and it was only a matter of time before their game was up and they were yelling, *Schnell, Franz! Das Boot! Das Boot*! as the constabulary finally entered to click on the handcuffs.

Hannay was a recognisable hero, like the Heroes of Nowadays in Kate's prize book. The news of the failure of Scott's expedition to reach the South Pole ahead of the unsportingly professional, dog-eating Amundsen had been telegraphed from Oamaru in 1913. The event was commemorated by an oak tree at the end of Arun Street and an annual essay competition on the topic 'My Visit to Antarctica'. Kate didn't actually like the thought of Antarctica much: it seemed too empty, too cold, too stuffy altogether in that little tent with Oates going out nobly for some time. But a prize was a prize. The heroes she received were Tenzing, Albert Schweitzer, a selection of RAF pilots — not including Findlay Todd from the photograph box — and someone called Freddie Spencer Chapman who was now just an ordinary English schoolmaster but who had once been an explorer in the Arctic and Tibet, a mountaineer in the Alps and Himalaya, lived alone with Chinese bandits and spent a year in the jungles of Malay with the Japanese army trying to hunt him down. Freddie was the kind of hero Kate selected from the lineup on the library shelves, as she herself was selected from the wooden benches at the Eveline Scout Hall.

I put on a great spurt and got off my ridge and down into the moor before any figures appeared on the skyline behind me. I crossed a burn, and came out on a high road that made a pass between two glens. All in front of me was a big field of heather sloping up to a crest that was crowned with an odd feather of trees . . . I jumped the dyke and followed it.

The Thirty-nine Steps by John Buchan

Love seemed so feeble by contrast. There was a whole section in the adult Library dedicated to love. The covers of the books were pink or pale blue with pictures on the front of young women in the arms of handsome doctors or pilots. All the other books in the Library were free, but these books cost sixpence a time to borrow.

Kate had a job after school sticking the little pockets into the backs of the new books. Her father had organised it.

'I've jacked it up with Miss Malloy,' he said. She could earn her own pocket money, and incidentally, she could also keep an eye out for him for anything that looked interesting — new novels, history, travel, anything at all — and put it on reserve, put him at the head of the list. Kate sat at her desk gluing in the pockets. She saw the women carrying their love stories up to the desk for issue, three or four at a time. She watched as they meekly handed over their sixpences, as though they were buying Tampax and the only person behind the counter was the chemist himself. As though they were purchasing a kingsize Fruit and Nut and intended eating it all themselves even though it was bad for them. The librarians scooped their sixpences into the till as the women stuffed love into their shopping bags and carried it off up Thames Street, along with the bread and a couple of chops for tea.

Books existed in a kind of hierarchy. There were serious books, about heroes and death and catastrophe. And there were frivolous books about love, which were not good for you and for which it was therefore necessary to pay a small admonitory fee. Some books were heavy and some were light, and contrary to the laws of nature, what was heaviest rose to the top of the hierarchy while what was lightest sank to the bottom. If love made an appearance in a serious, heavy book, it tended to be brutal or painful and ended perhaps in despair or death. If love ended happily at a tender kiss, a proposal of marriage, it was the bubble that made that book light, fluffy, frivolous.

She took the cork out of the bottle. It was ten past ten. She said earnestly, 'Dwight, if you're on your way already, wait for me.'

Then she put the tablets in her mouth and swallowed them down with a mouthful of brandy, sitting behind the wheel of her big car.'

On the Beach by Nevil Shute

Then there were the set texts.

There had always been class sets, beginning with the appalling *Janet and John* back in Primer One at Oamaru South. There had been *School Journals*, the only New Zealand stories Kate had ever read. They were crammed into cardboard boxes in the school library, which doubled as a sickbay. When Kate's nose bled, which it continued to do from time to time after the scarlet fever, she lay under a prickly grey blanket and looked at the class sets. They were illustrated in black and white: muscled gods heaved the fish that was the North Island from the ocean, Maui captured the sun and Rangi and Papa were torn asunder, grimacing, by their fierce sons. These stories were set in her own country but it was them that seemed alien and strange, and not the books Kate chose from the Library with their lolly-coloured pictures and smiling children in their plimsolls at the seaside.

The journals were akin to the one New Zealand book Kate actually owned: a prim little volume in a red cover, which her Auntie Mary and Uncle Frank had given her one year for Christmas: *Our Nation's Story*. Its pictures — The Signing of the Treaty, Governor Hobson — were faded and grey, as if they had hung too long in a dingy room. Boredom coated every page in a powdery mildew. The minute Kate peeled back the holly-leaf paper and saw it, she knew for an absolute fact that Auntie Mary and Uncle Frank truly disliked her and had not forgiven her for getting out of the car. She said thank you, of course, as expected, then used *Our Nation's Story* to stop her bedroom window rattling in a southerly. It fitted perfectly, jammed against the frame. Over the years it faded to a tolerable rosy pink, its dull pages toasted by the summer sun.

The set texts were as earnest as the *School Journal*, as dull as *Our Nation's Story*. They were wrapped in cracked clear plastic and covered with the evidence of previous readership: names going back to the 1940s, remarks scribbled illegally in the margins (*BORING!!!*), passages underlined in a variety of coloured inks. These were books intended to be read whether you liked them or not. They were texts, to be dismantled into their component parts, as a car might be reduced to a pile of scrap metal, valves and cylinders.

> *Mark caught the first aid box and pulled it open. 'And find the girl something to wear, will you? Now, keep still, and let me get that tied up.'*
>
> *'But Mark, what are you going to do?' I sounded infuriatingly humble, even to myself.*
>
> *'Do? Well, my heaven, what d'you think? I'm going to hand him over to the police myself, personally, and if I've got to paste the living daylights out of him to do it, well that'll suit me!'*
>
> *The Moonspinners* by Mary Stewart

The parts of the novel, as listed on the blackboard, were:

Themes.

Characters.

Setting.

Structure.

Under these headings, along with a brief biographical note concerning the author, the novel might be understood.

Miss Pollock stretches to the tips of her toes and writes in an even hand at the very top of the blackboard: *Mrs Gaskell wrote* Cranford *in serial form between 1851 and 1853. The village of Cranford is based on the actual village of Knutsford* . . . Here Miss Pollock takes a break from the blackboard and delivers a short peroration on the subject of pronunciation. Knutsford is to be pronounced 'Nutsford' with the K silent, the 'Knut' deriving from a common Anglo-Saxon Christian name usually rendered as 'Canute', 'a name made famous by the king who rebuked his courtiers' flattery by attempting to hold back the tide.' Miss Pollock adjusts her glasses and fetches a new stick of chalk up from the deep recesses of her MA gown. She turns back to the board.

. . . where the author spent her girlhood.

Behind her back, 4P copy the biographical note carefully. Then they move on to Theme One:

TIME.

In the back left-hand corner of the room, Maddie Greenleaf is writing 'Elvis Presley' as the 'He' the unknown 'She' meets in Consequences. She folds the paper and passes it underhand to Caro Williams, who writes 'Noddy's Little Car' as the Place Where They Met.

They were careful in their subversion. Miss Pollock was one of the old teachers, a stern New Zealander with her hair cut in a severe bob. There were several like her on the staff: single women of the generation that was simply recognised as 'old' — women who strode about the Gothic halls in billowing black gowns, whose nicknames and eccentricities were known to mothers, aunts and older sisters, women who worked year after year driving the causes of the Franco–Prussian War, the products of the Glasgow–Paisley–Motherwell triangle and Pythagoras' theorem into the chalky craniums of teenage girls. They were each reputed to harbour a secret sorrow, to have had a fiancé who died in the war, but Kate had observed Miss Pollock closely during the Anzac Day assembly, right through the head prefect reading about age not wearying them and Maddie Greenleaf banging her way through the chords in Jerusalem, and she had been unable to discern the slightest flicker of grief. It was impossible anyway, wasn't it, to imagine Miss Pollock — Polly — breathless in the arms of some airman.

'Oh, Polly! Polly!' he would sigh, running the tip of his finger around her orifices. 'My darling!'

The girls fell about laughing at the very thought.

Whatever sorrow the old teachers may have held within their

hearts, it had not rendered them frail. They were not to be trifled with, unlike the young teachers who had arrived from Britain as a kind of job lot to fill a teaching shortage.

The young teachers wore narrow skirts beneath their gowns, their heels were high and their hair was rolled up in French twists or fluffy and bouffant. They went tramping at the weekends or sang in Operatic Society productions. They were easily driven to distraction, teased to the point of tears.

'I thought coming out here might be a mistake,' said Miss Cameron, fresh from the Glasgow–Paisley–Motherwell triangle herself and here to teach biology, 'and you're every bit as stupid as I feared.' 4P stiffened among the dead dogfish, scalpels in hand. Not only had Miss Cameron lost her temper, she had insulted their country. They resolved to be intolerable. It was a point of national honour. Miss Cameron would not last anyway. None of the pretty young teachers did. Miss Bevan, who had taught them music last year, had sung in the Operatic Society's production of *The Merry Widow* and by the end of the second term she was seen driving around Oamaru in a red sports car with the young lawyer who had played the tenor lead. By the end of the year she was engaged and this year she was married. Soon she would be pregnant and that would be that. None of the pretty ones lasted. But the old teachers carried on for ever.

'*Theme 2*,' writes Miss Pollock in her quick clear hand, straight as a die over the black expanse of the board.

LOVE.

12.

---

*Blanchette felt a wish to return, but remembering the
stake, the rope, the hedge of the field, she thought that she
never could endure that life again and 'twas better to
remain where she was.*

The horn ceased to sound.

*The goat heard behind her the rustling of leaves. She
turned and saw in the shadow two short ears, erect, and
two eyes shining. It was the wolf.*

M. *Seguin's Goat* by Alphonse Daudet

Miss Schwartz had been in a concentration camp in Poland during
the war. That's what Virginia Craddock told them, and she knew
because her mother was chairman of the PTA. 4P knew a bit about
concentration camps. That was where that girl in Holland, Anne
Frank, had gone after she had lived in the cupboard. 4P regarded

173

Miss Schwartz with brief interest after Virginia told them about the camp, envisaging life in a cupboard, a breathless waiting day after day, like an endless game of sardines, only this time played for real, its conclusion the thump of jackboots on the stairs, the smash of a gun butt at the door. It made them shudder, but not for long. Nor did it make them kinder. They chattered, they played hangman in her classes without bothering to conceal the paper. They drew the gibbet quite openly, timber by timber, then the rope, then the circle of the little man's head, then the thin lines that were his body, arms and legs.

'Try E,' said Caro, and Kate added another arm. Caro would never guess 'rhythm', not in a million years.

Around them, 4P were plodding, one finger in the dictionary, through a tedious old story written by some tedious old man who had lived in a moulin, about Blanchette, the little goat. The warm air, the thyme-scented hills lay concealed behind a thicket of words as impenetrable as dry scrub. Miss Schwartz stood before them, her grey hair wild, her grey suit the exact same day after day, her hands making a curious continuous plucking motion at the folds of the gown that encircled her bony body.

There was a sudden commotion at the door. A deafening banging. KNOCK KNOCK KNOCK! 4P were startled, but only for a second. They knew it was just Angela Avery coming back from the toilet. It was a joke: they took it in turns to ask to be excused. One afternoon last week they had managed fourteen exits within a single period. That was today's challenge: fifteen or better.

'Mais non!' said Miss Schwartz, but the girl was desperate, she needed to go, right *now*, so she shrugged and let her leave. Angela was the fifth so far that morning. The rule was to stay out no longer than three minutes, which, allowing for a two-minute interval between requests, made fifteen a viable objective. 4P had seen Angela's head pass the window on the return circuit.

KNOCK KNOCK KNOCK! went her fist at the door. It was a joke. It was not necessary to knock. The oak shook, the latch rattled. KNOCK KNOCK KNOCK.

4P looked up with interest.

Miss Schwartz had frozen where she stood, then in one swift move she dragged her gown about her, over her head, and ducked down behind the desk. 4P went very still, Blanchette abandoned on her hillside, awaiting the wolf. The door opened cautiously. Angela looked around, pink and demure, then tiptoed with elaborate caution to her desk. Miss Schwartz emerged from hiding.

She stood before them, plucking at the fabric of her gown with skinny fingers. The room waited.

'You do not know . . .' she said, and suddenly she had gained inches in height; she possessed the full dignity of fury. 'You do not know . . .' She looked at the girls, plump in their grey serge with warm homes to return to, with a dance on Friday night to look forward to.

'Pah!' she said, as if they were not to be taken seriously, as if they were silly little girls lacking any real understanding. Her mouth worked as if there many words, a million words, piled behind trying for a way out but 'Pah' was all she could manage. 'Pah!' And she shrugged and left the room. 4P sat in silence.

'Well,' said Angela. 'That got Shorty going, didn't it?'

'Shut up,' said Caro. 'Just shut up!'

And they set to translation, unsupervised. In silence they translated the whole story, right to the end, where Blanchette fights all night with the wolf, hoping only to hold out until dawn. All night she fights bravely, gallant and alone, but when the stars have faded she lies down upon the ground, and permits the wolf to win at last and eat her up.

> *I was sent to Turkey and then to the Iraqi front . . . a deeply impressive event for a boy not yet sixteen years old.*
>
> *I remember every detail of my first encounter with the enemy.*
>
> *We were still being trained in our duties when the British — New Zealanders and Indians — launched an attack. Our little troop of Germans lay isolated in the vast expanse of desert, amongst the stones and the ruins of once flourishing civilisations . . . One after another my comrades fell wounded and had I been alone I would certainly have run away . . . Then suddenly, in my desperation, I noticed our captain who was lying behind a rock with icy calm, as though on a practice range, and returning the enemy's fire. It dawned on me too that I must start shooting. I let fly and, trembling, saw an Indian plunge forward, fall and move no more . . . My first dead man!*
>
> *The spell was broken.*
>
> *Commandant of Auschwitz: The Autobiography*
> *of Rudolf Hoess*

Kate did know, in fact, and not just from Anne Frank. She had found a book on the shelf behind the sofa at home. *Commandant of Auschwitz*. It was her turn on dishes and the table remained uncleared, but down here, behind the sofa, she was out of sight. Her mother was away. She had gone for longer this time. There had been a row about money, about her running around town running up debts for a lot of rubbish nobody either wanted or needed. (Kate's father meant *From the Spey to the Kilmog, Volume One, The Stuarts*, her mother's book about the family. She had taken it in to Mr

Fujamori, the printer at the two-minute silence, and he had run off a hundred copies for her, all nicely bound in blue cloth. It cost over twenty pounds.)

'What do you think you're playing at?' said their father. 'I can't afford to pay for that kind of nonsense.'

So one afternoon she left. She took a job at a hospital in Dunedin, working as a cleaner because her training was all out of date, but it was better than nothing. She had rung once, told Kate she was fine, she was earning her own money and was everyone coping?

Kate looked around the sitting room. The cat sat on the washing, licking its paws and wiping behind its ears. Dad had brought home pies for tea and then gone out. Maura was listening to her Beatles record.

'Yes,' said Kate. They were coping just fine.

'Good,' said her mother from her rented room across the road from the hospital. 'You haven't told anyone, have you?'

'No,' said Kate, because you had to cope and not tell anyone anything about your family. It was nobody else's business.

Kate sat behind the sofa and took down the new book. It was the usual war book: men in uniforms, baggy and rumpled for the goodies, smart for the Germans, with polished boots and peaked caps. Just another book about the same war they saw sometimes at the Majestic on Saturday nights, with brave airmen flying though they had no legs, or smart Cockneys and posh officers escaping from prison camps by digging tunnels and outwitting the stupid vicious guards. She flicked the pages, looking at the usual pictures of soldiers and suddenly there was a heap of sticks.

She looked more closely.

They were not sticks.

They were arms and legs. And they belonged to a pile of unimaginably thin human beings. And on other pages were more people, herded into bunkrooms, skin shrunken to the skull, chests concave so that every rib was evident. There was barbed wire and grey trains crammed with people and chimneys belching the smoke of burning bodies, a world of such horror that she had to run to the bathroom, where she was sick. A sour sludge fell into the bowl. And then for some reason she had to crawl back behind the sofa and look at them again. She had to turn to the beginning to read it all.

It began gently. It was almost like Heidi. A little boy rode about the hills on his black pony, Hans. He was going to become a priest, but he became a soldier instead. He was promoted to run a camp in Poland called Auschwitz. Some of the soldiers there found machine-gunning people upsetting. They drank heavily afterwards and a few committed suicide. So Hoess came up with a solution that had been effective on rats. He tried the gas out on 900 Russian soldiers and found it efficient: much less traumatic for the executors, though there continued to be some difficulties, especially with Jewish mothers who became uncontrollable if their children were removed from them first.

She read until she could read no longer and had to escape, running out into the sweet twilight air of the garden and the Nelsons' pigeons circling before settling for the night. That night and for nights after she read, not understanding it all, skipping some bits, while the dishes piled up in the sink and Maura and Paul sang in harmony that although she'd gone away, she loved him still (*yeah yeah yeah*!). Kate sat behind the sofa and encountered, for the first time, banal, unfathomable hate.

13.

These legendary personages are presented to the mind's eye in childhood; and the result is a hallucination that persists strongly throughout life when it has been impressed. Thus all the thinking of the hallucinated adult about the fountain of inspiration that is continually flowing in the universe, or about the promoting of virtue and the revulsions of shame: in short, about aspiration and conscience, both of which forces are matters of fact more obvious than electro-magnetism, is thinking in terms of the celestial vision.

Preface to *St Joan* by George Bernard Shaw

Lindisfarne was a cluster of barrack-like huts around a concrete-block dining-hall in a patch of bush next to a river. Kate unrolled her sleeping bag on one of the lower bunks in Aidan dormitory. Next door was Ninian, and beyond the toilet block with its rows of stalls and washbasins stood Columba and Cuthbert, where the boys slept. On the morning of Good Friday they had Weetbix at one of the long trestle tables in the dining hall, then gathered in circles for Bible study. Kate was in a group led by a divinity student called Glenn. He had a scrappy beard and wore khaki shorts. His fiancée, Noeline, was also at the camp. She wore simple cotton skirts gathered at the waist and plain leather sandals, and she had the most astonishingly hairy legs anyone had ever seen.

'Did you see those fetlocks?' said Angela Avery, who occupied the bunk above Kate's. 'She's hairier than him. Hasn't she ever heard of a razor?' Angela's legs were satin smooth, her lips were palest pink, her eyelids were laden with Maybelline blue and black eyeliner. Each morning she sat up in her sleeping bag applying her make-up in a little pocket mirror while the other girls squabbled over the single rectangle hung from a nail above the washbasins. Angela had been to Lindisfarne before.

Seated by the riverstone fireplace at one end of the dining hall, Glenn's study group turned its collective attention to the death and resurrection of Jesus.

Kate leaned against the mortared boulders and thought about St Joan. *St Joan* had been lying, price one shilling, among the usual assortment of books, plates, garden implements and daubs of Mt Cook viewed over a cobalt blue lake at Harris's second-hand. The book was unremarkable in khaki covers, but she picked it out because she had seen the play: not all of it, just the scene where St Joan convinces de Baudricourt, which had been performed at assembly by four actors who had pulled up at the school in a minibus.

'Hello!' they announced one by one in bright, perfect, posh voices.

'I'm Peggy Turvey.'

'And I'm Bernard Esquilant.'

Every word they uttered was punctuated by an invisible row of exclamation points.

'And we . . . !!!'

'Are the Southern . . . !!!!'

'Comedy Players . . . !!!!'

Kate had seen actors before. She had been with her mother to all the Operatic Society's productions, where people who were just the people she knew from the hardware shop and the florists on Thames Street were transformed magically in gingham and denim for *Oklahoma*, or in sailor suits and tropical white for *South Pacific* or crinolines and top hats for *The Merry Widow*.

'They are so gifted!' Kate's mother sighed, as the leads received their bunches of gladioli and waved from the stage at the Opera House. 'Such beautiful voices!'

Kate had a secret ambition to join them. Long ago she had sat watching the children in the Competitions, children who did elocution and tap, who wore proper make-up and sang in character in the Under-12 Song and Dance section. Maura had done ballet for a while, practising pliés in the hall against the dado. Kate had learned piano, struggling through scales and arpeggios in the front room, with all the china in the china cabinet rattling a frail tympani accompaniment. But to stand alone on stage, to perform 'Sweet Little Alice Blue Gown' in an elaborately flounced blue crinoline — that had seemed unattainable glory.

The Southern Comedy Players did not bother with crinolines. Nor did they bother much with sets. For one play they used the caretaker's stepladder and a couple of chairs to make a house, a car, a whole town. Then in an instant they had changed and were discussing cucumber sandwiches. Finally, Peggy Turvey in leather jerkin, tights and Carnaby Street kneeboots strode centre stage to persuade de Baudricourt to war.

One thousand like me can stop them!!! said the warrior maid, only seventeen yet already a leader of men. *'Ten like me can stop them with God on our side*!!!' Kate sat on the floor of the assembly hall, loving the moment when the shift happened. One minute the actors were faintly absurd, speaking with the plums in their mouths that everyone ridiculed as the sure sign of the pseud, the show-off and the fairy. But then — Hoopla! — they had slid into another skin and were butler, soldier, American teenager. It was extraordinary that so many kinds of people could exist under one skin.

So when Kate found *St Joan* in the Books for a Bob bin at Harris's she bought it. She took it home, shut the front-room door and set to finding out what happened to St Joan before and after the bit in the assembly hall. Before the play began, there was a preface. It was very long — pages and pages — but she read it anyway, and suddenly the words staged a revolution.

All the popular religions of the world are made apprehensible by an array of legendary personages, with an Almighty Father, and sometimes a mother and divine child as the central figures.

To the outside view nothing much might have appeared to happen. A fourteen-year-old girl sat reading in a patch of sunlight next to the china cabinet, a tortoiseshell cat asleep on her knees. But inside the reader there was tumult. A pen had blown a hole through a barricade of faith. Everything Kate had believed, everything she had been told about the world, her place in it, the purpose of existence, was 'a hallucination'. The plastic angel, the Virgin Mary, Gentle Jesus, Little Saint Teresa — none of them was necessarily true. Uncertainty came crashing in. She needed, desperately, to pit Gentle Jesus and the rest of them against George Bernard Shaw in a fair fight, fact for fact. The bearded saviour in the Rhododendron Dell versus the scrawny old vegetarian in his knitted Jaeger sanitary suit, or their proxies. In Glenn the divinity student she had found her man; in the dining room at Lindisfarne, the arena.

How could God, if he is Love, allow that pile of bodies at Auschwitz? He's supposed to know everything, isn't he, he's planned everything, so how could he plan for millions and millions of people to be gassed and burned? And weren't they killed because Christians had been going on and on for centuries about how Jews were responsible for crucifying Jesus? Look: it says right here: 'Crucify him! Crucify him!' So if God allowed all those people to die, maybe he's not Love. In fact, maybe he doesn't exist at all. Maybe he's just a hallucination, you know, like something we've been told, like Santa or the Easter Bunny, and then find out to be a lie. Maybe we've been told this lie because it stops people minding being sick or sad or poor because they'll go to heaven in the end so they can put up with their lives here and now . . .

Glenn couldn't answer.

He said it was natural at her age to doubt. He smiled. He referred her to the Bible. God was the truth. He was the Way, now and for ever.

'What were you going on about?' said Angela as they queued at the kitchen slide for dollops of pustular macaroni cheese. 'What was all that stuff about hallucinations?'

Kate shrugged. 'Nothing,' she said. Angela had a hard, bright eye ready to peck at the weird. It would not do to seem too earnest. 'Just trying to annoy Glenn, that's all. Aren't those shorts of his revolting?'

Angela relaxed. That she could understand. 'Well, it sure worked,' she said, and she sat next to Kate at dinner. A couple of boys from Papakaio sat opposite and after dinner, while the A Team were washing up, the hunky one who played for North Otago under-sixteens, said, 'You girls want to go for a walk?' And Angela said, 'All right.' So they went for a walk over to Columba, where Angela got the rep and Kate got his skinny mate whose name was something like Bing or Ding. The bunkroom was in darkness and filled with furtive sibilance as they stumbled hand in hand over boots and packs and unidentifiable bundles, which could have been sleeping bags or clothing or bodies on a bunk.

'Piss off,' said a voice from the gloom. Bing — or maybe it was Ding — drew Kate down beside him on a vacant bunk and clasped her in an urgent embrace. He dabbed at her in the dark, his lips leaving little damp patches on her skin tasting of macaroni cheese while his hands stroked and ventured around the waistband of her jeans and up under the sloppy joe to tweak at the edges of her size 32C Wonderform, when abruptly, 'What's going on here?' said an adult voice, and the bare lightbulb in the middle of the room was switched on. The campers scrambled from the bunks, tousled, dazzled, pink, avoiding one another's eyes. They marched over to the dining hall for a social. Glenn got out his guitar.

Bing — or maybe it was Ding — sat beside Kate at one of the trestle tables.

Michael row the boat ashore! sang Glenn, with Noeline clapping happily beside him, swaying in time to the music. *Al-le-luya*! Bing's arm lay along the back of the form seat. Kate was aware of him beside her, leaning closer. In the bunkroom he had been nothing more than mouth and body, skin and breath. Out here in the light she could examine him more closely. He had an odd receding chin, yellow wax in his ear and his hair was too short. His leg pressed against hers under the table.

Glenn had moved on to 'Where Have all the Flowers Gone'. Kate hated this song, just as she hated 'Ten Green Bottles' and any song with an insistent, inexorable structure. They made her feel trapped. There had to be the flowers, the girls, the soldiers, the graveyards, the flowers — just as the bottles had to fall one by tedious one until there was nothing but the smell a-hanging on the wall. Beneath the table Bing's leg was rubbing at her thigh, his hand pressed lightly at her upper arm. People would be watching. People would be assuming she was his.

''Scuse,' she said. 'Back in a minute.' And she stood up and went outside.

There was the first whiff of frost in the air and the sky was dazzling starry perfection. She went over to the toilet block and brushed her teeth, carefully, taking a long time, reaching into all the crannies, then she rinsed away the taste of kissing. By the time she emerged they were on to 'Oh Sinnerman', another circle, another trap. Poor Sinnerman, running hopelessly searching for concealment in unlikely places from the wrath of God. If only Sinnerman had known that God was just a hallucination he'd have saved himself a lot of effort. There was a flicker of light from the shadow beyond the kitchen door, a whiff of cigarette smoke.

'Hi,' said a voice from the darkness. 'I liked what you said, that stuff about Auschwitz.'

There was a boy sitting on one of the rubbish bins with his knees drawn up.

'Want a smoke?' he said. Kate had practised smoking in front of the bathroom mirror, holding a clothes peg in one hand with the wrist flexed elegantly as she drew in with narrowed eye. She was trying for something like Audrey Hepburn in *Breakfast at Tiffany's* and she had looked quite passable. But when she tried it for real one afternoon at Angela's, she had choked and spluttered and not looked one bit like Audrey Hepburn.

The rock told Sinnerman it wouldn't hide him because he shoulda been a-prayin', while Kate and the boy sat on the rubbish bins above potato peelings and macaroni leftovers, and smoked and talked, because the boy didn't believe in any of it either. He was here because his father was a minister, so he had to come, every year: but this was IT, definitely his last Easter Camp. It was all a load of crap, the opium — everyone said opiate but it was originally opium, that was what Marx had actually written — of the people. He stubbed his cigarette out on the dining-room wall and lit another.

The establishment always endorsed religion, because it was the perfect means of brainwashing the people, like it suited the rich if the poor were all happy to put up with whatever crap they got, rather than reaching for their guns and becoming revolutionaries. It was just like Marx said. Peter had actually read Marx: he'd sent away for an introductory book from the Communist Party in Christchurch and his dad had seen it and gone mad, raving on about Stalin and Hungary and gulags, and Peter had said to him that that wasn't the point: communism was an ideal, just like Christianity was an ideal. No one actually managed to live up to the ideal, but that didn't mean that the ideal was wrong. Communism was just putting into practice what Jesus taught. And that really finished it. His dad had taken the book and flung it in the fire. So much for Christian tolerance, eh? Peter had said that to his dad. He'd said to him, 'You are just a fascist. You're another Nazi book-burner.'

'Christ!' he said. And you could tell from the way he said it that he was trying the word out, seeing what would happen if he released the pin in it and flung it straight into the redoubt of faith. 'Christ!' He flicked his cigarette expertly into the darkness, where it arced and fell like a star. 'You should have seen the old man then! I thought he'd croak on the fucking spot!'

And that word too fizzled, but no thunderbolt fell from the outraged heavens. Instead, Noeline popped her head out the door and said, was that where they'd got to? And, in a way that brooked no denial, wouldn't they like to come in and have some supper? So they went in and there were all the campers drinking cocoa. The cocoa had a white membrane on its surface, like a layer of dead skin.

First thing next morning, Easter Sunday, they all walked through the bush to the top of the highest hill to see the sun rise. Noeline bounded ahead on her goat-like legs while Glenn volunteered to be tail-end Charlie. The campers straggled in the pre-dawn twilight, through drowsy trees, over a couple of fences

186

and up onto the crest of an escarpment that broke like a wave frozen in stone above the coastal plain. Away in the distance there was a gleam along the sea's horizon and the birds began to wake and call, one to the other. The crest of the sun rose, crimson through shining bars of cloud.

Kate watched it with elation, not because it symbolised the risen Lord (as Glenn was telling them) and the joy of the women coming to the empty tomb, but because it was not a symbol at all. It was not a stone rolling from a grave, but the sun. A star not created by God but with an origin greater, more awe-inspiring, more extraordinary than she could begin to comprehend. And she was here, alive, on this hilltop to see it, with Peter standing nearby, not wanting to hold her hand or kiss her or anything, but scuffing his shoe on a clump of Spaniard. Glenn was reading the bit about Jesus appearing on the road to Emmaeus when Peter looked up at her and crossed his eyes elaborately. Kate felt laughter bubbling in her chest beneath the sloppy joe, like the bubbles you see when you open your eyes beneath water, the ones that tell you in which direction the surface lies. The sun rose and the world was taking on its real colours, no longer the muted half tones of pre-dawn but vivid gold and green and blue. At last the campers were free to move off down the track to corn-flakes and toast.

Kate waited, concealed behind some matagouri from the scrutiny of tail-end Charlie, as the others straggled back over the fence and into the bush. At last she was alone, poised on some white rock, as smooth and white as a bare skull beneath her feet. The sun warmed her face and she lifted her arms to receive it, to the morning, to the sea, to whatever lay beyond the sea. For the first time in her life, she felt free of sin.

George Bernard Shaw had won, hands down.

14.

Life would go on. No more human contacts, other people's emotions washing at the brain — he would be free again. Nothing to think about but himself. Myself: the word echoed hygienically on among the porcelain basins, the taps and plugs and wastes. He took the revolver out of his pocket and loaded it.

Brighton Rock by Graham Greene

Their mother returned just before Christmas. Kate and Maura arrived home from school one afternoon to the house heavy with the scent of strawberry jam and there she was in the kitchen, stirring figure of eights in the sweet brew in the copper pan.

'Have a nice day?' she said, as if she had been gone only an hour or two. Then she showed them her Post Office Savings Bank book. The deposit column had sixty four pounds, two shillings and sixpence in it. Plenty for *From the Spey to the Kilmog,* and some over besides. Their father refused to contemplate the triumph.

'Bloody daft,' he said.

Their mother said she had prayed and God had told her to go home. She had opened the Bible as she did each morning, to find her instruction for the day, and it had fallen open at *If two lie together, then they have heat: but how can one be warm alone?* The day before, at work, the floor polisher, a great heavy thing with rotary polishers that slid about awkwardly on the lino, had wrenched itself from her grasp and driven a rent right across the floor of the entrance foyer. It was a sign. She had left her job that very day, packed the Morris, and come home.

And it was as well she had, for a few weeks later Pat collapsed on his way up Wharf Street reading the meters. Simply went very white and fell sideways into the vicarage hedge. The vicar's wife saw him fall and phoned Kate's mother. 'A touch of flu,' said Pat, irritable as he stood unsteadily and was driven home. But the joints at elbow and knee became red. They swelled to puffy balls of exquisite pain, too tender to be touched. The thistle shreds of metal from Alamein, the doctor said, were to blame. Though tiny, they were releasing poisons into muscle and bone. In the months that followed, the fingers on each hand began to twist in odd directions like the stems of a plant grown out of its proper place, under a wall or between stones. His legs became weak and spindly. Walking became progressively more difficult. He was forced to abandon his job in the open air, walking about the streets from house to house. He had to become an office wallah after all.

'Mahleesh,' he said. That meant there were others worse off than himself. His mate Walker, for example, out at Weston, his stomach shot to pieces and riddled with ulcers, the effects — long delayed — of a couple of years in a POW camp. He meant the young blokes who were dry bone and dust in the African desert.

The nights were worst. He could not settle. The slightest movement made him groan: fumbling for a cigarette, lighting it, turning a page, for he read all night sometimes. He began to talk: they could hear his voice arguing, agreeing, debating with an empty room. A pause while he read, then the voice raised in protest with a chest of drawers as his opponent, or the wardrobe. They could not hear the words precisely, but they became accustomed to going to sleep to the monologue. In the morning his light was still on and he dozed, propped up against the pillows, his glasses askew and one unwieldy hand holding the book open.

'All this she must possess,' added *Darcy, 'and to all this she must yet add something more substantial, in the improvement of her mind by extensive reading.'*

'I am no longer surprised at your knowing only six accomplished women. I rather wonder now at your knowing any.'

'Are you so severe upon your own sex, as to doubt the possibility of all this?'

'I never saw such a woman. I never saw such capacity, and taste, and application, and elegance, as you describe, united.'

Pride and Prejudice by Jane Austen

That year they studied *Pride and Prejudice*. The next, *Emma*. And *Northanger Abbey*. And *Persuasion*. Miss Pollock liked Jane Austen. To begin with, Kate would have said the set texts came a poor second to Georgette Heyer, but as the class shrank from thirty-five to twenty to the dozen who stayed on until the upper sixth, Arabella and her spirited sisters in their high-crowned bonnets and crimson ribbons began to seem thin paper things, all frill at the front but blank cardboard at the back by comparison with Emma or Fanny Price, and their courtships by Mr Beaumaris and his dandy tribe as boring as Ludo. Emma's fumbling progress toward love seemed closer, once decoded and understood, to Kate's own awkward experience.

Maura had a boyfriend, a surfer. She careered off with him to lie on the beach in her bikini, one of the chicks, while the boys paddled out beyond the breakers, bobbing like seals on the blue Pacific swells. She returned late at night in some beaten-up Holden station wagon with a stack of eight-foot Malibus strapped to the roof.

'You are being careful?' said their mother, and Maura shrugged and said, 'Course I'm being careful. Bazza is a good driver.' Which wasn't the question at all. When their mother attempted to elaborate — something about boys having no respect for girls who were not ladylike — she said, 'Oh, Mum!' and went into her room and shut the door. The radio switched on, the sewing machine whirred into action: a miniskirt in caramel cord, a little fitted jacket with a velvet collar, a pinafore dress with contrasting trim, a baby-doll dress in floral granny-print. The machine supplied a continuous drone to 'Do Wah Diddy Diddy' and 'I Wanna Hold Your Hand'.

Kate envied Maura the cheerful crush in the Holden at 2am. Hand in hand with a boy, Kate became shy and stupid. She didn't know what to say. She stood in the darkness in the Hall of Memories where all the boys took their partners after the Boys' High Ball, for a pash before the parents' cars arrived to collect their charges. Kissing and being kissed, touching and being touched, her body taking the lead while her mind stood back somehow, watching with astonishment what its owner was up to beneath the Gothic arches and memorial windows. At New Year she walked about Queenstown with Maddie Greenleaf and Caro Williams and some boys they had met on the beach at Frankton. Hand in hand with one of them, she was as usual struck dumb, dawdling with the others in a monosyllabic daze away from the crowds milling about the mall, a fight breaking out down towards the waterfront, up a quiet street past the library where they found the door to the reading room open. The tables were Victorian: massive slabs of totara that took the weight of several writhing teenagers with only the mildest of breathy creaking.

I decided I'd just see old Phoebe and sort of say good-bye to her and all, and give her back her Christmas dough, and then I'd start hitchhiking my way out West. What I'd do, I figured, I'd go down to the Holland Tunnel and bum a ride, and then I'd bum another one, and another one, and another one, and in a few days I'd be somewhere out West where it was very pretty and sunny and where nobody'd know me and I'd get a job.

Catcher in the Rye by J.D. Salinger

Sheldon Fein from New York was lean and tanned and he was reading Dos Passos in the common room when the minibus pulled up and the sixth-form geography class emerged to study cirques, drumlins and hanging valleys.

Geography was deadly. It consisted of Mr Slooten handing each girl a copy of Cotton's *Geomorphology* on the first day of the first term and saying, 'Here: summarise this.' The book was massive. It occupied the desk like a terminal moraine, dense with fact. The class settled to confused paraphrase, tracing maps and ruling off headings in red ink while Mr Slooten read the paper and sat idly picking his nose and gluing his discoveries into a large white handkerchief. He did not come on the field trip. The class was entrusted to a couple of the young English teachers, who wore khaki shorts and proper tramping boots and stopped to photograph weird stuff on the way, like shearing sheds and letterboxes. The drive had taken hours because they had to keep stopping for Angela Avery, who had insisted at Omarama on a vanilla milkshake and two steak and kidney pies that had clearly been sitting in their little glass cabinet for a couple of uneventful decades. The class emerged at last from the reeking van, pale and grateful for air that tasted cleanly of ice and cloud and leaves.

And there was their hitchhiker. They had passed him just north of Twizel, lean and brown, standing on the side of the road with his thumb held out nonchalantly at the passing traffic.

'Stop! Stop!' said Angela. 'Pick him up! We've got a spare seat!'

But Miss Paget had just laughed and glanced at Miss Cameron and said, as she accelerated onto a straight, that she thought they had quite enough on their hands without adding a hitchhiker. Kate, who was in the back seat, turned to see what had happened to him but he had vanished already in the white cloud of their dust.

But when they arrived, there he was already, like the hare in the story, gone ahead of them somehow while they were stopped for photos or to allow Angela to throw up. He laid aside his book as the sixth-form geography field trip burst in and he said 'Hi!'

'Hi!', like in the movies.

He was Kate's first real American. When she had been younger — in the fourth form — she and Heather McFadden had sometimes pretended to be American. They talked American loudly on the street and hoped that strangers would not recognise them as coming from here, from Oamaru. They hoped they would think they came from somewhere wonderful like Los Angeles, in their bobby sox and straight skirts. But Sheldon was the real thing. He didn't have to pretend. He came from Noo York. He sounded like Jack Palance. He stood in the kitchen while the sixth form cooked sausages for tea and because there was some extra (Angela was still suffering from the pies) they invited him to join them. He accepted with alacrity and sat between Kate and Caro, talking animatedly and not noticing that Miss Paget and Miss Cameron seemed cross and did not hand him the bread when he asked for it. He talked as they ate and as they cleared the table and did the dishes, about movie stars, because Angela asked him if he knew any.

He did: he had actually been to the same high school as Marlon Brando.

'What's he like?' said Angela, but Sheldon said Marlon was a lot older and had been in the same grade as his uncle. (He said 'grade' just like in the movies.) He talked about a movie he had just seen, *A Knife in the Water*. It was Polish. (Polish? There were *Polish* movies?) by someone called Polanski. (Movies were '*by*' someone?)' Roman Polanski,' he said. 'That's a name you should look out for.' He helped Caro spell it properly when she copied it into her notebook. He talked about American things, like Kennedy's assassination — which was not at all as they said it was on TV, the work of poor, mad Lee Harvey Oswald, but an evil conspiracy of right-wing oil barons in collusion with the CIA. And of course he knew, because he was American. Kate tried out some of Peter's Marxism on Sheldon and followed it up with a bit of George Bernard Shaw and he scooped it all up and mentioned anti-Semitism among other things, so Kate tried *Commandant of Auschwitz* on him too, and he knew about that because his uncles and aunts had actually died in Auschwitz.

Sheldon was like actual history. He was like current events and TV and movies, he was like the *world*. He talked as the sixth form sat about playing five hundred, and after they had all climbed into their sleeping bags he came and sat on the end of Kate's bed and she and Caro and Maddie talked with him in whispers until the birds started singing, and it was time to head out in the wake of a dauntingly muscled ranger in boy scout shirt and shorts who marched them over a grubby glacier while the two English teachers asked bright, interested questions about birdlife.

Before they left for the glacier, Sheldon had handed Kate a tiny American flag and his address in Noo York, should she ever be over that way. He made it seem the most casual, easy thing in the world. That she could simply be in the neighbourhood of apartment 1A, 92 Horatio Street, Brooklyn. That she, Kate, could be strolling down that street and think in an offhand kind of way, 'Oh, I think I'll drop in on Sheldon, that American I met at Mt Cook.' Could she ever do that? Could she ever be in Noo York?

'Here you are,' he said. 'Been great talking with you.' And he leant over and kissed her, a fraternal kiss, the kiss of fellow citizens in this wide world. She walked all day on the glacier, not minding the disappointingly mucky ice where she had been anticipating silvery perfection, not minding the muddy tracks or the fog that hung heavy as lounge curtains over the tops, or the rain that dropped at last, soaking through her thin plastic windbreaker. She had her hand furled around a little American flag, an address in Noo York, a wider vision of her future, which until now had consisted of passing one exam after another, then going to varsity, then becoming a teacher in Oamaru. And finding love, presumably. Engagement ring, marriage, babies.

Except that her experience of love so far suggested that she was destined to spend her entire life in furtive grappling in a selection of the notable architectural gems of New Zealand.

15.

Their names dropped musically like small fat bird-notes through the freckled sunlight of a young world: prophetically he brooded on the sweet lost bird-cries, knowing they never would return. Herrick, Crashaw, Carew, Suckling, Campion, Lovelace, Dekker. O sweet content, O sweet, O sweet content! He read a dozen of Scott and liked best of all Quentin Durward, because the descriptions of food were as bountiful and appetising as any he had ever read.

Look Homeward, Angel by Thomas Wolfe

'*I wonder by my troth . . .*' murmured Richard Burton into the drowsy ears of the upper sixth, '*. . . what thou and I did till we lov'd?*' The Virginia creeper around the windows had shed its crimson leaves and gone to bare twig over winter. Now it burst into fistfuls of fresh green. *Were we not wean'd till then? But suck'd on countrey* *pleasures, childishly?* The record crackled slightly under the needle.

Exams arrived with the green leaf and the summer: end-of-year exams, then Schol. They were all sitting Schol, the biggest class ever to do so at the school. Caro and Angela and Maddie, Kate and half a dozen others, all of them except Virginia Craddock the daughters of parents who had not gone to university themselves.

These girls were specially blessed.

They had received The Opportunity.

It was engraved in capitals like the title of some Hollywood epic.

SPARTACUS

EXODUS

THE TEN COMMANDMENTS

THE OPPORTUNITY

Deprived of a university education by the Depression (another Hollywood word: THE DEPRESSION) and its twin, THE WAR, the parents of the girls in 6A were certain that this was what their offspring deserved, like free dental care, cheap medical treatment, crime-free streets, solid state-houses if required and a universal Family Benefit. The girls took the obligation entailed seriously. They finished all their essays more or less on time, they studied for their exams, sitting in the sun with their skirts rolled up to tan their legs while revising the causes of the First World War and bits of *Pro Milone*. Virginia Craddock kept a little notebook in which she recorded all their marks so that she could predict with absolute accuracy who would be Dux, who would get a Scholarship, who would win and who would lose at every stage of the competition that operated, unacknowledged, alongside the chat about movies and the school ball.

Kate's father would have liked to go to university. If he had not had to leave school at fourteen, he would have read arts. He looked through the university calendar Kate brought home from school, deciding what he would have chosen. Philosophy, he thought, and history and literature, of course, and maybe this 'anthropology' — that looked interesting — and classics, an arts degree being The Only True Education.

'The rest is just training,' he said. 'Medicine, law, all the rest of it. You can pick those up later if you want, after you've had a decent education.'

He would have read arts, if he had had The Opportunity. He was clever enough. He could answer all the questions on 'King of Quiz', pressing an invisible buzzer on the chair arm and beating the lot of them.

'Ah, well,' he said, laying the calendar aside, taking up his walking stick and setting out on the route march up the hall to the car and the carpark and the office at the Power Board. 'Mahleesh.'

Kate's mother would have gone too, had a shining roof not diverted her to her True Vocation, and then there was Uncle Tom, his career cut short by billions of besieging bacteria. But Kate was well and she was able and she had The Opportunity.

When she was studying for the first of the national exams, School Certificate, her mother had moved out of the back bedroom. She went down to Harris's second-hand and bought a writing desk with a fold-down front and a bookshelf, and when Kate arrived home they were all set up in the back bedroom, her books arranged on the shelf, the desk against one wall with a kitchen chair and a cushion made from a sugar sack with lazy daisies embroidered on the top.

'But where are you going to sleep?' said Kate.

'Oh, don't worry about me,' said her mother. 'You need to do your swot and you can't do that in a shared room.'

Her mother slept instead on the foldout bed in the front room. By day it was stored in the hall cupboard and each night it was wheeled through and set up between the china cabinet and the piano.

'I don't want you sleeping in the front room,' said Kate. 'I'm fine sharing with Maura. Truly.'

She hated the guilt of displacement. She also hated the foldout bed and its hint of the temporary visit, as if their mother had landed only lightly in the house and could as readily pack up and go. As if she were merely visiting. And yet . . . And yet . . . It was so good to close the door on her own room. Here, she could sit on her own bed and listen to the Hit Parade, or write poems of loss and anguish for the school magazine:

I too have met the deer and know their ways.
Their breath has seared me. Their red eyes gaze
At me from darkened corners . . .

Or learn her lines. She played Madame de Correbas, the clever aristocrat who eluded the clutches of the vile mob by her talent for disguise in *To Save the Queen*!, the dramatic tale of Revolutionary France that was the school's entry in that year's British Drama League's One-Act Play Festival. ('A most promising young actress!' wrote B.J., reviewing the triumph for the two-minute silence.) She was also Macbeth in a tartan skirt and picnic-blanket cloak, and she was Count Diego in *Violetta*, wearing her mother's old nursing cloak and cardboard buckles tied to her school shoes.

And she swotted, memorising the names of the Great Lakes, the four repercussions of the Treaty of Versailles and key speeches from *Hamlet*. Her mother popped in from time to time, hoping she was not interrupting and bearing tea and biscuits: peanut biscuits, because peanuts were 'brain food', like fish in parsley sauce and sweetbreads. They would ensure Kate's brain was in tip-top condition when the exams came, just as years of sea-bathing and sleeping with the windows open had ensured her body could put up a fairly determined resistance to any infection considering a takeover. Kate ate her peanut biscuits and swotted and at the end of that year it all paid off: she passed her exams. She got a prize for English:

the stories of Katherine Mansfield, bound in blue leather with the school crest — *Dulcius ex arduis* — stamped on the cover.

The first book she had ever read that mentioned mutton sandwiches.

And little girls grouped in the sliver-sharp hierarchies of the playground, the dawdle home between banks of dry grass, the two-storeyed house, the kids who lived beyond the boundary: the minute adjustments that signified class in the classless society, so much more subtle than a world where goodies dined at the club and went down to the country for the weekend and the baddies dropped their aiches. Kate recognised here an intricate and familiar world. She remembered the Creeches and Flying Fanny. She remembered tea at Virginia Craddock's: the strange salad with oil instead of condensed-milk mayonnaise, the sour orange they called a grapefruit that arrived on her plate instead of the fruit she had anticipated, those expensive little purple berries she had tasted when she had had scarlet fever. She remembered the airy expertise with which Virginia and her brothers and sisters sliced their strange fruit. *What is the capital of Germany? Who wrote* A Tale of Two Cities?

Kate recognised the Kelveys. She recognised the Burnells. It was like coming upon her own reflection, unexpectedly, in a darkened room.

The one question was, 'Have you seen Burnells' doll's house? Oh, ain't it lovely!' 'Haven't you seen it? Oh, I say!'

Even the dinner hour was given up to talking about it. The little girls sat under the pines eating their thick mutton sandwiches and big slabs of johnny cake spread with butter. While always, as near as they could get, sat the

Kelveys, our Else holding on to Lil, listening too, while they chewed their jam sandwiches out of newspaper soaked with large red blobs.

The Doll's House by Katherine Mansfield

Kate had a job for the summer working at the Albert Residential Rest Home. The residents rested in rows in sunrooms overlooking Friendly Bay and the wide sweep of the sea. The women sat at one end of the building, the men at the other, with matron's flat and the office in between, and a dark dining room where festive arrangements of silver pinecones replaced the usual plastic daffodils, and the smell of a century of mutton stews hung like a fog.

Matron walked about with the white wings of her veil spread and a dog, a wheezing pug called Moppet, at her side for the patients to pet. Her husband acted as handyman around the place. He was a balding, doughy Australian who spent most of his time working on his car, a white E-Type Jag, in the drive in front of their flat. The old women sat with afghans spread over their knees in red and purple and citrus green. They bowed low before the afternoon soap and the tinsel tree blinking on and off, on and off in the corner, while the old men smoked, perched about the rockery behind the laundry like so many elderly gnomes, for Matron had forbidden cigarettes in the building after Mr Posket fell asleep and set fire to his bed. They sat among the sempervivums rolling skinny twigs of Park Drive, then shuffled home to their cubicles.

The Home had originally had open wards, designed for the care of the indigent poor. Now each inhabitant lived behind a plywood dividing wall of cupboard and chest of drawers on which their children clustered in wedding dresses or graduation gowns or turned side on in the photographer's studio as if they were smiling over their shoulders while walking out the door into the glow of a brighter future. The old women stood among them, not as they were now in their cardigans and slippers, but as they were before the children even existed, when the old women's hair shone as if it emitted light itself and their lips were full and red. The old men stood stern in khaki or as one of the team, arms folded after a season playing on the wing for Old Boys, lean and running away from the pack. The photos had to be dusted.

'You be careful with them pictures,' said Mrs Oblowski as Kate flicked a duster lightly, for on Tuesdays all surfaces had to be dusted before morning tea and it was a rush when there were more beds than usual to change, sheets to strip quickly and the whole damp mess dumped in the linen basket. 'Give it here.' A skinny hand with fingers like twisted vine took firm hold of the duster. She wiped her photos carefully, taking her time over each one.

'What's going on here?' said Audrey, who was head cleaner, popping her head around the partition. 'What are you up to, dear?' She called all the old people 'dear' except for Mr Depree in the men's wing who you had to keep an eye on. 'Don't turn your back on him ever,' she said. 'He'll be onto you quick as a flash, even though he's pushing ninety.' She called him 'you randy old bugger', but quietly, so that Matron could not hear. Not that Matron was much better off, with a husband who tried it on with anybody. He'd had a go at Pania who did the cooking, called her a black bitch when he'd bailed her up one night in the pantry and she wouldn't come across. They discussed it in the staffroom over buttered scones at morning tea. Should they say something to Matron? Should they let it pass? 'Let it pass,' Audrey counselled. No point stirring up trouble.

Mrs Oblowski dabbed ineffectually at a photo of a man holding up a six-foot marlin. Dab dab dab.

'You'll be all day, dear,' said Audrey. 'Why don't you let Kate here do it?'

Mrs Oblowski kept firm hold of the duster. Dab dab dab.

'That's what she's paid for,' said Audrey.

Dab dab dab.

'Now you just give that duster to me, dear,' said Audrey. 'And you have a nice rest.'

'I've had a rest,' said Mrs Oblowski. 'Plenty of time to rest. I like to be useful.'

She got up at night sometimes and laid the tables in the dining room: all of them, with all the cutlery, if you weren't on the lookout.

'The boys'll be in soon,' she'd say. 'They'll be wanting their dinners. They've been gone a long time.'

Audrey shrugged.

'Suit yourself, then,' she said. 'If you want to dust, there's fifteen more to do down the corridor.' When Kate returned that afternoon with the tea trays, Mrs Oblowski lay on her bed, eyes closed, arms folded across her chest, and clutched in one hand, the pink and white check of her duster.

Six pound a week, triple time on Christmas and New Year. Kate bought a fawn duffel-coat, a fawn ribbed turtleneck, a suede miniskirt and a pair of brown Mary Janes. She tried them all on.

'So, let's have a look at you,' said her father. He surveyed her with satisfaction. 'Now, don't you look the student!' he said.

'Is that what they're wearing these days?' said her mother, regarding the miniskirt. It ended several inches above the knee.

'Yes, it is,' said Kate, though to be honest she had doubts herself about her thighs. All the biking to and from school in all weathers had left her with muscles of iron and legs that would not have looked out of place in a scrum.

Her mother's doubts were becoming irritating. Now that The Opportunity was here, she seemed to be regretting its arrival.

'You are sure you want to go?' she said. Beside her on the kitchen table lay another shoebox stuffed with cards: she was doing her mother's side. *Falconer, Alice. b. Kenmore, 1884. McGregor, Isobel.*

b. Dunedin 1859. Grant, Jane. b. Cromdale, Sctld, 1832.

'Of course,' said Kate. Though to be honest if the others — Caro, Maddie and the rest — had not been going, she would not have gone either. She would have liked, ideally, to become an actress, after her success as Madame de Correbas and Macbeth. But that would have involved going to London, she supposed, like the girls in those Noel Streatfield books she had read when she was a child. Dunedin seemed altogether simpler. It was where everyone was going.

'Because you don't have to leave Oamaru,' said her mother. She stuck a little label onto the back of a photograph. A sepia print of a wedding couple, both bride and groom clearly mightily impressed with the seriousness of what they were about to do: the begetting of ancestors. The bride stood by the chair, one hand on the groom's shoulder. The groom stared at the camera, jaw clenched beneath a thick moustache, as if something furry had died on his top lip. 'You could just stay here, and get a job, like Heather McFadden.'

'I don't want a job like Heather McFadden,' said Kate. Heather worked for the BNZ, seated behind a desk in the echoing hall of one of the Doric temples on Thames Street. Kate had been in to see her to say goodbye.

'With you in a minute,' Heather had mouthed, expertly dealing fistfuls of twenty-dollar bills. Her hair was permed, a poodle frizz replacing the page-boy bob she'd had when they used to bike home together, on the lookout for the Weston bus. Her make-up was china doll.

'Thank you, sir,' she said at last, with a quick professional smile. She slid from her high stool and nodded briefly at the supervisor. The supervisor looked significantly at the clock. Forty-five minutes, the look said, and NO LONGER. Heather's sandals clicked across the polished floor.

'Come on,' she said. 'Quick. Before they decide we're too busy for lunch breaks.'

They went for cappuccinos at the Rendezvous, for old times' sake, though they skipped the corn rolls. Heather was on a diet.

'I've got this dress put aside at Mamselles,' she said. 'It's gorgeous. Halter neck, white. It looks stunning but it shows every ounce.' She was going to a wedding in February: her boyfriend Gary's brother was getting married at Duntroon and it was going to be her introduction to the family. She wanted to make a good impression.

'You have a corn roll, though,' she said. And Kate said no, she could do with losing a few pounds. They settled into the booth nearest the street.

'So, what are you going to do in Dunedin?' said Heather.

'English,' said Kate. 'And History and French and Anthropology.'

'What's that?' said Heather. 'Anthro-wotsit?'

'Not sure,' said Kate. 'The study of people.'

'Oh yeah?' said Heather. 'Like social studies?'

Kate picked a bogey of candle wax from the wine bottle on the table.

'I think so,' she said. 'The set texts are about Mexico and Samoa.'

'Sooner you than me,' said Heather. 'I hated that stuff: lamb exports and steel and the Glasgow–Paisley thingummy. Why are you doing that?'

'I just thought it looked interesting,' said Kate.

'Is that right?' said Heather. She was going out that evening with Gary to Dalgety's end-of-year barbecue. She had a pair of white matador pants and a red top with a boat neck. She'd seen just the shoes too, in Tremewans: white sandals with a flower on the strap across the toes.

'And it'll come in handy for teaching,' said Kate.

Or maybe the black slingbacks? Heather looked at her watch. Half an hour before the supervisor went bananas. She reapplied a slick of Frosted Peach, pursing and straightening her lips in the mirror of her compact.

'Come on,' she said. 'Help me choose.'

They went next door to Tremewans and spent the half-hour among slingbacks and t-straps. Heather surveyed her neat ankles in the floor mirror and walked up and down saying, 'What do you think?' in a pleasant agony of indecision while Kate stood by saying, 'Those make your legs look longer,' and 'Not the ankle strap,' while wondering if she did indeed want to spend a lifetime in the company of lamb exports and the Glasgow–Paisley thingummy.

She had no idea what she was going to be doing in Dunedin. In *Seventeen* magazine there were pictures of beautiful girls heading off to college with complete sets of matching luggage in madras checks, but that was America and therefore probably irrelevant. University in Dunedin would be more likely to be common rooms where brilliant chaps discussed the ultimate imponderables of human thought or delivered lectures to rooms stuffed with brainy Quiz Kids. But she could not be sure.

So when her mother suddenly offered this other opportunity, the one that required no particular effort to imagine, that would simply be an extension of the life she had lived so far, it infuriated her. How tempting to take a job at the BNZ, to go out with someone from Dalgety's, to go to barbecues and a wedding at Duntroon in a new dress. But what, then, had been the point of all the swot, of the foldout bed in the front room, of the fish that had to be eaten because it was brain food? What had been the point of the peanut biscuits? Crumbs lay like silt along the binding edge of every volume.

'Heather seems very happy,' said her mother, landing as usual with absolute precision, like a bird with needle-sharp claws, on just that spot where Kate was tender, voicing exactly that uncertainty squirming beneath the skin. It made Kate furious. It forced her to be sure.

'Of course I want to go,' she said. 'I don't want some stupid job in this stupid town.'

'It doesn't have to be a stupid job,' said her mother. 'There are plenty of opportunities here for a clever girl.'

'Not for me,' said Kate. She could hardly breathe in this room, in this house, in this street, in this town. 'I'm not staying here. I'm not going to have a horrible marriage and settle to some hideous dead-end job.'

I'm not going to be like you hung in the air between them, sharp and shimmering as the onset of a migraine.

Her mother slid the wedding photograph into the shoebox where it belonged. *Stuart, John. m. Falconer, Alice. Feb 22, 1901.* Her forehead wrinkled with concern.

'You won't go and overdo it, will you?' she says.

'No,' said Kate. 'I won't overdo it.'

'You won't swot too hard?' said her mother.

'No,' said Kate, knowing what came next.

'Because remember what happened to Tom.'

'I'll be fine,' said Kate. 'Just fine.'

'Well, if you're sure . . .' said her mother.

'YES!' said Kate. 'YES YES YES, I'm sure!'

And she slammed the door on the kitchen and went to her room where she slammed the door on the house, on the whole shoebox stuffed full of family.

16.

There was nothing in the afternoon but themselves. When she arose, he, looking on the ground all the time, saw suddenly sprinkled on the black wet beech-roots many scarlet carnation petals, like splashed drops of blood; and red, small splashes fell from her bosom, streaming down her dress to her feet.

'Your flowers are smashed,' he said.

Sons and Lovers by D.H. Lawrence

'Now,' said the tutor, flexing the Metaphysicals so that they cracked at the spine,

The foe oftimes having the foe in sight,
Is tired with standing, though they never fight.

Paraphrase, please?'

Silence. The tutorial group kept their heads down and eyes

averted. Outside on Albany Street builders were demolishing one of the old houses. The smell of dust and diesel blended with the usual Dunedin bouquet of chocolate and brewers' yeast and burnt coffee and the chill salt air off the harbour. The class were acquiring the knack of criticism. Under their scrutiny, literature fell apart into its component parts like a .303 in the hands of a bunch of cadets, until they could do it fast, eyes closed and under fire. Then they reassembled it into a kind of parallel structure in accordance with the critical principles of Leavis, with due reference to Leach or Wilson, Knight or Williams. They were learning to detect influences, constructing genealogies of literary connection as complex as the Stuart family tree: medieval to Renaissance, Renaissance to Enlightenment, Enlightenment to romantics, Edwardians and moderns. They ignored biography, other than a passing acknowledgement of Coleridge's opium-eating, which contributed no doubt to the eerie pleasure dome; or Eliot's conversion to Anglo-Catholicism, which must have contributed to the shift from the neuraesthenic despair of *The Wasteland* to the certitudes of *The Cocktail Party*; or Virginia Woolf's death by drowning, which lent poignancy to the characterisation of Clarissa Dalloway.

Under this regime Donne was no longer a dreamy wallow, but strong-lined, the subject of hour-long analysis invoking Thomas Aquinas and corruption derived from contrariety and Aristotle and Ovid and someone called Persius. Nor was it all sweet *good morrow to our waking soules* but a tougher love.

'"The foe",' said the tutor. 'Who or what is "the foe"?'

The tutor was blond and square-jawed. He was young, not one of the older lecturers who tended toward tweed jackets and brainy glasses. This tutor — Dr Brokenshire but just call me Jack — wore a frayed shirt with faded jeans and bare feet and sometimes rode a white horse along Cumberland Street among the traffic, bare-headed, bareback.

He leaned back now in tutorial room 221 and put his hands behind his head. Tufts of blond hair exploded from beneath his T-shirt. His armpits seemed tender and private, white where his skin was otherwise tanned from the wind and the rain and the horseback riding. He regarded the current crop of freshers dispassionately from behind tinted glasses. They avoided his scrutiny: the pretty ones with the pruned private-school vowels in the twinsets and camel coats; the earnest unadorned ones; Eric from Clyde who attended tutorials infrequently, preferring to read up on stocks and shares in the caf at the Student Union; Cleary who was skinny and acned and had had a poem already in *Matagouri*.

Kate had looked it up. 'Homage to Salvador Dali' was a skinny poem, the words scattered about the page like fingernail parings.

flesh slit
like vel
vet
screams
slice
sil
ence
at
the shrine

of
Our Lady
of Per
petual
suckers

Cleary said little in tutorials but she regarded him with respect on account of

flesh slit
like vel
vet.

Next to Kate sat Claudia: full-breasted with sleepy, lidded eyes. She had been in a play already, as one of the Chorus of Women in *Lysistrata*: the one who stripped to reinforce the central theme of the play, the sexuality that strove against the militarism of the men, just as love strove against the current aggression in Vietnam, as the programme note explained. Kate had wondered about auditioning for *Lysistrata*. She had dawdled past the hall in which the auditions were taking place, pretending another destination: a friend to visit nearby, perhaps. As she passed the entrance, an elderly man in a beret had emerged, together with a younger man in bike leathers.

'Well, ciao!' said the young man, snapping down the visor of his helmet. And 'Ciao!' said the older man, and the bike revved away in a fine blast of black smoke. 'Ciao!' with an accomplished casual wave of the hand. Chow? thought Kate. What's that? Chow? She had known then that she could not attempt an audition. She suspected that Madame de Correbas was no preparation for the Chorus of Athenian Women, and when she saw the ivory-smooth expanse of Claudia's naked back it was confirmed.

Claudia yawned loudly.

'So?' said Jack. 'Any takers?'

Silence.

'Delwyn?' he said.

'The man?' ventured Delwyn. Jack snapped back onto all four chair legs. He leaned across the desk.

'Don't be coy,' he said, and Delwyn, who was one of the earnest ones, a plain moon-faced girl from Tuatapere, flushed and said she wasn't being coy, and Jack sighed and said, 'So let's be more precise, shall we? Let's be a little more mature.' And Claudia yawned again and said, 'The penis. It's a penis.' Jack smiled at her and said, 'Thank you, Claudia.' Then he read the whole poem . . .

Off with that happy buske, whom I envye
That still can be, and still can stand so nigh . . .

noting the shift in pronunciation the rhyme entailed, and the puns on 'stand' and the characteristic epigrammatic structure and the imagery in which the classical has been aligned with the erotic, and the tutorial scribbled it all down, just as mature as could be. And all Kate wanted to say was, 'Why does she leave her shoes on until last? Doesn't everyone kick their shoes off first when they're getting ready for bed?' But that might have betrayed her essential immaturity. Maybe everyone in such a situation left their shoes on.

Madame stripped beneath the man's discerning gaze, line by line, her body becoming a landscape, a glimpse of Cythera, while beneath the desk a foot nudged at Kate's ankle. She moved her leg to the left. The foot followed. She looked down surreptitiously and there it was: large and bare, square calloused toes with tiny tufts of fair hair at the knuckles. The foot was not meant for her but for Claudia, of course, but what could she say? How could you point out its mistake? Better to leave it undisturbed to wander at will, while the tutorial group turned their collective attention to the 'Nocturnall Upon St Lucie's Day'.

So this was university. Not common rooms filled with pipe smoke, nor Quiz Kids. French was nihilism on the beach in Algeria, and History was Renaissance Italy, and Anthropology turned out to be slides of skulls thick and lumpy as the attempts of a novice potter before experiment and repetition refined jaw and eyebrow ridge. And excavation, proper archaeological excavation, on a tiny headland at Purakanui. The students hacked away at bracken to expose bare earth where lay no golden tombs of kings or hoards of buried silver, but the traces of cooking fires and the echo of people talking, like the keening of seabirds around the cliffs. Nothing remained of Mapoutahi but some post holes, which showed up as darker circles on exposed earth, and a single broken fish-hook, like a question mark of white bone.

English was *The Prelude*, which at first seemed like so many fusty lines found in a closed room, faintly absurd and over ornamented, their exact purpose uncertain. But in lectures the lines were taken out, dunked in cold water. Their meaning became clear. Here was a madwoman on a muddy hillside, here was a boy rowing breathless with terror over a dark lake while the mountain's vast bulk loomed and came after him. English was Dr Dalziel, another in that lineage of single academic women Kate had encountered at Waitaki, lecturing on Jane Austen. (Who else?) A little carved statue of the Virgin Mary stood like an admonitory finger on the shelves behind her desk. That year's Burns Fellow roamed the corridors like some old swagger, bearing poetry like lollies in the drooping pockets of his jacket. Kate passed him sometimes seated cross-legged beneath a tree in the park outside the museum, surrounded by pale acolytes, another grubbier version of Jesus among the children in the Rhododendron Dell.

The university was images of disorder in the natural kingdom and references to blood and fire and The Great Chain of Being; it was Grendel's mother stalking the swamp and the pilgrims riding down in that flowery spring to Canterbury and a couple of tramps hanging about talking nonsense until the beautiful boy arrived instead of Godot and Clara bending over the cowslips and Paul spilling flowers in her hair and Don Juan going on and on, like some swollen version of 'Ten Green Bottles', country after country, until you just wished, really, that he'd shut up and stop.

Huh, Dilsey said. Name ain't going to help him. Hurt him neither. Fools don't have no luck changing names. My name's been Dilsey since fore I could remember and it be Dilsey when they's long forgot me.

How come they know it's Dilsey when it's long forgot, Dilsey, Caddy said.

It'll be in the Book, honey, Dilsey said. Writ out.

The Sound and the Fury by William Faulkner

In the evenings Kate walked back along George Street looking at all the clothes she could buy if she wanted: a tartan mini-kilt, a red woollen baby-doll dress, a pair of stretch jeans with a white cord belt. She entered the shops where the clothes hung like empty skins on their hangers, like a person she could slide into if she wanted. She felt their fabric, held them against her body in the full-length mirrors while the assistants looked on, poised to strike. She tried things on, twisting to look at her changed self repeated endlessly from the front, from the sides, a new kind of self in this new skin vanishing through a long hall of diminishing mirrors, until she disappeared. Then she usually put them back. Her Albert Home money would only go so far.

She walked up York Place, to the very end, where Di sprawled in the hostel lounge smoking Sobranis and playing her guitar and Gaylene sat on the stairs knitting while she talked to her boyfriend back in Timaru, 'Yes, I love you too,' her fingers going one purl two plain and never admitting to the boys she picked up at the Cook, who rolled through her bedroom window at all hours until her room-mate said she'd rather sleep on the sofa in the lounge than spend another night with someone's boot landing on her head.

Across the hall, Philippa's door stayed firmly shut because she was desperate to get into med. She emerged at erratic hours to cook a freeze-dried chicken curry in the kitchen, leaning against the wall wearily watching the dots of green and red swell into rubbery peas and rubbery carrot. And upstairs, Sandra practised her violin — some tricky phrase, over and over, the music drumming its fingers as she waited for Gaylene to get off the phone because her boyfriend was at Lincoln and the only time she could get through to him at his hostel was around six and Gaylene knew this and was just so inconsiderate. And Maryeve, who shared the back bedroom with Kate, was peering into the mirror and trying to fix a false eyelash in place.

'Bugger and damn,' she says. The eyelash is gripped between a pair of tweezers like the caterpillar of some extravagant moth. Maryeve swears grandly and emphatically, having just emerged from ten years' pupation in the pale shell of a convent school dedicated to producing young ladies who can play the piano, ride a horse and recite selected speeches from Shakespeare. 'Bastard,' as the eyelash wriggles and glues itself to her right nostril.

She is wearing Kate's suede mini. Kate dumps her caseload of Dickens onto her bed.

'Want a hand?' she says. 'That's my skirt, by the way.'

'Yeah, but it looks better on me,' says Maryeve, which is true. She has skinnier legs. 'You can have my turtleneck, the red one. It looks better on you.'

And that is true too. Kate has bigger breasts and narrower shoulders. She grasps the eyelash firmly with the tweezers and holds it against Maryeve's eyelid, where it alights and stays put. Maryeve flutters at herself in the glass.

'Fab,' she says. 'Are you going to get changed?'

'I can't go out,' says Kate. 'I've got an essay due tomorrow.'

'Oh, bugger the essay,' says Maryeve. 'Don't be so boring. You can do your boring essay when we get back.'

'No, I won't,' says Kate. 'I'll just go to sleep.'

Maryeve is shuffling through Kate's clothes, which hang at one end of the rack by the boarded-up fireplace.

'You can have some of my diet pills,' she says. 'They'll keep you awake. You'll be brilliant.' Maryeve's pills worked like a dream. She is thin, Twiggy-thin, her eyes are bright, her energy levels are high and her essays are always on time. 'So put this on . . .' She is holding out Kate's corduroy pinafore. 'It's a bit boring but it will look all right with the turtleneck and you can have my boots if you like.' Italian boots. Soft black leather with little zips at the ankle. Dickens is waiting in her bag, reaching out to grab her shoulder with his big heavy hand. *Darkness and light, night and day. Discuss the development of this theme in Dickens' Great Expectations.* Maryeve dances the boots before her.

'They'll look good on you,' she says.

Kate takes the boots.

Because the university was also parties with the furniture stacked in the back garden under the clothesline and a crush of bodies on the stairs and in the kitchen and overflowing onto the street and there's punch in the washing machine especially for the girls, some concoction of pineapple juice and ginger ale and a couple of bottles of vodka and maybe a dash of absolute alcohol pilfered from the lab and a few lonely orange slices adrift like life-rings after a collision. The Stones are playing 'Honky Tonk Woman' and someone is leaning against the gas stove in the grease-encrusted kitchen and saying, 'But Marcuse says . . .' and someone else is saying, 'You're fulla shit, man. You know that? Fulla shit.' And the toilet door is locked and someone is thumping on it and someone has thrown up over the agapanthus by the back door and someone is leaning against the wall in the hall saying to a girl that he's seen her around and is she a model in her spare time? And someone is pouring Kate a martini in a silver shaker he is carrying in his jacket pocket and she's knocking it back because it tastes disgusting though it seems to be the drink everyone prefers at the pictures: in *Dr No* and *Breakfast at Tiffany's* they drink martinis. And within minutes the room is rolling and the floor is sliding away from her and the room is hot and the boy with the silver shaker is guiding her outside through all the people who only a few moments ago were strangers but now she loves them all. So she hugs as many as she can on the way through. And him too, the boy with the silver shaker who has such nice hair. It is curly like the skin of a newborn lamb.

'Get off,' he says, shrugging her hand aside, but it is so sweet, his hair, the way it curls. Then they're outside and she's lying under the clothesline and it is beautiful too. She had never noticed how beautiful a clothesline can be, like a web with stars pinned on to dry and someone has put on the Beatles and everyone is singing that they live in a YELLOW SUBMARINE and the ground is rising and falling like the sea and she's singing too and her voice sounds the best it has ever sounded. Then the boy is kissing her and his tongue is wet but nice, like a little fish in her mouth, and then they roll a little further on the dark grass and suddenly there is the most sickening smell and the boy is pulling away, he's sniffing, and he has the most amazing pointy nose, especially when he sniffs, and he's sitting up and saying, 'Fuck! Dog shit! I've got dog shit on my trou!' and that is the funniest thing that has happened all night.

It really is.

Kate laughs as he twists to reach the back of his trousers and then he's standing up and saying, 'What's so fucking funny?', which is even funnier, and then he's gone and she is left there, all by herself, singing under the clothesline. It's lovely out here, riding along under the web of stars, the old house set adrift and sailing off into the Dunedin dark, yellow submarine, yellow submarine . . .

'Bugger off,' says someone from the open doorway and there's Maryeve tripping on the steps and then her face is floating among the stars and she's saying, 'Come on, let's split. This party's boring. Full of pseuds.'

She gives Kate a hand to stand up. 'Upsy daisy,' she says.

Then they're walking up George Street through crowds of importunate parking meters and pushy shop-fronts and a car pulls alongside and a boy leans out and says, 'Evening, girls, nice night for an orgasm!', which is funny but Maryeve tells them to bugger off, because she's starving.

'Let's get a Chinese,' she says. So they go through the Octagon and up to Foos, which seems to be the only place open at this hour and there, serving on tables, is Jugs Creech from Oamaru, with her thin fair hair teased bouffant and her lips white as if they had been frozen and her feet in gold stiletto slides.

'Hi, Kate,' she says. 'Whatja been up to?'

'Hi, Jugs,' says Kate, and Jugs says she is not Jugs any more. She's Jade. Then she takes their order (One chow mein, Charley, and one egg and chips) and sits down to talk while they eat because her feet are killing her and the boss can like it or lump it. The place is quiet. Just a man slumped in a corner behind one of the faded pink Formica tables, his head thrown back, his mouth slung open like an empty pocket.

'One of the regulars,' says Jade. 'He just comes in to talk, really.' And she shows them a photo of her fella, who's an American sailor, called in six months ago on his way to Vietnam and he's been writing ever since. The fella is bare-chested and lean as a ferret. 'He took these of me,' adds Jugs, passing over the whole package. She leans back, eyes narrowed, smoke hissing from her pale lips, as Kate and Maryeve shuffle through the collection. Jade in a black negligee, on all fours, snarling at the camera. Jade lying on a bed, one hand tugging at the strap of her petticoat, the other resting on her crotch. Jade pouting, poking out her tongue, winking over one bare shoulder.

'He's going to send them to a magazine,' she says. 'In the States. And look!'

She holds out her left hand. She has a ring: a gold ring with an engraved eagle with ruby eyes.

'Real rubies,' she says. 'And when he gets back to America we're going to get married. In Vegas!'

The man in the corner stirs. 'Where the fuck . . .' he says. Then he slurs back to sleep.

'So I'm going to live in California!' says Jade. 'I'll be almost in Hollywood!'

Kate thinks about Jugs as they climb the hill toward York Place. Halfway up they stop to sit on the steps for a while, just sitting, looking out over the city, all its muddle contained within shining lines of longitude and latitude.

'Garnets,' says Maryeve. 'Those were garnets. They were absolutely not rubies.' She knows about such things. She has a diamond and ruby ring she inherited from her grandmother. And a pearl necklace. And a real pigskin shoulder bag. She knows the brands of cars, says she is not going to settle for anything less than a Porsche, and if you're going to marry, you might as well marry someone with money. 'They might even be just glass. Red glass.'

A motorbike revs down Princes Street and off toward St Kilda and suddenly Kate feels sad. Unbearably sad, for the yellow submarine and the gold stiletto slides and the man's open mouth and the eagle with the glass eyes. Sad for the motorbike disappearing into the dark, which is a kind of metaphor, isn't it, for all human existence, for they will all get old, won't they, and they are all just riding into the dark, aren't they? And it is just so sad, you know, so sad . . .

'Come on,' says Maryeve. 'I'm getting a cold bum.'

17.

I was to leave our village at five in the morning, carrying my little hand-portmanteau, and I had told Joe that I wished to walk away all alone. I am afraid — sore afraid — that this purpose originated in my sense of the contrast there would be between me and Joe, if we went to the coach together.

Great Expectations by Charles Dickens

Kate went back to the Albert Home for the summer. The matron had changed. The old one had been pushed over the cliff by her husband, the bald Australian. Audrey told her all about it as they cleaned the windows in the men's wing.

'I knew he was a bad lot, that one,' she said. 'But I never ever thought he'd be capable of murder.'

He had waited for a foggy winter's night, then he had followed

Matron as she went out to take Moppet for a walk, just as it was getting dark. He'd pushed her, over there, beyond the fence, and she'd fallen a hundred metres straight down. She'd have died, no doubt about it, said Audrey, except that the wet weather had brought down a slip, so she landed on a whole heap of soft clay. She had broken her shoulder but she still managed to crawl to the road, where a worker for the port company had found her on his way home and rescued her. It was lucky, because there weren't many people about. (Kate had seen that for herself: the bay was a less populous place than it had been in the days of Friendly Bay and the beachfront promenade. Oil silos occupied the land where the merry-go-round had stood, the kiosk had been demolished, the swings were broken and a grey slick like a scum of mutton fat floated on the water.) Matron had survived to lay charges and now her husband was in jail. Turned out he'd been having it off with the new cook, silly cow, never did take to her, said Audrey. Seems they'd planned the whole thing — meant to make it look like Matron tripped and fell. So the cook was in jail too.

'Best place for 'em too,' said Audrey, polishing vigorously. 'I mean to say, it's like a book, like on TV, but you never think the things you read about really happen, do you? Not here, not to people you know.' She straightened and surveyed their handiwork. The sea glittered behind clear glass, the little town was rubbed up to a brilliant sheen. 'It just goes to show,' she said. 'It just goes to show . . .'

'So what's varsity like?' said Maura. She was cutting out a dress: the pattern pieces for bodice, skirt and sleeves were pinned to a length of blue floral fabric. She still had a year of school before she took up The Opportunity.

Kate picked a piece of cotton from the floor and wound it around her little finger.

'All right,' she said.

By August, Gaylene had been pregnant to one of the boys from the Cook. She didn't know which one, nor did she appear to care much. The wages of sin had not been pain, in her case, nor agony nor leprous sores. On the contrary, her skin had cleared up overnight to a peachy bloom, her hair was a glossy fall, her breasts swelled impressively to a 36D and she never had a moment's morning sickness. She spent the final term — because the administration permitted her to stay to sit finals and she had paid her rent in advance — with her feet up on the sofa, knitting tiny white matinee jackets, her Child Development notes spread on her belly and one eye on the TV. Her parents seemed equally unperturbed. She was going back to live with them until the baby came and maybe her Timaru boyfriend would still be around, maybe not — she wasn't much bothered either way.

Philippa was twitching and wild-eyed and sobbed in her room. Di had joined a jug band and spent hours rehearsing in the cavernous cat reek of a deserted cinema in South Dunedin. Sandra's boyfriend, the aggie at Lincoln, had stopped returning her calls in August and for weeks she pounced on anyone passing her door to talk it over. She came and perched on the end of Kate's bed, repeating for the fiftieth time that he had said he loved her and they had been going to get engaged on her twenty-first birthday and their parents knew and everything — it was practically official — and she'd actually looked out this dress in a magazine, a white sheath in off-white Thai silk, and his sister was going to be the bridesmaid in pink, and why would he change his mind, just like that, when everything was organised? Maryeve had decided to chuck it all in and become an air hostess. That way she could fly around the world and meet people who weren't boring like the people in New Zealand but had some style.

Maura carefully cut out a neck facing. Scrunch scrunch scrunch.

'Is that all?' she said. 'It's just "all right"?'

'Yeah,' said Kate. 'It's hard to explain.'

Her mother had not asked. She had simply made a quick scrutiny of Kate as she walked in the door and said she was looking peaky and had she been overdoing it? She made chicken for tea: Sunday food, Christmas food, as a special token to mark her return.

Her father had thumbed through all her books, except for the Dickens. He couldn't stand Dickens.

'But *Great Expectations* is a classic,' said Kate. 'You'd like it if you tried.'

'Tried him,' he said. 'He's overrated. Calling a book a classic is just a way of selling it to people who don't know what they like for themselves.' He seemed disappointed in the university for not being more adventurous, for not constantly re-evaluating the canon. He reached over to the table beside his chair, wincing with the effort. 'Now this,' he said, fumbling the top volume from the pile, 'is a great book. Have you read this? *The Tin Drum*? I'd take this any day over your Dickens.'

He became animated when he talked in the day, but at night they heard the muttered argument conducted without ceasing with whatever it was that had him pinned down there in the front bedroom.

The house seemed smaller, darker than she remembered. There were those faded patches on the hall, worn from years of leaks and buckets. They depressed her more than she could say, and the loose handle on the fridge still jammed your fingers if you weren't paying proper attention, and the back door rattled mightily then flew open in a southerly as if something had entered unannounced, unless a knife had been shoved into the jamb to keep it shut. On Mondays the washing machine went chunka chunka chunka and the iron went thump hiss thump hiss every Tuesday and there were still fish and chips every Friday, though it was no longer strictly necessary post-Vatican Two. Kate stayed out as long as she could, worked every shift available, and when she had to be home she vanished between the covers of whatever books lay around.

'Mm-hmm,' she'd answer if her mother said she was just popping out to post a letter and could Kate keep an eye on the potatoes. 'Mm-hmm,' but not really hearing, not really there. Miles away, with her head in a book. When she did emerge she was irritable. 'What? Why didn't you say? No, I didn't hear you.' The potatoes burnt black, gone to cinders in a ruined pot. She wanted the irritation, the argument, the raised voices and slammed doors. She invited them in. They made her feel separate.

Their mother insisted upon a holiday before Kate returned to Dunedin. One last holiday together as a family.

'A what?' said Kate.

But their mother was determined. They would go on holiday — and not just to the Power Board's crib at Hakataramea. No. They would go to Takaka, where she had spent a holiday once before the war with her friend Rita McIvor from Public. They'd been about the age Kate was now. They had saved all their money and gone by train. They had stayed at Takaka with some cousins, connections on the Stuart side, who had a marble bath in which a Duke of Gloucester had washed his royal body on some visit to the dominion. Rita was so impressed! They'd had baths every night, just to say they'd done it. And they had visited a spring, she said, with water so pure they could dive down and from under the water they had looked up and could see every star. It was the purest water in the world. And there was an old lady, she said, who fed eels with a silver spoon. Oh, she said. It was just wonderful. Takaka was just wonderful. They had to see it for themselves. She would drive, so Pat would be comfortable in the front seat.

So there they were, for definitely, absolutely the last time, crammed in with bags and bedding and cake tins filled with bacon-and-egg pie and afghans 'for the trip' in the back of the new Triumph Herald, which had been specially adapted so that Pat could drive it the mile or so to the office. With interminable slowness they chugged up the Main North Road past Timaru (*Look, look, there's Caroline Bay*), through Christchurch (*Aren't the gardens lovely? It's called the Garden City, of course. When Rita and I were here, the daffodils were out, and you should have seen them: all along the banks of the Avon. It was such a picture . . .*) Along the road past Kaikoura. (*Keep an eye out for seals. We saw three seals here, right there, on that corner, just lying there like a lot of old dogs . . . oh, there's one. No . . . No . . . that's just a rock, but it could easily be a seal.*) To Blenheim. (*My mother's second cousins lived in Blenheim before they went off to Rhodesia. They were Grants and none of the children married, wasn't that strange? Not one . . .*) To Takaka. (*Thank goodness the road's tarsealed, such an improvement, though these curves are still terrible, aren't they? You all right in the back? Not feeling sick? I've got some barley sugars. Go on, have a barley sugar . . .*)

Paddock and beach edged past, slowly, slowly. Their father sat with a book open on his lap, hardly speaking at all. Maura had the window permanently wound down so that everything flapped and blew about, but she would otherwise be sick. She was never sick in the Holden when Bazza or Crooksey skidded out to Kakanui, but here, knees jammed between sleeping bags and boxes, the temperature edging toward the mid-thirties, she was overwhelmed with nausea. Kate's elbow strayed over the centre line drawn invisibly between them.

'Get off,' said Maura.

'Get off yourself,' said Kate. So much for maturity.

They tried to find the house with the Duke of Gloucester's bath, driving down one winding gravel road after another.

'I'm sure it was around here,' said their mother, peering hopefully through some scrappy macrocarpas.

'Why don't you ring?' said Kate. 'Won't they be in the phone book?'

'I don't want to be a nuisance,' said their mother. 'They'll be old now. Leonard would be . . . what . . . in his eighties? They'll just go to a lot of trouble if we ring in advance, making afternoon tea and whatnot. They were very hospitable people. We'll just drive past and if they're home, maybe we'll drop in and say hello. It'll be here somewhere. Let's just have another look at that map . . .'

A farmer approached them on a bike, dogs surfing the switchbacks with their ears folded back by the wind on the rear carrier.

'You people looking for someone?' he said from a cloud of white dust.

'The Stuarts,' said their mother. 'Their house is around here somewhere, isn't it?'

The dogs had leapt from the bike and were sniffing at the strangers.

'Lenny's place?' said the farmer.

'That's right,' said their mother. 'Leonard.'

'Had a stroke,' said the farmer. 'Years ago now. Gettouttathat, Blue. Went up to Masterton to his daughter. Don't know if he's still alive.'

'And the house?' said their mother.

'Burnt,' said the farmer. 'To the ground.'

They found it finally. A rim of blackened stone foundation blocks, a couple of chimney stacks standing like exclamation points at the end of an overgrown drive of tangled monkeypuzzle trees. They wandered about kicking at bits of brick, some twisted metal. By the fence an old bath stood under a tangle of rusted wire and dry grass. Their mother dragged at the mess.

'This might be it,' she said. 'Yes. I'm practically sure . . .'

'I thought you said it was a marble bath,' said Kate. She was hot. Thistles scratched at her bare legs. 'That's not marble. It's porcelain.' Her mother straightened up. She looked around at the bare foundations, the gargle of magpies overhead.

'Such a shame,' she said. 'Such a shame.'

There was a sign at the spring where the purest water in the world burst from a crevice in the earth. It forbade swimming, along with fires, dogs and camping. There was a track instead leading to a viewing platform and a special place where you could stand and look through a glass partition at the pond life, all identified in silhouette for the information of visitors.

They watched the bubbles of perfect water rise in shining columns to burst on the surface above waving tendrils of pond weed.

'But you can't see the stars any more,' said their mother. An eel unfurled from right to left like a grey pennant waving. Its eye passed them by. A steel stud.

'Oh, what a shame,' she said. 'I wanted you to see the stars.'

And there was a sign on the gate where the lady fed the tame eels, saying that for Personal Reasons, a Family Bereavement, the feeding of the eels was cancelled that week. Kate shrugged. It was raining, a sudden drenching cloudburst that flooded the road and left the car stuffy with condensation.

'I wouldn't want to get soaked just to look at a whole lot of fish anyway,' she said.

Her mother turned to her a bright, desperate face.

'But it is so wonderful,' she said. 'Like something from a fairy-tale. The lady sits by the river and the eels lie across her feet. She feeds them cat meat and blancmange. You can hear the scraping of their teeth on the spoon.'

It did sound interesting, but Kate pushed the momentary flicker of regret to one side. She wiped a clear space in the fog and looked moodily out the window. She wanted this holiday to be a disaster. She wanted it to be completely and totally awful. She wanted shops to be shut and roads to be impassable and camping grounds to be noisy. She wanted it to be so bad that no one could ever say she should go on such a holiday again.

And finally it was over. The holiday was at an end and Kate could climb onto the train at the beginning of a new term. She could sit alone looking out the window like the mysterious woman on some enigmatic mission on the Oriental Express. She could view the waves at Katiki and think how beautiful they were without prompting, while strangers glanced at her and wondered if she harboured some deep and secret sorrow. She could thunder through the tunnels around Purakanui and burst at last into the harbour where the clock on the church at Port Chalmers pointed the time north, south, east and west.

18.

What is a course of history? Or philosophy, or poetry, no matter how well selected, or the best society, or the most admirable routine of life, compared with the discipline of looking always at what is to be seen? Will you be a reader, a student merely, or a seer? Read your fate, see what is before you, and walk on into futurity.

I did not read books the first summer; I hoed beans.

Walden; or, Life in the Woods by Henry D. Thoreau

The books became a flood. Tamburlaine shouting, Edward screaming, both the Richards, II and III. Cleopatra gliding on her gilded barge, Romeo and Juliet growing cold within the tomb, *Twelfth Night*, *The Winter's Tale* and a couple of dozen sonnets.

Kate stood in the path of it all, trying to maintain her balance. There was the business of discovering what exactly it was that was funny about Bartholomew Cokes and his Numps, and what exactly it was that was serious about the crash site at the end of *The White Devil*.

There were the Americans. A trio of lecturers all rumoured to be Quakers in revolt against conscription and Vietnam had come ashore and established a kind of beachhead before the British canon with *The Scarlet Letter* and *Moby-Dick* and *Huckleberry Finn*, big books with expansive rolling prairies of verbiage, rolling oceans of prose. There was Benjy slobbering by the golf course and Whitman beating his individual drum and Robert Frost pausing in a yellow wood and Eugene's catalogue of the south: *musty cotton baled and piled under long sheds of railway sidings; and odorous pine woodland of the level South saturated with brown faery light* . . . And *Walden*, which performed that trick of being simultaneously a kingdom in virgin bush and a domestic pond with a railway line jagged across one border.

There was *Troilus and Criseyde* and Bacon's *Essays* and *The Pilgrim's Progress* and *Gulliver's Travels*, which was not after all a story for children but bleak and full of fury. And in a cell alongside the Houyhnhnms blessed with reason and the bestial Yahoos lay St Margaret struggling with the devil, and outside, stalking the moorland, the shaggy figure of the Wanderer, and the Seafarer fearful of that soft dawn where the sword slips beneath the heart like a lover. *That passed away. This also may.*

There was Spenser going on and on about the Faerie Queene and that interminable quest until you just wished he would stop. Just SHUT UP and STOP!

But it was all right after all, because that year, Kate fell in love.

He was tall and wore thick black-rimmed glasses and he had the most beautiful hands Kate had ever seen. Broad in the palm with long slender fingers. They were what she noticed first when she sat beside him for the first read-through of *The Duchess of Malfi*. He was with his mates: the stocky one whose name was Mack who was going to be Antonio, and the thin one with the floppy brown hair, like the picture of the young Wordsworth on the cover of her *Collected Works*, who was called Gowdie and who was going to be the Cardinal. The tall one — Steve — was a Gentleman of the Court. He spoke rapidly and quietly so that it was necessary to concentrate. And as he spoke he prodded the air in curiously awkward gestures as if there were some distance from brain to fingers and they operated with a degree of independence. Kate noticed this, though she was concentrating on the text because she had offered to be prompt. She looked at the text, marking changes and cuts as the director suggested, but seeing always to her left, the hand spread on the knee, sensing the restless jittery energy of him.

She met him next morning in the library. He appeared without warning around the corner of the 821s.

There is the muted sound of people talking at their desks beyond the shelves, the whispery stillness of book row upon row, all their words hushed between covers; there is the smell of old paper, and old glue and a whiff of chip fat from the Student Union cafeteria next door. He walks toward her and when he sees her he makes a little ducking movement with his head as if he might slip sideways down the long aisle between the eighteenth and the nineteenth centuries. But he decides against it almost immediately and continues toward her instead and she for her part walks toward him and they say 'Hi!' as they pass. She does not drop her books in charming confusion, nor does she regard him with eyes heavy with wonder and celandines in her hair as his gaze penetrates to the very soul of her being. But there is a kind of quivering in the air after he has passed, like dust motes jittering in the sunlight through the high windows by the 821s.

At rehearsal that evening, Steve stood near her while Claudia, who was the Duchess, rehearsed the closet scene with Antonio.

She could feel him arrive behind her, standing a metre or so back, watching from the darkened auditorium. She did not need to turn to know he was there. That same quivering accompanied him, running its fingers the length of her spine, so that she was simultaneously following the text and watching the play and listening to that quiet voice at her back. Jack was blocking the scene.

'Bring me the casket hither, and the glass . . .' says Claudia, walking across stage, and — 'No, no, no,' says Jack. 'You are preparing for bed,' he says. 'You are about to go to bed with your lover.'

'Yes?' says Claudia. 'So?'

'So, you move down right,' says Jack. 'To the chair . . . over . . . here.' He places his hands on her shoulders to guide her to the correct place. 'To your dressing table, here.' And he drags a table before her. 'Where you seat yourself,' he says, 'flirtatiously. No — not like that. More languidly. In anticipation of the pleasures of the night to come . . .'

Steve has moved a little closer to Kate's chair. He is right behind her now, talking in a whisper to his mate the Cardinal.

'You get no lodging here tonight,' says Claudia.

'And you . . . Mack . . . Antonio . . . will sit . . .' Jack guides Mack into place, '. . . here.' Mack sits. 'Not like that,' says Jack. 'You're an aristocrat, remember? You are in your mistress's chamber, your wife's chamber. You look like you're having trouble taking a crap.' Jack waits for the laughter. Mack leans back, legs spread. He takes a car key from his jeans pocket and spins it, he smiles a slow smile; he could be Paul Newman, he could be Hud.

I must lie here, he says.

'Not sure about the keys,' says Jack, 'but otherwise fine. Terrific. Now the two lovers begin to spar with each other. Claudia?'

But Claudia is already teasing. She lets Cariola dress her hair while she keeps her back to Antonio. She bends her neck and the glossy fall of her hair catches the light.

My lord, says Cariola, the plain earnest student from Kate's tutorial group, *I lie with her often: and I know she'll much disquiet you.* Claudia has given her her comb as a prop.

'Don't turn your back on the audience, Delwyn,' says Jack. 'And use your upstage hand to comb with.'

'But it's really hard because I'm left-handed,' says Delwyn, fumbling with the comb.

'See, you are complain'd of,' says Mack. The comb catches a tangle in Claudia's thick, curling hair.

'For she's the sprawling'st bedfellow,' says Delwyn, tugging.

'Ow!' says Claudia and 'Masking!' says Jack. 'Delwyn! You're masking the Duchess! Move left.'

'I shall like her the better for that,' says Mack, and in one smooth move he has taken the comb from the maid's hand and is combing Claudia's hair himself.

'Hang on, Mack,' says Jack. 'Let's just stick to the blocking as I've got it here.' He has it all set out in dozens of tiny diagrams in the margins of his script. He frowns.

Mack draws the comb slowly through the thick fall of Claudia's hair. It fizzes with static electricity and clings to his hands.

'But I think that's what he'd do,' he says. 'He'd take over without her knowing, just to tease her, eh?'

'But I've got you crossing later, for the kiss,' says Jack.

'But we could do the kiss like this,' says Mack and he lays aside the comb. He turns to Claudia. 'You say, *I'll stop your mouth.*'

'I'll stop your mouth,' repeats Claudia. And then she turns and reaches up. She draws Mack toward her and she kisses him. A long and languid kiss. The kiss of a woman anticipating the pleasures of the night to come. Antonio puts his arms about her.

'And then,' he says, 'I embrace her and say, *Nay, that's but one, Venus had two soft doves to draw her chariot. I must have another.* And I kiss her too.' And he kisses Claudia. A kiss such as Paul

233

Newman might deliver. The hall is quiet, watching.

'I'm not sure about that,' says Jack. 'I think it's fiddly. It would be better if he approached her like this . . .' And he demonstrates, walks upstage, turns, crosses to the dressing table, sweeps Claudia into his arms. She breaks free.

'No,' she says. 'It doesn't feel as good. What Mack's doing feels more natural.'

'Okay,' says Jack. He's annoyed. 'What do the rest of you think?'

'I like the hair combing,' says the Cardinal.

'Me too,' says Delwyn. 'It's awfully hard with your right hand if you're left-handed.'

Jack sighs. 'All right,' he says. 'We'll keep the hair combing. Now . . .'

Steve is seated next to Kate. She looks up at him.

'Hi,' he says. His arm brushes her bare skin. She lets it lie there, every tiny hair prickling against his.

When I wax grey, I shall have all the court
Powder their hair with arras, to be like me:
You have cause to love me, I ent'red you into my heart.
Before you would vouchsafe to call for the keys.

The Duchess of Malfi by John Webster

The cast party was red paper glued about a bare lightbulb above a contemplative buzz of people who sprawled on cushions and carpet at Claudia's flat on London Street. Someone had produced a couple of joints. Marijuana. The real thing. A skimpy blue cloud smelling of burnt cabbage hung over the ladies and gentlemen of the court as they passed the joint from hand to hand, breathing 'Far out' and 'Good weed', as if they had been practising the lines for months and had simply been waiting for the authentic props to arrive. Kate did her best to inhale without coughing, then with watering eyes lay back waiting for something to happen. A blast of euphoria, or sudden enlightenment or something, anything. Her nose seemed to have gone completely numb. Around her, the courtiers smoked and drank Asti Spumante from an assortment of Marmite jars and coffee mugs. They laughed. They smiled at one another: Bosola and Ferdinand, the Duchess and all the other inhabitants of that dog kennel that had been the court of Malfi. They were all a little in love with one another, though the play was over, dwindled to a little point, a kind of nothing. The bodies had piled up, stabbed and strangled.

That was the most difficult part: making the deaths authentic.

'It's the major challenge of this play,' Jack had said at the first rehearsal. 'We have to work on making death *real*.' Even so, on several nights there had been muted giggles from the audience as Bosola killed the Cardinal and Ferdinand killed Bosola and Bosola in his death throes managed to kill Ferdinand. But now the dark symbolic set with its black cubes of pinex had been dismantled, the hall had been cleared and all that carefully choreographed tragedy was the stuff of memory.

'*Help, help, help I am slain!*' said Mack in a squeaky falsetto and they laughed: they fell about laughing as he collapsed at Claudia's side. He was good at dying. His was commonly voted the best death by far, with a twitching kick, a gargling of blood in the mouth, and the final touch: a trickle of red dye from a capsule he had concealed in his hand until the right moment, when he transferred it to his teeth and snapped it in two. He lay by Claudia, with whom he was now living: unofficially, of course, though he had admitted it publicly at the Live-in at the Student Union to protest against the ban on mixed flatting.

'A standard morality is being imposed upon individuals capable

235

of making their own decisions about where and with whom they want to live,' he had declaimed to a room crammed with outrage. 'In Berkeley they demand free speech on campus! We demand the freedom to live where we please! In Selma Alabama, Blacks demanded their civil rights. We demand the civil right to live with whoever we please! The Accommodation Officer has no place in the student bedrooms of this city! I will live where I want to and I will live with the woman I love!' The audience applauded, they cheered. 'Right on!' they yelled as he took Claudia's hand and raised it, as if together they had entered some arena. James K. Baxter had followed with a lengthy ode about mixed flatting and 'dipping his wick' in a flat on Castle Street, but it was Mack's declaration that earned the standing ovation. It was the most thrilling and romantic moment Kate had ever witnessed. She had leapt to her feet in her sleeping bag and cheered with the rest.

So far, the university administration had not risen to Mack's challenge. The citizens of Malfi sprawled about the illicit flat, arms flung comfortably around one another. They had become a kind of family, formed by the play, as if they had indeed survived some tragedy, come through it together. They called themselves the Malfiosi. Then someone put on some music and they all danced. 'GLORIA,' they sang. 'GLORIA,' jumping up and down until the house piles shuddered. And sometime late, just before the night coloured to twilight and dawn, they began to find coats and scarves, they looked for their shoes beneath the cushions, they hugged one another in the hall, they said, 'It's been fantastic, you were fantastic,' and a little unevenly they drifted off home. A police siren spiralled the length of George Street and hand in hand, Steve and Kate walked back to his flat.

1. Off with that girdle

A villa on Clyde Street. BSA bike in pieces in the hall, a room with an old door on trestles doubling as a table, an anglepoise like a heron bent over a pool of light, a plaster garland of ivy about the distant scotia, coal dust on the carpet and on wrinkled sheets.

2. Unpin that spangled brest-plate that you weare.

The glow of a street lamp behind sagging drapes. The thud of the front door as flatmates return from the lab at 4am, a record turning on the spindly-legged record player. 'Bluebeard's Castle,' says Steve. 'Fantastic, isn't it?' Ping, bong, zing in an apparently random series of notes. It is like no other music she has ever heard. His hand strokes the long curve of her back, brushes across her breasts, the long fingers run rings around her nipples.

3. Off with that happy buske

The unzipping and unbuttoning, the unleashing of belt buckle and the undoing of shoelaces, the stretch of elastic and of nylon, the unpeeling of tights and socks, the fumble at fastenings. The texture of new skin, its hair black where hers is fair, thick where hers is sparse, curly where hers is straight.

4. Off with your wyrie coronet and show

The sour-sweet smell of the body's crevices, the pleated press of lips, the curious muscular motion of the tongue, the taste of sweat, the chest with its rack of bone beneath taut skin, the tender spaces at the back of the neck, the crook of the arm, the ankle, the wrist, the curve of the sole of the foot, the curl of the ear, the soft round bud of the lobe.

5. That hairy diadem that on you doth grow.

The press of bone, the small bruises left on thigh or forearm, the indentations at either side of a man's spine above the hip bone, the hands stroking, squeezing, pressing, the hard plate of shin bone, knee opening knees, the prodding of the penis, the weight of a man, the stretching of the body to take him, to absorb him, the light from the street making him a dark silhouette, the rushing of blood within the ears, the voice moaning and it is her voice making sounds it has not heard before, not pain though they sound like pain. And there is something delicate and deep within her stretched to bursting and then it breaks and she is released to crying out and the blood comes, not much, just enough to leave a stain like a moth's wing on grubby linen.

6. Off with those shoes; and then safely tread
In this love's hallow'd temple, this soft bed.

And when they went to bed that night, and on all the nights after, they always kicked their shoes off first.

19.

. . . a glorious time,
A happy time that was; triumphant looks
Were then the common language of all eyes;
As if awaked from sleep, the Nations hailed
Their great expectancy: the fife of war
Was then a spirit-stirring sound indeed,
A black bird's whistle in a budding grove.

The Prelude by William Wordsworth

Steve's brother got arrested up in Wellington, scaling the fence into the American embassy.

Ho Ho Ho Chi Minh!

Dunedin was less fortunate in that it had no embassies. They marched anyway, down to the Octagon where they gathered, for want of anywhere better, between the Star Fountain squirting jets of coloured water in time to the Beautiful Blue Danube, and the statue of Robbie Burns. Mack and the other organisers occupied the plinth and addressed the crowd.

'This war is a war of national identity! It is not, as the media would have us believe, a kind of holy war between two powerful ideologies: communism versus capitalism! The NLF is fighting a war of liberation, and history shows us that such wars will never be won by the invader. We demand an immediate end to the bombing of Vietnam!'

'YES!' yells the crowd beneath the thoughtful gaze of the Scottish bard.

'We demand the immediate withdrawal of New Zealand troops from Vietnam!'

'YES!' yells the crowd with even greater fervour.

'We demand an end to WAR!'

'YES!' yells the crowd, and the shout sends the pigeons roosting on the ornate nineteenth-century corbels of the town hall into flurried flight.

'What's happening, dear?' asks a woman outside Arthur Barnett's with her string bag full of shopping as they pause momentarily on the march back down George Street, homemade banners buckling in a brisk southerly. 'Is it Procesh?' She looks hopefully up George Street for the comical floats, the Maidenform Brass Band hooting and thumping.

'It's a demonstration,' says Kate. 'Against the war?' she adds as the woman looks puzzled.

'Oh,' says the woman. 'Well, you've got a nice day for it.'

Hey hey LBJ, how many kids did you kill today?

The crowd straggles off toward the Student Union for Forum and songs by members of the folk club.

'I'm not saying that US policy in Vietnam is good. (*So what are you saying?*) Bombing is definitely immoral but Thomas Aquinas in the *Doctrine of the Just War* (*Thomas who? What the fuck would he know?*) says that an aggressor must be fought by such means that will result in the lesser evil. (*Who's the aggressor here? It's their country for God's sake! Thomas Aquinas is talking a load of CRAP!*) And let's not forget the US is in Vietnam because it was invited in by the South Vietnamese government (*By their South Vietnamese stooges, you mean!*) And New Zealand forces are there because we have military obligations to our allies. I mean, it's all very well to preach pacifism but who's going to rescue us when the dominoes start falling, eh? (*Ah, siddown, you fascist prick!*)

Then Di from York Place and an earnest young man sporting a prematurely patriarchal beard asked how many times the cannon-balls had to fly, the chords strumming from D to G to D, the harmonica wailing.

Her father approved.

'Good on you,' he said. '*All that is required for evil to triumph is that good men do nothing!* Remember? That's what Burke said and he was damn right.' He'd had a go himself back in the thirties when things got tough. Same old story: government and big business and the press and all the rest of the bastards hammering away at the working man, trying to wreck the unions, which were the only thing standing between civilisation and the jungle. By uniting, the working class had won back in 1935: got decent housing, health care, education, all the things that had got them to where they were today. All the things that had contributed to creating the uniquely fortunate lives of Kate and Maura. All the things that had blessed them with The Opportunity.

'They were back again in force in '51, of course,' he said. 'But they'll never be able to turn history around completely. So you lot get stuck in with your demonstrations.'

He pats her on the shoulder awkwardly with his buckled hand.

'You take them on, the Americans and that nincompoop

Holyoake. (Hand us my cigarettes, will you?) "Kiwi Keith"! The man who said he'd educated himself walking barefoot behind the plough reading Charles Dickens' *Origin of Species*! Charles Dickens! Can you believe it?'

He fumbles with a cigarette, fits it between his lips.

'The man's not fit to run a raffle, let alone a country.'

The cigarette jiggles as he reaches for a match.

'Men for Mutton, that's what it is, pure and simple.'

He winces as he tries to strike a match, so Kate reaches over and does it for him. He inhales deeply, eyes narrowed.

'If I weren't laid up here, I'd come down and join you and get stuck in myself.'

Mr Leopold Bloom ate with relish the inner organs of beasts and fowls. He liked thick giblet soup, nutty gizzards, a stuffed roast heart, liver slices fried with crustcrumbs, fried hencod's roes. Most of all he liked grilled mutton kidneys that gave to his palate a fine tang of faintly scented urine.

Ulysses by James Joyce

Once a week Steve and Mack and Gowdie ate not at the Student Union caf where everyone queued for chips, but at the Alhambra across the park. The Alhambra had menus in red plastic covers and the Maryland Fried Chicken arrived with a pineapple ring attached to the crumb coating, beetroot carved in crinkles and a radish shaped like a rosebud on top.

Steve was at ease in such sophisticated surroundings, just as he knew about not clapping in the middle of concerts. He had taken Kate to hear an orchestra, the first time she had ever heard one where the strings easily outnumbered the brass and were not there to accompany someone singing 'Some Enchanted Evening'. The hall was strangely silent: no rustle of lollies, no programmes with photos of the performers listing their off-stage hobbies and occupations (*Greer Polson (Dolores) works in the offices of G.T. Gillies. Hobbies include ballroom dancing and taxidermy!*) The volume of the orchestra was equally astonishing with no handy switch to turn it down. They were seated near the cellos and basses and the sound thrummed beneath their feet and up through every bone to resonate about the heart. It was marvellous. When the first piece had crescendoed to a conclusion, Kate clapped. Steve placed his hand quickly over hers. 'Two more movements,' he whispered. Nobody else had moved a muscle. Then fortunately, the orchestra stepped off into the theme from *Elvira Madigan*: Swedish fields, leafy lanes, the beautiful circus acrobat, the lovesick young officer.

'I liked that,' she said as they walked back to the flat on Clyde Street. But Steve said it was ho-hum, the usual stuff — Mozart, Tchaikovsky — and when would New Zealand orchestras ever perform anything from the twentieth century? Anything at all: Copeland would do if they couldn't quite stretch to Berg or Webern. Steve knew about concerts because his mother played the piano on the radio in Invercargill. Steve knew when to clap at concerts, just as he knew about foreign films that had subtitles and were generally in black and white and about virgins being raped or women going mad on Swedish islands inhabited by dwarfs or Italian circus freaks or Spaniards experiencing visions of the Virgin. Kate sat in the dark watching a horse's eyeball being cut in painful and exquisite close-up. No intermission, no Nibble Nook, no Hollywood twinkle. She sat hand in hand with Steve and afterwards was able to discuss quite dispassionately the technique by which one director had achieved a greater degree of authenticity and impact in his depiction of human pain, or death or suffering, than another. She was able to sit with absolute maturity as one of the segregated all-women audience that the censor decreed, watching Leopold Bloom considering *the dark tangled curls of his bush floating, floating hair of the stream around the limp father of thousands, a languid floating flower . . .*

'I wouldn't exactly compare it to a water-lily,' she said afterwards. They were lying in the vast claw-foot bath in Steve's flat, discussing the central issues amid clouds of swirling steam. 'An orchid maybe . . .' Steve was rubbing lemon-scented soap into her foot and washing it off, separating each toe. 'Or a snapdragon . . .'

She could feel his feet pressed against her sides beneath the warm water. Condensation dripped frog-plop from the clouded ceiling. The skin of his feet was tender and hairless below the ankle bone and the second toes crossed slightly over the third toes because of the small shoes he had to wear as a child when his feet began to grow at a great rate and new shoes cost a fortune. She loved the little mound of the anklebone, the ticklish sole. The candle sent their shadows slipping around the misty walls. *And his heart was going like mad and yes I said yes I will yes . . .*

The Alhambra was peaceful, even when crammed with people eating their Maryland Chicken. A guitar played music she now recognised as being by Albeniz, probably performed by John Williams. She knew such things now: she could identify the strange fluting of the countertenor in the Deller Consort and the rich malt of Janet Baker singing Bach oratorios and Fischer-Dieskau singing Mahler. She had been learning them, LP by LP, as she sprawled on Steve's bed, dawdling before the re-emergence into the world beyond that small room. The music formed its intricate lacery of sound about the Alhambra, notes splashing into the gardens of the earthly paradise. The student caf was strident with law students making their pitch for a position on Exec, but here at the Alhambra, Steve and Gowdie and Mack were engaged in more subversive business. They collaborated each week on a satirical column for the student newspaper: *Proctorscope! The Column that Gets Right to the Heart of the Matter!*

All over the city, smoke has risen this week from bonfires lit by rioting students demanding the right to cohabitation. 'Give us Bread!' 'Free Speech!' 'Sink More Piss!' are the slogans heard on every side . . .

Inflammatory student activist Fritz Weatherby, long banned from the Otago Campus, may be attempting to smuggle himself back into Dunedin. Known and dreaded for his uncompromising stance on anything at all, he is believed to have changed his name to Amos the King . . .

The University Council has appointed as Generalissimo Morass Jell, with a mandate to quell dissent and restore the Duke of Edinburgh to his role as our leader by Divine Right . . .

They wrote parodic letters to the *Otago Daily Times* and the *Listener*:

like the soaring lines of St Peter's Basilica in Rome and the Wellington Chief Post Office, they remind me curiously — and strangely (mirabile dictu) — of the je ne sais quoi of Nachsichtigkeit evident to the sensitive listener in the 1916 volume of Debussy's Prelude, so movingly rendered by an unnamed pianist of Radio Free China last night. You might inquire what the hell this has to do with music in New Zealand; I would reply, taking a stand with Goethe, who first said, I believe, 'Der Mensch muss denken . . .

Bruce Mason and his music criticism were fair game. He was pretentious; he aped English manners and an English accent; he was *old*.

Steve and Mack and Gowdie did not stand for pretension. They aspired to robust simplicity. Steve's dad was a cabinetmaker, Gowdie's was a wharfie out at the port and Mack's dad worked at the railway workshops.

'Consider, if you will,' boomed Mack over the Maryland Chicken, 'tea Pie-ringer!'

The table at the Alhambra was a centre from which the assault on all that was phoney could be planned and executed.

The first time Kate went with Steve to the Alhambra the place was crowded. Gowdie looked up as they came in.

'Dobbo!' he said, 'You're late, you bastard.'

There were only three chairs at their table. They had never previously needed a fourth.

'Hang on, I'll get another chair from out the back,' said Maria, who ran the place. She returned a few moments later with a kitchen chair, which she handed over the heads of the other diners. ''Scuse me, scuse me, sorry about this . . .', the heads of strangers ducking over their plates while Gowdie and Mack waited to resume their conversation. Kate felt herself sweating with embarrassment, until at last she was seated, back safely against a corner wall, thighs straddled about a table leg. She had never eaten in such a place before, where you picked the food from a menu rather than directly from a glass case with lamingtons and sausage rolls lined up for the taking.

'Have the chicken,' said Steve, casually, as if choosing were easy.

'Brokenshire hasn't read the whole thing, I'm sure of that,' said Gowdie, jabbing his fork into a crumbed drumstick. 'Ten bucks he'll fall for it.'

They were composing a fake essay supposedly from a second-year student about a non-existent canto of *The Faerie Queene*.

'How about a temple called "The House of the Seven Earthly Delights"?' said Mack.

'On the "Isle of Deliria",' said Steve.

'Yeah, yeah!' said Gowdie, delighted. 'That'll be where Artegal shags Lascivia.'

'How'll we sign it?' said Mack. All essays had to have a name in the top right-hand corner.

'Put Donkin's name on it,' said Gowdie. Donkin was running

for student president. He was clean-cut, private school and belonged to SCM. He was an off-the-peg, fully assembled, ready-made joke.

'You could tear off one corner,' said Kate. 'Like, rumple it, make it look like it's been stuffed in a bag or something.'

They looked at her. They seemed surprised to find her there.

'Yeah,' said Mack. 'That'd work.'

Gowdie scribbled something illegible. 'See?' he said. '"D.J. Donkin". But you can hardly read it. That'd do.' He hadn't heard what she had said.

'Tear off one corner,' said Mack. 'It's less obvious.'

Gowdie underlined the signature. 'Donkin's got it coming to him, the cunt.'

Steve glanced at Kate. 'Bastard' was unremarkable, or 'prick' or 'wanker'. 'Fuck' was a slight risk. But 'cunt' was pushing it. There was a slight pause as they listened to the word land. It sounded like a slap.

'Donkin and Brokenshire in one hit,' said Gowdie. 'Think about it.'

The vote went for tearing off one corner. Steve was pleased with her contribution.

But Gowdie had not glanced once in her direction, and when they parted, Mack and Gowdie heading north toward the Cook and a quick beer before classes, Steve and Kate heading south toward Clyde Street, it felt as if something had been broken.

After that, Steve did not always go to the Alhambra on Tuesdays. Sometimes he bought a dozen oysters at Joe Tui's and cooked his one speciality at the flat: oyster soup. In Invercargill they ate such food as a matter of routine. He and Kate sat with their feet curled around the rickety chair legs in the kitchen eating broth tasting of the sea and the salt air blowing in from the Antarctic over the wide stretches of Oreti, and after they had wiped their bowls clean he took her hand and they walked down the hall among the motorbike parts, over the puddles of oil on the flowery mead of the Axminster to his room.

'Have we got time?' she asked.

He kissed her.

'Always,' he said. 'For this.'

She was on the pill so it was safe. There was no risk of pregnancy, no fear of the furtive trip to Christchurch, the bloody knitting needle, no fear that she might end up as the body beneath the packing case in some sordid garage in Hornby. No risk either of the brisk engagement, the speedy wedding with the luxuriant bouquet of lilies held before the spreading waistline. No risk of the sudden change of plan, the job up north, the lone journey to some home in Wellington where she would peel potatoes with the illegitimate mothers on one side of the corridor for the dinners of the legitimate mothers whose rooms occupied the opposite, sunnier side. No risk of the child handed over to strangers, the bound breasts, all secretions suppressed, and everyone saying nothing and just getting on with things. She had made sure of that by going to Student Health, where for the first time she had lain on her back while a complete stranger examined her vagina with all the professional detachment of a mechanic checking for an oil leak, then supplied her with a prescription. One tiny pill a day to preserve her from fruition. She was safe.

20.

Cover her face. Mine eyes dazzle: she died young.

The Duchess of Malfi by John Webster

Claudia wanted everyone to come to Queenstown for New Year: all the Malfiosi.

'We've got a crib at Frankton,' she said. 'There's heaps of room.' Now that the university year was ended and summer had come they were reluctant to let one another go. Homes seemed impossibly claustrophobic, parents more irritating, towns more populated by tedious people who had not lived as they had all lived, stabbing and poisoning and surviving the moment when Gowdie had a few beers too many at the Cook and had to be rapidly sobered up for the eight o'clock curtain, and all the other moments that were theirs and belonged only to them, the true Malfiosi.

Everyone brought sleeping bags. They slept on sofas and

mattresses dragged out onto the lawn, for the nights were perfect, the sky clear. They drank wine and beer and ate the fruit they had bought on the way up: trays of nectarines and peaches and cherries.

They taste of musk, methinks, said Claudia, juice trickling down her chin. Mack kissed her full sweet lips. *Indeed they do,* he said.

At night they drifted out onto the lake in a couple of canoes, trailing their hands in the deep dark water so that the pattern of stars became random squiggles on the surface.

They sprawled on the beach one morning, in the shadow of the willows. One of those blue days, the lake one brilliant dazzle, the Remarkables cut into the sky with just a sprinkling of snow still on the tops. The air was warm though it was still early. Children were running up and down with buckets, carrying water to pour into moats they were building in the sand. Someone was water-skiing far out on the lake, swooping about in wide circles. The canoes bobbed at the end of the little jetty. One floated a little apart, its nose raised to the breeze.

'Bugger,' said Mack, sitting up and dragging off his T-shirt. 'One of the canoes has come loose. I'll get it back before it drifts too far.' Kate lay with her head on Steve's leg. The wind brushed through the long tendrils of the willow branches so that they swept like the long hair of a chorus of women, all in one direction, then all in another, and sunlight glittered and left rainbows caught in her eyelashes. She watched through sprinkles of light as Mack ran — ooh ooh ouch — over scorching sand, stepping high, clowning for his audience, whoever they might be. He ran along the jetty, raised his arms operatically, and dived in. Kate closed her eyes. When she opened them again, the canoe had drifted a little further out. She could see its painter trailing in the water. Of Mack there was no sign. Claudia was turning over. She was sitting up. Out on the lake there was no thrashing of arms or legs, no flick of fair hair. Nothing.

He had drowned. When they ran to the end of the jetty, all of them tripping and stumbling with a sick cold fear making them clumsy, they could see his body floating just below the surface, arms and legs limp before the current, the heart stopped in mid-beat by the shock of the icy water.

So this was how death came: no bloody dagger, no poisoned Bible.

She had not expected that it would be like that, of course: daggers and poison were literature, they were theatre. But she had expected something more dramatic: a day like the day when the rain fell, drumming steadily on the roof, leaving small ponds among the motor parts in the hall. Damp patches the shape of India had drooped from the edges of buckled wallpaper. The Waters of Leith rose within hours from a gutter trickle between concrete walls to a raging flood dragging down whole trees and boulders to the harbour. Rain dripped down the chimney onto the fire so that the lumps of coal fizzed, sending out little puffs of ash that settled like foam on the carpet, and the ferry had gone aground somewhere near Wellington. Neither she nor Steve had ever been to Wellington but they could imagine it. The cars parked bumper to bumper below decks, the people assembled on the deck. The radio had crackled from Steve's desk, balanced on a *Collected Shakespeare* as the ferry listed and sank and ordinary people from ordinary places like Timaru and Blenheim leapt into the churning water and were carried ashore or driven out into open water as fate and the elements decreed, dying only a few metres from suburban streets.

Blow winds and crack your cheeks!

She had expected something like the train tumbling into the river in the long-ago year of the Queen's visit, when the main street was hung with boxes of gladioli and carnations and gypsophila and the gold medal was pinned to her cardigan. She had expected chaos, the water pouring into the carriage, the Christmas presents torn from the racks, the people drowning . . .

Not this.

Silence. A blue day. The sky lifted like a banner overhead, the last thing seen the pebbles beneath clear water, all as simple and true as if they had been laid to a design, one by one.

But then, Mack was always the best at dying.

21.

'Do you think we should get married?' said Steve one night, not long after the return from Queenstown. Life seemed serious suddenly. Finite. It seemed necessary to act. His skin felt smooth as sunwarmed stone. There was always a kind of whirring about him, a buzz of nervous energy. He felt alive, and right now Kate wanted very much to be alive. At the mention of marriage she felt a bubble form in her chest the way it always did when she was excited.

She turned the word over in her mind. She tested the strangeness of it. Something that happened to other people, something that she had read about for years, could happen to her. She could be Princess Grace on the steps on the palace witnessing the Explosion of Joy over the Principality. She could experience the final page in all the sixpenny rentals: that blissful wedding that followed the kiss as naturally as night followed day. She had, of course, already experienced the part that lay beyond the wedding: the moment of ecstasy when *there was no further need for words.* The end of university loomed. What lay beyond — that awkward space between childhood and death — was a blank. Marriage filled the gap and solved the problem in just eight letters.

'Yes,' she said. 'Yes, yes.'

This was the year of the *Songs of Innocence and Experience* balanced on a shining thread above the hallucinatory abyss; the year when the angel fell headlong from heaven in the blind man's vision, *dark dark dark amid the blaze of noon.* In that year, her third at university, Joseph Andrews and Tom Jones and Tristram Shandy packed down as a cheerful scrum, Hamlet tried to make up his mind as the bodies piled up centre stage, Lear carried Cordelia in his arms, howling, howling, Fanny came to Mansfield Park and Robinson Crusoe ventured offshore in a proto-colonial direction. Pope nipped and snapped in couplets like rows of sharpened teeth and Mr H leapt from the cupboard in pursuit of that dodgy virgin, Pamela. And the wanderer dreamed of home, and of kissing his wife under a single sheet.

She sat in tutorials trying on marriage. She wrote her name surreptitiously in the margins of notes on *Tristram Shandy*: Kate Dobbs. Mrs K. Dobbs. She suffered brief regret at the monosyllabic ordinariness of it, at the loss of the pleasingly alliterative Kate Kennedy, at the abandonment of Irishness for Uncle-Tom-Cobbley Englishness. But at least the name did not make her absurd.

Imagine if Steve's name had been Pate, for example. 'Kate Pate'. Her mother had a cousin who had married a man called Arnold Smellie. It had made her bitter, her mother said. Ridicule was a high price to pay for love. Kate Dobbs. The name had a clunky sound, like solid timber, like sensible shoes. Kate Dobbs. Steve and Kate Dobbs.

Steve bought her an engagement ring. It was a diamond solitaire with a chip on each platinum shoulder. Kate had never worn a ring before, nor bracelets, nor necklaces, hating the sensation of metal against her skin. Rings particularly appalled her. They slid on readily enough, then they stuck. She became frantic at their immovability, soaping her knuckle wildly to help them slide off. It was akin to the claustrophobia aroused by a tight sweater caught over the head. But this ring was different.

She wore it for the first time on the night they went to see *Long Day's Journey into Night* at the Regent. She sat in the dark while Katharine Hepburn, tremulous with morphine addiction, fluttered about the dark house like a pale moth, and the lumpish sons squabbled, and Ralph Richardson, shorn of any quizzicality, became another of those literary dark male brooders. As the family writhed toward catharsis, Kate looked down at her hand. In the dark the ring twinkled. She had read somewhere that that was a test for a true diamond: it should cut glass. She had tried it out that afternoon, scratching her initials, KSK — her soon-to-be-abandoned maidenly initials — on the window of her room at the flat. And it should gleam in the dark.

Her right hand was held in Steve's hand. Her left hand had the ring like a little star.

She was engaged. The word sounded giddy: like a new haircut, or red shoes. It sounded silly and serious, all at once.

> *'That was in the winter of senior year. Then in the spring something happened to me. Yes, I remember. I fell in love with James Tyrone and was so happy for a time.'*
>
> *Long Day's Journey into Night* by Eugene O'Neill

Mr and Mrs Patrick Kennedy of 55 Greta Street, Oamaru, announce with pleasure . . . The words in the two-minute silence were forced to their formulaic order. Their natural sequence had been appropriated by convention.

Convention also dictated an engagement party at the flat in Clyde Street, with the Doors on the stereo, several crates of beer and punch made from ginger ale and half a dozen bottles of Pimms. The guests brought presents: a wooden salad bowl, a coffee pot, a set of whisky glasses, an electric clock. Caro organised a kitchen evening and there were more presents: another coffee pot, kitchen scissors, and a Mood Barometer with hands labelled Him and Her that could be turned to points ranging from Lovey-dovey! to Watch Out! Maddie gave her a nightie in a brilliant orange psychedelic print.

'Thought you'd like it for the honeymoon,' she said as she poured Cold Duck into a tea cup.

For the honeymoon retained a certain aura.

Caro slept regularly with a med student: a tall med student who she said made her feel at last delicate and tiny, like a porcelain shepherdess. Maddie had had a succession of disastrous relationships. She said musicians were hopeless, being romantic and neurotic, but she continued to bring them home where they retreated to her room for some brief, generally unsatisfactory sex, followed by intense and equally unsatisfactory conversation. Despite evidence to the contrary, however, the myth of pre-marital chastity was politely maintained.

. . . announce with pleasure the engagement of their older daughter, Kathleen . . .

In fact, when Kate announced her engagement to her mother, the response had been more muted.

'What about your job?' she had said.

'What job?' said Kate. 'I don't have a job.'

'Teaching,' said her mother.

'I can still teach,' said Kate.

'Not when you've got children,' said her mother. 'I thought teaching was to be your calling?'

'We're not going to have children straight away,' said Kate. 'And teaching's not my calling. I just took the studentship for the money. I don't know yet what job I want.'

'You should do law,' said her mother.

'Law's boring,' said Kate.

'It looks interesting on *Perry Mason*,' said her mother.

'It's not like on *Perry Mason*,' said Kate. 'Not really. Not in New Zealand. It's divorces and real estate and stuff like that.' Caro was doing law. The books on her desk were enormous, dense with detail: Adams on Criminal Law. Cheshire and Fifoot. Caro sat at the kitchen table with her law student friends discussing snails in ginger beer, the indefeasibility of title, contract and negligence. It should have been interesting: The Carbolic Smokeball Case! Donoghue v. Stevenson! Frazer v. Walker! But in reality, the discussion revolved around tiny points of debate. There was no grand sweep, not around the kitchen table at any rate, no sparkling dialogue, no revelatory climax, just dry resolution and precedent.

Her mother Tip-exed a mistake, dabbing at the manuscript with the little brush. The maternal side was nearly ready for the printer.

'You could do good if you were a lawyer,' she said. 'If you didn't have the distraction of a family to take care of, you could help other people. You could become an MP! We need women MPs.'

'I do not want to be an MP,' said Kate. 'Now, where's the Windolene?'

The windows in Maura's bedroom where Steve was to sleep were grimy. Kate had already visited Steve's home in Invercargill and the windows there were polished, the furniture gleamed: the Queen Anne bedroom suites made by Steve's dad, the dining table under its baize cloth, the eighteenth-century longcase clock in the hall — all bore the satisfied glow of furniture properly waxed and cared for. The roses in the garden were pruned, the edges trimmed. For days before Steve's first visit Kate vacuumed the floors and tried to apply some polish to furniture scuffed beyond redemption.

'Who is this boy?' said her mother. 'He must be quite something.'

She seemed amused. Her father too. Kate thought she saw them wink at each other, for the first time that she could ever remember in collusion. They thought her cleaning was funny. They had never had guests to stay, not even family. They had never had anyone over for a meal. They had never gone out to a restaurant with red plastic covers on the menus. They had no idea how other people lived. Kate scrubbed the bath viciously with half an inch of Ajax.

'He is something,' she said.

'I'd better make a cake then,' said her mother.

The visit did not go well, despite the clean windows. Steve seemed curt, her father was uncomfortable, struggling to sit at the table, his stiff hands fumbling to hold knife and fork properly. Her mother flustered, endlessly asking this strange young man if he'd had enough to eat, endlessly apologising.

'Here you are, Steven. Have another helping.' ('He's very thin, isn't he?' she had whispered to Kate out in the kitchen as she tipped the carrots into one of the serving bowls making its inaugural appearance from the china cabinet in the front room. 'He looks like he's outgrown his strength.' 'He's just fine,' said Kate.)

'You'll have to eat up,' said her mother. 'When you're swotting so hard. My brother Tom . . .'

'Mum!' said Kate, but it was too late. Her mother was launched into Tom and the TB and Waipiata.

'I was up at Waipiata once,' said Steve. 'At a health camp when I was seven.'

Her mother was triumphant.

'You see?' she said as they dished up the pudding in the kitchen into a crystal bowl she had received at her own wedding twenty-five years before, with the silver spoons released at last from white tissue paper. 'A shadow on the lung!' She tipped some cream into a bowl rimmed with stylised orange trees. 'That boy will have to watch it if there's TB in the family.' She loaded his plate with pineapple upside-down pudding and a small hillock of cream. Steve tried hard, but Kate could see him struggling.

'Something wrong?' said her mother, seeing his spoon falter.

'No,' said Steve. 'It's delicious. It's just that I've had plenty, thank you.'

Her mother looked disappointed. 'I know it's not very nice,' she said. 'I should have added more sugar.'

'It's great,' said Steve, but her mother was not to be comforted.

'Is it?' she said doubtfully. 'Are you sure you won't have some more then?'

'Mum!' said Kate. 'He's not hungry! He's had enough!'

'If you say so, dear,' said her mother, and she took up the cream bowl as if it were heavy burden. 'I'll get it better next time.'

'They're not always like this,' said Kate, when they were able to escape at last and walk together on a blessedly empty beach.

'It doesn't matter,' said Steve. 'My parents are exactly the same.' (They weren't. They played violin and piano duets in the living room after dinner. They called lunch 'luncheon'. They drove a Riley. They had a Labrador called Rusty. His mother was secretary of the National Party. His father had a cabinetry factory employing fifteen men. He was a city councillor. They didn't bother much with church, but if they did go, they were Anglicans.) The beach stretched away undisturbed into heat haze; the sea rolled in; there were tiny beetles of iridescent green scaling the marram grass in the hollows of the sandhills.

. . . to Steven, oldest son of Mr and Mrs Clarence Dobbs of 'Sevenoaks', Invercargill . . .

Convention required dress fittings in a workshop whispery with tulle and satin: frills or simple sheath? White or cream? Train or no train? Fingertip veil or full-length? There were invitations to send. One bridesmaid or two? Trumpet Voluntary or Mendelssohn? The reception to plan for. The Gold Room at the Central Hotel or the Homestead Wedding and Reception Centre? Beef or chicken? Trifle or pavlova? The photographer. The flowers . . .

The honeymoon was the one thing that required little thought. Steve had a scholarship. They were going to England.

It was not quite so far off as could have been wished: but it was probably far enough, her radius of movement and repute having been so small. To persons of limited spheres, miles are as geographical degrees, parishes as counties, counties as provinces and kingdoms.

Tess of the D'Urbervilles by Thomas Hardy

The wedding was recorded on Super 8 by Kate's cousin Bernard, who had given up on his chemistry degree after only a term and moved into television. ('What's that lad up to? He's throwing away his Opportunity!')

Bernard filmed the entire event from odd angles: from between the straw wedding hats of Caro and Maddie, from ground level among a shrubbery of legs and shoes, and, to finish, the wedding party walking down the church path and coming to a halt on the steps so that they were perfectly framed by a sign painted on a shop wall across the road advertising Lane's Emulsion: 'Good Health in a Bottle!'

Their families came to see them off. Steve's parents kissed them both and wished them good luck. Maura gave her a brief hug. 'You're so lucky!' she said. She still had two years to go at university, and it was torture. French and German and a teaching studentship. She had come second, however, in Miss University, in a purple halter-neck dress she had made herself, and she was working part time in a clothing shop near the Octagon. The management was hopeless, she said. Absolutely no sense of design. They still hung the clothes on those plastic dummies with the pointed feet and the vacant smiles. But she was going to turn it around. She had done one all-white display with a Vespa Supersprint in the window and a model with the visor down sitting astride it in a kind of Courreges print and white boots. The boss had not been too sure but they'd done ten times their normal business that week and she was going to be allowed to try another.

'Tell me what they're wearing in London,' she said. 'And if you can find me some really good boots, I'm a size six. Remember?' She wrote it down in Kate's address book, along with her body measurements, just in case.

Her father hugged her awkwardly. His arms were crooked permanently now at the elbow.

'Well,' he said, 'enjoy yourself over there.'

'I will,' she said.

Three years suddenly seemed like a long time.

'You could come and visit,' she said. 'You could come and stay in our flat.'

The vision rose, complete and unlikely. Her family, transported across the world to an English bedroom with counterpanes and casement windows and church bells chiming down a leafy lane. Now that she was abandoning them so definitively, she had a sudden urge to hang on to them all. She wanted to take them with her. But her father was saying, 'Now why would I be wanting to do that?' And when she said well, he could look up his relations, he could go back to visit Dundee, he laughed and said he could remember as much as he wanted of Dundee and he hadn't kept in touch with the relations and where would they get the money for a trip like that anyway?

'No,' he said. 'You just go and have a good time.'

Anything could happen in three years.

'If you're ever in Hodges Figgis or Blackwell's or Foyles or one of those second-hand places,' he said, 'and you see anything interesting, just pick it up for me. You know what I like: travel, history, Pacific exploration, that kind of thing. I'll send you the money. All right?'

'All right,' she said.

She held his hand. His bad hand.

'That's the girl,' he said.

Her mother had stayed up the night before, baking biscuits for them to eat on the way.

'But the tin's enormous!' said Kate. And it was: the largest cake-tin available, with a picture of the daffodils by the Avon on the lid, squeezed into a pink plastic string-bag. It was filled to bursting with ginger crunch, afghans, coconut squares and peanut biscuits, with layers of greaseproof paper in between. 'I don't know if we'll be able to take it on board.' They had already checked their luggage in.

'Nonsense,' said her mother. 'Of course you will. A great big plane like that.'

'They have weight limits,' said Steve. The woman at the desk was very particular. 'And there might be Customs as well. They have rules about what can be taken in and out of a country.'

'But they won't be bothered about a few biscuits, surely,' said Kate's mother. Nobody knows. Nobody has ever flown before. 'I'll go and have a word with her.'

'Don't do that,' said Kate. 'They're busy. They won't want to be bothered about biscuits.'

'But we need to know,' said her mother. 'We need to know for sure.'

'They'll have plenty of biscuits anyway on the plane,' said Steve. 'They do full meals.'

Her mother looks defeated at that. She stands holding the string bag as the crowd mills about.

'Packet biscuits,' she says. 'I thought you might like something from home.'

'We would,' says Kate. 'We'd love it.'

Her mother smiles at that. 'I'll come up to the desk with you, and ask them,' she says, and she follows them when they move toward the escalator, holding the string bag with the daffodil tin.

'I don't like these escalators,' she says, but Steve is already rising away from her, and so is Kate, so she steps onto the tread. Kate hears the intake of her breath behind her, and a kind of frantic scrabbling. She turns. Her mother is hanging on to the moving handrail and fighting to keep her balance as the stairs move upward. The string bag has caught on the edge of one of the steps and tipped her back, she's falling, she's grabbing for support but the steps are moving too fast and the tin has fallen open. Ginger crunch, peanut brownies, afghans are tumbling out onto the metal treads and rising in little crumbling heaps toward Kate who is trying to walk back down to help but she is holding her coat in one hand and her bag in the other and she can't get back.

'Kate!' calls her mother. Kate!'

Kate gets to the top then runs back down the stairs and by the time she is back her mother is being lifted to her feet by a stranger, she is dusting herself down. She is fixing her hair and gathering what is left of the biscuits into the tin.

'Well, that's taken care of that,' she says. 'They're ruined. You can't take them now.'

'Of course we can,' says Kate. 'Look, there's heaps that are all right. See: these ones are fine.'

She wants them now, more than anything. The afghans, the ginger crunch, the peanut brownies.

'No, they're not,' says her mother. 'You can't eat them after they've been on the floor.'

But Kate is on her hands and knees, picking up whatever is unbroken, stuffing them back into the tin and her mother is saying, 'You'll have to pack them properly or they won't fit,' so they pack the tin again carefully, while Steve stands by keeping an eye on the time and as the final boarding call is made she hugs her mother and her mother hugs her fiercely, closely, and Kate loves her so much she can hardly speak to say goodbye.

Then somehow she and Steve are on the plane and home is vanishing to a rim of cloud on the horizon. They fly out over the ocean and on across the astonishing crimson continent that is Australia with its hour after hour of deserts squiggled with dry valleys and serpentine creekbeds. She nibbles an afghan and feels the threads stretch that hold her to home. They stretch and stretch until they are so fine as to be almost invisible.

22.

When they came down again, they were in England. They were living in a flat that had eighteenth-century woodwork and rooms so small you could stretch and touch each wall with the tips of your fingers. It backed onto a pub with head-cracking beams and a mynah bird that cried from its cage night and day with a peculiar frenzy, 'Have a cigar! Have a cigar!', its own true language having been lost somewhere, somehow, in transit.

Behind the pub stood a college wall of dressed stone, with some mean, defensive metal along the top. Along the street were the Bodleian and the bookshops, the banks and the bakers and double-decker buses and students on bicycles and women in belted macs towing little shopping trolleys to a market where rabbits were hung by their heels.

She had known how it would be. A thousand books and millions of words had prepared her, so that this place was as familiar in some ways as the jagged framework of the Kakanuis, the knuckles of limestone beneath drought-brown paddocks, the shingle rivers in their willow fringes.

Without her knowing it, Kate's imagination had been colonised.

Beyond the city the whole country possessed the same curious familiarity. Paintings she had known since childhood in the *Arthur Mee's Encyclopaedia* appeared on a gallery wall, swollen to enormous size and no longer a uniform decorous sepia but brilliant blue and crimson, and the flesh of the plump goddesses viewed in close-up was a whole melange of pink and sulphur yellow and bruised purple. Places she had read about materialised, but smaller, more intimate than she had imagined. Westminster Abbey was almost domestic with its cosy buried family of worthies. The great peak of Snowden when they climbed to the top was accessible by train. The places on the Monopoly board were within hand's reach: the purple bits, the blue bits, Pall Mall and The Angel, Islington. Winter that year was for the first time in her life the way it was somehow, by endless definition in books and pictures and Christmas cards, *supposed* to be. Snow fell on branches to which a few crimson leaves clung, crumbly with poetic pathos. Then in spring the walled gardens of the colleges burst into Easter white and yellow and little churches in the country smelled of damp plaster and lilies, and a figure of St Christopher strode toward the door through a cartoon wriggle of water studded with ochre fish. This was the rectory where Sterne had written *Tristram Shandy*; this was the sofa on which Emily Brontë had lain, this was the river in which Virginia Woolf had drowned.

The contemporary mythology became actual too. She went with Steve to hear The Who perform *Tommy* in a crowded ballroom in London, and she lay on the grass in a field near Bath listening to Jefferson Airplane and Donovan and Country Joe. Songs to which she knew every word became live. Portaloos overflowed with turds and piss and a boy wandered alone in some private terror among the monstrous crowd, whimpering. 'Who am I? Where am I?'

They heard James Dickie reading from *Deliverance* in a dark room by the Thames, drooped drunkenly over the lectern, and Lowell hovering hesitant in the shadows of a stage as if he would rather not read his poetry to a live audience at all. They crammed into a pub in Liverpool to hear Adrian Henri reading poetry as if it were rock'n'roll. *Oh. Oh. Oh. Oh for the wings of a dove.* And they went to theatres where Shakespeare and Sheridan were performed by actors for whom the language sat easily on the tongue. They saw Olivier emphatically upstaging everyone within reach, and Maggie Smith delivering her own peculiar brand of silvery malice. They went to Scotland and France and over to Ireland because everything had shrunk to a few hours' hitching, lumbering along the motorways in trucks full of bacon or tinned fruit. They heard Irish actors making sense of the tramps in *Godot*. They heard the prisoner sing in *The Quare Fellow.* They saw the premiere of a play by Beckett. It was a bare stage and five minutes of recorded breathing before the curtain fell. The audience sat uncertainly at the fading of the lights. Was that it? Five minutes? No actors? Just breath? Should they clap? Should they leave? Someone clapped tentatively. They all clapped. It wasn't a con. It was brilliant. A devastating comment on the human condition. All drama reduced to its bare essentials. Another work by the master.

She had been colonised, yet colonisation can never be more than partial. There is only so much room in any colonist's luggage: only room for a single chair, a single engraving of Edinburgh from Calton Hill. The coloniser introduces rabbits but not foxes; sparrows but not ravens; dairy cows but not badgers; trout but not carp; rats but not voles. Kate's literary colonisation had been partial. It had omitted vast and crucial amounts of detail — all the detail that lent the picture complexity, contradiction and context. She had absorbed a notion of this place as odd as the architecture of the bank buildings at home in Oamaru, which made a passable imitation of Doric at the front, yet were pure New Zealand corrugated iron at the back. Without her being aware of it, her imagined world had been a synthesis. Roman soldiers had marched over Central Otago high country, somewhere around the Rock and Pillar. Milly-Molly-Mandy's village had been surrounded by acres of sheep paddock. In reality, the village was as likely to be surrounded by an estate of semi-detached houses with miniature herbaceous borders modelled hopefully on Sissinghurst. She had loved Richard Hannay, but when she met his modern manifestation at some college sherry party or on some Sunday ramble over muddy fields, he turned out to be a pompous Monday-Clubber who swirled his Oloroso or knocked the mud from his brogues and said, 'New Zealand, eh? If I can't get a decent job here, I might consider New Zealand.' New Zealand, it seemed, was the Empire's booby prize, trailing somewhere behind Canada, which was boring, and Australia, which was vulgar — though the Australians could be amusing. They spoke like Barry McKenzie. They said things like 'crook'; they called the English 'Pommy bastards'. They called girls 'sheilas'.

Australia was a bit like America: vulgar, but too big to be dismissed. Whereas New Zealand was more like Canada. Just plain dull.

Meisse ocus Pangur Ban,
cechtar natha fria shaindan . . .

Myself and White Pangur are each at his own trade.
He has his mind on hunting. My mind is on my own
task.

He points his clear bright eye against a wall. I point my
own clear one, feeble as it is, against the power of know-
ledge. He is happy and darts around when a mouse sticks
in his sharp claw, and I am happy in understanding some
dear, difficult problem.

'The Scholar and his White Cat' by an anonymous
ninth-century Irish poet

Steve was occupied. He was studying medieval languages: medieval Welsh, medieval Irish, Icelandic, Catalan and Provençal. He had met his tutors. One was muddled with gin by 10am, the other wore a stained suit and sandshoes that smelled richly of something very ripe and very fungal: an aged Stilton, perhaps, stored creamily between the toes. Mercifully that tutor was also terrified of contracting any infection and conducted tutorials in his garden, marching in Socratic fashion round and round the rosebeds. Another crop of graduates had popped up like annual weeds between the cracks, and must be endured.

They were acting, of course. Everyone was acting. The jolly porter with the pale eyes peering through the gatehouse window like a pig in its crate, the girl in the bakery leaning on the counter chewing a cud of dull resentment, the Ratty-and-Mole denizens of the senior common room, the busy booming women doing good at Oxfam, the Irish tramps swapping a confused yarn for a handout — they had all been sent around from central casting to try out for the film in which they were all engaged: *Carry On Up the Dreaming Spires!*

The graduate students also had their roles. The Australians were tough and clever. One, a philosopher, moved in with Steve and Kate for a few weeks between flats, and for a time the kitchen was taken over by a Melbourne-and-Sydney push who sat about the table drinking treacle-thick espresso coffee and arguing ethics. Some of them had rented a house in North Oxford that retained an acre of pear trees and quinces and gnarled apple trees. They were vehement about animal rights, they ate no meat and they dropped a lot of acid, when the talk would cease for a few hours while they lay in the sun beneath the apple trees, their eyes splintered by the inner vision.

Next door to Steve and Kate were flats occupied by Americans. The men studied PPE as the prequel to a few years at a reputable law school back in the States and a career in government. Their wives took temporary jobs, the kind that could be dropped in an instant to go off cycling down the Loire or to drive the Mini to Morocco. They lived a temporary life, making temporary adjustments to living in this weird place where no one seemed to have heard of tacos or chilli mix, while they waited for the return home, when their careers could be resumed in earnest.

The Canadians were a less uniform federation. The Rosenbergs from Montreal lived in a top-floor flat a few doors down Holywell Street. David was studying mathematics. Toba was pregnant and spent her time buying furniture at auctions, which she painted in folk-art garlands of fruit and flowers. Tony from Toronto was studying medieval versions of the life of St Eustace. Military commander under the emperor Trajan? Came face to face with a stag in the forest while he was out hunting on a Good Friday? A stag with a crucifix between its antlers? Converted on the strength of that vision and got martyred by being roasted along with his family? Probably never existed? That St Eustace?

'It doesn't matter if he existed or not,' said Tony. 'People took him seriously, even if he was fiction. They needed him to exist, evidently. That's what's interesting.'

The English graduates seemed to include an extraordinary number of young men who knew an awful lot about Renaissance musical instruments, which they built from scratch and on which they performed in long concerts of painstaking authenticity. The exceptions included a stocky Scottish economist who had stood as the Liberal candidate in one of those gallant, hopeless attempts on a rock-solid Tory seat near Glasgow. And a solitary Cockney, notable, he said, for being one of the four per cent of Oxford students who could genuinely claim to be working class.

There were the South Africans, like Colin and his beautiful blonde wife, who had hitch-hiked from Johannesburg to England and arrived tanned and leggy in faded shorts at the tag-end of summer. A one-way trip. Colin had had some bruising brush with the South African police. They did not plan to return.

Some of the New Zealanders did not plan on returning either. They faded instantly into the English woodland, following the precedent of the men who had come to Oxford before the war, done sterling service breaking enemy codes and fighting with the guerrillas in the hills of Yugoslavia and being generally brilliant and wily and brave, and who now spent a pleasant retirement in the bar at the Vicky Arms. There they drank beer from monogrammed tankards kept for their personal use while fondly remembering a small-town, sugar-sack New Zealand of hard-case jokers and compliant sheilas. They were not English. They were not exactly New Zealanders. They had become some bluff monologuing hybrid: the 'colonial'.

Who am I? Where am I?

> *When I finally left Wally or Sid at Rugby Park corner of a Saturday or Sunday night I'd trudge the rest of the way home in the rain wondering what the hell was the matter with me, whether I was a different breed or what, and why it was always me that was left, and thinking that in some other country somewhere things mightn't be like that at all and people would see what I really was instead of what I'd always been.*

> *The Quiet One* by Dan Davin

Kate trundled the washing back from the laundromat. There was one of those little shopping trolleys in a cupboard at the flat and it was indeed just the thing for hauling dirty clothes and soap powder the four blocks to the machines. The rackety wheels caught in the cobbles and paving stones and bumped over the front step. She tipped their clean things onto the sofa. Shirts, pants, socks, all still a little damp because she had suddenly become frantic to get away from the portholes with the roiling mass of clothing, the dreary woman counting out shillings, the pile of magazines with the covers missing.

'Who are you?' said the little heap of damp washing. Its voice was thin and whingey.

'Well,' said Kate, 'I'm a wife.'

'A wife,' said the washing. 'That's what you wanted, wasn't it?'

'Yes,' said Kate. She picked up a sock and tucked it into its mate. 'That's what I wanted.'

'So you've got what you want?' said the washing.

'I suppose so,' said Kate.

'So, what's a wife?' said the washing.

'I don't know,' said Kate. 'This, probably.'

'Washing?' said the washing. 'Cooking? That sort of thing?'

'Yes,' said Kate. 'That's what my mother did and she's a wife.'

'But she hated it,' said the washing. And Kate had to admit that the washing was right. Her mother had never, to Kate's knowledge, identified herself on official forms as 'housewife' but always as 'Nurse, ret'd'. But day by day, this was indeed how she had spent her wifely life. Washing. Cooking.

None of the books she had ever read were of any assistance. Wives were not generally the heroines of novels. They hardly featured at all in the set texts, and if they did, their wifely lives were not given an especially encouraging report. Emma Bovary and Anna Karenina were bored by marriage. They were restless and unfulfilled. Such wives ended up eating arsenic in desperation or flung themselves under trains. More usually wives were peripheral creatures who hovered in the shadows, becoming that compliant thing — a mother — who washed and cooked and smothered the hero while fading discreetly toward irrelevance. *She moved about at the little tasks that remained to be done, set his breakfast, rinsed his pit-bottle, put his pit-clothes on the hearth to warm* . . . In the books that did not qualify as set texts, the sixpenny rentals and the rest, wifedom was the condition to which the heroines aspired but it was never described. After the kiss, there was of course *no further need for words*. Being a wife came without written instructions.

Emma, once so careful and dainty, now went whole days without putting on a dress; she wore gray cotton stockings, and lit the house with cheap tallow candles.

Madame Bovary by Gustave Flaubert

Kate looked around at the other wives in Oxford. Toba went to the Graduate Wives' Club. Kate went with her to a meeting and found herself balancing a cup of instant coffee and a chocolate digestive and seated next to someone who was introduced to her as Princess something. From Iran. Or Iraq. Kate missed both details in a momentary flurry of wondering if you called a Princess 'Princess' or used their proper name. She managed a tentative 'Hello' before the bosomy memsahib who ran the club and the associated second-hand furniture depot next door swooped down and carried off Princess whatever-her-name-was to meet a compatriot. Another wife from Iran. Or was it Iraq?

Kate did not think she had a future as a Graduate Wife. Doing good was one thing. Being done good to was quite another.

She tried the temporary job instead.

A wall of cardboard boxes stood along one side of the art history department reading room. The Victoria and Albert had handed over to the university its entire collection of ancient glass magic lantern slides.

'So,' said Kate, 'what do you want me to do?'

The secretary was sweet and Belgian and had learned her English from American movies.

'Ya sort'em,' she said. 'Ya knowwhaddamean?'

Kate had no idea what might prove useful to Oxford's students of art history. Would anyone want to consult Queen Victoria's collection of silver dogs? Was Puvis de Chavannes likely to stage a comeback? Or Moreau? The slides were frail and covered in dust. She sorted and sneezed and hiffed every third one or so into the bin, where they snapped in a dozen pieces with a satisfying crack. When that job was finished she worked for a time at the Bodleian, gluing new titles into the catalogues. The catalogues were massive volumes alphabetically indexed, and each new entry was typed onto a little strip of paper that had to be glued into its proper place on the page. When a page became filled, all the little strips had to be lifted gently to accommodate the new arrival and glued back into place. It was pleasantly fiddly, a reversal to childhood and gluing stickers in a scrap album.

When she tired of that, she found a job at Pergamon Press, copy-editing *Solid State Electronics*, a daunting compilation of inscrutable equations, and the *European Journal of Cancer*, which was worse, with page after page of mice sporting unusual tumors. The office was open plan and a place of endless distraction. She sat at her desk checking equations and captions while the little dramas — the flirtations and the fallings-out and the reconciliations — unfolded on all sides: the man with the limp from the art department who was chatting up the Scottish woman with the big breasts in technical books, the man from accounts who suddenly flung all his papers onto the floor and walked out, never to return.

After work she and Steve went swimming in English rivers that ran deep and slow over sucking mud and clinging tendrils of weed. They drifted on a lazy current, between banks lush with English flowers whose names she had learned long ago — purple loosestrife, Queen Anne's lace — while the summer storms broke overhead and hammered the surface to dimpled pewter.

There is a willow grows aslant a brook,
That shows his hoar leaves in the glassy stream.

Hamlet by William Shakespeare

There were marches in Oxford too. Kate and Steve marched — *Ho Ho Ho Chi Minh!* — down Cornmarket where conservative bystanders pushed through the column to cross to the other side of the road, saying, 'Excuse ME!' to register the full force of their opposition.

The Cockney working-class student was puzzled. It was his first time.

'I thought there'd be more opposition,' he said. 'Police and that.' He seemed almost disappointed. He had been hoping for blue meanies, truncheons, Alsatians unleashed on the crowd. Tear gas and rubber bullets. The paving stones outside Tescos torn up to make barricades.

'No,' said Steve. 'It's usually like this.'

A man with an umbrella had stepped from the pavement and was approaching the column, arm raised like Moses intent on parting the Red Sea. 'Excuse ME!' he said.

Steve and Kate felt like seasoned campaigners. The British had sent no troops to Vietnam, so in a way their protest was more peripheral, their role less central. But New Zealanders were actually fighting: lads from Taihape and Tuatapere were distributing Agent Orange, defoliating vast areas of the country, maiming children and killing villagers, alongside the Thais and the South Koreans and the Filipino allies.

What do we want? NO WAR. When do we want it? NOW!

The march ended up somehow at Christ Church, where Steve and Kate found themselves with a few others, skirmishing with squawky young Tories in the Fellows' Garden. They milled about trading insults. Some had grabbed the Get Out of Vietnam placards and were using them to thump the protesters. Fights had broken out amid the herbaceous borders. A yelping pack was pursuing a boy in jeans and embroidered Indian shirt: they were running and blocking and bringing the boy to the ground in an efficient public-school tackle. Kate was consumed with rage at them: at their stupid well-bred faces and their heavy-muscled thighs in their stupid trousers and their unassailable assurance and their condescension and their stupid braying voices. She loathed them at that moment with an overwhelming tribal loyalty to whoever opposed them. She let the rage consume her. It burst in stars behind the eyes. She shoved one of the Tories hard between the shoulderblades. He was not expecting it. He tumbled with a startled 'Fuck!' into the rockery, legs flailing.

'You guy are such PRICKS!' she said, and fortunately a kind of middle-class restraint still operated when it came to women and she was not thumped in return but let go, free to walk off between the marguerites and delphiniums.

She was a member of the Protest Tribe.

The tribe marched and protested a lot that year. They occupied the Clarendon building, cramming into the university offices among desks and filing cabinets all stuffed to bursting with Secret Files detailing the political activities of students. They sat-in, surrounded by the subtle lies and protective deceit of the establishment as the speeches droned overhead and the police assembled in the courtyard. And that Christmas, her second in Oxford, Kate and Steve and half a dozen other New Zealanders began a student newspaper.

The *Oxford Strumpet. All the news that's left.* They pinched the byline, but the title was original. They came up with it one afternoon in the sitting room of the flat in Holywell Street.

'The Clarion?' said someone, maybe Rob, who was from Auckland and studying English at Balliol.

'The Bugle?' said Jenny, who was his wife.

They were trying out names. Newspaper names. They had discarded The Reporter and The Chronicle and moved on to the brass section.

'The Monday Club's already nabbed The Trumpet,' said someone, maybe Chris, who was from Wellington and was studying Peruvian land reform at Linacre.

'The Strumpet?' said someone else.

They liked that.

Mmm, they said. Yes. *The Oxford Strumpet.* They tried the name aloud, sprawled on the sofa and the carpet, wrapped in an assortment of eiderdowns and sleeping bags. The heater sent out tiny hopeful tendrils of heat into the refrigerator chill of the flat. Upstairs their shoes in the cupboards were growing woolly coats of white mould. Little mustard-coloured toadstools flourished on the downstairs skirting boards. Beyond the window cars slushed along Holywell Street. They had all been out walking, a brisk trip across winter fields to the pub and back. No one was quite sure who suggested the paper. It simply evolved that afternoon and before they knew it, they were typing up features on an ironclad Remington in a room off a narrow alley-way behind the Student Union.

Clonk went Kate's fingers in thick woollen mittens on the solid keys.

Clonk.

Clonkclonk clonk.

— *Strumpet comes as the siren of radical change in the Oxford student press! The monochrome boredom and political irrelevance of Oxford's student papers is challenged!*

Clonk clonk.

— *Strumpet will present a critical examination of the university; its ideological role in shoring up the capitalist structure of the state; its position as a landowner in Oxford.*

Clonk clonk.

— *Oxford colleges pay their staff less than half the recommended minimum wage!*

— *Elections for the presidency of the JCR at Keble rigged!*

— *How the Tory Anti-union Laws will work!*

— *A South African prison described by a graduate student with first-hand experience* (Strumpet: *What tortures were used?* Evans: *Beating, kicking and genital torture. One man's cock was placed on a table and pierced with a nail hammered through a board . . .*)

Reviews of kinetic sculpture, books with subtitles like 'Notes on Imperialism', movies.

— Mick Jagger's Ned Kelly a Real Shitkicker!

— Strumpet will provide a new criticism of local films theatre and exhibitions: an antidote to the banalities of student reviewing in Oxford ...

Clonk clonkclonkclonk.

They pinched cartoons from America, from England, from anywhere at all, in a wild samizdat grab. They pasted up Fat Freddy and his mates onto sheets of A4 paper, along with the articles, a satirical column by Steve featuring the adventures of Warden Tytte and the student radical Randolph Raspberry Whyppe, and some advertisements for upcoming events. They took it around to the printer in a cardboard box on the back of someone's bike. And when it was printed, they stood on the street and sold it.

'*Oxford Strumpet*!' called Kate, on the corner of the Turl in her long black cloak and knee boots. '*Oxford Strumpet*,' called Jenny in her long coat and boots from the opposite corner. Oxford passed them by glancing incuriously in their direction. 'Are you really?' said a man in a mac. 'How much?'

The administration was less indifferent. The article about the rigged ballot at Keble touched a nerve. They insisted upon a retraction. A triumph! A response from that immovable solid beast, the Establishment, and they had hardly started!

'The printer's refused to print any further copies,' said Rob as the editorial group crammed into the office. 'They insist we print an apology.'

'Why?' said Chris. 'We were right about the Keble ballot. I checked all the facts with half a dozen sources.'

'Just the same,' said Rob. 'They've given us the words of the apology. We have to print it on the editorial page.'

So they printed it but across the page in large block letters they pasted the word BULLSHIT.

They found another, braver printer, Morse Ambler, who took it on and they tried even harder with the next issue. An article on the university's attempt at censorship, another on student cohabitation, which earned an immediate threat of disciplinary action. Better and better! They were joined by some Trotskyites from Balliol and an American cartoonist with a real mean streak.

Clonk. Clonk.

— *Today the women's liberation movement is a vanguard movement. Its nature is to challenge basic structures . . .*

— *On Thursday Rhodes Scholars presented a petition to the Warden of Rhodes House expressing their deep concern that there have never been any black Rhodes Scholars from South Africa or Rhodesia . . .*

— *The bourgeoisie will do their best to prevent a truly left-wing government. They will use what armed force they can muster to depose it. Our task in the working-class movement is to prevent this . . .'*

Clonk clonkclonk clonk.

The *Strumpet* crowd protested at Heath's visit, where Rob got dragged from the crowd by a gaggle of plainclothes policemen all wearing identical pink paisley shirts. They took him off into a lower room at Balliol and when they re-emerged, Rob could barely walk and his fly was undone.

'Quick!' said Steve. 'Quick! Take his photo!'

Rob looked like Jesus being tormented by the centurions. He looked like Che Guevara, minus the bulletholes. They printed the photo on the front page of the next issue.

They turned up to offer their solidarity to the striking picketers at Cowley. 'Bugger off, you lot,' said a large angry man holding a megaphone.

They turned up at Rhodes House when the New Zealand embassy came scouting for talent. Some New Zealanders attended in shirts and ties, clearly hoping for placements in Rome or Paris, but most were there to hear Rob read out *our objections to New Zealand's craven involvement with the United States in the vicious imperial war in South East Asia and our solidarity with the people of South Vietnam.*

'Yeah!' yelled the crowd. 'Right on!' And 'Thank you,' said the man from the embassy, wrapping it up and tapping his papers smartly, top and sides, on the desk. Clearly, there was little in Oxford to recruit to the government's cause that year.

23.

The summer vacation approached. Kate and Steve hitch-hiked to
Italy where Maddie now lived. She had gone to Florence to study
Pallavicino but in the first week her washing blew from its line on
the balcony into the room of the Italian architect downstairs, just
like in the movies or sixpenny romances. She had gone down the
dark stairwell, carefully rehearsing the Italian for, 'Excuse me. May
I have my washing back, please?' The young man who opened the
door had eyes the colour of cooking chocolate. In his hand he held

her blue silk panties and a white lacy bra. He was laughing. He let her stumble through her sentence right to the end, because, he told her later, she was enchanting — her accent was terrible, she could have been asking equally well for a glass of milk or the way to the Uffizi, but she was so beautiful standing there in the dark at the foot of the stairs trying to shape her lips to the expressive outlines of the Italian words. They had married within the year and now lived in a flat a block from the Arno.

'And I'm so happy,' she said, hugging Kate and kissing her in the European fashion on both cheeks. 'Soooo happy!' Every morning she crossed the Ponte Vecchio and all the shopkeepers emerged calling 'Ciao bella!' at her as she passed, with her waist-length snow-blonde hair flying. Their flat was built within the curve that marked the walls of an ancient coliseum. A line of faded slime green marked the place to which the river had risen when it overflowed its banks, indifferent to the fact that this was a capital of culture. In the squares and galleries, Venus drifted ashore upon her cockleshell and the two Davids posed for their photographs above the tour groups waddling like so many ducklings behind their leaders' umbrellas.

'They're too obvious,' said Maddie. 'Come and I'll show you something special.'

The tombs were Etruscan. Husband and wife lay side by side on the couch of their tomb at the eternal feast, their lips curved in secretive connubial smiles. Clearly they had not expected Death, this bony guest who came knocking at their door unannounced and much too early, and interrupted their dinner. Dried wreaths of marigolds had been hung about their necks. They shed their petals like so many yellow teeth.

'I'll never go home again,' said Maddie. 'Giovanni hates leaving Florence and I don't want to either.'

She drove them out to a friend's farmhouse in the country. Stone steps worn at the centre from centuries of contadini feet; a fireplace like a whitewashed cave; creaking wooden shutters thrown open upon rows of vines from which Maurizio made his own wine. Each bottle bore a label: 'Della Vigna di Maurizio e Tapa'. Tapa was Maurizio's dog. They picked wild strawberries from between the rows of vines, keeping a sharp eye out for the snakes, thin as boot-laces, that dozed among the prunings and dry grass.

'What about your mother?' said Kate.

'What about her?' said Maddie.

'Don't you worry that she might miss you? I mean, you were all she had,' said Kate.

'No I wasn't,' said Maddie.

'But your father . . .' said Kate. 'The accident? The motorbike crushed by the northbound express? The accident when you were only a month old?'

'All rubbish,' said Maddie, popping a strawberry into her mouth. 'My father is alive and well and running a Tegel chicken franchise in Foxton. Mum walked out and left him with two kids.'

Kate stopped picking. She sat back on her heels.

'You're kidding!' she said.

'Nope,' said Maddie. 'I've got a brother and a sister. So . . .' She shrugs, an Italian shrug. Lips drawn down, hands upturned. 'I'm not all she's got. And this is my home now.' The rows of vines, the warm white stone of the farmhouse, the plain below the village with its borders of poplars. It was all so simple, so orderly compared with the complicated view from the Bella Vista guesthouse on Wansbeck Street.

They ate the strawberries in glasses of Maurizio's red wine as the sun flared in baroque swags of pink and purple.

'Remember drinking Cold Duck?' said Maddie.

Giovanni was puzzled. 'You drank ducks?' he said.

'It was a kind of wine,' said Maddie, picking a strawberry from her glass. 'I don't know why it was called Cold Duck. We thought it was so sophisticated, didn't we, Kate?'

'Yes, we did,' said Kate, and she laughed too at their simplicity. The strawberries had grainy skins. They popped on the tongue, releasing a tiny shot of sugary juice. Truth to tell, Kate would have preferred fat berries with whipped cream and spoonfuls of icing sugar, but that would have been an admission of naïveté. Those were the kind of strawberries favoured by people who would like Cold Duck. The sun set over blue hills like the hills glimpsed through the windows of paintings of the Madonna: hills through which a white road winds toward a distant plain. They had come so far along that winding road leading from Cold Duck to Maurizio's own vintage.

When the Dromedary went to the Bay of Islands, the maiden followed us over-land, and again taking up her station near that part of the vessel in which she supposed her protector was imprisoned, she remained there even in the most desperate weather and resumed her daily lamentation for his anticipated fate until we finally sailed from New Zealand.

Journal of a Ten Months' Residence in New Zealand
by R.A. Cruise

Her mother wrote: *How nice for you to meet up with Madeleine! Her mother tells me she seems quite happy over there. I saw her down town only last week at the Farmers' sale. Must close as it is nearly 5 o'clock and I must get the tea on. Lots of love. PS Do remember to boil the water when you're travelling, won't you? Mrs Craddock spoke at the Spring Afternoon at Church about their trip. She said that everyone else on their tour came down with tummy bugs in Italy. The food was terribly rich and did not agree with them. She was very careful with what she ate and never drank anything but boiled water and she was the only one who did not have any problems.*

The printing was squashed around the edge of the main text, up the right-hand margin and upside down across the top. Kate tracked the text. The aerogramme featured a photo of the Treaty House at Waitangi. One arrived with absolute regularity every Friday, written and posted on a Sunday afternoon.

I saw Mrs McFadden outside the butchers last Tuesday. She tells me Heather is moving to Napier. She's had a baby (boy, 8lb 12oz). I think she said his name was Craig. It was a difficult birth evidently, but mother and babe both well now!

Oamaru, it seemed, was full of mothers, who met one another on the street and exchanged news of their daughters: Maddie in Italy, Caro in Auckland, Kate in England, Virginia Craddock who was studying volcanology in Hawaii, Marilyn Rasmussen who was in the navy, all the daughters who had flown and come to roost elsewhere.

The mothers write about people their daughters can scarcely recall any longer. Their faces have begun to melt into one another. The mothers mention names that their daughters begin to confuse. They cannot quite remember who has married, who has had a baby, who has moved elsewhere. Kate's mother encloses clippings from the newspapers: a news story about someone Kate vaguely remembers from kindergarten or horror stories about overseas: an earthquake in Turkey; a bomb blast in Belfast.

You will be careful won't you? Kate's mother writes. *But I'm nowhere near Turkey,* replies Kate. *And I'm not planning on going to Belfast in the near future.*

The mothers meet and chat with their bags of shopping and the dog tugging at its leash, outside Mr Budd's dairy, or over the counters full of sale-price lingerie at the Farmers', and they weave the web that tweaks, ever so gently, at their children's ankles.

Kate did not write as regularly. It was too difficult. She sent postcards of the Duomo, the Eiffel Tower, San Marco, the Little Mermaid. There was only room on the reverse for *Well, here we are in Florence/Copenhagen/Paris/Venice! Having a great time. Saw* . . . and there followed a resumé of things seen and places visited. No mention of the woman on the Lido who stripped off all her clothes and stalked grandly up and down shouting 'Scheisskerl! Arschloch!' until her husband lunged at her and the two of them struggled, tumbling to the ground with hands gripped about each other's throats in some dreadful murderous marital rage. A ring of outraged Germans had formed about them. 'Ruhe!' they said. 'Unverschämt!' The woman's legs, Titian-plump, kicked, exposing a shock of startling red pubic hair.

No mention of the man who pulled a gun on them in the tenth arrondissement. He had seemed almost bored as they fumbled in their pockets for money, and when they had handed over what they had, thanking God the traveller's cheques were safe in Steve's left shoe, he said, 'Merci.' 'Merci, m'sieu, ma'mselle,' then he left, walking briskly as if he had an appointment elsewhere and was running just a trifle late. No mention of drinking wine in a camping ground near Paris, so gloriously cheap at two francs a bottle, nor of becoming lost on their way back to their tent, nor of waking under an elm tree to a bleary Monet of a morning, the Seine glinting in a multitude of dabs of pearly colour.

Nor any mention of staggering about a room in Denmark with some students, drunk this time on schnapps, which left the body incapable but the brain curiously detached. They staggered two steps to the left, arm in arm, someone's hand groping at her bum, then a step to the right. They were singing some lugubrious Faroese ballad of at least ninety-four verses. No mention of throwing up twice in the tent afterwards, nor of the decision to move the tent, nor of the tent taking on a mind of its own once partially dismantled so that it seemed simpler, after all, to sleep where they were; nor of waking soaked with dew. Wet green grass, a cow licking her face with its big soft heavy tongue, its soft brown eyes like a lover's only an inch or so from her own.

No mention of the cave near Trieste where they walked along a slippery path beside a river into the interior of a hill. Among stalactites and stalagmites stage-lit in red and blue stood a little fish tank. A sign in several languages said that the creature it housed was the Human Fish, Le Poisson Humain, Der menschliche Fisch. The Human Fish's little swollen head blindly nudged at the glass, its pink hands fought for a grip on the sheer surface, its tiny feet paddled about seeking a way through to the dark river that churned at the tourists' backs, surging from one crevice to disappear into another and filling the air with its deafening roar. They stood watching the little pink foetal fish, hearing the sound of water, which could have been the sound of blood rushing in the ears. Then the guide waved her torch and the tourists straggled on to the waterfall signposted as Lover's Leap, La Corniche des Amoureux . . .

She mentioned nothing, in other words, on the reverse of the great sights of Europe, of anything that moved her, or caused her to laugh afterwards, or grimace, or feel slightly ill. Nothing, in fact, that she would tell a friend.

Her parents seemed so very far away. At Christmas her mother sent a tape, painstakingly assembled with many stops and starts and promptings.

Helloooo, deeearr, she said.

Did she always speak so slowly? Did she always roll the 'r' so markedly? She sounded foreign.

Bernard came to visit your father last month and brought us this tape recorder so we could send a message this year. He tells me it's what people do these days instead of cards. Click. Scratch. Click. *How are you? We're both well.* Click. Click. Long pause. *Ooh — I think this is going. Is it going? Can you hear me?* Click. Click. *Yes, well, we've had a lovely summer so far. Not too much rain.* Click. The tape trailed off after ten minutes of hesitant report on the garden, a brief account of Auntie Annie's operation for varicose veins, and a resumé of the talk at this year's Spring Afternoon, which had been about smuggling Bibles into Russia. Click. Click. *Well, I can't think of any more to say,* said her mother. *But Happy Christmas. We'll be thinking of you. Lots of love. Bye . . .* Her voice trailed away into silence. She did not know what to say either.

When Kate rang home, feeding shillings into the phone on the Turl, their voices counted each other out, colliding midway like two bodies fighting to get through a narrow doorway . . .

'What time is it over there?' said her mother, at the same time that Kate asked how they both were.

'I'll get your father,' she said after they had compared the time and the weather and established the exact cost of the call.

There was some fumbling and muttering and then her father came on the line. On the phone his voice still bore a Scots lilt.

'How are you?' said Kate.

'Not bad,' he said. 'Have you got me any books?'

A Young Woman of Otaheite, bringing a Present.
A Canoe of the Sandwich Islands, the Rowers Masked.
A Night Dance by Women, in Hapaee.

Captions to engravings in *A Voyage to the Pacific Ocean* by
Capt. James Cook and Capt. James King

When Kate first arrived in England she had been unable to read. Three years of study had left her with acute literary indigestion. Reading induced a kind of nausea. But she continued to visit bookshops to buy books for her father, scouting through piles of dusty volumes for the Pacific. She found him a copy of Cruise's *Ten Months' Residence in New Zealand,* a book with tattered covers about the everyday life of the Patagonians, another about Easter Island, a book about Polynesian methods of navigation. For five pounds she picked up a volume of engravings of Cook's third voyage, unbound but complete. They had been lying on a table in a dusty corner. She had to lift them closer to the light from the little square-paned windows that opened onto a narrow alleyway.

The light falls, pale and northern, on grey images of palm trees about lagoons where canoes slip over grey water. Grey men paddle a canoe, the muscle of shoulder and torso delineated as carefully as if they were Gaulish warriors. These men have travelled across the ocean tracing starlight and the journeys of gods. They have followed currents and winds, clouds and the flightpaths of land birds and the trails of luminescence emitted into the ocean by islands.

Grey sailors in tricorne hats sprawl before a group of women dancing in exquisitely engraved firelight. Light catches the graceful curve of an upraised arm, the bare breast, the sheen of oiled skin. The crew have their backs to the artist but you can sense the excitement, cocks stiffening against nankeen: these dancers are women any ordinary sailor could fuck in exchange for a nail.

It's a lie, of course: the tiny squirt of disease is already at work, breeding beneath the skin. A chief's son lies in irons on the *Resolution* for stealing one of the ship's cats. Behind the sailors' backs, beyond the rim of firelight, stalk resentment and mistrust. Kate has read since that those dancers were intended as distraction. While Cook and his men sprawled at their ease, the islanders intended to avenge the insult to their chief's son by killing the

Englishmen and seizing their ships. They had that day witnessed English sailors soundly defeated by island boxers in the arena, they had seen English marines fumble in their drill and fire their muskets missing the mark. *They seemed*, wrote Cook in his journal, *to pique themselves in the superiority they had over us.* To recover some reputation, he ordered the gunner to prepare a fireworks display that evening. It was successful. The islanders were impressed. The assassination never eventuated. The sailors in the engraving owe their lives to fire-serpents and flowerpots, sky rockets and water rockets that could travel a distance underwater before bursting forth to explode in a shower of sparks.

There is no hint of that in the engraving: simply grey firelight, the mesmeric sway of grey palm trees, the garlands of grey flowers in the dancers' hair.

Kate stood in the grimy bookshop where the owner sat at a desk, sniffing from hayfever, dust allergy or the beginnings of a summer cold and writing with pen and ink. She could hear the regular sniff sniff sniff and the careful squeak of the pen. She looked at the engravings. They reminded her of the *National Geographic*. She has a memory of children giggling on a wet afternoon at Millerhill and the Divali woman veiling her face in an attempt to hold the camera at bay. A Young Woman of Otaheite brings a gift to Captain Cook and his men. She walks toward the observer, smiling coyly with one hand raised charmingly to her cheek, like some antipodean, barefoot Pinkie, white muslin dress and ribboned bonnet replaced by a crinoline of tapa cloth that leaves one breast bare. The hands are elegant, the bare feet pointed. Another young woman dances wearing a starry hat and a bustle of pleated cloth. She smiles also at the observer. The engraver has captured the softness of her skin as cleverly as he was able to capture the gleam of northern snow or the glow of firelight, but the Divali woman was right to be suspicious.

The images of the engraver were grey, filtered through steel. Kate stood in the shop and was overwhelmed suddenly by a longing for what was absent: for colour, for blue and green and white, and for that brilliant, unflinching Pacific light. She longed for the white sand of an empty beach on a clear day, for the sound of waves breaking after they had crossed thousands of uninterrupted miles onto white sand, not the fret of channel water on shingle; for sand dunes and white gravel roads; for the jagged rim of mountains; for braided rivers milky with snow melt; for the scent of sheepshit and muddy paddock; for the tang of sea salt not diesel; for a whole host of sensations that she had not even known she was missing.

As soon as we had reached the limits of perpetual snow, my two native attendants squatted down, took out their books and began to pray.

Travels in New Zealand by Ernst Dieffenbach

New Zealand became the world imagined. She began frequenting the library at Rhodes House, that chunky monument to imperial ambitions and corporate greed, gone all respectable now with gardens and polished wood and no longer strained with the mess and mayhem of the new empire taking bloody shape in Vietnam. In the moderated hush of the library, Kate began to read again, and for the first time she read about her own country. Missionary accounts, explorers' tales, journals official and unofficial. She read Dieffenbach's account of the ascent of Taranaki, with Heberley the whaler for a companion. Sustained by maize cakes baked for him by one of '*E Kake's*' *female slaves* and with some flowers in his pocket that he identified as a viola, a primula, ranunculus, myosotis and a daisy, he reached the summit, where the pair were immediately enveloped in dense fog. Dieffenbach nevertheless set to *try the temperature of boiling water with one of Newman's thermometers and found it to be 197, the temperature of the air being 49 that taking 55 as the mean of the temperatures at the summit and the base, would give 8839 feet as the mountain's height.* The European stood in the fog on a sacred peak, discovering numbers and facts — and, incidentally, the skeleton of a rat.

The lights came on mid-afternoon and she walked home along the streets of Oxford among all the other young Dieffenbachs in their greatcoats and knee boots shuffling through the fallen leaves of trees whose names — elm, beech, oak — she knew better than she knew the names of the trees in her own country. Where did she belong in all this?

On the lofty peak in the fog of experiment?

Among the New Zealanders on the lower slopes reading their books?

Where am I? Who am I?

The day is early with birds beginning and the wren in a cloud piping like the child in the poem, drop thy pipe, thy happy pipe. And the place grows bean flower, pea-green lush of grass, swarm of insects dizzily hitting the high spots, dunny rosette creeping covering shawl cream in a knitted cosy of roses . . .

Owls Do Cry by Janet Frame

It had not been necessary to read New Zealand literature at university. The New Zealand authors taught were Sargeson and Glover, and they made their appearance as a kind of savoury afterthought following the main course, which was substantial Wordsworth and hearty Dickens. Kate had consulted them briefly: a cat was dropped into the fire in a coal range by a monosyllabic moron, while the poems were about swaggers and beetled seamen and a woman shopping:

In her basket along the street
Rolls heavily against her thigh
The blood-red bud of the meat.

There had been something brutal and foreign and repellent about New Zealand literature. It was as sticky as Baxter *dipping his wick on Castle Street.* He had been too old to possess a viable wick. He had been grubby. When he had delivered a couple of lectures on New Zealand poetry he hunched over the lectern, fixing the few rows of students who bothered to attend with a bleary eye and speaking with a slow, deliberate emphasis. But it did not matter. You did not have to remember what he said, nor read Sargeson or Glover. You could safely bypass New Zealand literature altogether, for all you needed to pass the exams were *Fair seed time had my soul,* and *I grew up Fostered alike by beauty and by fear* and *Whan that Aprill with is shoures soot* and a selection of images of blood and fire from *Macbeth*.

Kate had known of *Owls Do Cry*, of course. She had known about Janet Frame. Janet Frame came from Oamaru. Her great uncle or cousin-once-removed had married Kate's mother's second cousin. Or something like that. That was what Kate's mother had said. He was brainy. He had invented a special light for railway engines that shone around corners but he had been duped by the manufacturers and never made a penny from his invention. Or something like that. The disappointment disturbed him. He became difficult. He took to the drink. Or something like that. The marriage had not lasted.

Janet Frame was a writer, but not as famous as Oamaru's other writer, Essie Summers, whose husband was the minister at Weston and whose books sold by the million overseas. Janet Frame had lived in a house near the Botanic Gardens, in one of the wild gullies beyond *Sequoia gigantea* and *Fagus sylvatica*, which the Adventure Club had made its mission to explore on Saturday mornings. Janet Frame had gone mad. Cracked up. Broken down. She had ended up at Seacliff, that dark castle over the hill from Millerhill where the mental people lived. Like Kate's Uncle Tom, who had to be locked up for their own good.

Essie Summers wrote happy books that people liked and were prepared to pay sixpence a time to read. Janet Frame wrote uncomfortable books. It was said that real people featured in her books. Recognisable people like Maddie's grandmother, Mrs Greenleaf, who ran a corner dairy and gave the children in one of Janet Frame's books sweeties. Sometimes Janet Frame had been less kind. Teachers at Waitaki had been ridiculed, people who deserved greater respect. And doctors at Seacliff, who had only been trying to do their best, and were not at all the bullies they were painted as. Of course they had been upset when the dark castle caught fire. But what did Janet Frame want? Did she think that people who had cracked up, people who were not all there, who were mental, could be let loose to wander at will about the hills, singing and carrying on and looking in the windows of farmhouses where normal people were getting ready for bed or listening to the radio? Was that what she wanted?

Kate read *Owls Do Cry* in Oxford. She liked the roses around the dunny on the first page. There was a teacosy sweetness about the roses. She went on to read with a sickening sensation of recognition. The dump where Francie burned was the dump she and Maura had raided for old telephones to pull to pieces and springs on which they had attempted fantastic feats of flight across the neighbours' fence. The woollen mill was the mill they drove past sometimes in the scarlet Standard, and the little shovel scoop of Friendly Bay was where she had sat with her sister waiting for their jellyfish to melt in the sun. The hospital, where Daphne and the women waited in their red dressing gowns for nine o'clock and the terror of shock treatment, was a Gothic version of the place they had visited to collect Tom for his Sunday dinner. Was this the horror to which he returned after lamb and mint sauce?

See. Forget. Go blind.

A smell hung about the book: the cabbagey pong of human confinement, a menstrual stink, the reek of rotting fear that is also the sweetness of dunny roses. There was anger in the text, and a stern rebuke. This was the unmistakable sound of the Kelveys having their say at last, and it was not calculated to reassure. Lil was saying to all the world, 'This is how it felt. This is how it was for us, the stinky kids. We weren't sweet, we weren't satisfied with our glimpse of the little lamp. You might have thought we had been comforted, but that was as it was reported by the writer occupying the escritoire in the front room of the big house. This is the dark truth of the washerwoman's cottage.'

Toby looked over at his mother. She had a piece of butter paper in her hand and was greasing the girdle for the pikelets that would be made on the coal stove, the batter dropped in spoonfuls on the smoking girdle, and rising and bubbling and browning and being thrust quickly to sweat under a warm folded tablecloth. Amy Withers always made pikelets for peace . . .

Owls Do Cry by Janet Frame

There was the butter paper and the girdle, for the first time. There were the pikelets and the coal range. Kate wanted desperately to escape the book, to close the door on that airless room and run away.

But the story had her by the wrist and it was saying what it had to say with such appalling beauty that she was caught. She had to read it in one breath, right to the end where Bob Withers sat in the Old Men's Home *built on the Cape and all day and night the inmates moved within sound of the sea. And Bob was deaf, and he sat alone, and slobber trickled down his chin, and his voice had grown thin like a thread, and the day burned on him as hot as the stove ready for pikelets if there were anyone in the world to make them.*

She had to read it all, because the Old Men's Home was the place where she had polished the windows and she knew what lay outside: the wide blue of the Pacific and the complicated little settlement that had planted itself on its shore.

24.

We go across the yard. ('Excuse me for taking you in this way but I don't think the front door has been opened since Papa's funeral, I'm afraid the hinges might drop off'), up the porch steps into the kitchen, which really is cool, high-ceilinged, the blinds of course down, a simple, clean threadbare room with waxed worn linoleum, potted geraniums, drinking pail and dipper, a round table with scrubbed oil cloth. In spite of the cleanliness, the wiped and swept surfaces, there is a faint sour smell — maybe of the dishrag or the tin dipper or the oilcloth or the old lady, because there is one, sitting in an easy chair under the clock shelf.

Walker Brothers Cowboy by Alice Munro

The three years in England came to an end, but Steve's thesis remained unfinished, so they decided to go to Toronto where he could work on it a little longer with other, perhaps more helpful, supervisors. He flicked through the stout blue volume that was the university calendar.

'Look,' he said. 'There's a Drama Centre there too.'

Ten years after Madame de Correbas, Kate could study theatre.

They flew out from Heathrow, rising up through bleary cloud above the serpentine curves of the river moulding peninsulas of terraced houses and high streets with Boots the Chemist and Barclays and laundromats and building societies. Higher yet, they flew above hedgerows and woodlands and the little bosomy hills of the countryside. And out over the ocean and when they came down again, they were in Canada.

At first glance, Canada was white slabs of concrete carved into a sky of the most dazzling blue. Cars the size of pool tables swept down eight lanes of freeway before turning onto inner-city streets lined with horse chestnuts bearing candelabras of creamy blossom. It was all a surprise.

Kate knew nothing of Canada, other than some distant recall of the names of the Great Lakes. Canada was the piece that lay like a thick slab of pink icing on top of that other part of the continent which was fruit-cake thick with *I Love Lucy* and *The Summer of Love* and *Catcher in the Rye* and bourbon-and-coke and Bob Dylan, Henry James, *The Graduate*, highway diners, hamburgers, Manhattan, LA, Marilyn Monroe, the Monroe Doctrine, the Confederate South, the Constitution, the Declaration of Independence, Abe Lincoln, convertibles, Cadillacs, Thunderbirds, Walt Disney, Walt Whitman, *The Waltons*, the White House, 'The House of the Rising Sun' and a million other random facts.

Kate had read just two Canadian books: *Anne of Green Gables* by L. M. Montgomery and Robertson Davies' *Fifth Business*.

The country was as shy, as understated and elusive as her own.

I stepped briskly — not running, but not dawdling — in front to the Dempsters just as Percy threw, and the snowball hit Mrs Dempster on the back of the head. She gave a cry and, clinging to her husband, slipped to the ground.

Fifth Business by Robertson Davies

They moved into a flat on Bay Street. It was a skinny house clad in brick-patterned tarpaper that peeled psoriatically at soffit and corner. It stood a little lopsidedly like a jerry-built kitchen cupboard on a corner, one block north of Bloor. Bay Street headed north until it ended, presumably, in the vicinity of Hudson Bay. South, it passed between the cliff faces of the downtown office blocks until it met the waters of Lake Ontario. Bloor Street ran east–west. Follow it far enough and it passed over an infinity of prairie, rose over vertiginous mountains and came at last to the distant Pacific. Follow it east and you came after a few thousand kilometres to the White Way of Delight.

Kate pushed up the window of their room. The sash cord had broken, exactly as the sash cords back home always broke, and the window had to be wedged open with a *Collected Shakespeare*. Outside the room an ash tree sent reflections dancing all over the ceiling. She looked out at their new view. The scale of the place, the expansiveness, was exhilarating. You could stretch as much as you wanted here, and never touch either wall.

Across the hall was Kevin from Kingston, who was studying medicine and lived in a room decorated with posters of women bursting like ripe fruit from black leather astride an assortment of big bikes. His ambition was to lure nurses, preferably ripe, preferably clad in black leather if at all possible — though he wasn't fussy — back to this room, which he managed surprisingly often, given that he had hedgehog hair, thick specs and square yellow teeth like a row of wooden pegs. When a woman landed, he switched on an ultra-violet light that he had rigged to pulse in time to Led Zeppelin, his chosen music for fucking to. All night the flat vibrated to drumbeat and the grunts of mutual pleasure.

Downstairs on the first floor lived Tony, still studying his medieval saints, and across the hall from him, Clara from Alberta slept during the day, emerging as night fell to drop a tab before setting to work on one of the massive canvases that occupied the walls between her bedroom and the bathroom. She slashed at the canvases with a palette knife, producing thick intestinal tangles in savage primary colours. The bathroom was best approached with caution after midnight. Clara stood aside reluctantly as you edged past, her eyes glittery and blank as bottle-glass, the knife in her hand dripping thick blobs of bloody red onto the carpet.

Their landlord lived a few blocks away in the Annex. He called around from time to time to sit and drink coffee. William was only twenty-eight, not much older than any of his tenants, but he seemed already middle-aged. Maybe it was the suit: the tailored suit of fine wool, the white shirt, the silk tie. He worked at the stock exchange, dabbled in real estate and was determinedly set on his first million by thirty and retirement by forty. When he called round, he loosened the tie and said visiting the flat reminded him of grad school, which felt like a lifetime ago.

Two weeks after their arrival, he drove them up to Georgian Bay to 'winterise' the cottage. Houses here had to be tucked in, evidently, before the arrival of a winter more savage and determined than any Kate had previously encountered. They required special attention before being abandoned to the elements until the spring.

'And you've got to see the fall colours,' said Tony.

'Oh indeed,' said William. 'The fall colours are compulsory.' They said it the way people at home said, 'You've got to see Waitomo.' Or Mount Cook. Or the geysers at Rotorua. As if they were mentioning sights that were at once iconic and the clichés of a million postcards, a million souvenir calendars, a million placemats.

They may have been a cliché but Kate was unprepared for the exuberance of trees. Trees at home behaved with due restraint. They were subtle. They exhibited a kind of understated chic in shades of green and brown, season after season. Here the seasons clearly demanded something more dramatic. She looked out the window of William's Volvo as they swooped past two-storeyed farmhouses and their attendant barns standing white and bare-boned against the rococo red and gold of their woodlots. She sat in William's boat as they carved a deep wake between little pink islands upthrust like bare knees, skinned elbows, each bearing on their crests a twisted jackpine, a cottage with its flag lowered in deference to winter's coming and a grove of golden leaf. William's cats, Tristan and Isolde, meowed from their cages, thrusting out desperate paws like prisoners confined to some unspeakable Burmese jail. When the boat drew at last into one of the little islands, their cages were opened and they leapt forth to vanish, tails erect, into the brilliant wood.

The cottage stood solid and rough hewn overlooking an expanse of water turning gold in the setting sun. The air was already cold and scented with damp leaf and the end of summer and after dinner they sat by the fire and drank whisky because William said it was high time they learned to distinguish Laphroaig from Glenmorangie. Above the mantel hung a little row of wizened skins.

'What are those?' said Kate, sniffing for the vanilla tones that made such an unmistakable contrast, so William said, with the Islay tang of peat and seaweed.

William was selecting a cigar.

'Philistine foreskins,' he said. 'Part of my collection.' He rolled the cigar appreciatively, sniffed at the furled leaf. 'I lure innocent young men up here and when I've had my wicked way with them, I toss their bodies into the water. But I always claim a souvenir first and nail it to the wall.'

'They're rattles,' said Tony. 'Snake rattles. There are quite a lot around here.'

'So don't go putting your handypandys into any crevices,' said William. 'You have no idea what may be lurking there.' He struck a match, inhaled then exhaled luxuriously and stretched his boat shoes toward the fire. 'The cats catch them,' he said. 'They are formidable hunters, aren't you, my dears?' The cats curled like velvet on his lap, resting between forays.

That night Kate lay listening to the strangeness of this place. The rustling of golden leaf, the yowling of cats reverting to the jungle, the cry of a bird somewhere out on the lake, of deepest despair, as if something irretrievable had been lost here for ever. She felt very small, like a child who had yet to learn a whole new language.

The next morning Tony showed her how to paddle an Indian canoe. They crossed the channel to a larger, neighbouring island while William fixed the shutters and Steve, the cabinetmaker's son, helped him, happily wielding a hammer with a couple of nails clamped between his teeth. From mid-channel, Kate could hear the rap of their hammers echoing weirdly in the cavities of glaciated rock and the sound of William's voice raised in a cheerful tuneless baritone. *O contadi*! he sang, to the brilliant morning.

Tony held the canoe steady as she stepped awkwardly ashore, then he walked ahead of her into the woods. Golden leaf covered the ground, golden leaf gathered overhead. He had on a red T-shirt with a little hole torn at one shoulder. Suddenly he lifted his hand and they both halted. Ahead, in a clearing, stood a young stag. They had approached him downwind and for just a second they were close enough to see the red flicker of his tongue tasting the air. He turned and saw them then, and once, twice he stamped his hoof, like some Spanish dancer in his pointed shoes, then he leapt to one side. There was some crackling of twigs and he had vanished. Gold leaves spiralled about dizzily where he had stood. Tony turned to her and his face was shining and Kate looked up at him among the flying leaves and thought, I love you.

The thought arrived from nowhere, unexpected, startling. She loved Tony, standing there with his rumpled hair and his ripped T-shirt and worn jeans. She loved Steve too of course, hammering away out there in the sunshine. She had assumed until then that marriage was a kind of inoculation: one jab, one set of vows, and you were preserved from falling in love with anyone else for life, but she'd been wrong.

For just a second, the possibility stands there, tasting the air: the kiss, the furtive liaison, passion in the afternoons behind drawn curtains once they return to the city, another life entirely. Tony is looking down at her. He reaches out and peels a leaf from her arm, gently as if it were another layer of skin.

'Me too,' he says, though she has said nothing. 'I love you too.' And the possibility leaps aside and disappears. They'll do nothing further, say nothing more about it. But she loved him then. She'd love him always.

I love the subway. Not its denatured surfaces, not its weatherless tunnels, but its mad anonymous, hyperactive, scrambling and sorting; the doors sliding open in the station, the rush of people, their faces declaring serious and purposeful journeys they are undertaking . . . I like to think at the end of each of these rushed, wordless, singular journeys, there is someone waiting, someone who is loved.

The Box Garden by Carol Shields

Steve and Kate had no car, so they lived within the confines of the city. She loved the crowd waiting for the lights outside the subway entrance at Bloor and Bay, at the foot of the canyon where a small particular current always eddied, snatching at bags and briefcases and tossing women's skirts around their waists. She loved Queen's Park rattling with fallen leaves and the streetcars heading out to the Beaches, people resting bare arms on the windowsills in the last of the Indian summer and the press of all their languages on every side.

She loved kitchen tables in flats off Spadina or College where the talk was about events and people she had never previously heard of: Tommy Douglas, Joey Smallwood, the Winnipeg General Strike, the October Crisis and the War Measures Act and Emily Carr and federation and Louis Riel and Rene Levesque and the purging of Waffle from the NDP (they all voted NDP). NDP. CCF. RIN. FLQ. She loved the eccentricity that seemed to lurk below the earnest public decorum of Canada, where the country could be governed by a man like MacKenzie King who conducted a war on the basis of advice from his dead mother, whom he believed to inhabit the soul of his dog.

She loved hearing her friends talk about the places they had left to come here to the city: the Mennonite farm in Manitoba, with its acres of blue-flowering linen flax a misty ocean; the father who preached to his congregation in eighteenth-century German; the baby brother who died and was kept in a baby bath full of ice while the women of the community prepared his funeral; the crack in the earth from which snakes emerged after overwintering to mate in great seething knots in the weak spring sunshine.

They talked about canoe trips into the deep forests of the north, or skating parties along prairie drainage canals, the skaters spread out in a line moving across a disk where there were no hills or forests to break the perfect round bowl of the sky and its circular horizon.

Winter came to the city, and ice rinks formed in the parks where portly men, serious and pink-cheeked, skated about balanced on a single blade with one leg lifted elegantly behind, and the lights came on in the afternoon and the stores were filled with a dozen different contraptions for the toasting of sandwiches and a hundred different machines for the manufacture of the perfect latte. She loved winter evenings knocking a puck around a deserted schoolyard with garbage bins for goals and everyone playing hard, though she never quite got the rules.

'Just slam it,' said Tony, passing to her from the left. That seemed to be the only rule that counted.

Then spring arrived overnight: one minute it was slush and grime, the next the lawns had been rolled out and the flowers were fully formed and the smell of last year's dog shit was sweet and noxious in the cool clear air and the chestnuts held knuckles of leaf. She loved the Beaches on an early summer morning, the joggers on the boardwalk, the sound of someone singing from an upstairs window, and hot summer nights when the Portuguese families played cards until after midnight on their porches and the Chinese ladies talked across the width of the street, their bamboo fans flapping like moths' wings in the light from the open windows and the air was soft and heavy around them all as a woollen blanket.

They left the city infrequently, and when they did it was usually by train. Kate looked out at the townships along the way with their wide, empty streets and plain houses. Railway lines are sneaky things, designed for glimpsing the back door, the back yard, the heap of wrecked cars, the shambling downtown, not the bright perfect face presented to the road. She looked out at the towns and the farms and swamp and forest as the train, horn blaring, carried them up to Montreal to visit David and Toba, who had returned from Oxford to a house crammed with the astonishing clutter required for the nurture of small children: baby buggies and little bicycles parked in awkward hallways, swings on springs hung in doorframes, an avalanche of Lego over the living-room floor, the only uncluttered place the little back bedroom Toba used as a studio. Between nappy changes she painted: not the folk-art designs but tiny images of the sky, 'because that's what you notice when you come back to Canada, all that sky', overlaid with details painstakingly copied from Mantegna, Vermeer, Holbein. A cherub's upturned face, a pearl earring, 'because it's all I've got time for, and anyway, I like details. You can learn a lot from studying details.'

To have my closet inviolate, to be sole empress of my tea-table, which you must never presume to approach without first asking leave. And lastly, wherever I am, you shall always knock at the door before you come in. These articles subscribed, if I continue to endure you a little longer, I may by degrees dwindle into a wife.

The Way of the World by William Congreve

The Drama Centre had its offices in a miniature version of an Oxford college, complete with St Catherine's bell and the standard ex-services porter breathing lunchtime ale through a waxed moustache. Robertson Davies presided. He strode magnificently each morning across the park in a Tennysonian hat and swinging a walking cane Kate suspected might be malacca. She passed him sometimes on her way to classes in dramatic theory and practice.

The students were a varied lot and plays at the centre were performed in a corresponding Babel of accents: Canadian of every provenance — rural Ontarian, prairie, eastern seaboard; a pick-'n'mix from south of the border; English, both posh and regional; Scots; Irish; German; Australian. It did not seem to matter here. *The Way of the World* was about love and malice and what it meant was more important than uniformity of diction. Rehearsals went on late into the night and repaired afterwards to a café on Bloor Street where the cast ate French fries and steamed pudding among a mêlée of late workers and insomniacs: the kind of men who sat for hours over a coagulating coffee, probably planning how to concrete their landladies into the basement. The kind of women who tottered in from temperatures edging toward zero in halter tops, hot pants and silver wedge-sandals.

'Well, here we are,' said Donna, a law student who was playing Foible. She was picking all the currants from her pudding and arranging them, *tinker tailor soldier sailor*, around the rim of her bowl. 'All looking for love on the twilit streets of the mean city.'

She was plump as a pudding herself, not to mention sporting a fierce squint and problematic facial hair.

'Jello in a sack,' she said, resignedly spooning up custard. 'It's just as well I've got a fabulous personality.'

But she was also a gifted mimic. In her hands, Foible was running off with the play.

Humh (says he), what, you are a hatching some plot (says he), you are so early abroad or catering (says he), ferreting for some disbanded officer . . . Night after night, the cast was reduced to that helpless hysterical rehearsal giggling that made the director sigh and say, 'Okay, you guys, take five.'

Seated in Vic's, Donna arranges the currants on her plate *rich man poor man beggar man* and performs episode 503 in the long-running soap that was the Disastrous Love Life of Donna Da Silva:

the Date With The Man Who Worked With Her Cousin In Detroit. The Jazz Buff.

She had bought these new shoes, death-defying stilettos, micro skirt, shoulder-length earrings, the whole catastrophe, and he turned out to be five foot, a fact her cousin had omitted to mention. But never mind: they went to this place downtown — leather couches, jazz band, pocket-size dance-floor — and they were getting on fine. He talked, she sat and said a-ha, a-ha, the way they mistake for intelligence, and then he suggested they danced and he was one of those guys who throws you about, spins you out, reels you in and she was trying not to fall off the stilettos and then suddenly the band switched to slow and sexy and he came in for the clinch and he was whispering something against her neck and she nodded and Jesus, there was this ripping sound — brrrrrt — and whaddya know, his hair was caught in her earring. No kidding, it came right off, and there she was with some kinda squirrel hanging from one ear and this little bald guy was jumping about like Rumpelstiltskin hissing 'Give it back! Give it back!'. But she couldn't and the more he hissed the more hysterical she became but finally she got it disentangled and he snatched his hair and went off to the men's room and just disappeared. Left her high and dry with the bill to pay.

'So,' says Donna, *doctor lawyer Indian chief*, 'I don't think I'll be dating anyone recommended by any member of my family again. Not ever.'

She has them exactly: the irritable little man, the hopeful idiot who is herself. She makes a gift of her embarrassment and frustration, the story-teller's gift, to the cast of rakes and ladies gathered in the steamy warmth at Vic's.

Three nights a week Kate also worked late at the university library. Her job there was to issue books, alongside a stern Lithuanian who supervised the night shift. Valda wore a permed blonde helmet and was a passionate advocate of colonic irrigation. Between student enquiries, which she dismissed with brisk disdain, she described its benefits in graphic detail.

'Iss amazink vott iss in 'ere,' she said, patting Kate's stomach. 'Meat. In beeg lumps zat rot and steenk.' She was in love too, with Max, who had been a businessman in Budapest but had been unable to find comparable employment here. He wore a suit and tie nevertheless to do the shelving, bowed slightly when encountered on the stairs and maintained a dignified demeanour at all times. The library extended several floors down. Silent secretive places where the smell of old paper mingled with the furtive pong of orange peel and chewing gum, though the rules were clear. NO EATING. Valda made it her duty every evening on the hour to patrol the stacks evicting wrongdoers. She returned with her hands full of unwrapped candy bars, bananas and peanut butter sandwiches.

A girl arrived one night at the desk, breathless.

'There's a man downstairs,' she gasped. 'He's crawling between the desks and the wall. He . . . well, I had my shoes off while I was reading and he started rubbing his . . . well, his *dick* on my feet. He's down there still. On C Floor.'

'On C Floor?' said Valda. 'Zat is strange. Zis man, with ze feet, 'e is usually on B Floor. I shall call Mr Korda.' She pressed the buzzer to summon Max. He materialised instantly from the stairwell in his grey suit like the ghost of Hamlet's father emerging from the trap, immaculate even in death. Valda meanwhile was leaning toward the girl, who had run barefoot up three flights and was holding in one hand a half-eaten apple. Her eyes snapped.

'You haff been eating!' she said.

Kate walked home from rehearsal or library along the midnight streets, planning how to tell it. From the corner, she could see a light shining in their window on the top floor. Steve would be working, seated at the table they had found in a bin one night on Forest Hill: a perfectly good dining table along with two matching chairs. They had carried it home where it joined the other trophies in their room: the bed from another bin in the Annex, an awkward find that had to be carried with difficulty along the dark streets, Steve at the back, Kate at the front. The easy chair that was missing only one leg had come from Cabbagetown, where someone was busy rehabbing one of the old worker's cottages. Beside the easy chair in the window embrasure stood their most valued find: the silver ashtray borne aloft by an ecstatic dancer. It was amazing what people here threw out. All their clothes came from bins too, or the Salvation Army Store. Winter jackets, jeans, a couple of curtains Kate had stitched together and wore with a tasselled cord as a belt. She loved roaming about this city scavenging, improvising their shared life.

Steve straightens up as she opens the door, wiping his eyes clear of the after-image of words. He had work too, translating a coffee table book on Viking art for Phaidon, its original Danish as convoluted as the tangle of serpents on a bronze shield.

'How was work?' he says.

Or, 'How was rehearsal?'

And she tells him the stories she has planned on the way home: about Donna and the jazz buff's toupée, or Valda and the foot fetishist from C Floor. They lie together on their pilfered bed, arms around each other, laughing and telling the inconsequential tales that those who sleep together under a single sheet exchange at the end of every day.

25.

When a great political movement takes place, it is not consciously led nor organised: the unconscious self in mankind breaks its way through the problem as an elephant breaks through a jungle. Finally . . . the whole political business goes to smash; and presently we have Ruins of Empires, New Zealanders sitting on a broken arch of London Bridge, and so forth. To that recurrent catastrophe we shall certainly come again unless we can have a Democracy of Supermen . . .

Preface to *Man and Superman* by G.B. Shaw

They studied film history with Josef Skvorecky. The knights of the Klan galloped to attend the Birth of a Nation, prescient battalions of workers in striped uniforms marched through the distorted streets of Metropolis, the little aeroplane circled through towering cities of cloud bearing the beloved leader to the ecstatic crowd. The students in lecture room 101 heard for the first time the superman's rhetoric of blood and brotherhood translated from the usual stiff-legged comedy routine to a deadly poetic.

The vast army carries shovels as soon they will bear guns, they plant trees as soon they will plant bones. The mass is reduced to the individual.

Where are you from? calls the comic, the good joker.

From Kaiserstuhl! replies one honest worker.

From the Saar! replies another.

One people! One leader! One Reich! And it is so wonderfully filmed, so queasily seductive.

A pram bounces down the steps, a mother screams silently at the loss of her son, an army fights upon a frozen river.

Skvorecky was newly arrived from Prague and the winter that had followed that fine spring. He was puzzled at the students' lack of understanding.

'How can you not see that this is political allegory, not a re-creation of history?' he asked. Ivan the Terrible? The tyrant? The despot? Stalin? The children of a generous sample of western democracies nodded and noted it down. *Ah yes, of course. Now that you point it out . . .* Skvorecky stood at the lectern, tears in his eyes at their comfortable ignorance of irony.

Shakespeare was Clifford Leach, a brilliant and patient man, blessed with the gift of turning a student's fumbling question into the subject for informative discourse. And Robertson Davies was Shaw. His tutorial style was the provocative debate: no essays, no end-of-year exam, just talk around a table. Students had been demanding an end to the old methods and old structures — so let them try the new.

A democracy of supermen, he muses. His voice is rich, his brows most definitely beetle. He regards the students seated around the

313

table over half-frame glasses. 'Do we agree?' he says. 'And if not, what would we propose as the ideal form of government?'

The students doodle knotted lines on their notepads. They cross-hatch all the capital letters in SUPERMAN. Assessment for the course is, however, based on the quality of their reply so finally they are all flushed out onto open ground.

'Some form of socialism, I suppose,' says Kate when it is her turn.

'Indeed?' says Robertson Davies. 'And what might we mean by the term socialism?' He gives the word a hollow beat. Kate feels herself step out onto an icy street with her back to the enemy.

'Some form of government that guarantees equality of opportunity for all,' she says. She can hear her voice rise at the end in the New Zealand fashion, signifying some lack of conviction, but it had worked for her, this socialism, so why should it not work for the world?

'For the purpose of engendering universal happiness, I presume?' says Robertson Davies. He has put a stone in the snowball. Kate can feel it coming. No matter how carefully she treads, the ball will land between her shoulderblades.

'Well, that's a lot to ask of any sys—' she begins, but Davies is speaking. '*A lifetime of happiness!*' he declaims, as if centre stage at the Old Vic. '*No man could bear it! It would be hell on earth!*' Kate looks around the table. None of the other students will meet her eye. She is on her own, out here on slippery ground. She makes one final desperate appeal.

'I just think there might, you know, be a chance that people might be happier, you know, that there'd be more kind of general happiness under a socialist government than any, you know, other kind of universal government I can think of, if you see what I mean . . .' She has lost them. Lost the other students, not to mention the chance of an A — in this course anyway. She is rapidly sliding toward a B, maybe a C. Robertson Davies takes out a pocket watch and turns the little knob on its top rapidly back and forth. *What socialism will look like when it takes its final form*, he says, *we do not know and cannot say.* Do you know who said that, Mrs Dobbs?' Kate shakes her head. He holds the watch to his ear to check its steady reliable tick. 'Vladimir Ilych Ulyanov,' he says. 'Whom history remembers as Lenin.'

The ball lands. Ice slides down her collar.

As played by Robertson Davies, Shaw was no longer the iconoclast who had smashed the hole through which she had escaped religion. He boomed at her. He corrected her. He was becoming irritating.

He had learned to take tobacco: and when he was assur'd he would die, he desir'd they would give him a pipe in his mouth, ready lighted; that they did: and the executioner came, and first cut off his members, and threw them into the fire; and after that with an ill-favoured knife, they cut off his ears and his nose, and burn'd them; he still smoked on, as if nothing had touch'd him; then they hack'd off one of his arms, and still he bore up, and held his pipe; but at the cutting off the other arm, his head sunk, and his pipe dropped and he gave up the ghost.

Oroonoko by Aphra Behn

'Aphra Behn,' said her MA supervisor. His wife wrote a regular column for the *Globe and Mail* on the history of food: one part history, the other good old-fashioned gourmandise. Tonight, for dinner, they were making pasta. It was taking hours. First the special gluten flour, then the eggs, then the repeated stretching of the dough through a silver mangle they had bought in Florence on their last visit to Italy. He poured Kate another glass of some aperitif that tasted of artichokes and removed all the plaque from her teeth. It was also making her rather drunk. 'Seventeenth century,' he said. Strands of tagliatelle emerged from the machine. They were all rather drunk, in fact. Kate hung some tagliatelli across the backs of a couple of kitchen chairs. The room had become a cat's cradle of pasta. They were becoming trapped in a web of pasta. For afters they were going to have a medieval cheesecake, flavoured with elderflowers. 'I think you'll like her,' said her supervisor. '"The Admirable Astrea". She's quirky. Look her up. She's in the library.'

And there she was, the next morning, occupying half a metre of shelving in a distant corner of the stacks. Kate was feeling slightly bilious from pasta and cheesecake at 1am, but Aphra Behn did indeed look quirky and not in the least astral. She was rather solid, with a determined chin. The only biography was brief and filled with surmise. She might have gone to Surinam, she might have spied for the English in Holland. She had certainly written a lot of plays and short stories featuring libidinous nuns and dashing rogues. Kate had never heard of her before but she liked the look of that dimpled chin. Here was someone who had not composed elegant verse at the escritoire of some country estate, but scribbled hard for her life in the scrum that was Grub Street.

Kate chose *Oroonoko* for her essay topic — an account, supposedly an eye-witness account of an uprising by slaves in South America. There was a good deal of feathered prose about it, but forcing it forward was an unflinching documentary sense of outrage. A woman with a chin like that could very likely have travelled so far, and returned to write for the first time of the savagery that underpinned the Palladian elegance of the country estates and the enlightened debate within the city. Her presence there in the far corner of the stacks hinted at a different version of literary history than the one Kate had encountered so far. She was the tiny bayonet tip that hinted at a forgotten, buried army.

I am not so credulous as to believe that it has been coincidence that has been responsible for the disappearance of more than one hundred good women novelists before Jane Austen in favour of five men (Defoe, Fielding, Richardson, Smollett and Sterne) . . . In the face of the verdict of the men of letters it is my contention that women were the mothers of the novel and that any other version of its origin is but a myth of male creation.

Mothers of the Novel by Dale Spender

BA. MA. PhD.

Why not collect the set?

It was all part of that great gift, The Opportunity. And when it came to choosing a topic for a PhD, Eliot was the man. He was big: a rock-like eminence on the literary landscape. He was a set text and books about him occupied several shelves at the centre of the stacks. He was serious. He had most likely been born in a three-piece suit and suckled uttering Greek tags.

Prologue. Doris and Dusty.

Parodos. Arrival of Wauchope, Horsfall, Klipstein, Krumpacker.

Kate began work on a manuscript outline for one of Eliot's unfinished works, *Sweeney Agonistes*. The outline was rough: a couple of sheets of notepaper with pencil scribblings. She liked that, just as she preferred sketches, or the cartoons for paintings. The red outlines that lay underneath all those layers of laquer and polish were so much more satisfying than perfection and completion. She liked the jagged hint of the writer at work, the second thoughts, the scratchings out. It was like stripping away the wallpaper surface and finding a rougher, more expressive pattern underneath.

Agon. Sweeney monologues.

Parabasis. Chorus 'The Terrors of the Night'

For two years Kate examined these scraps of notepaper, just as others around her were examining Icelandic love poems, or the political speeches of MacKenzie King or a saint's life as it was recorded by various medieval monks.

Scene. Entrance of Mrs Porter. Debate with Sweeney. Murder of Mrs Porter.

She loved the jazzy coalescence of the dialogue Eliot had completed before a sudden conversion to High Anglicanism rendered him certain and boring. She loved the way the play scooped up contemporary anthropological speculation about the rituals that lay at the roots of drama: the ancient death rituals and the celebration of human frailty that lay behind tragedy, all the way through from Antigone to Bonnie and Clyde. Or the fertility rituals that lay perhaps behind the romantic preoccupations of comedy. She loved the daffy romanticism of Cornford and Frazer and the other anthropologists and their visions of orgiastic coupling in Arcadian woods, the sacrifice, the crack of the symbolic egg, the imagery of rebirth, the sacred marriage of the goddess and the god newly restored to youth and vigour. She loved the passion with which people adopted such visions, as the twentieth century came thundering down on them with nerve gas and aerial bombardment. She loved the fact that these scraps of play had been written just at that point when the most primitive instincts of aggression ran slap bang into sophisticated chemical and mechanical technologies in that great culling from the flock of all those young men who were most energetic, most idealistic, most likely to smash down the palace gates and cause trouble. She loved the way these scraps of notepaper bobbed about on the Zeitgeist like a little paper boat.

I knew a man once did a girl in . . .

But stripping away the wallpaper also exposed patches of damp rot. The same man who was capable of this sour, syncopated brilliance was also capable of sniggering doggerel of the *King Bollo and his big black queen/With a bum as big as a soup tureen* variety. It was like coming upon the great man stripped of his suit and discovering him in only his underpants and his underpants were saggy with loose grey elastic and had holes in the crutch. She examined his photograph in the rotund biographies and saw him standing next to that pale wraith of a wife who appeared to float a foot or two from the ground and who emanated such pure misery that it was difficult not to suspect him of some private failing. But T. S. Eliot was her topic and she could not afford at that moment to doubt him. She had to persist in adding another stone to his sizeable cenotaph.

Germaine: My God! My God! My stamps! There's nothing left! Nothing! Nothing ! My beautiful new home! My lovely furniture! Gone! My stamps! My stamps!

Germaine falls to her knees beside the chair picking up the stamps remaining. We hear all the others outside singing O Canada. A rain of stamps falls slowly from the ceiling.

Les Belles Soeurs by Michel Tremblay

They travelled down to Washington for Nixon's anti-inaugural, hurtling down the freeway jammed in the back of a rattling Chevrolet driven by Kevin, who was planning to volunteer at one of the paramedic stations. The minute they crossed the border they were in a familiar movie. The radio played 'American Pie' and they sang along as the Chevrolet passed through the scenery that had accompanied movies as long as they could remember. Skyscraper cities, black neighbourhoods, farms with post-and-rail fencing and white barns.

The White House was a few blocks from the flat where they were staying with one of Kevin's friends. They marched up Pennsylvania Avenue, and the chanting belonged here, truly, for the first time. They were taking part in the original rather than its distant imitation. That night, Kate got up from their mattress on the floor of the friend's flat. The room was high-ceilinged and decorated with exquisite Georgian plasterwork abruptly interrupted by flimsy subdividing walls. The windows were generously proportioned to let in rational amounts of light. The air beyond the panes crawled with sirens, strange cries, a sudden burst of furious shouting like the barking of wild dogs. Elegant Doric columns ornamented its porch, but the vestibule stank of piss and when Kate switched on the light in the kitchen the walls shimmered with the nutbrown bodies of cockroaches scrambling for cover. It was curiously beautiful, this shining wall, the whisper of dry carapaces.

In the morning the bathroom on the landing was locked from the inside.

'Shit!' said Kevin's friend. 'Another of those fuckers.' He hammered at the door. There was some vague movement behind the polished oak, like something dragging itself with infinite pain across the floor.

'Get the fuck outta my bathroom!' yelled the friend.

Silence.

'Get the fuck out, shithead, or I'm calling the cops this time, you hear?'

There was a muttering from behind the door, a fumbling at the latch. The door opened slowly. A young man knelt on the floor, rubber still twisted around his arm, his eyes rolled back to the white.

"'S cool,' he muttered, dragging himself up the icy face of the bath. "'S cool.'

He swayed in the doorway, like a sick cat whose fur was matted and its tail filthy and its eye dropped from one socket, then stumbled somehow back down the stairwell holding tight to the sinuous curves of the maplewood banister.

'You guys watch your feet when you take a shower,' said the friend, making a quick examination of the bathroom. 'Could be needles or sump'n. I'll make some coffee.'

And that, too, felt familiar, like something they had seen on TV.

Canada was not a movie, though it was fast becoming one. Kate sat in theatres among audiences seeing rural Quebec on screen for the first time, or the wide empty streets of Sudbury. In the dark the audience squirmed with sweaty embarrassment, sensing the most minute inauthenticity, as actors struggled with the business of being themselves rather than theatrical Regency swells or Southern belles. In the dark the audience watched their country become something more than a momentary reference to meet legal distribution requirements. The coffin was carried across a snowy field they recognised from somewhere north of Montreal, the uncle was like their uncle and the recognition was both painful and amusing, like the faint hysteria at a family funeral when your very own Uncle Bill or Auntie Eileen, having consumed one drink too many, insists upon grabbing the microphone and standing centre stage to sing 'Bye Bye Blackbird'.

———————————

I hadn't reminded my father of the game. I was afraid he'd show up and embarrass me. Twelve years old, and ashamed of my old man. Ashamed of his dialect, his dirty overalls, his bruised fingers with the fingernails lined with dirt, his teeth yellow as old ivory. Most of all, his lunch-pail, that symbol of the working man . . .

Of the Fields Lately by David French

Each week Kate wrote reviews for the student newspaper. Two plays a week, from bleacher seats erected in the echoing machine rooms of former factories, from warehouses and railway sheds and rooms above electrical stores off Yonge Street. Plays in English and plays with the vinegar tang of joual. Plays based on interviews with Ontario farmers or nineteenth-century feuds between Irish settlers, plays featuring Quebecois transvestites and Newfoundlanders, plays satirising Canadian government policy, or improvised comedy, or versions of that play that was being written in various settings and various languages everywhere in that decade: the play about the working-class boy or girl who leaves home and goes to the city to take up their Opportunity, and the guilt and love and anger that erupt when the boy or girl returns.

The writers reached for big bleak moments. Their sets had taps that squirted real water in lovingly recreated rural kitchens, or they opted for symbolic simplicity: eight panels of perspex to create the walls of offices or hotel rooms, a row of lanterns marking the road lines of Ontario. Buying a ticket to these productions came with no guarantee. No foreknowledge of the text, no preconceptions. Audiences cringed or walked out loudly before half-time announcing, 'Pack of bushers!' before slamming the door. But when the actors and the playwrights and the technical crew and the designer got it right, the audience laughed — that startled laughter at something so familiar that it had not previously been considered worthy of comment. They went quiet and still and attentive, drawn into the wonderful intimate ritual of let's pretend.

Kate sat scribbling notes in the half-dark while a young man wearing nothing but a green ribbon around his penis sang soulfully to thirty people assembled in a former soap factory on a cold winter night. The seats were wooden benches and they were hard and a distinct draught cut the backs of her knees and she loved the risk they were all taking: of embarrassment, boredom, failure, probably pneumonia. All on the chance of witnessing something new and true. The naval ensign had been replaced by a maple leaf but it still felt like something glued on, as if the country were still getting its tongue around a new anthem. Expo had closed and its buildings stood empty: flimsy futuristic domes and towers of perspex and ply waiting to be filled with something.

There were novels, too, where she found the places she had glimpsed from the back seat of a car on the way to Georgian Bay or from the train. The books took her around to the back door and let her into the place where passions seethed around scrubbed kitchen tables and that faint sour smell was the smell of a dishrag in a bucket. These places were recognisably the places her friends here had left when they rode away on the bus from the shores of Lake Huron or some rail stop out west toward the towers of the shining city. They reminded her of the place she had left herself. The post office might not be built of stone, but it occupied the same prominence on the main street; the general store might not be the Farmers' Co-op, but it had the same socks and racks of shirts. And the people were familiar: the couple glimpsed parked up in a car, 'though they had no business to be there', the man who told jokes but said nothing of what he thought or felt, the chorus of neighbours who watched and gossipped. Their speech had a different rhythm, but in the frugal silence between the words Kate detected an echo of home.

She began to exist in two worlds: one was the customary literary world, the common room inhabited by Shaw, Eliot, Cornford and a pachyderm tribe of important men. The other was the Canadian world of small rural towns, bare yards and high-ceilinged kitchens. People laughed in that world in a way that no one ever laughed in the common room. The grand men were clever, but their room was classical and cold. The Canadian world was composed of scraps of speech woven like the scraps that had been once an uncle's good trousers or a child's frock into a serviceable rag-rug, something to be placed before the fire, somewhere you could stand and warm your feet. It was waxed linoleum, scrubbed oil cloth. Kate opened the door to this room and took a good look around.

26.

We negotiated the stairs of the back porch, which were overgrown with empty bottles of all kinds, beer bottles, milk bottles, wine and Scotch bottles and baby bottles, and found Clara in the garden sitting in a round wicker basket chair with metal legs. She had her feet up on another chair and was holding her latest baby somewhere in the vicinity of what had once been her lap.

The Edible Woman by Margaret Atwood

She was walking home to the flat one night feeling full of words. They filled every crevice of her brain, packed down solid like the stuffing in a cabbage. She could burst from so many words and all their contradiction. When that happened, she reached out and touched something real: a tree trunk, big and solid as your mother's leg when you were small and in need of comfort. A leaf bud, furled like a tiny fist. A daisy poking its yellow head through the gaps in a rotting picket-fence. Their solid, seasonal presence, flowering, setting seed, dying back each year, held her steady.

A chestnut lay on the path, still in its prickled green hood, though one side was cracked, and in the crack she could see the nut lying snug in its white moulding. She broke the case and took the nut out. It fitted, smooth and cool and rubbed to a high finish in the palm of her hand. She held it tight while she crossed the road and just at the corner where the leaves had piled deep, she thought, I could have a baby. The thought rose unbidden and would not go away. That night she lay in bed stroking the curve of her belly. Beneath its skin lay tubes and eggs and all the apparatus required for birth, not much better understood than when she was twelve.

A baby.

She pushed the idea aside. The world was too full of babies already; it was irresponsible even to consider procreation while millions starved and resources to feed those already on the planet were exhausted. More pragmatically, they were sharing a flat; they had only their student grants and a couple of temporary jobs to live on; they were thousands of miles from home. Kate had never babysat a child, she had not the faintest idea when they talked or walked, nor the slightest notion of how to care for one. She had never read a single book that described birth: death had been there in every kind of explicit, groaning detail, but birth was generally marked by a row of asterisks, a change of subject, an abrupt move to an adjoining chapter. In movies, birth happened off screen as ear-splitting shrieks from an upstairs room while the hero paced below boiling water, presumably for cups of tea all round once the hideous ordeal was over. She knew nothing about birth nor about babies, but she rolled over anyway, that bubble of excitement already rising like pure water within her, and put her arms around Steve.

'Steve?' she said. 'Why don't we have a baby?'

Steve turned toward her.

'What?' he said.

'A baby,' she said. 'We could have a baby.'

'When?' said Steve. 'Now?'

'Yes,' she said. She could hardly speak for the excitement of it.

Steve stroked her hair.

'But what about your thesis?' he said.

'What about it?' she said.

'I thought that was what you wanted,' he said. 'To finish a PhD?'

'I can still finish,' said Kate. 'People do all sorts of things and have babies.' She did not want to think about such niceties. She did not want to think at all. She felt like a child at Christmas, an excitement all the greater for the fact that this time she herself would be the parcel, a baby wrapped within the tissue of her own skin. She wrapped her legs around Steve's and nuzzled at his neck.

'You sure?' said Steve, and yes, she said, yes yes yes yes.

Within a week she knew she was pregnant.

'I think this drug thing must be wearing off,' I said mildly, 'because it seems to be getting worse and worse, can you give me something else please, quick?'

'Oh no!' they said, 'not yet, you've a long time to go yet, we have to leave something to give you later on.'

'Oh,' I said feebly, 'What a pity.'

'Never mind,' they said, 'you're coming along nicely,' and they turned and went back to their row of seats outside and had just resumed their conversation, though in more muffled tones, when I heard myself start to moan rather

violently and they all came rushing back and within five minutes my child was born . . .

The Millstone by Margaret Drabble

A summer night, too hot to sleep, the Chinese ladies talking downstairs. Their new flat is near the market in one of those streets inhabited by successive waves of immigrants. Only a few years before, it was Jewish. The holes for the mezuzah are still there on the doorframes and a few elderly middle Europeans hold out behind elaborately crisscrossed net curtains. But that tide has retreated up onto the lake terraces and now the street is Chinese and every yard is cultivated with spinach and rows of lettuces and on this hot night the old ladies do not seem to sleep at all, but sit out on their porches playing mah jong and talking to one another across the width of the street.

Their voices rise and fall like the comfortable clucking of birds and there is the click of west wind and east wind, the flap flap flap of bamboo fans. Steve has settled to a light restless sleep, one hand flung back behind his head. Kate lies beside him, feeling the baby squirm within the taut skin of her belly. She can feel it roll over and when she places her hand against her skin there's the nudge of heel or elbow and the smooth curve of the baby's back. She slides out of bed, fills a glass with water from the fridge, sits on the sofa by the open window. The chestnut tree outside is all lit up with candle flowers and its leaves move in the breeze that comes up after dark from the lake. She peels her nightie away from her body so that the breeze can lift it too, making a sail of fine white cotton. She picks up her book.

> *Martha allowed herself to be held upright by the mud and lowered her hands through the resisting water to the hard dome of her stomach. There she felt the crouching infant, still moving tentatively around in its prison, protected from the warm red water by half an inch of flesh. Her stomach stretched and contracted; and the frog swam slowly across the water, with slow, strong spasms of its legs, still watching Martha from one bright eye.*
>
> *A Proper Marriage* by Doris Lessing

After the pale blue slab of Georgette Heyer consumed in adolescence, Kate had read few novels written by women. She had studied even fewer: Jane Austen made the cut but she was often on her own, scribbling on her little ivory tablets in a corner of the common room occupied by all those magisterial men. Virginia Woolf was taken seriously and so was Sylvia Plath, but they were depressing. They killed themselves. They cracked up from the unnaturalness of their occupation, destroyed by too many words. Kate avoided them, fearful of contagion. Some superstitious dread warned against contact. Some vapour rising from *The Bell Jar* or *The Waves* could be breathed in from their pages, bearing with it distress, despair, self-destruction. Kate wanted to be in the dining room making easy chat with the winners, with the sleek and the successful people, not kneeling with her head in a gas oven and a pile of dirty dishes in the sink.

But who could tell Kate about birth?

In the first month of pregnancy Kate went to the library and looked up the books. There were books with profiles of a pink sac and tubes, and books with grainy photographs of women with contorted faces squeezing out a head the size of a basketball. It looked so hideous that Kate shoved them back on a lower shelf and exited hurriedly in the direction of fiction.

Her baby stretches now, pressing uncomfortably on bladder or kidneys or something vital, and there is a niggling at her back that could be a cramp or could be nothing. She can hear Steve breathing steadily in the next room. A siren so distant it is no more than a kid's toy seesaws northward. The sound of the leaves is like the rush of blood through myriad tiny tubes. The baby lies curled in its warm dark watery world. Kate can no longer curl, but she arranges some cushions on the floor and manages a passable position for half an hour or so. She lies and reads novels. Novels written by women who mention among other things the hard dome of the pregnant stomach and leaky breasts and the fluffy brain that seems to accompany gestation and the sensation of a body squirming beneath the skin and kitchens cluttered with nappies and toys and the mess and the discomfort and the reassuring pleasure of it all.

Someone had given her a copy of Doctor Spock, with its cute 1950s cartoons and instructions on what to do if confronted by spots and odd swellings. But Doctor Spock was just as incapable as the diagrams and photos of telling her what she really wanted to know right then: how any of this business of having a baby might actually *feel*. Only the novels could do that.

Water soaking the bed at 4am. The sick drag at lower back.

'Shall I make bacon and eggs?' said Steve, dragging on jeans and socks and fetching the suitcase they had had packed for weeks. They had read that it was important to have a protein meal, as labour could be prolonged. So he made bacon and eggs, trying to move quietly so as not to disturb the others in the flat downstairs. The eggs lay on the plates like unblinking yellow eyes, the bacon had a foetal curl.

'I don't think I can manage it,' she said, and she pushed it away.

Steve ate her share while she had a cup of tea, then he tiptoed off to call for a taxi.

The others in the flat heard them moving about anyway. They stood at the foot of the stairs saying, 'Well, good luck!' as if they were heading off to a particularly arduous sporting function. 'Good luck and, well, you know, have a good time!'

Then the hospital with the Portuguese woman crying 'Mae de deus!' and the Italian woman moaning 'Jesu Maria!' and someone close to Kate who could have been Kate herself crying something loud and unintelligible and the nurse with the crooked teeth whisking in to check and measure as if she were some creature who had washed up, huge and dumb, onto the beach of the narrow bed. And the fist clenches and unclenches, steadily taking a firmer grip and Steve rubs her back but he can't rub away the tidal suck of pain and the pain is building so she can no longer see anything but a night sky bursting with stars and she's rising to a crest and suddenly it is beyond pain and there are no words for this, this is sensation beyond words, and then there is a head bursting from between her legs and a face turned upwards, crumpled, sticky with blood and creamy lickings of wax, and she is born, and Kate puts her nose to her daughter's damp skull and she smells like nothing and no one Kate has ever smelled before and there are no words to describe that either. Simply overwhelming love.

'What'll we call her?' says Steve, entranced by the way she grasps his finger. 'See that? That's supposed to prove we had fur once and she's got an instinct to hang on. Like the Moro reflex. They're supposed to be able to step, too, if they're placed on a flat surface, and they can swim . . .' He has read the books with the diagrams of the sac and tubes. He knows all the facts.

'Hannah,' she says. They had not planned a name. It had felt like a risk to choose a name before she was there, with her arms and legs, before she was there to receive it.

Steve considers.

'Hannah,' he says. 'Why did you think of that?'

'It was in a book once,' Kate says. *Hannah Wright, Her Booke*. She has not thought of it in years.

'I like that,' says Steve. 'Yes. Hello, Hannah.'

Hannah looks back at them with those depthless blue newborn eyes.

27.

*I had lovely enlarged boobs which leaked milk every time
she cried. The pull of the toothless infant mouth on one's
nipples is highly erotic, I discovered. It induces ecstasy.
The little hand on one's breast and the tiny piggy grunt-
ings are a delight.*

Brother of the More Famous Jack by Barbara Trapido

Kate sits with her feet up on the heater with the whole city to themselves. The nights are cooler now and the old ladies downstairs have
retreated indoors. She sits alone with the soft slup slup slup of
Hannah suckling. Her milk arcs from the unsuckled breast, leaving
wet patches on her nightgown that smell of faintly of cheese.
Hannah's hands knead at her flesh rhythmically and she remembers
the half-wild mother cats at Millerhill and their ecstatic purring as
the row of blind kittens lined up at their bellies.

They spent that summer in Iceland, walking about in a land-scape where geysers spouted simply from the middle of a green field, with no announcement, no information board, no guard-rail nor tourist hoopla. The blue bubble rose as regular as breathing, and swelled to an enormous globe straining within the meniscus before its extravagant feathery release. Children played in huts on lava fields barely covered by stunted trees and had to be called in by their mothers to sleep, and men mowed their lawns, stripped to the waist in the creamy light of 3am. Steve saw the hills and valleys with their knee-high forests and steaming lakes covered with stories: this was where Snorri had bathed, this was where the man had written to his beloved that she was a tree of ribbons, she was a white ship upon the ocean. Rock and scoria were overlaid with tendrils of language. Words burst from the ground with the exuberance of wildflowers.

Inflation was also exuberant. When they got home after that summer they were broke. So Kate got a job at a publisher's, working on a new children's reading series. The system was phonic. She was employed to write little stories with lots of words including clusters such as 'au' and 'aw': *The awful dragon was caught by the paw.*

For six months Kate commuted to a cubicle an hour and a half away by subway and bus, in an office park filled with white build-ings arranged like so many toasters or shiny appliances, along roads where provincial officials had made a bid for glorious posterity: Walter. G. Obscure Dignitary Drive. Arthur B. Manager Place. The partitions beween the cubicles were flimsy and reached to head height so that every conversation, every phone call, every sniff or giggle or sneeze fluttered over the top and landed on the sur-rounding desks. Maggie, who occupied the cubicle next door, had conducted a survey.

'Hey,' she called from her desk, 'would you believe it: ninety-five per cent of the characters in these stories are males, and that includes four dogs and three donkeys and maybe a cat, though it's a bit indeterminate. The females are all princesses or mothers. And not a single one of them, whether male or female, is identifiably Canadian. So what do you make of that, eh?'

'Rubbish!' called Murray from Marketing who was passing. But somewhere in the celestial hierarchies that governed this Canadian subsidiary of an American branch of a global conglomerate, someone agreed with Maggie. Now the stories not only required vowel clusters, but heroines and a Canadian setting. *Jean sees the beavers among the trees by the stream . . .*

Kate coped: baby, job, thesis, reviewing two nights a week. Other people coped. Toba had babies and did her painting. Donna Da Silva had a baby and a job in a downtown law firm. She had given in and gone out with the son of one of her mother's friends, someone she had avoided for years as the man who was 'just right' for her: aspiring surgeon; handsome according to her mother; great sense of humour.

'Okay!' she had said. 'Okay! I'll go out with him!'

And he was nice. He wasn't good-looking — but then he'd been told she was beautiful too, so that was a relief. They were married within the year and she'd become pregnant (not entirely by accident) a month later. Donna coped: her waters broke during finals. She acted it out for them one night at dinner: the surprise, the recoiling of students seated within splashing distance, herself as the resolute student answering every last question before departing for the hospital. She had a job and a nanny who arrived at 8am to a row of bottles filled with expressed breast milk keeping cool in the fridge.

She coped.

Eva, who was their doctor, coped. She worked full time with two children whose photos, mounted in silver frames, stood among the prescriptions and note-pads on her cluttered desk.

Maggie at work coped. She had worked full time since her son was six months old. She was single too.

But Kate, standing one morning on the platform at Bloor and Bay waiting for the train and the commute out to the phonic clusters, was overcome by panic. The wind rushed from the mouth of the tunnel. The train was roaring toward her, and for no particular reason she could understand, she thought, 'I could jump'. The edge of the platform was a clear line: on this side stood the usual people unconcernedly reading their papers or consulting their watches. On the other side of the line sat death. She had read about the people who jumped and how their deaths caused delays in the system. She felt her back break out in a sweat at the sheer possibility.

Of course she wouldn't jump. Who would care for Hannah? But once the thought had arrived, it had her in its clammy grip. She pushed her way back to the rear of the platform so that the other commuters made a wall of bodies between her and oblivion and pain and terror, and the train came as it always did and she climbed on and sat in a corner, trembling. From that morning on she dawdled in the corridor until the train was in the station, then emerged to join in the rush for the doors. But when she left the bus to walk along the verge of John C. Councillor Cul-de-sac to the office, the terror was lurking there too, like the wolf in the fairy tale, behind every tree trunk, at the corner of every blank building. The earth became unsteady, tipping about like water beneath her feet, the sounds of cars and air conditioners and her own hurried breathing amplified and she had to run — awkwardly, on wedge-heeled sandals — for the relative safety of the office.

Then the terror spread. It seeped out to flood the supermarket on Saturday mornings. The aisles became narrow canyons of tins and cartons; the front doors were unbearably distant; the sound of the music that was supposed to soothe her into letting down her money, to indulge in some frenzy of purchase, as a cow is persuaded by country music's greatest hits to let down its milk, that same selection of easy listening became amplified, distorted, and she

336

had to leave the trolley where it stood in the middle of the cereal section and walk as fast as she could without drawing attention to herself, to the exit. She bought from then on at a Macs Milk where the mark-up was astronomical but the doors were less remote.

Something made her panic, something was breathing down her back, making her want to run. But where? Eventually even the apartment became unsafe. The terror could come upon her as easily as she made the bed or cleaned the bath. She closed her eyes then, tried to breathe steadily, hoped that it would pass. She told no one, not even Steve.

'Are you looking after yourself?' said her mother on one of those trans-Pacific collisions that were their phone calls. 'You sound tired.' Even from several thousand miles away her antennae were attuned. 'You're not overdoing things, are you?'

'I'm fine,' Kate said, then changed the subject. 'How's Maura?'

Maura was living in London. She was working in a costume-design department in the West End. She was married to a bass guitarist. She had sent a wedding photo: she wore a loose cream satin pyjama suit and carried half-a-dozen arum lilies. She looked very cool and very elegant. Cat Stevens lived in the flat downstairs.

Kate sits in her cubicle composing stories like acrostics. The terror starts. The floor begins to tilt and she could slide right off into nothing, into chaos. She can hear Maggie speaking in the cubicle next door but none of the words make any sense. They are just birdsong, babble. She can feel her heart begin to accelerate to a bongo beat; sweat is breaking out along the line of her shoulders. She is going to scream.

'So what do you think?' says Maggie, looking over the cubicle wall. Then, seeing Kate's face, she says, 'Are you okay?'

'No,' says Kate. 'I think I'm cracking up. I think I need to see a doctor.'

Maggie drives her into town to see Eva. Eva adjusts the photo of a little boy riding a merry-go-round elephant.

'So, what are you going to give up?' she says. Kate notices the tremor in her hand, the dark rings around her eyes. 'It's hopeless trying to do everything. Just hopeless.'

'The job,' says Kate. 'That's what I'm going to give up.'

She resigned that afternoon.

Maggie rang.

'Murray's ecstatic,' she said. 'He said he'd had a bet with someone in editorial — I don't know who exactly — that you wouldn't last. He said women with children never last.'

'Sorry,' said Kate. 'God, I'm so sorry.' She had just let down every woman on the planet. She had failed fifty-one per cent of the world's population. She had dashed the hopes and ambitions of an entire generation. She wanted Maggie to forgive her, but Maggie said nothing. Hannah was dragging herself up onto the sofa and heading for the dials on the record player.

'Look . . . I've got to go,' said Kate. 'I'm truly, truly sorry I've let you down.' The record player suddenly boomed into life.

. . . *TWINKLE LITTLE STAR* . . .

Maggie was saying something but it was totally inaudible.

'Bye!' said Kate. And 'Sorry!' again, and that was that.

HOW I WONDER WHAT YOU ARE!

Hannah looked around at her, laughing.

28.

Cody, searching for something to say, happened to look toward Prima Street and see his family rounding the corner, opening like a fan.

Dinner at the Homesick Restaurant by Anne Tyler

What tugs us home? A memory of a garden with an overgrown lawn sprinkled with constellations of daisies where children tumble barefoot. White sand edged with a woven mat of marram grass, the sea treacherous with sudden holes, a tangle of driftwood at a river-mouth and men like dry sticks standing guard over yellow plastic buckets where there is the silvery flitter of whitebait trying to find their way through to the undisturbed, dark reaches. Hillsides covered with houses the colour of boiled lollies, every one being its own place and bugger civic coherence. A constant wind stirring everything up: newspapers on a city corner, dust on a white road, a wind capable of forcing itself through every crack so that the wall-paper bellies like a sail and joists creak and houses sound like boats at a tenuous mooring. The intensity of life lived personally, where every single issue is the work of your cousin's best friend's husband or your next-door neighbour's nephew's girlfriend and there is no possibility of anonymity. We come home: eels drawn back by the scent of water across thousands of kilometres, birds flying back to the nest from beyond the equator, guided by memories of light down the bare tracks sketched on magnetic fields.

So here they are. Kate's mother is holding her grandchild in her arms and Kate feels as if she has given her a gift and she is saying, 'She's got the Falconer hair, hasn't she?'

It was true. After that initial mop of baby black, Hannah's hair had grown thick and wavy and red. All the time Kate had been away being herself, thinking herself so free and independent, she had been carrying that gene, nested like a little bird somewhere on some chromosome or other. She had been carrying her entire family, generations of them, within the dark pockets of her body.

'And look, Hannah,' said her mother, holding up a whole box of Cadbury's Milk Tray. 'I've got something for you.'

'She doesn't eat chocolate,' said Kate.

Her mother was surprised.

'Why not?' she said. 'She's not diabetic is she? That's a terrible thing. It's on the increase, too . . .' She looked alarmed.

'No,' said Kate, 'she's fine, but we don't give her junk food.' When they had left Canada someone have given her a recipe book: *Laurel's Kitchen*. Chard Pie, Yeast Butter and careful tables showing the precise amount of thiamine in a cup of rolled oats. There was a photo of Laurel and her friends in LA: long skirts, hair pulled back in demure buns, the keepers of the keys to the health and well-being of their families, their neighbourhoods and ultimately the planet. Junk food had no place in Laurel's kitchen. Nor would it stand a chance in Kate's.

'Och,' said her mother, relieved, and selecting a strawberry fondant. 'One little chocolate isn't going to do her any harm.'

'It'll rot her teeth,' said Kate.

'But your teeth are fine,' said her mother, stripping off the silver foil. 'And you used to love chocolate. She did,' she said, turning to Steve, enlisting his support. 'She took money out of my purse and spent it on chocolate at the shop. She made herself sick.'

'I didn't know you knew about that,' said Kate.

'Of course I knew,' said her mother. 'It was those darn Creeches. They were a bad influence.' Hannah had the chocolate in her mouth already. 'There, darling. Is that nice?'

'Yum,' said Hannah, holding out a sticky hand. 'More cho'lit.'

'She won't eat her tea,' said Kate.

Her mother took Hannah off for rides in the Morris. Tollie perched on one cushion so she could reach the pedals and Hannah perched on another so she could see out the window. They arrived home hours later, cheerful and chatty, for they seemed to understand each other effortlessly and enjoyed long and involved conversations. Hannah generally returned bearing some treat: an ice cream, or a packet of yellow Styrofoam bits.

'They're cheese,' said her mother. 'Not chocolate. They're a new thing. The girl at the supermarket tells me they're very popular.'

Her father had struggled to his feet when they had first arrived back, as if they were visitors. Eight years she had been gone, and the house still smelled of fried onions and Sunlight soap and tobacco smoke and old timber. The back door still rattled. The fridge handle still pinched unwary fingers. Some things had grown in the time they had been away. The ribbonwood by the bedroom window overtopped the roof and knocked at the walls. Some things had shrunk. This old man, for instance, struggling to his feet with the aid of his stick. His head reaches only to her shoulder and when she hugs him he seems all bone.

'So, how was it over there?' he says, and she tries to explain, but he's tired and there's too much to say, and anyway, *The Two Ronnies* will be on at eight o'clock. He likes that, her mother says. He gets up for that specially. Normally he stays in bed and when he wants something he calls out.

'Oi!' he calls from the front bedroom. 'Oi!'

And she goes through to see what he wants. They seem to have arrived at some accommodation now that they are on their own. Her mother occupies the kitchen during the day and has moved back into Kate's old bedroom now that it is no longer needed to facilitate swot. Her father stays in bed. They live at opposite ends of the house, meeting when he requires washing, or a bedpan.

'So you see,' says her mother, 'all my training didn't go to waste after all. It was meant to be. I'm still a nurse. No one else would put up with him.' She butters a scone and puts it on a plate, glances over at what Kate is doing. 'He likes a spoonful of sugar in his tea,' she says. 'Since when?' says Kate. 'Since always,' says her mother. 'He's always taken a spoonful of sugar in his tea.' 'No he hasn't,' says Kate. She's sure she would remember such a thing. 'Yes he has,' said her mother. 'Always.' She would know, of course.

Kate feels foreign, as if she might never have lived here, in this house with these people. She feels a little lost. She sounds different, evidently. 'You've got an accent,' said her cousin Graham when she went to visit him at Millerhill. He had taken over the farm and leaned back against the fence, arms folded, in swannie and woolly hat, while she told him about Toronto: forty-five different nationalities in the city, the tallest tower in the world, five months of winter. 'Izzat right?' he said. 'Jeeze, you sound just like an American.'

The whole country had taken on a dreamlike quality. The place she had imagined had subtly altered. Shops had sprouted new fronts, houses had disappeared, leaving gaps in which flats had been inserted like false teeth. Friends had children already old enough to ride about on little bicycles; marriages that she had left in the first flush of confetti and optimism had already plunged into divorce and reassembly. There had been a Labour prime minister, there had been bands and outdoor music festivals, and friends had gone off to grow sweetcorn in communes in the Hokianga and returned to the city where they had bought their former student flats and were scouring the demolition yards for stained glass and kauri doors. They spent hours now scraping paint from crevices around dados and taking their children to Playcentre.

Steve had a job at Massey, and Kate, pregnant again, settled into being a mother. Motherhood would be a New Zealand synthesis of whole-food Californian with a dash of Margaret Drabble. There would be a long wooden table with a white jug filled with daisies, and around the table on a variety of Windsor chairs discarded by some rural church in favour of padding and stackable plastic would be children with names like Octavia and Ben, and they would eat homemade yoghurt and homemade muesli and wear little denim Oshkosh overalls and home-knitted sweaters — homespun if she could possibly manage it, home-dyed with onion skins — and Clarks sandals on their feet so that their bones would grow properly. They would go to Playcentre where the mothers sat on the steps in embroidered muslin shirts and jeans or long skirts, drinking coffee and breast-feeding the youngest while the older children learned about quantity by filling up plastic bottles with water, or learned about unbridled power by pushing one another off the tyre swing. They would go to the library on Saturday mornings and they would choose two story books and two non-fiction; they would go to music appreciation classes on Monday afternoons to develop their aesthetic sense and to Tiny Y's to build physical confidence.

> *I walked out of the house this morning and stretched my arms out wide. Look, I said to myself. Because I was alone except for you.*
>
> *Between Earth and Sky* by Patricia Grace

A tall dark woman with her hair in a thick plait was attempting to spread plastic sheeting on the playdough table one-handed while balancing a two-year-old on a hip that had vanished more or less beneath the swelling of an ample late pregnancy.

'Here,' said Kate. 'Let me . . . my God! Caro!'

'Kate!' said Caro Williams. 'What are you doing here?' They held either end of the plastic and unfolded it and it was simple once there were two of them, to spread it evenly over the table and peg it in place and distribute lumps of pink playdough and the ice-cream cartons full of rolling pins and cookie cutters. Then they stopped Caro's two-year-old from eating a purple felt-tip and washed some coffee cups and found Hannah's bankie, a scrap of satin ribbon that was all that remained of her baby blanket and that wriggled off constantly with snake-like cunning down the backs of sofas and into impossible crevices, and then they sat, idly molding scraps of playdough, and Kate told Caro the record of her adventures and Caro recounted the narrative of her life thus far. It was a broken narrative, as such conversations always are, making allowance for what had to be done. Not the unbroken meditative prose of the study, but a jumpy, fractured tale, moving from past to present, from here to there.

'The worst year was Theo's intern year,' said Caro. 'I didn't think we'd survive, no, Harata, don't put it in Hannah's hair, it'll stick, it's terrible stuff to get out, we nearly divorced, truly, it was awful, he was working twelve-hour shifts, longer sometimes, and we'd only just arrived here, so I didn't know anyone and we already had Harata, she was, what's that sweetie? Yes, it's beautiful cake, mmmm, mmm, yes it's delicious . . . she didn't sleep, she had colic and I didn't expect it to be like that, you know? I thought it would be all Laura Ashley rosebud curtains and after six months I would be going back to varsity and it was all going to be sweet and she did this . . . mmmm, mmm, yummy, thank you, that is the best cake ever. Oh, it's not cake? It's a rabbit? Oh, sorry, sorry, I've just eaten your rabbit, well, never mind, look, we'll make another one. But she did this projectile vomiting, and it really did project, everywhere, it was amazing, and we had about two hours' sleep a night and I truly thought I was going mad.'

'Me too,' said Kate. She was rolling bits of playdough into sausages for Hannah's playdough fry-up. 'Not the vomiting, Hannah didn't have colic or anything but she just liked being awake, Hannah you need to blow your nose, here you are, big blow, that's a good girl, so we'd be dead and she was ready to party, you don't want to do playdough any more? Yes, we can do drawing instead, let's get some felt-tips. And we were both trying to do theses and then we ran out of money and I got this job and was commuting an hour and a half each way and it was hell, it truly was . . .'

She was able to hint to Caro about the panic. She could make a joke of the terror. She could turn it all into a story and when Caro laughed, it was all right again.

It was a bitterly cold day, with snow falling. Just after nine o'clock the Maori, numbering about a hundred and fifty men, women and children, marched slowly out into the snow. Turning their backs on the little village they had raised in the tussock, they began the long trek back down the Waitaki valley to the coast. Thompson counted 30 drays and wagons, 100 horses and about a hundred dogs in the sad procession. As the people marched, a column of smoke rose in the sky behind them: the police were burning their homes. Only the house in which Te Maiharoa lay sick was left standing in a field of ashes, and Duncan Sutherland made brisk arrangements to buy up the abandoned firewood.

Te Maiharoa and the Promised Land by Buddy Mikaere

Twice a week Kate left Hannah with Caro, who minded her while Kate taught drama at the teachers' college. Just four hours a week but it meant changing, from jeans and a saggy sweatshirt with play-dough glued to the sleeves, into skirt and lipstick; it meant that The Opportunity had not been entirely wasted on her. It was a small gesture of propitiation to her father's mother coughing and scrubbing, to the jingling of the foldaway bed in the front room.

And twice a week Kate minded Harata while Caro went to lectures at the university. She was studying sociology. She was going to write a thesis on Maori health. Her father had died at 52 from a heart attack, both her grandmothers from TB.

'But I thought one of your grandmothers was Italian?' said Kate. 'The one who was an opera singer, who rescued the wounded soldier?'

'Good story, wasn't it?' said Caro, stretching comfortably on the worn-out sofa on the verandah. 'English and Nga Puhi on one side, Irish and Ngai Tahu on the other. It was just more glamorous to be Italian in 1959.'

The children were playing house under a table. The garden was sprinkled with plum blossom. It was the garden Kate had imagined when she was away, with the daisy lawns and the barefoot children, though her imagination had not allowed for the hens. Where the

346

vision had included lush rows of nourishing vegetables there stood some bedraggled silverbeet and a few devastated cabbages. Everything else had been tugged up by Mrs Tooky and her little flock. They could not be contained. She and Steve had tried high fences and clipped wings but the birds simply flew like eagles over the wire, landing where they fancied. Their eggs were perfect and golden-yolked, but they were never laid in the special straw-filled boxes in the hen-house. They could be found only in nesting places of the hens' own choosing, beneath the roses in the hedge. Gathering their eggs left a tracery of scratches and scars. Hens, Kate had discovered, are deeply subversive of any imposed order. They pecked about the verandah-edge now, looking deceptively peaceable, as Hannah and Harata wheeled their dolls' prams up and down the overgrown gravel paths.

Kate and Steve had tried giving Hannah cars and trucks to play with. She had wrapped the little red tip-truck up in a blanket and called it Charlene.

'It's nature, I guess,' said Caro, arranging a cushion under her back and reaching for her coffee mug. Fistfuls of stuffing burst from the sofa's shabby crimson velvet. 'I don't suppose it really matters. So long as we draw the line at those Barbies with the big boobs.'

'Too late,' said Kate. 'My mother's already given her a Barbie: Ballerina Barbie. She's all dressed in pink. Hannah adores her.'

Kate had not known about Maori health. She had not known about Maori anything really, other than a pa built with burnt match-sticks, some stories in black and white of sky fathers and earth mothers, a charcoal outline of a creature with spread wings painted on the roof of a limestone shelter. How could she have grown up in this country and known so little? She hadn't even known, it seemed, the lives of her closest friends. Caro and her Italian opera singer grandmother kneeling in the snow to bind the soldier's wounds with her petticoats had been like Maddie's widowed mother and the father who had died so tragically on the railway track. Just a story.

29.

Kate shared an office at the teachers' college with an older woman whose name was Stanley.

'It's for an uncle who died in the First World War,' Stanley said. 'It could have been worse, I suppose: one of his cousins was called Bertrude.'

She looked like a Swedish grandmother, with white hair in a tangled bun and pink cheeks and bright blue eyes and a soft body dressed in layers of loosely floating cotton and muslin. Their desks nudged each other in the tiny office so that they climbed in and out, careful not to dislodge minor avalanches of paper and books. Stanley was writing a history of the Waihi strike.

'The what?' said Kate.

The Waihi strike. The one where a striker was booted to death by Harvey the Pug and his strike-breaker mates, newly released from prison for the purpose, in a paddock behind the union hall? The one that united Bob Semple and Paddy Webb and the others in opposition to the government and a London-owned mining company? The one that was broken by John Cullen, who went on to lead sixty-seven police to Maungapohatu to capture the prophet Rua on a sly-grogging charge? Two Maori dead at the end of that day, four constables wounded and six Maori prisoners taken off to Mt Eden. The same John Cullen who retired to a cabin beneath Ngauruhoe, where he recorded every detail of the mountain in full eruption above him, the earth shuddering, the fiery rock bursting in the air above his fierce and unforgiving Old Testament head.

Stanley had talked to old people who remembered Waihi during the strike: men and women who had been children when it began. A tubby little boy who had delivered *The Maoriland Worker* on his pony to the strikers' houses, a sweet-faced little girl whose uncle had been on the strike committee, a little boy whose mother had carried him on her back through the bush to Paeroa and safety when the strike-breakers were running amok.

'The thing that got me,' said Stanley, 'was the washing. One of the women told me that she and her sister had a clean starched pinafore every day, and at lunchtime they ran home, and after they had had their dinners, their mother gave them each a clean pinafore for the afternoon. She did the washing in a tub with a wringer, in Waihi, with dust from the mine blowing everywhere. Yes . . .' said Stanley. 'It's the washing that's amazing . . .'

She wrote that down, and all the other things the people told her, and it became a book. She pulled it out of the brown paper parcel and laid it on her desk.

'Would you look at that!' she said. 'My book!'

The book had a black cover and a photo on the front of strikers bearing a placard: *If Blood be the Price of your Cursed Wealth, By God We Have Bought it Dear!* A real shiny new book.

Steve and Kate went up to the book's launch in Auckland. They stood with the crowd at the graveside of the murdered striker. Fred Evans had been carved in noble profile. An old man stood beside his cenotaph, stooped and craggy and still speaking of brotherhood and solidarity. And all the way home, as they drove past Taupo with its shining islands and the bare pointed hills, and the little townships with their pubs and boarded-up shops, and the long straight roads cutting across the Manawatu, Kate thought about the washing, and about her grandmother scrubbing away at the Protestant linoleum in Oamaru so that her children might have The Opportunity, and that history was not something external — the reunification of Italy, the four causes of the First World War — but something palpable, contained within a washtub, a police baton.

'No one was writing about it and all the old people who remembered it were dying,' Stanley said. 'So I thought: I'll give it a go. I'm not an historian but I can write down what they tell me. It can't be too difficult.'

'Is that all there is to it?' said Kate.

'Well, yes, I suppose so,' said Stanley. 'I mean, if we don't write it down, who will? If we want history and literature, we've got to do it ourselves.' She paused. 'Said the Little Red Hen.' And she held her book to the light so that she could see the photo on the front clearly.

Kate wrote a play for the students based on Stanley's book.

On the big rock-candy mountain, they sang.

There's a land that's clear and bright . . .

The mountain at Waihi had gone, reduced to a crater. The dazzling peak of Martha Hill had vanished, its crest white, not with snow or ice but with aeons of regurgitated gizzard stones, for the same stone that held veins of gold was good for the digestion of moa. It was the glistening of the peak that had drawn the prospectors to it in the first place, but now it had disappeared along with the big birds that stalked about its summit like Mrs Tooky and her mates, their heads dipping, their beaks pecking to gather up the beautiful white stones.

30.

It was a man and he was standing with one arm outstretched, on the highest span between two islands.

The Silk by Joy Cowley

She was reading when the fluttering stopped. For nearly six months she had been pregnant. For the past two, the baby had been flying about beneath her navel. As she drove Hannah to Playcentre or stood in the queue at the supermarket or talked to the students at teachers' college she could feel it. Her baby was flying in the dark, underwater world that was her belly, kicking its tiny feet, like a little penguin. The Human Fish, Le Poisson Humain. It tickled. She had to resist the urge to scratch at her belly, knowing the cause was beyond her reach. The baby was conducting its own existence.

Kate turned a page. The tickling stopped. She read on, waiting for it to begin again but it didn't.

She finished the chapter.

Nothing.

All that week she went about as usual, driving down Albert Street, teaching, picking up Hannah from Caro's, going to the cinema on Saturday night. She could not remember the movie afterwards. Even its name eluded her. She had had her hand on her belly in the dark. She was waiting for the fluttering to begin again, for the baby to begin flying.

Nothing.

Silence.

Stillness.

She didn't want to fuss. She waited until the following Wednesday before ringing the doctor.

'I wonder if I could make an appointment,' she said. 'I think there may be something amiss.' It was weird how she became formal when she was frightened: she'd never used the word 'amiss' in her life before. It was like 'misled': a word read but never spoken. Even when she read them she often mispronounced them, as 'ay-miss' and 'mizzled'. 'I think the baby might be . . .' and she fumbled here, before settling for 'no longer viable.'

The doctor listened, leaving the chilly little pawprints of the stethoscope across the white globe of her belly. 'Hmm,' he said, straightening. 'It's unusual at this stage but it does happen. We'll let nature take its course, but if it should come away when you're at home, just pop it in a bottle, would you? I'd like to take a look.'

Kate left the surgery and for a month she waited — driving to Playcentre, teaching, going to the movies — until the doctor said it might be dangerous to wait any longer and she went into hospital and finally cried. She heaved and sobbed as he tried to place a catheter between her open legs until he said a trifle irritably, 'Do try to be still.' She hiccoughed to silence and in an hour or two there were some contractions and something small and scratchy emerged.

A little black bud, withered and dry as a husk. Something that would have rattled, had she popped it in a bottle.

The second death came one afternoon six months later.

Kate was pregnant again. She was painting Hannah's room. It was dark blue and she was stencilling a border of giant daisies around the walls. The furniture was piled in the middle of the carpet and covered with the old Japara tent they had used for camping. It was no longer big enough to accommodate them but just the right size for a drop-sheet. She tripped over it as she ran for the phone in the kitchen.

'It's your father,' said a voice she did not at first recognise. A light empty voice, like a child's. 'He's gone.'

'Where?' said Kate, though she was just playing for time, waiting for the thought to land.

'He's gone,' said her mother. 'I took him in his cup of tea and he was going. I've laid him out. I did it myself. You don't forget how, even after years and years. Not when you're a trained nurse.'

Kate's legs had folded under her like a newborn calf's. She sat on the floor.

'Heart failure,' said her mother. 'That's what the doctor said. The funeral's on Saturday.'

Her voice floated, a few inches above the ground.

'Are you all right?' said Kate.

'I'm fine,' said her mother. 'I've phoned Izzie. She's driving up. She'll be here in an hour or so.'

'I'll be down tonight too if I can get a flight,' said Kate. 'Or first thing tomorrow. Just as soon as I can. Okay?'

'Yes,' said her mother. 'Don't worry. We'll cope.'

When she hangs up Kate stays sitting on the floor. She can't cry. Her throat is too tight for tears, too tight to call out to Steve who is just outside the back door whistling as he mends the chain on his bike. Hannah and Harata are giggling somewhere close. They have left their books scattered about. *Mr Gumpy's Outing*. *The Very Hungry Caterpillar*. *Richard Scarry's Busy Busy World*. Kate sits looking at a picture of rabbits on bicycles that her father had given Hannah for Christmas, along with a pop-up book of dinosaurs. She looks at the rabbits while a fantail, brisk and busy, flutters about the kitchen on the lookout for insects. Phweet, it says, flirting with her from the curtains. Phweet phweet phweet. Its black eyes button-bright, its little moustache perky with knowing. The bird that laughed when the man tried to wriggle away from death.

Maura flew out from London, and together they helped their mother lay out the cups for the funeral tea. They emptied the china cabinet, using cups that had never to Kate's knowledge been used before. Some still had stickers on the bottom reading, in faded ink, 10/6d. Their mother baked.

'You don't have to do that,' said Kate. 'We'll order some in.'

'It's never as good as homemade,' said her mother, busily creaming butter and sugar. 'I'd rather do it myself. That way you know it's done properly.'

Their father lay safe from the bustle in his burial shroud down at the undertakers. They had not expected the shroud.

'The Irish shroud,' said the undertaker. 'Not many ask for them these days.'

Pat had looked like a monk in the plain woven habit: collarless, his crooked hands folded over a crucifix. He had become someone austere and celibate, member of some fraternity of death. They could scarcely recognise him as their father.

Kate spoons cake mixture into paper cups: pink, green, pale blue. The tabletop is already covered in plates of cakes and bacon-and-egg pie. Sausage rolls are lined up ready for the oven on the bench.

'Just a half spoonful,' says her mother, 'or the dough will spill out of the cases.' She rinses the mixer. 'It's not true what's on the certificate, you know,' she says.

'What's not true?' says Kate.

'Heart failure,' says her mother. 'That's not true.'

Two weeks ago, she says, Mulherron came to visit. His mate Mulherron. The man from the truck. Then one who had prayed all the way out through the gap between Bir Abu Batta and Matta, yet had no memory of it.

'He'd never visited the South Island before,' says their mother. 'But his wife had died so he decided to come down to see Pat. He's got an orchard up near Havelock. He drove down in his campervan.'

She is busy pricking the pastry on the sausage rolls with a fork. 'So I took them in a cup of tea,' she says, 'and I left them to talk. But I had the door open, so I could hear what they were saying.'

The men sat by the fire, grown old now, when they had last seen each other young and fit and strong. They had talked about the war: about mates who hadn't made it, about mates who had come back and were farming or working for the Ministry of Works, the usual chat. Their mother had listened, popping in to freshen the tea, bring some more scones. When he'd gone, Pat had been quiet.

'You know how he got,' says their mother, popping the rolls in the oven. 'Moody.'

That night as she was getting him ready for bed he had suddenly started talking: about a bloke who'd been running beside him and fallen sideways and both his legs had been ripped off, good bloke too, from Taranaki, finished just like that and Pat had had to keep going, he didn't know where the hell he was, what he was doing, he'd gone over some sandbags and he'd looked down, and there were a couple of lads in the trench. German lads. Fair hair. That's what he'd noticed first: fair hair. You could see it in the dark, and these two lads were just huddled there in a corner, arms around each other, looking up at them coming over and not doing anything. Just waiting.

'So he killed them?' says Maura.

'Yes,' says their mother. He said he was covered in blood, they all were, when they finally got through. Blood and dust and shit, their own and the blood, sweat and shit of others. (She said 'bowel movements' of course, not 'shit'. 'Their bowels moved,' she said.) They had to be doused with water before they could peel off their uniforms. Blood, dust and shit had set as tight on them as a second skin.

'He said other things too,' she says. 'He talked for hours. I don't know if he knew I was there or not. But I just sat and listened and after a while he went to sleep.' She reaches for the mixing bowl. 'I had no idea,' she says. 'None of us have got any idea.'

He died a couple of weeks later. All day he kept calling to her.

'There's someone at the door,' he had said. Two lads. He could see them from his bed, standing at the front door knocking.

'I thought it was those Mormons,' says their mother. 'They're nice enough boys but they always come when you're busy.'

She had been typing, writing up her mother's mother's line, but she had lain it aside when Pat called, taken off her apron, checked her hair in the barometer that was always set to Fair and opened the door.

'There's no one there,' she had said to him, but he could not be reassured.

'There is,' he insisted. Two lads. Fair-haired lads.

She had returned to her typing, the thread of connection interrupted, and ten minutes later he'd be calling again.

'They're back,' he said.

All day, until late afternoon when he became quiet. As it was getting dark, she had taken him a cup of tea.

'As soon as I opened the door, I could hear the breathing,' she says. The air rattling in his chest as if it were full of stones. The pause, the gasp, the retrieval of breath, the rattle. As if the air were considering its next move . . .

'I couldn't believe he was on his way out,' she says. 'I sat and held his hand but it was only a few minutes before he was gone.'

She pauses. They stand in the kitchen and somewhere in the air around them is the sound of gunfire, the howl of young men running at other young men, the slipping of blade into flesh.

'He'd managed to take all his painkillers,' she says.

The squat brown bottles by the bed with their little white pebble pills, leading a way through, between the dark eminences.

She had laid him out. She had tidied him up, emptied the urine bottle, straightened the bedclothes, scooped the pill bottles into a rubbish bag. She had prepared him for inspection with professional precision, then she had rung the doctor.

'What did the doctor say?' says Kate.

Her mother is concentrating on separating the white from the yolk. She tips the broken shell back and forth until the white has fallen in sticky strands into the basin.

'He examined him, of course,' she says. 'He knew.'

But he put heart failure on the certificate. Tollie switches on the mixer. Over the whirring she says that he was always a nice chap, right from the start when he first arrived at Public as an intern and she was in charge of theatre. He was a decent man. The egg whites puff up into soft white clouds, full of air and holding their shape, light as a gentle lie.

Heart failure. Though it could as easily have been kidney failure or liver failure. There was little need to explain anyway. Pat had been ill for so long, the war playing itself out slowly over decades, that no gloss was required.

'You won't say anything, will you?' says their mother. 'Just keep it quiet. It's nobody else's business.'

The oven bell rings like the Angelus. The sausage rolls are done to a turn.

Their mother worked all that night, as if she were baking for a journey. Kate was restless in her old bed, her sleep broken by the sound of pots and plates from the kitchen. Maura said she slept poorly too: she thought she had been woken by groaning from their father's room, but that was impossible.

Kate could not cry at the funeral. The tears had formed a sago-lump that lodged in her throat. Dry-eyed, she listened to the priest dispatching our dear brother Patrick in a cursory Irish rattle. They stood and knelt and followed the coffin out in the prescribed manner. Then the poppies drip drip dripped into the trench below the cannon marking the Returned Servicemen's last stand on a little hilltop in the cemetery and someone made a wavery effort at the Last Post. She could hardly bear that drip drip drip nor the soft slurp of commiseration over tea and cakes back at the house. Her father's chair still bore the print of his back and the last pile of library books waited to be returned on the table next to his bed.

'You'll miss your dear daddy, won't you?' said Aunty Annie, her eyes watering copiously and coconut sprinkling her bosom. She planted a wet kiss on Kate's cheek. Maura was standing across the room, still jetlagged from the flight. She was wearing black, but black cut in a fitted sheath and jacket with silk lapels and a little black net hat. She caught Kate's eye and made a 'Let's get out of here' gesture with her head and the little black net flower on her hat nodded in general agreement. Izzie was with their mother, helping her pour the teas. Everyone seemed happy with platefuls of sausage rolls and bacon-and-egg pie.

So they leave. They walk along the street, not talking, just side by side down the hill, past the Garden of Memories and the Post Office, past the Power Board to the Library.

Where they return his books.

31.

What age am I waiting for to come to myself?

Xenophon's *Anabasis*

So here is Kate reading in her room by the sea, about soldiers and their long journey home. It is years now since her father's death, years too since her mother turned her face to the wall and let the cancer take over.

She had not been to see a doctor but simply ignored the symptoms, dismissing them, when Kate enquired, as a touch of flu, an upset tummy, nothing to worry about. She had said nothing to Izzie either, though they saw each other every week. When Kate visited Izzie to tell her of her sister's death, she found her getting Ted dressed. He had begun to wander and it was only a matter of time before he would have to go into a home, but in the meantime, Izzie coped. He hunched on his chair carefully counting the spots on his pyjamas. Izzie's hands shook so much that she had to lay aside the hairbrush. 'But who will I tell all my secrets to now?' she said to Kate. ('Thirty-three, thirty-four, thirty-five,' said Ted.) She smoothed his skimpy hair with a wavery hand. 'Who?'

Tollie may have said nothing of disease, but she had planned her funeral carefully nevertheless. Every time Kate visited her in the little house in Dunedin to which she had moved after Pat's death, she brought down the sphinx box from the mantelpiece.

'You see this?' she said each time. 'This has everything you'll need. This is my will, this is my bank book, and all the bills will be here, paid up to date.' She laid them out on the table as meticulously as if she were preparing for an operation. Objects in the house all bore a sticky label glued to the base: *MAURA* on the bottom of half the cups and saucers, *KATE* on the remainder. *MAURA* on the sewing machine, *KATE* on the Remington. She had planned the funeral tea.

'Just a cup of tea,' she said, 'and some cakes from the Astoria Bakery. They're not as good as homemade, of course, but they'll do.'

She had even, it turned out, planned the service. When they opened the sphinx box after her death they found a video. *TO BE USED AT MY FUNERAL.* Bernard had been over to visit and while he was there, she had asked him to film her doing one of the readings: *Praise him with the timbrel and dance! Praise him with psaltery and harp!* Then she made a brief account of her life.

Well, I was born at Millerhill in Otago on the South Island of New Zealand. My father was a farmer and my mother taught piano in the district. They were both descended from Scottish early settlers.

She was wearing her dancing dress for the occasion, the toffee-coloured silk with the string of amber crystals and the matching earrings. She was very formal, sitting upright on the piano stool and facing the camera. A little nervous, but determined.

I spent a happy childhood playing with my sisters, Isobel and Anne, and my brother Thomas. When I was sixteen I discovered my vocation, which was nursing, and went to Oamaru Public, where I spent twenty happy years. I married Patrick Kennedy in 1945 and had two daughters, Kathleen and Maura, who have been a great joy to me. I just want to say that I love you all. So goodbye, until we meet again in heaven.

She turned to the piano, stretched her fingers as she always did before beginning to play. There was a cut in the film while the operator moved the camera to profile.

Now let us sing, said the determined little figure on the screen. She played a couple of chords. The tuning on the piano was uncertain, the tone jangly, but the introduction was recognisable enough.

Love divine, all loves excelling, sang their mother. And the congregation at Millerhill joined in while she played, vamping a little in the bass when the chords became too difficult. *Joy of heaven to earth come down.*

She had arranged it all. She had done it all herself.

The church itself at Millerhill outlasted her by only a couple of years. It was rarely used. The families who had once occupied its pews on Sunday mornings had vanished as the district shrank. Where once there had been thirty smallholdings, each sufficient to sustain a family in some comfort as the wool cheques rolled in and the English dutifully ate their butter and fat lambs, there were now only half-a-dozen big farms. Each enclosed its quota of old cottages falling to ruin, or renovated by city people wanting a weekend retreat. The farmers had become agribusinessmen; their wives commuted to the city, which was only twenty minutes away, now that the twists of the old roads had been made straight. The school closed first, then the hall was sold to a weekend potter. The church was demolished and its timber and furnishings went off to rehabbed kitchens in Maori Hill. The only sign of its former existence was the tribal cluster of Stuarts and McGregors and Todds rotting down companionably on the hillside looking out to the sea and the jagged silhouette of the Horse Range.

Kate's mother is there, among her own people. Pat lies 200 kilometres to the north, buried beneath his white wooden regimental cross. Kate's two daughters have grown up. They lead intricate lives of their own. They have walked round Annapurna, gone climbing in Peru, driven around Australia in a clapped-out Toyota, fallen in and out of love several times, been to university, worked as applepickers and waitresses and on offshore islands with seabirds and tuatara, and they have told Kate something about all this, but the rest belongs to their secret private lives and is none of her business. She and Steve are no longer married. After twenty-five years the marriage reached a standstill. That's all. It stopped and they got off and walked in different directions. She became seduced by the thought of solitude.

And then suddenly the cabin was in front of me, the sunset making its windows reflect gold as if it had lit itself up for me: and I was home.

Gaining Ground by Joan Barfoot

She lived alone for a time, then she met another man. Rory is strong and kind and she loves him too and they live together in a house like the Little House, with its orchard full of apple trees. The bare branches burst into pink blossom every spring and are heavy with fruit every summer and hens peck about their trunks, finding bugs and worms and talking their contented talk. Kate picks the apples and stores them in a room on the southern side of the house where the air over the winter smells more and more sweetly of apples until it is almost fermentation and decay, and then, just in time, it's spring and the whole business can begin again. The house is at the end of a twisting gravel road. The sea washes into the bay a hundred metres from their door and at night they sleep to its regular breathing.

Every morning she walks up the valley into the bush where birds are busy leading their extraordinary lives and the creek chatters along the way creeks usually do. She walks as far as the waterfall. The creek tumbles here over a lava face into a pool surrounded by gnarled fuchsia. They drop their tiny red earrings into the dark water. Kate puts her hand into the water and wishes those she loves a good day. It's a bit like praying, the praying you do when God has disappeared for ever over the rainbow. It's probably pointless, just a ritual. Sometimes it seems to work: her daughters are happy, and Caro and Maddie and Donna and the others. Other times, it fails. Babies die and are found like white china in their cots. People crack up, break down, they are knocked from the bikes or they change to an earlier flight, as Tony did one summer morning on his way to a conference in California, and fly at the hands of angry men into a shining tower.

The studies of circles and waves benefited from colossal investments of effort by man, and they form the very foundation of science. In comparison, 'wiggles' have been left almost totally untouched.

The Fractal Geometry of Nature by Benoit B. Mandelbrot

Last year Kate went back to Canada. She visited Toba and David, their children grown, their house calm and orderly. Toba took her to her studio. They walked together over snowy ground to a former soap factory where Toba flung open the doors. Inside, the walls had been whitewashed and paint spattered the concrete floor like fallen leaves.

An entire wall was covered in one vast canvas. 'Mandelbrot's Garden,' she said. 'We rented his house in Oxford last year when David went on sabbatical. It was ghastly: one of those dank, gloomy, academic houses. But the garden was something else.'

The canvas was made up of hundreds of tiny squares, each painted exquisitely in the colours of flowers.

'I got into the habit of painting tiny things when the kids were small,' she said. 'Remember? I thought it was a handicap, that I'd never be able to paint anything big. Then one day, I realised that if I put all the little squares together they made a bigger square.' Now the canvases are huge. They hang here in the soap factory and in galleries in Ottawa and New York.

Up close, the grid was obvious. A tightly measured pencilled scaffolding was still visible the width and length of the canvas on which squares of colour had been painted, end to end and side by side until the whole wall was concealed. From a distance, the scaffolding disappeared and all that was visible was a garden. All that was clear was colour and the perfect form of a sufficient mass of apparently random elements.

Once upon a time, in a barnyard, there lived a little red hen.

The Little Red Hen (trad.)

So Kate sits reading Xenophon in the week that war begins. In time, this war will be declared over. It will be called a victory. Baghdad will be occupied. In time, Hussein's two sons, Uday and Qusay, will be killed, along with a third man and Qusay's teenage son. Their faces will be shaved and reconstructed and they will be laid out beneath a makeshift awning for the inspection of the world's press:

Qusay the strategist, the reliable son, and Uday the playboy, who was the favourite of their mother, Sajida. Their flesh will be reconstructed and Uday's leg will be amputated and laid alongside his body, so that the pins that had been inserted after an earlier assassination attempt can be seen and the relic verified. In time, Saddam Hussein will be dragged from a hole in the ground. In time, the whole appalling fairy tale of this war will fade into another story.

But all this is yet to happen. Today, Kate is reading in her father's book about Xenophon and his part in the attempted overthrow of the High King Artaxerxes. The name is familiar but she takes a moment to identify it.

Artaxerxes.

Son of that other Artaxerxes who makes a brief appearance in her mother's book, the Bible. She looks it up, and there he is: Artaxerxes I. The good king who gave his cupbearer, Nehemiah, permission to return to Jerusalem to supervise the reconstruction of the city's walls. He features as a model employer, providing his servant with letters of safe passage and timber for the walls from the royal forests.

He is a minor figure, soon forgotten in the businesslike report that is Nehemiah's contribution to biblical history: a marginal character, like his son, Artaxerxes II, who merely supplied the focus for Cyrus's insurrection and appears in person for only the split second it takes to dispatch his younger brother. They are both, Artaxerxes I and II, father and son, peripheral to the stories in which they appear, however powerful they may have been in their day, however they may have lived as men before whom other people prostrated themselves trembling. The narrators have stepped forward and elbowed them off the stage of history: one a Jewish cupbearer, the other a Greek mercenary. But Kate likes finding them there, nevertheless, Artaxerxes I and II with their freight of double Xs, one in her father's book, the other in her mother's. It feels like a link, a kind of union.

There is war and terror in both the books in which they have their cameo roles. There is also the recurring miracle of the birth of children, the gleam of a woman's bracelet, the curiosity of seashells discovered on an inland wall, the sight of wild asses galloping through scented scrub. There is wonder in the arrival of all this in a small room at the end of a gravel road on an island neither writer even dreamed could exist.

Kate reads in her room by the sea. Episode five of *McGibbon*, the Marlborough Sounds mystery, lies disarticulate on her desk. Her last episode. She won't write any more. She is going to write a novel instead. A novel about real life, as it is lived, and as it is read. She has decided to write about books and their beautiful, simple power.

Outside the window, kereru are stripping the fruit from a ngaio. The leaves on the apple trees in the orchard are starting to turn. When she reads now, she is looking from the corner of her eye for little references to old age and the progressive death of the body and how that might feel. While she reads everything co-exists: past and present and future, friends and family, the living and the dead, apple trees and wild asses, tyrant and infantryman, birth and the sea, doughnuts and newspapers and hens pecking about in a garden.

Book book, they say.

Book book.